He came on like a windmill in a storm. The steel-capped butts of his staff struck divots on the trail, sparking on a flint once or twice. For a second I regretted pissing him off.

I stepped quickly to the side and threw a knuckle shot at his throat. He was too mad to anticipate the move, but he was still quick enough to lean back out of the way. He kicked at my crotch, but I caught the blow with a knee. He shouted as the spike on my kneecap pierced his foot.

My new bone structure had that going for it. Who needed a cup?

He battered me with either side of the staff, but the strikes came from the obvious four quarters. I caught them all with my bony elbows and knees. Just before I saw the flicker of sanity return to his face, I caught the staff with both hands and did what I hate most.

I bit.

Even before my "episodes," as the boss called them, my smile would send the barber running from a block away. After the fire, my jaws were more like a rusty bear trap.

Luckily for Fong, I didn't go for his face. Instead, I clamped my teeth on the staff. It split with a satisfying crunch. A yellow flash dazed me for a second, but it sent Fong flying back a good four yards. Spitting out the splinters, I tasted enamel and fragments of gold.

Fong gaped in disbelief, but it was Burning Cloud Devil who cried out, "Impossible!"

"What?" I said, dusting myself off an arm at a time. "I told you I could take him."

"The Eight-Figured Staff," smiled Fong. "M... you have destroyed th...

"If you liked it so m...
in my face."

The Pathfinder Tales Library

Master of Devils

Dave Gross

paizo
PUBLISHING

Cover art by Lucas Graciano.
Cover design by Andrew Vallas.
Map by Robert Lazzaretti.

Paizo Publishing, LLC
7120 185th Ave NE, Ste 120
Redmond, WA 98052
paizo.com

ISBN 978-1-60125-357-6 (mass market paperback)
ISBN 978-1-60125-358-3 (ebook)

Publisher's Cataloging-In-Publication Data
(Prepared by The Donohue Group, Inc.)

Gross, Dave.
  Pathfinder tales. Master of devils / Dave Gross.

  p. ; cm. -- ([Pathfinder tales])

  Portion of title: Master of Devils
  Set in the world of the role-playing game, Pathfinder.
  ISBN: 978-1-60125-357-6

  1. Imaginary places--Fiction. 2. Good and evil--Fiction. 3. Fantasy fiction. 4. Adventure stories. I. Title. II. Title: Master of Devils III. Title: Pathfinder adventure path. IV. Series: Pathfinder tales library

PS3607.R67 P74 2011
813/.6

First printing August 2011.

Printed in the United States of America.

Chapter One
Falcon-Head Sword Gang

R un for it, boss!"

Jeggare arched an eyebrow the way he does when I defy the natural order by commanding him. Arnisant didn't need telling. The wolfhound lowered his head and nudged the count down the slope.

Behind me, the bandits unleashed another volley. We'd seen them touch the arrowheads to their firepots, but the flames were invisible in the afternoon sun. They'd taken a lone shot now and then to see when the boss's warding spell expired before spending ammunition on full volleys. Clever lads, but adding the fire was pure meanness.

I looked for a Radovan-sized gap in the flaming cloud of arrows. The spread was denser than before, despite the casualties we'd inflicted. Spinning into the thinnest patch I could see, I batted away a few arrows. One creased my cheek. A couple others caught me in the hip and thigh. The rags tied beneath the arrowheads splashed flaming oil over me.

I hit the ground and rolled. The arrow in my hip snapped away, but the other stuck fast. Fire spread up the shaft and onto my leathers. I dropped my blades and grabbed the arrow in both hands, snapping it short. My hands barely tingled as I choked out the flame. A little fire doesn't bother me much.

The arrows, on the other hand, hurt like hell.

I grabbed my big Chelish knife in one hand and the Varisian starknife in the other. I rocked back up to my feet and braced for another volley, but the bandits had a better idea. The instant they'd fired, they lit more arrows and charged the hill.

Between the count's spells and my crossbow, we'd already killed maybe a dozen bandits. There were still twice that many left. I reckoned I could cut down five or six if I was lucky, give the boss a head start. After that, I didn't much like my chances.

The bandit chief was a proud one, announcing his identity with an ensign waving a tall red banner at his side. To show my appreciation for the help, I threw him the big smile. A few of his men balked when they saw what I have instead of proper teeth. The chief pointed at me and shouted in Tien.

"Kill that devil!"

I threw the starknife. The chief tugged his standard-bearer over as a shield. One of the four wide blades of the starknife sank into the ensign's chest. Another split his chin and sent a line of blood across his face and onto his leader's cheek. The chief grimaced and backpedaled away from the corpse. I hoped that ensign would be the only dead bodyguard when this thing was over.

"Shoot!" yelled the chief.

The brigands raised their bows and fired. I leaped away.

Too slow.

Most of the arrows hit my legs, but some of the archers led their target. The oil soaked my clothes, and I grew a halo of fire. The arrows stuck out in every direction, pain tearing at me no matter which way I moved. When I tried to roll off the flames, another dug into my arms, my ribs, my spleen.

Terrific screams and curses burst out of me.

The Tian bandits didn't understand a word of Taldane, the common tongue on the other side of the world. Some laughed and shook their swords as I thrashed in agony. Their chief ordered them to shoot again.

Asshole.

The second volley hurt worse than the first. One fiery arrow passed through both of my cheeks and hung there like a horse's bit. I chomped it to splinters and spat them out.

I felt the heat as the flame poured down my throat and up into my sinuses. I was past feeling the difference between the fire and the wounds. I was ablaze inside and out.

Then came the change.

The arrows inside me disintegrated. My clothes peeled away in flakes, and all my blackened tools fell to the ground. Every joint in my body twitched and cracked.

I still didn't know the why, but the how was that fire brought out the devil in me.

The pain didn't subside. I was baying, the voice coming out of me no longer my own. Even the language was different. I recognized it as the tongue of devils.

My monster voice told the bandits what was going to happen to them next. They couldn't have understood the words, but there was no mistaking my tone. They dropped their bows and scattered before fleeing into the woods from which they'd launched their ambush.

I squinted at the retreating figure of their chief, weighing the big knife in my hand. It looked as small as one of my throwing blades, but that was an illusion. It was the same size as ever. It was me that had gotten a lot bigger.

My fists were the size of hams, with claws where my nails had been. Bony spurs jutted from my knuckles. From what little I'd seen the last few times I'd been immolated, I was spiky at every joint and angle.

Slapping out the last guttering flames, I tallied my wounds. Most of them looked like little more than blackheads on my copper skin. None felt worse than a snakebite. It felt like my internal heat had already mended my flesh and eaten up the arrows inside me. That much I was used to after the first few times I got lit up.

Despite the boss's nagging, I'd never done a serious inventory of the changes fire made in me. There was one thing that had been gnawing at my curiosity, and I felt a burning sensation where you hate to have one. I peered down at my crotch.

About what I saw there, the less said the better.

I went to the fallen ensign and ripped the chief's banner from its frame. Its embroidered silk looked mighty fancy for a bandit chief, but that's not why I wanted it. I tied it around my waist with the dead man's bandolier, figuring, out of sight, out of mind. I pulled the starknife out of the ensign's corpse as easily as I might have plucked a dandelion. The change made me crazy strong.

Above me the light shifted. My first impression was that the sun was falling toward me. The way things were going, I wouldn't have put it beyond possible. But the light didn't come from the sun.

A big fireball crackled through the sky, a black tail of smoke curving behind it. It looked like one of the boss's favorite spells, only slower. Branches withered as it swooped down just above the trees. It was headed my way, so I moved.

It corrected course, coming at me again. I ran ten yards to the side. It shifted again.

Damned thing was definitely coming for me.

Probably fire wouldn't even singe me now that I was full fiendish, but I still didn't want to get hit. Just as I tensed to run again, a voice boomed out from within the blaze.

"Excellent ki!"

The fireball floated to the side and settled on the hill. The flames subsided, revealing a man inside.

He looked small to me, but I guessed he was bigger than the average Tian. That was one of the few things I liked about Tian Xia. Even before I got big, I was a finger or two on the tall side, even among the men.

The stranger had thick black hair and a beard, both frosted with gray at the edges. His faded robes were old and patched, and he wore a lumpy bag slung around his muscular chest. An empty scabbard hung at his left hip, but his right arm was missing just below the shoulder.

"Who the hell are you?"

"A true devil!" He spoke a dialect of Tien I hadn't heard, but I understood him all right. I'd been picking up the language a few phrases at a time, and it had been more than a week since the boss had to cast a spell that let me understand our bearers.

Despite the one-armed man's dialect, I could tell it was me he was calling a devil, not himself. He added something in the infernal speech.

"I don't understand that devil bullshit," I said. When I've changed, I understand what I'm saying because I'm thinking it, not because I understand the words coming out of my mouth. Yeah, it doesn't make sense to me either. "Talk human."

He switched back to Tien. "I am Burning Cloud Devil, King of Heroes."

"Your mama must be real proud."

He stroked his beard and strutted back and forth like an actor, not a regular person. "Show me your skill!"

I shot him the tines. Back home, that was a great way to chase off a coward or start a fight, but he cocked his head, not getting it. Still, he had to know I was giving him the brush-off. He threw back his head and laughed.

His voice boomed like thunder. The sound battered my ears and knocked me on my ass. I rolled back up to my feet.

I could smell his breath ten feet away. It was all eggs and pickled cabbage. As I raised a hand to wave away the stink, he closed the distance quick as a wink and struck me on the forehead. I fell backward, but he was already behind me. He caught me on his knee and chopped me across the chest.

I jabbed with an elbow, but he was gone. My momentum threw me off balance. I fell flat on my back.

"You have no skill." He sounded astonished and disappointed. "None!"

My witty retort was little more than a wheeze, but I got back on my feet. I showed him the big knife.

He smiled and beckoned me closer.

I took the invitation, but I took it slow. He shook his head and scoffed at my cautious approach.

"What sort of hero are you?" His eyes flashed, and he shot darts of green light at me.

I've been stung by magic, once even on the tender bits. That time it hurt enough to make me flee a girl half my size. Still, that pain was nothing compared to Burning Cloud Devil's magic bolts. They smacked my cheek harder than a bouncer's slap.

I had something nasty to say to that, so I said it. It translated just fine.

"If you wish revenge, come take it." He leaped into the branches of the nearest tree. The distance was way too far for mortal muscles to carry a man.

Son of a bitch had to be a wizard. Witch. Sorcerer. Something like that.

Usually I know better than to fight a magician, but I was hopping mad after that sting in the face. I ran after him.

The woods were thicker than they'd looked from the top of the hill. I lost sight of Burning Cloud Devil in seconds. His laughter rang out from the side opposite where I thought he'd gone. His clothes were dark, but now and then I caught a glimpse of his flashing eyes among the black boughs.

"Where the hell are you?"

He struck me from behind, a hard smack on either shoulder. My muscles trembled where he'd touched me, as if his fingers lingered where they had struck to dig deep into my flesh. By the time I turned to stab him, he was gone, except for that mocking laugh. I ran blind through the woods.

Felt like minutes. Could have been hours.

I trampled saplings in the gloom until the stone-hard bole of a tree knocked me down. It hurt, but it knocked some sense into me. What the hell I was doing? I shouldn't be here. I should be with the boss.

Burning Cloud Devil's laughter grabbed my attention. The boss could wait a few more minutes. I chased the voice into the yellow-green light of a forest meadow. Spring buds had begun to color the branches. Ridges of brown-and-white fungus formed shelves on the surrounding trees. The place looked like a dryad's library.

The first shot threw me across the clearing. I hit another tree hard enough to shake loose a rain of crumbled fungus. Even in my big devil body, the impact hurt. But the pain gave me strength.

I leaped back at him.

I dropped the starknife and caught Burning Cloud Devil by the hair just as he tried to leap away. He killed my other hand with a knuckle shot to the wrist. I lost the big knife.

I pivoted and swept my elbow to the back of his neck. Even before I get ugly, my spurs are enough to break a breastbone, maybe even sever a spine. He shrugged, and the six inches of bone protruding from my elbow barely scraped his neck.

"Such power!" A hopeful smile spread across his black beard. "But power without form is useless. You must become my disciple."

I said the two words that best described my feelings on the matter.

Nothing got lost in translation that time, either.

His smile vanished. My body shuddered, pain breaking out in a hundred places as he struck me faster than I could see his hand move. He hit me with his fingers and thumb, the sides of his hands and the heel, never with a closed fist.

He ripped the strength out of my arms, one after the other. He jabbed the inside of my thighs, deadening my legs. Everywhere he struck felt like an icicle through my body. He poked my neck in three or four spots, and I couldn't move my head. Finally he punched me all around my heart and throat. He stepped back to observe the results.

"You are a wave, not a stone." He shook his head. "You are made of molten spirits. I will forge you solid."

His fingers traced Tien characters in the air, and their paths lingered like a blood trail. I didn't know what they meant. I should have paid more attention when the boss tried to teach me the local writing.

Burning Cloud Devil took a low stance, feet spread wide, knees bent. His body trembled, blurred, and fell still. He showed me his hand, like a priest offering a benediction. White witch-light played over his palm.

He struck me on the chest. It hurt, but not as bad as I figured after his little preamble.

He drew back his hand, and I felt invisible filaments of my heart float up to twine about his fingers. When he gripped them I felt the blood stop in my veins. He relaxed his grip, and my pulse returned.

"This fiendish body rides your soul until I release it," he said. "Now you are an alloy of your mortal and infernal selves, and I am your master. You will obey me until you have learned my ultimate technique. With it you shall slay my sworn enemy."

"What the hell did you hit me with?"

Burning Cloud Devil looked smug, as if he'd hoped I'd ask that question. "It is my penultimate technique: the Quivering Palm."

Chapter Two
White Tigers

By my reckoning, our predicament constituted the twenty-third time Radovan had been obliged to delay an attacker while I withdrew from the field. In my memory library, I left a mental note to add an extra purse of gold to our next accounting.

More imminently, I intended to repay Radovan's courage by ensuring his efforts were not in vain. If I could reach the scrolls in my satchel, I would awe the bandits with a mighty spell.

Our bearers were in full rout, their once-stubborn pack animals now perversely eager to follow their handlers. They carried off all of the expedition's supplies, the bulk of our money, and the remaining healing potions we would require in the unlikely event that we should survive the attack.

The guards had been the first to flee, kicking their horses into a gallop moments before we spotted the bandits brandishing their eponymous falcon-head swords—flared and hooked things somewhere between falchions and machetes. Collusion between our men and the robbers was now all but certain. I regretted my failure to heed my initial suspicions about the port functionary who recommended them. In the future, I would insist that Radovan personally select our guards.

The treachery was only the latest in a series of disheartening misadventures.

What began as a mission to collect the husk of a celestial pearl from an agent in Minkai became a full-blown expedition across Tian Xia. No land in all of Golarion lay farther from Absalom and the headquarters of the Pathfinder Society, the august community of explorers and scholars to which I belong. Yet while my masked superiors in the Decemvirate arranged for a conjurer to teleport us instantaneously to Minkai, upon arriving we found the provider of our return transport murdered and the object of our mission stolen. Rather than return empty-handed, we secured sea transport to mainland Tian Xia and marched across half of the Successor States to entreat the King of Quain for an identical husk from his royal vault.

I spied my satchel under the arm of a bearer mounted on my steed.

"Halt!"

The man replied with an insolent smile. His irregular teeth resembled stained wooden pegs.

"Come back here this instant!"

He slapped the reins and vanished over the next hill. With him went all of my personal belongings, including my precious spellbook. If only I had kept all of my riffle scrolls on my person, I should have reduced him to cinders, horse and all.

Arnisant butted my hip, urging me to continue our inglorious retreat. He had already dispatched two of our attackers, but his instinct was that of a guardian, not a berserker.

As we crested the next hill, I dared a glance back. There stood Radovan bristling with fiery arrows. In an instant he became an inferno. I held my breath in anticipation of the metamorphosis. In a flicker of flames, it was done.

Seven feet tall and covered with long bony spurs at every joint, Radovan's infernal form resembled the nightmare of a shiver addict. Steely coils roiled beneath his copper skin, which now flowed across him as if turned to molten metal. Even in his original form, Radovan's teeth were the stuff of street legend in our home city of Egorian. After the change they resembled a mound of shattered blades left by a retreating army.

While many of Radovan's devilish qualities were the product of his unfortunate parentage, these new fiendish transformations were something else entirely, and began during our investigation into a diabolic cult. Unfortunately, I was not witness to the first incident and had observed others only during the distraction of combat. If only Radovan had acceded to a few experiments under controlled conditions, through research and consultation I might have guided him into a fuller understanding of his condition.

Always it was a great conflagration that triggered the change. From my extemporaneous observations, I knew that Radovan's usual resistance to fire was greatly enhanced in his present state, so he was in no danger of incineration. His strength increased in proportion to his size, and conversely his temper shrank.

I was happy not to count myself among the brigands.

The whinny of my stolen mount captured my attention. Two hills away, the horse reared up in defiance of its untutored rider. Alas, it did not manage to shake the wretch from the saddle. I pointed at the thief.

"Arnisant, fetch!"

The loyal wolfhound streaked forward, and I ran after him. Briefly I regretted not having prepared a second scroll to summon a magical steed. The one I had cast earlier for Radovan, who could not approach a natural horse without causing a fracas, had already expired. While I could not ride the fiery red mount I had conjured for him, it might have at least allowed him to escape after securing my retreat.

Arnisant closed in on the thief. Whether in fear of the massive hound or from a misguided obedience to its usurper, the horse bolted. By the time I crested the third hill, it was clear that even Arnisant could never catch up. I whistled to call him back to my side.

Back at the site of the ambush, Radovan faced our attackers alone. There could be no question of his loyalty, and I more than half suspected he would fight to the bitter end to buy my escape. Were he simply a hireling, I should have left him to his duty. Yet over the years and especially in recent months, he had become more than a servant to me. I would not allow him to sacrifice himself.

With Arnisant at my side, I sped back to the fight.

Expecting a scene of carnage, I was dumbfounded to find only a number of abandoned bows and a single corpse clutching the empty frame of a Tian war banner. Near the crest of the hill on which we first made our stand, an immense heat had scorched a circle into the grass. Nowhere could I see Radovan.

Our attackers, however, soon returned.

They held their swords at the ready, wary of the spells they had seen me unleash. I felt my belt for any scroll I had overlooked earlier, but of course my tally was correct. None remained.

"Seize him," commanded their chief. He was tall and becoming, apart from the scar that drew an arc from his left eye to the edge of his lip. His wavering tone told me that something had shaken his confidence, and I knew what that must be.

Radovan yet lived.

There was no way this man and his minions could have defeated my bodyguard in his infernal state. While I did not know where Radovan had gone, I had only to delay the brigands long enough for him to return and rescue me.

The first brigand to approach shouted as Arnisant intercepted him. Seconds later, the man shrieked as he saw his severed fingers in the wolfhound's jaws.

"Kill the dog," said the chief. The bandits lifted their bows.

"Arnisant," I said in Taldane. "Fetch Radovan."

The hound never hesitated. He was a pewter-colored blur following Radovan's invisible scent trail, out of range before the first of our foes could shoot an arrow.

"You have defeated me, gallant sir," I said, addressing the bandit chief in his native tongue. I bowed and offered the chief my sword in the local fashion. "My family will pay a handsome bounty for my safe return."

The bandit tilted his head, an expression I had seen more than a few times in recent weeks. The Tian did not expect to hear their language spoken by an outlander, especially one so obviously half-human. He waited until one of his men snatched the blade from my hands—a wise if rude precaution—before approaching to feel the embroidered fabric of my coat. I bristled at his unseemly gesture. This prince of bandits was taller than the average Tian, only three inches shorter than I, and of a deep copper complexion that would have caused my fellow Chelaxians to wonder whether he, like Radovan, had a touch of infernal blood. He nodded, perhaps judging by the richness of my attire that I could easily compensate him for the lives he had spent capturing me.

Without warning, he kicked me in the chest, knocking me to the ground.

"Take his clothes," he ordered his men. He tugged loose the scarlet kerchief at his throat. "I want them."

Hours later, we prisoners trudged along, bound in pairs by rough leather manacles. Guards flanked us on either side, as well as before and behind our miserable train. The bandits had captured three of our unfaithful bearers—alas, not including the thief of my horse and satchel—and added them to half a dozen other unfortunates who were to be sold as slaves.

My companion was a sweaty peasant named Mon Choi. He explained that he had been taken the previous day by the notorious Falcon-Head Sword Gang, who prowled the nearby hills in hopes of kidnapping pilgrims to the famous Dragon Temple.

Mon Choi was one such hopeful, or had been one until his capture. Now the brawny farmer expected to live a short life in servitude. In other circumstances, his tale might have provided an interesting footnote in my next dispatch to the Pathfinder Society, but I was barely listening to him. At any moment, I knew, Arnisant would return with Radovan.

The worst indignity of the march was enduring the torment of wearing the bandit chief's garments. Not only were they coarse and damp, but I was more than half certain they harbored a colony of lice. My skin crawled so much that I could not know whether it was in my imagination or upon my flesh that a hundred tiny mandibles gnawed.

The bandit chief luxuriated in my fine Chelish garments, although to me he appeared no nobler than an orc swathed in velvet. He had even taken my jewelry, although he lacked the intellect to appreciate the magical powers inherent in the rings and medallion.

How I loathed this lowborn brigand who failed to perceive the value of treating a noble captive with courtesy. While they live half a world away, the customs of the Tian people are not so alien from those of my native Cheliax that I would accept any apology for his monstrous behavior. Once Radovan arrived, I would see the bandits beg for the forgiveness that I was in no vein to grant.

From the back of the column, a man screamed. I turned, already smiling in anticipation of rescue. Yet it was not Radovan who had caused the alarm.

A huge white shape soared over a low hill above the road, leaving a trail of blood on the spring grass.

"The white tiger!" A terrified brigand stood alone where his companion had vanished.

The bandits panicked as deep growls sounded from the cover of the nearby woods. I discerned at least three separate sources of the menacing rumbles from both above the trail and below.

"Slay the captives!" shouted their leader.

To his credit, there was more decisiveness than fear in his voice. Despite its imminent threat to me, I admired the logic of his order. If his men were to leave fresh corpses as tribute to the beasts, they might buy time to escape.

"Watch out!" shouted Mon Choi. He pushed me aside and raised his hands to catch the sword our nearest captor slashed at my head. He caught the blade on the leather straps that bound his manacles together. Wrapping the straps around the blade's hook so that the bandit couldn't withdraw, he sawed his bonds back and forth, freeing his hands.

I hesitated, astonished by my companion's prowess. Of course a temple aspirant would need a modicum of martial skill, but I had mistaken Mon Choi for a bumpkin with more ambition than ability. For my part, I stamped on the bandit's insole, causing him to hop, curse, and release his sword. Mon Choi caught the grip of the blade and brandished it at the bandit, who needed no further incentive to flee.

"Your hands," said Mon Choi. I raised my manacles, and he cut the thick leather thongs.

More screams heralded the arrival of two more of the gargantuan feline predators. While they did indeed resemble white tigers, they were the size of draft horses. Their ice-blue eyes glittered with pitiless hunger. One had already pinned a pair of bandits under its enormous paws. Blood from the first man's opened chest dripped from the big cat's whiskers, while the terrified screams of the other man rose above the cacophony as the beast tore out his vitals.

"Run." I demonstrated my meaning.

"We cannot outrun the tigers!"

"We need not outrun the beasts." It was time to employ my enemy's stratagem. "We need only outrun as many men as it takes to fill their bellies."

"You are wise, foreigner," said Mon Choi, passing me within twenty strides.

Just as I began to fear he would leave me behind, an arrow struck him in the calf. Mon Choi tumbled to the ground. I looked back and saw the bandit chief drawing another arrow from his quiver.

I ran to Mon Choi. Half of the arrow shaft protruded from either side of his leg.

"Go, brother," he said, clutching my garment. "I am dead!"

Gripping the fletching side of the arrow, I broke it short. Mon Choi screamed.

"The dead feel no pain," I told him. "Thus, you live."

Mon Choi gaped at something behind me. I turned to see the bandit chief striding toward us, aiming his arrow directly at my face.

"It will not be I who—" said the brigand. Before he could unleash his arrow, one of the enormous tigers fell upon him. He vanished like a mouse beneath an alley cat.

Mon Choi emitted a shriek at the sight of the butchery behind me. I took the opportunity to pull the arrowhead-side of the shaft through his leg, altering the tenor of his scream. He glared in indignation until he realized the favor I had done him, whereupon his expression dissolved into an unbearable epitome of gratitude. I tore the sleeve from his shirt and tied it around the wound.

"Thank you, brother." His tone of sincerity was most cloying. I nodded away his thanks, not to mention his inappropriate address to a count of Cheliax. I helped him stand, and we hobbled away together.

"This way." He pointed up the western slope.

Lacking better knowledge of the locale, I obeyed his advice. At the top of the hill, Mon Choi pointed to the mountain rising to the west.

Halfway between the mountain's foot and its summit rested a walled compound the size of a small town. Over centuries, its stone walls had absorbed the green hue of the moss that spread like liver spots upon its surface.

The compound was shaped like a great wheel with four spokes, its quarters sectioned off by interior walls and climbing the steep slope in a series of terraces. Prominent among its many clustered buildings was a stone temple in the classic Tian style. From any greater distance, the signs of human labor would have been invisible, so seamlessly did the structure merge with the existing topography and foliage. Through the plentiful trees within the walls, however, I spied the hint of many other buildings.

"Dragon Temple," said Mon Choi. "Those who enter its gates are safe from all beasts and spirits."

"What of brigands?"

We staggered to the crest of the next hill before I dared to glance back. There was little left of the brigands or their other captives. A few other fortunate men had escaped the slaughter, but one or another periodically attracted the attention of one of the tremendous tigers. One of the great beasts turned its massive head toward us.

We fled with as much celerity as three good legs could muster.

"There!" shouted Mon Choi. Four hundred yards away, a procession passed beneath the first of four gates leading up the road to Dragon Temple.

The gate was a freestanding archway with three tiers of tiled roofs. Huge statues flanked it. One was a stone representation of a foo-lion, those grotesque brutes that appear at once feline and canine. The other was a bronze depiction of the fabulous stag-lizard creature known in Tian Xia as a qilin.

Regardless of my curiosity about such details, the nature of the statues would not aid our escape. My heart sank as I noted no walls attached to any of the first three gates, nor any guards outside the central compound nearly a quarter of a mile away. There was nothing to prevent the tigers from chasing us down and devouring us.

Nothing but our own legs and determination.

We hastened down the first slope, narrowly avoiding a tumble as we crossed a game trail where bloodstained earth and a scattering of bones suggested that we remained in the tigers' territory. Mon Choi gripped my arm as a growl thundered behind us.

"Hurry!"

The guards of the procession turned at the sound of the tiger. There were twenty men, each bearing a spear with a thick red tassel beneath the blade. They flanked a sextet of muscular porters bearing a covered palanquin. At the head of the procession rode a robed figure of such fair complexion and hair that he might have been an albino or a ghost. Even from such a distance, his air of command was unmistakable. He snapped open a fan and closed it again before pointing it toward the gate. The gesture was an order, for the bearers and guards turned toward the next gate and marched double time, leaving us to fend for ourselves.

Mon Choi cried out for help, but it was to no avail. Any of my peers in Cheliax would have done precisely the same upon seeing a pair of peasants fleeing a dangerous animal, especially when escorting a precious passenger.

We ran. The tiger pursued. The earth shuddered at its every bound.

We made it halfway to the gate before Mon Choi stumbled, taking me down with him. My ankle twisted as we hit the earth.

The great tiger flew inches over our heads and slid down the rocky slope beneath the trail.

We scrambled to our feet, gasping at every agonizing movement. We resumed our retreat as the tiger bounded up toward us. At first it slid upon the loose stones, but its scythelike claws dug into the soil. In two leaps, it closed half the distance.

My ankle gave out, sending a bolt of agony through my leg. I fell.

Before I could voice a cry for help, Mon Choi lifted me over his shoulder like a sack of grain. Screaming at the pain of his own wound, he dashed through the gate and collapsed.

Outside, the tiger unleashed a defiant roar. It directed its attention not at us but rather at the guardian statues. The tiger glared at their impassive stone faces. The standoff reminded me of the samurai of Minkai, the island nation we had visited before landing on the shores of Tian Xia.

At last, the duel was decided. Its tail drooping low, the tiger ran back to the remains of its feast of brigands and slaves.

Mon Choi and I lolled in the dust, our strength exhausted. The palanquin and its guards had long since vanished behind the walls of the inner compound. Thinking ourselves alone, we clutched our injuries and groaned.

"What are you doing?"

The speaker was an ancient man whose skin had shrunk and darkened to the complexion of stained walnut. He wore the white robes and prayer beads I had come to associate with various sects of Tian monks. On his shoulder rested a light bamboo fishing pole.

Mon Choi rolled over and slapped my arm with the back of his fingers. "Kowtow, brother," he whispered. "Kowtow three times!"

I am not averse to the courtesies of bowing, but I am not accustomed to prostrating myself before any presence less august than that of a prince. Considering my circumstances, however, I deemed it best to comply with Mon Choi's advice. Careful not to aggravate my injured ankle, I placed my hands on the ground, fingertips touching. I bowed three times, my head upon my knuckles.

The old man frowned, no doubt dissatisfied with my obeisance. I felt his eyes lingering on me, no doubt considering my appearance. While my straight black hair and almond-shaped eyes were not unusual in this part of the world, my height and long, tapered ears no doubt marked me as a foreigner even before I spoke.

Out of the corner of my eye, I saw Mon Choi peering across at me. He kept his head down, so I did the same. A rivulet of perspiration formed on his neck and spattered in the dirt. We waited an interminable period before the old man sighed and spoke again.

"Very well, you may stand." He looked with longing toward a pond between the first and second gates. "You do not look like much, but I accept you both as applicants to Dragon Temple. You are late, so your first trials begin at once."

Chapter Three
King of Heroes

Desna weeps."

Burning Cloud Devil tilted his head. "I do not understand."

"Desna is what we call Lady Luck."

"I am familiar with the Resplendent Goddess of Fortune. But why is she melancholy?"

Desna weeps.

On our way back to find the boss, I explained to Burning Cloud Devil that we'd been ambushed by bandits. That was all the prompting he needed to expound on the difference between luck, fortune, and fate, and which of those powers had brought me to his attention.

It was fate, he said. He had bargained with many devils in the past, but none had been able to master the techniques he taught. He needed someone both infernally strong but full of mortal life. Back in Cheliax, they call my kind hellspawn. He called me a semi-devil.

I called him a few things back to see which ones translated through to Tien. Burning Cloud Devil smiled, but I saw he was remembering every insult for later.

He kept shoving a sheet of yellow paper at me, demanding I sign a compact with him. In exchange for becoming his disciple and slaying his enemy in a year, he'd unlock me from my infernal form.

I said I wouldn't even consider his crazy demand until we'd returned to the spot where he'd found me. He surprised me by agreeing, since it was fate that he had found me where he did. Sometimes crazy works in your favor.

At first I thought he wanted me to kill some fellow called Dragon. After all, he called himself Burning Cloud Devil, and he was no more devil than . . . well, he was no more devil than most any other fellow you might meet. The more he talked about his enemy, however, the more I started to realize he meant for me to kill an actual giant-flying-wyrm dragon.

With my bare hands.

The man was beyond optimistic. The boss would talk some sense into him, pay him off, or stupefy him with some of his big words and convoluted sentences. Or, if that didn't work, magic.

The one thing I learned from Burning Cloud Devil's yakking was that I was never going to get used to Tian Xia. The only reason I was here was to look after the boss, who'd been sent by his bosses in the Pathfinder Society to fetch some magic pearl, or the shell of one, or something like that. The whole thing was shady, if you ask me. Someone in his little explorers' club was jerking him around, and I didn't like it. Neither did he.

He might not have liked the reason for visiting, but the boss loved Tian Xia. All the way cross-country from the eastern shore, he pointed out every curious landmark and told me what he'd read about it in one of his thousands of books. When we ate, he explained what was in the hundred different shapes of dumplings. When we drank—not too much, and for that so far so good—he gave me a lecture on how the local wine was really more like beer because of the way it was fermented. If he weren't here on business, it'd all be research for a book of his own. He couldn't be happier.

Me, not so much.

The food was all different, and you had to ask for a spoon or else they expected you to eat with a pair of sticks—although I was getting better with those. Darned near everyone wore robes, not just the priests, and being polite was a lot more complicated than it was back in Cheliax. Plus, the rules on manners changed from province to province, as I'd learned the hard way a few times. The worst part was that in most places the women were too shy to talk to strangers, especially foreigners. Especially foreigners with devilish good looks. I was lucky to practice "hello, sweetheart" before they scurried away.

Don't even talk to me about the language, not that I could speak it at the moment. Tien was ten times harder than the Varisian I'd learned. They didn't write with proper letters but these complicated symbols that meant whole words—and different words for the same character, which you had to figure out from the context. I couldn't read more than a few words, and even then it was a throw of the dice whether I got it right.

Now Burning Cloud Devil explained that they change the names of the gods. "Resplendent Goddess of Fortune," my spurs. He needed some educating.

"Desna smiles, see?" I said, shooting him the big smile. He didn't even blink at the armory in my mouth. Good for him, tough guy. "She smiles, you have good luck—fortune, fate, whatever. She weeps, you have a bad day. A real bad day."

Burning Cloud Devil grunted agreement. "Desna wept over me thirty-five years ago. But now I think she is beginning to smile again."

"You've got to be careful," I said. "Sometimes Desna laughs."

He frowned at that. "Why would she laugh?"

"Because sometimes you only think she's smiling," I said. "That's because you don't understand women."

Another joke that didn't translate, I figured. Burning Cloud Devil stopped walking and turned toward the sunset. I was impatient to get back, but I let him ruminate a minute.

Whatever Burning Cloud Devil had done to make me a stone instead of a wave—or to forge an alloy out of me, or whatever—I could feel that I wasn't coming down out of the big and spiky anytime soon. I had a bad headache and an anxious feeling that squirmed like a winter eel in my stomach.

Still, I'd calmed down enough that I realized my blunder. I had to get back to the boss, and fast. Those bearers could not be trusted, and there was every chance the bandits had found their balls and returned to finish the job.

Just as I was about to nudge Burning Cloud Devil, he started walking again. He also started talking, and how.

"Long ago, my name was Black Mountain. I was the greatest hero of Quain. None could stand before me, neither the greatest swordsman nor the most enlightened monk. By fist or by sword, all fell. The defeated begged to become my disciples, but I refused. None were worthy of learning my Twin White Palms technique, against which even the Mighty Abbot of the Red Desert Monastery perished.

"One morning the Golden Swordswoman of Qiulin came to challenge me. She fought with bravery and skill, eluding my Flowing Strikes and keeping me at bay for hours. As the sun set, so chivalrous and beautiful was she that I was tempted to feign defeat to please her. Yet so heroic was her demeanor that I would not dare to tender such an insult. If I had pretended to lose, even out of admiration, she would have rightfully scorned me.

"Rather, when I exhausted her stamina and showed her that death lay in my palm, she renounced her name and begged to be my disciple. I accepted her pledge, dubbing her Spring Snow, for I knew that her once-cool heart had sought out my warmth that it might thaw.

"Together we reigned over the heroes of Quain, but only for one month. By then I knew I wanted her not as a disciple but as my wife. As a wedding gift, I promised her the wish granted once every twelve years by the Celestial Dragon."

"You don't say."

He puzzled over that. "I *do* say."

I hadn't told Burning Cloud Devil what the boss was looking for, so I couldn't figure how this could be a trick. After things went sour in Minkai, we'd been on our way to ask permission of the king of Quain to acquire a magic pearl for the Pathfinder Society. What were the chances this could be the same one?

This Celestial Dragon was supposed to produce its pearl about a year from now. The boss was hoping he could finesse the king into letting him have the shell left after the pearl's magic was used up. He had all but told me the Decemvirate expected him to fail. If it were up to me, I'd tell the whole pointy-headed gang to climb their thumbs, but the boss saw it differently. A matter of honor or something. So here we were, on the other side of Golarion.

"Go on."

Burning Cloud Devil continued his story. "Together, Spring Snow and I overcame the trials of Iron Mountain, defeating all of its guardians and reaching the Gates of Heaven and Hell before the royal envoys. We barred the way behind us and summoned the dragon down from Heaven. We would use the pearl's wish to ensure that we would remain together forever—the strongest vow I could offer.

"The Dragon refused to surrender the pearl to Snow, declaring her no virgin. That was true, since we had already consummated our marriage. But we would not be denied. If it would not give us the pearl, we would take it by force.

"Snow was magnificent. She leaped upon the dragon before I could prepare my mightiest strike. It was too soon, and the dragon was ready." Once more, Burning Cloud Devil stared off into the distance. His eyes misted, but he kept walking, so I didn't complain. I couldn't leave him behind, since during my mad pursuit I'd completely lost my bearings.

"I get the picture," I said. "The dragon killed your wife."

Burning Cloud Devil turned to me, an anguished look on his face. He gave me a curt nod, paused, and nodded again. The second one looked like thanks for not making him say it.

"I get why you want revenge," I said, and I meant it. There were a couple of people whose deaths I'd avenge. Hard.

"I meant to have it the moment Snow perished. Before, we had sought only to defeat the dragon, not to destroy it. As an immortal, the dragon was invincible to all but my ultimate technique, the Twin White Palms."

He grasped his stump with his remaining hand.

"The dragon bit off your arm."

"I fought through the guardians of Iron Mountain and wandered Tian Xia for thirty-five years. Everywhere I found an oracle or a conjurer, I offered myself as his disciple. I learned to summon devils to do my bidding. I recited ten thousand sutras. Yet no combination of minions and spells was sufficient to slay an immortal dragon. The only skill I possessed that was capable of slaying my nemesis was useless to a one-armed warrior."

"There must have been some other fighter who could learn your technique," I interjected.

"There were many! But none would agree to act as my hand, fearful of the judgment of Heaven. I tested the devils I had learned to summon, yet none of them had the ki necessary to perform the Twin White Palms. That is what makes you the perfect disciple. You are a human man suffused with the power of Hell. Your mortal ki combined with your infernal might will overcome the dragon's defenses."

"That remains to be seen," I said. "I told you, I've got to make sure the boss is all right first."

"If you refuse me . . ." He clenched his fist, and I felt his fingers in my heart.

"Yeah, yeah," I bluffed, but it came out a hoarse rasp. Maybe the boss had a spell that would cut Burning Cloud Devil's hold on me.

We reached the site of the attack as the last rays of light drowned beneath the western mountains. Burning Cloud Devil conjured a bright yellow flame in his cupped palm and threw it at my head. I flinched, but I didn't feel the slightest heat. The light danced atop my head like a torch flame.

"Knock it off."

"Why would I do that?" said Burning Cloud Devil. "Do you not need the light?"

The fact was, I didn't so much need the light. Even before I go all spiky, I can make out everything but the detail in darkness. So all right, the light was helpful. But that was beside the point. I didn't like his putting crowns of fire on my head. People see something like that on a guy who looks like me, they get the wrong idea. I was having a bad enough time before the transformation. I didn't need his making it worse.

I squinted at the tracks in the gloom. Among them lay the blackened remains of the tools I'd kept in my now-disintegrated jacket. They were useless even if I'd had a place to put them. I found my lucky coin in the ashes of my clothes. It was a little worse for the fire, but I could still feel the profile of an ancient prince on its face. It reminded me of a couple of women I had left back in Ustalav. I tucked away the thought with the coin.

By the trampled ground, I could see that the brigands had returned. Judging from the tracks, so had the boss and Arnisant, although the hound had run south. Everyone else had headed northwest.

"All right, enough with the halo," I said. "Get this thing off my head."

Burning Cloud Devil dismissed the light with a flick of his little finger, the nail of which he left long. "I weary of this," he said. "If we do not find this boss of yours soon, I insist you answer my demand. Become my disciple, or—"

"Yeah, yeah, I heard you the first time." I pointed to the tracks. "A bunch of bandits got him."

"The Falcon-Head Sword Gang roams this region in the spring," said Burning Cloud Devil. He lifted his beard with his wrist. The gesture reminded me of the way the boss pinches the bridge of his nose when he's thinking.

"'Sword Gang' sounds like these guys. They went that way. I figure we creep up on them, nice and quiet like. Kill the sentries, slit as many throats as we can before they know we're there. Bust up the rest if they don't have sense enough to run."

"They must be miles away by now," said Burning Cloud Devil. "You were fortunate I found you when I did. They are notorious cannibals."

"Then we'd better get marching," I said. "Unless you can conjure up a couple of horses." That's what the boss would have done. It was one of my favorite of his tricks. The steed he conjured for me always looked like it came from Hell, complete with brimstone smoke for a mane.

"Horses?" Burning Cloud Devil scoffed. "I have something much faster." He drew big circles in the air, each leaving a faint orange trace behind. He spun on his heel, forming a globe of fiery threads.

"I see why they call you Burning Cloud Devil."

When the last thread of fire fell into place, I felt the earth tilt as we rose off the ground. I fell into the bottom of a flaming sphere as we flew across the countryside. I could see through the walls about as well as looking through a bonfire. Flames crackled all around us, along with the muted sound of barking.

"Wait," I said. "That sounds like the boss's dog."

Burning Cloud Devil either didn't hear or didn't care. "The trail leads this way." Standing above me, the wizard pressed the back of his first two fingers against his left eye, then the right. Magic glimmered over his irises, and I could tell he was following the tracks I could no longer perceive.

We flew for maybe half an hour before landing. I saw by the light of the fading sphere that we stood amid a field of bloody bones. Scraps of armor, arrows, and bows were strewn in all directions. Lots of swords with those beak-shaped tips, which I finally connected to Burning Cloud Devil's "Falcon-Head" remark.

"We are too late," he said. "The dragon was here."

My belly felt tight as a drum. I couldn't breathe. I banged against the warm inner shell of the flaming ball and shouted, "Boss!"

The fireball vanished. I could make out the shapes of mutilated corpses and other detritus, but no details.

"Give me some light," I said.

"But you said—"

"Give me some goddamn light, you son of a bitch!"

His lips whitened. If he'd attacked me, I wouldn't have minded. A fight was what I felt like at that moment. Instead, he flicked a scrap of magic light at the big knife. I held it up and searched the ground for any sign of the boss.

All too soon, I found it.

There wasn't enough of him left to fit into a coin purse, but there was no mistaking his embroidered Chelish coat and one of his riding boots. He would have wept to see the state of them, after all the hours he'd spent keeping them at a high polish.

I knelt there a while. At first I tried to straighten the bloody clothes and lay the lone boot, foot still inside, in the appropriate place. I tried to find the other one, but I gave up after an hour's search.

Burning Cloud Devil sensed the meaning of what I'd discovered, and he gave me my space. I heard him messing about with the other remains, probably looting them. I didn't give a damn about those ones.

It felt wrong to leave the boss's body alone, even if it was almost entirely gone. Any moment, I figured I'd embarrass myself in front of the Tian wizard by crying my guts out, but it didn't come. My face was hot, but everything inside felt ice cold. I didn't know what else to do, so I used a dropped sword to cut a line in the earth beside him, outlining a grave.

Burning Cloud Devil clasped my shoulder and almost lost his hand for his trouble. "Allow me," he said

I let him pull me away. He slapped his chest and drew a series of characters in the air. When he pointed his stiffened arm at my outline and drew swift spirals at it, the earth churned and blew out to form a pile beside the grave.

When it was deep enough, I lifted the remains and climbed into the hole. There I laid them gently in the earth and whispered a couple of things that nobody else needed to hear. When I climbed out, Burning Cloud Devil gestured, but I waved him off.

"I've got to do this part myself," I told him. He withdrew from the light of my knife, and left me alone until I'd finished pushing the last of the earth back into the hole. I stood there for a while before realizing I had my feet on the boss's grave. I moved back and sat on the ground. Sometime later, Burning Cloud Devil joined me. He didn't say anything, just sat beside me. Neither of us said a word as the moon oozed past two constellations. He waited for me to break the silence.

"You say this was the work of your dragon," I said at last.

"He claims all of the land within the sunset shadow of the Wall of Heaven Mountains as his territory," said Burning Cloud Devil. "In spring, he gorges himself on the flesh of mortals."

Chapter Four
Dragon Temple

The ground rushed up to buffet my aching body. This time I was too weak to keep my skull from bouncing off of the hard-packed ground. Once more I reevaluated my decision to remain within Dragon Temple rather than to be expelled into the tiger-infested wilderness. At least in the jaws of a beast, the end would come swiftly.

"Brother Mon Choi wins," declared Master Wu. The squinting instructor of combat scowled at me, no doubt resentful that the late arrival by Mon Choi and me required him to stage another bout of contests after he thought the year's first trials concluded.

The humiliation of my defeat at the hands of the other new acolytes, who had been training for days before our arrival, was nothing compared to the burning shame I felt when my wounded comrade hurled me to the ground in the wrestling trials. While Master Li bolstered us with his healing touch, the pain in my ankle suggested that Mon Choi must also be far from his peak condition. It was small consolation that he had won the title of Second Brother in wrestling, defeating all but the champion, First Brother Kwan.

Yet with one throw, Mon Choi had all but sealed my fate as Last Brother in each fighting style taught by Master Wu. One by one, my fifteen fellow aspirants had defeated me in five of the Six Sacred Weapons of Irori: fist, pole, knife, spear, and now wrestling.

"The foreign devil is even weaker than he looks," whispered Brother Karfai, he of the absurd topknot sprouting from the exact center of his pate.

The foreign devil has keener hearing than you realize, I thought.

Karfai's comment evoked a humorless nod from Kwan, who had prevailed in every style both before and after our late arrival. Neither Mon Choi nor I had demonstrated the least ability to appropriate that title. Kwan whispered back to Karfai, "The outlander is too old for such exertion."

The pity in his voice was more shaming than Karfai's dismissal of my strength. While I had lived well more than ninety years, my father's elven blood granted me the vigor of a human boasting one-third my years.

Well, perhaps a human boasting half my years.

It was now more than an hour after sunset. Four bronze braziers and a ring of tall torches provided ample light for our contests. We stood in the proving grounds of the temple compound's easternmost district, flanked on three sides by a dormitory, an armory, and a great shrine to Irori.

Irori was the god of enlightenment, known in my homeland as well. Vudrani monks spread the deity's doctrine of physical, mental, and spiritual perfection throughout Golarion. It had taken hold in countless monasteries throughout the western continents of Avistan and Garund. Here in Tian Xia, Irori was worshiped not only by warrior monks but by a significant portion of the population.

Upon our arrival, Master Li had cautioned us that neophytes were forbidden to trespass beyond this easternmost courtyard, named the Cherry Court for the trees that thrived in plots between its buildings. The other three courts were also named for their fruit trees. Beyond the interior walls of the temple, I saw the light of colored lanterns shining on bare tree branches, peach to the south, plum to the north.

Judging by their appearance and demeanor, our instructors were, with two exceptions, no more than forty years old. Master Wu's iron-colored hair suggested that he might have been more than fifty, although he moved with more agility and grace than any of the young men, except perhaps for First Brother Kwan. And the grand master of Dragon Temple, Venerable Master Li, might have been sixty or eighty for all I could discern. His diminutive stature and weathered skin may have exaggerated his years, but beneath prodigious white eyebrows, his eyes shone with intelligence and vigor.

Mon Choi offered me a hand up, but I stood on my own power.

"Forgive me, Brother Jeggare," he said. "I did not mean to hurt you."

"There is no need to apologize . . . brother." Referring to a base farmer by such an intimate term required a supreme effort. I had neglected to transpose my names when introducing myself to Master Li, but now I was grateful for the error. It was considerably less disagreeable that these common men should address me by my family name than by a more personal appellation.

I dusted myself off and straightened my back. Towering over the other brothers was no advantage in our contests. What the others lacked in reach, they

more than compensated for with speed and power.
Most of them had been raised as laborers, hardy young
men who had worked all their lives for the opportunity
to learn from the masters of Dragon Temple.

Despite my foreign origin, I was not without some
understanding of fundamental lessons taught at the
temple. My library in Greensteeples included dozens
of volumes concerning Tian Xia, from horticulture to
painting to silk production to the historical chronicle of
the now-fractured Empire of Lung Wa. And, thankfully,
the various martial arts, which I had long desired to
study under the tutelage of a native practitioner.

With my youthful interest thus whetted, the arrival
of a Tian diplomatic mission in Egorian had given me
the opportunity to strike up a friendship with a young
clerk named Song Chu-yu.

In my role as Count of Cheliax and Accessory to the
Royal Court, it was my honor to introduce Song to such
local splendors as the Grand Opera, the Royal Palace,
Blackrose Gardens, and a hundred other icons of
Egorian culture. He was a frequent guest to my home
at Greensteeples, where he taught me such customs as
the chadao tea ceremony and the Thirty-Six Forms of
Exercise for Internal Fortification.

For decades after Song's return to Tian Xia, I practiced
the skills he taught me. Alas, for more decades since,
I had neglected them. Thus, my practical skills were
incommensurate to those of my peasant rivals.

"The final contest," announced Master Wu. "Swords."

Kwan smiled, and the other brothers looked at him
with a mixture of trepidation and envy. I sensed they
had suffered at his hand in the previous contests. My
own smile I buried in my heart. At last, I hoped, I would
not find myself the least of the brothers.

Master Wu declared the terms of the contest. Because this was our introductory trial, the first combatant to strike his opponent would prevail. It was incumbent upon each aspirant to acknowledge a touch, and the master promised harsh punishment for any recalcitrance.

My first opponent was Runme, whose former profession I deduced by the stink of fish that lingered on his person even after a trek of hundreds of miles from his home town. He showed me a yellow smile, obviously pleased to have drawn so weak a foe in the first round. When the master called start, I parried his hasty attack and rapped him neatly on the skull.

Runme hopped and rubbed his head so violently that there was no need for further confession of his loss, but Master Wu glared until he yelped, "I am hit! I am hit!"

The quick and surprising conclusion to our match distracted Mon Choi's opponent so profoundly that he found himself poked four times in the chest and stomach before he, too, called out defeat. Kwan dispatched his opponent an instant later. Within half a minute, the remaining contests concluded. Master Wu paired off the eight victors, and I faced Mon Choi.

We bowed before engaging our practice swords. For an instant, I recalled the gratitude I felt when Mon Choi carried me through the outer gate to safety. Yet I had already performed the arithmetic presented by Master Wu at the beginning of the trials. The only avenue by which I could escape the mantle of "Least Brother" and the ignominy of kitchen duty was to prove myself First Brother of Swords.

Mon Choi grimaced as we crossed blades. He was more cautious than Runme, but he had no greater understanding of defending the four quarters of his body. I lured him into an attack on my legs and smacked him smartly on the shoulder as I retreated.

"I am struck!" His grimace turned into a beaming smile. "Well done, Brother Jeggare! You have sword skill."

His approval filled me with shame, but only for a moment. Grateful as I was for his earlier assistance, I could not allow sentiment to interfere with my advancement.

The penultimate match pitted Kwan against Karfai and me against a snaggletoothed carpenter named Harbin. Harbin had placed near the top in all of the other contests and second in knives.

Radovan would have excelled in a contest of knives, I thought. I wished he would arrive soon to spare me further indignity among these common louts. Then we should continue our journey to Lanming, where I would present my petition to the king.

Harbin's confident stance as we bowed suggested his skill with the twenty-inch-long butterfly knives would translate well into a contest with the three-foot-long wooden swords. My prediction proved accurate. Harbin demonstrated such precise blade control and fluid footwork that he had me on the defensive within seconds.

My first mistake was employing the Elliendo defense. When deployed against a fencer of nearly any school in Avistan, it is nigh impenetrable so long as one need not advance. Unfortunately, Harbin's nimble shifts in stance required both a broader spectrum of parries and the occasional adjustment to my own posture. As my rivals had already noted, for a man of my age, especially after my encounters with the bandits and the tigers, such strenuous defense was trying.

Harbin's eyes glittered as he saw a shadow of desperation cross my face. Emboldened, he redoubled his efforts to draw my defenses from the extremes of each quarter, high and right, then high again and low. The tip of his sword struck a divot in the hard-packed ground, an inch from my toe. I knew I could bear only seconds more of his assault before making a fatal error.

To succeed, my rally would need to be surprising, even audacious. So be it, I decided. If I were to know my final defeat in these trials, I chose to fail with a display of élan.

Having observed the movements of the other aspirants all evening, my body began to recall the martial forms I had learned so long ago. With them in mind, I reevaluated the situation.

Harbin depended approximately one-fifth more often on attacks to my upper and right quadrants. While I had little hope of a successful riposte, I knew I could almost certainly parry one strong attack from above. When it came, I moved my sword to block as I advanced in the motion I had learned from Song Chu-yu as Crane Steps Forth.

Harbin's sword struck the earth again, deflected slightly by my own weapon. With my extended right foot, I pushed his ankle and allowed him to fall over my body, twisting to avoid acting as a cushion to his fall. Surprised, Harbin wasted half a second turning to transform his fall into a roll. It was an elegant recovery, but it allowed me time to shift my wooden blade beneath him. He fell upon its edge, while I added my other hand to the grip to ensure that I would not drop the weapon.

Harbin slid down the edge of my sword and recovered his stance. His counterattack was too swift to deflect. He struck me in the chest and upon each shoulder. When I declined to admit defeat, he poked me again and again, until Master Wu stepped in and slapped the sword from his hands. The blow was so powerful that the wooden blade flew across the practice ground to clatter against the wall of the dormitory.

"I won," declared Harbin. "The foreign devil has no honor. You all saw!"

"Kowtow," said Master Wu.

Harbin grinned at me, relishing what he imagined was my admonishment. His grin vanished as Master Wu kicked his legs out from under him and stamped a foot upon his back. The master looked at me with an indecipherable expression and announced, "Brother Jeggare wins."

The other aspirants stared at me with expressions of astonishment. A few glared resentment or outright hatred. Mon Choi beamed with an emotion I could only interpret as fraternal pride, which caused me all the more discomfort because it seemed so unaffected. Alone among the disciples of Dragon Temple, Mon Choi appeared to wish me well.

"Brother Kwan," said Master Wu, sweeping the other brothers from the center of the court with a gesture. "You face Brother Jeggare."

Kwan took his place across from me and offered the martial bow, a flat palm against the fist that gripped his sword. On the backs of his hands I saw the tattoos of a raptor's talons. I returned his gesture, my own gaze trying to penetrate the veil of his eyes. Was he angry? Nervous? What weakness could I exploit in this man who had triumphed in every other contest?

"Now!" said Master Wu.

Kwan allowed me no time for further speculation. He forced me to retreat with a blinding central attack. His blows were so fierce that I tightened my grip lest he disarm me and end the duel before it had begun. Just as I lifted my rear foot to retreat another step, he swept his sword low at my ankles. Independent of thought, my front leg thrust just hard enough to raise my feet above the sword. I landed awkwardly, stepping out of line to my right.

The motion was not what Kwan had expected, but only because I had performed the defense so poorly. His sword licked out where my shoulder should have been had I dodged as I had intended. I attacked his knee to buy time. He withdrew to the left, chasing me in a spiral path back toward the center of the court.

I stood my ground, employing a coarse but effective Andoren defense that requires two hands on the grip, leaving virtually no opportunity for ripostes. Let Kwan weary himself by chopping my blade while I recover my breath, I calculated.

And then I saw it. Kwan dragged his left foot whenever he shifted stance. Traced in the sand of the courtyard, I saw the arcs and whorls of our fight. Patterns have long been a specialty of mine, and in an instant I saw these for what they were: a sign of weakness. He was not wounded, nor infirm in the leg, but he had a bad habit.

A bad habit that I could exploit.

With a feinted step to the left, I abandoned my defense and attacked Kwan's feet. He stepped back, again dragging his left foot to form curves in the sand. One more, I knew, and he would be an instant slower on that side. I lunged for the toe of his slipper, turning my blade at the last moment to thrust at his belly.

With a piercing whoop, Kwan flew above my blade and kicked me solidly in the sternum. The blow sent my point out of line, and his sword came down to rap me firmly on each shoulder. Had we been fighting with steel swords, he could have lopped off my head.

I fell flat on my back, and he landed with a foot on either side of my body. Almost idly, he kicked my sword away.

After a second's hesitation to command my lungs to move once more, I gasped, "I am struck."

The other aspirants cheered, Mon Choi among them.

Kwan stepped away and waited for me to stand of my own strength before bowing again. I could not bring myself to resent Mon Choi's fickle transfer of admiration. Unlike Karfai, Kwan behaved with impeccable honor and skill. Moreover, I noticed a twinkle in his eye as his gaze slid from the arcs he had drawn in the stand. As he withdrew from the duel, I noticed that he no longer dragged his foot.

Kwan was as cunning as he was strong.

I bowed again, this time to express sincere admiration. He nodded back to accept the gesture, but only barely. He knew exactly how much he deserved the acclaim.

"It is confirmed that Kwan is First Brother in all weapons," said Master Li. His old man's voice had begun to sound musical to my ear. It had a hint of the mysticism I had detected in the voices of priests and ascetics, but without the practiced affectation of pretenders. "Brothers Mon Choi and Jeggare are now officially disciples of Dragon Temple. And Brother Jeggare, while Second Brother in sword, remains Least Brother until the second trials. For two hours each morning and each evening, he is First Brother of Kitchen."

My "brothers" bowed formally at the pronouncement of my new title, but few could constrain their titters. Only the cool of the evening breeze could soothe the resentful flush of my cheeks.

"Kowtow!" bellowed Master Wu. We hit the ground in unison, our heads turned to Master Li, but the old man sighed and looked longingly at his fishing gear. He was not the intended object of our submission.

Both masters turned to bow at the pale man and the noble he escorted, flanked by their twenty spear-bearing guards. We shuffled crablike to present our heads to the visitors.

We aspirants—disciples now—had caught scant glimpses of the visitors since Mon Choi and I arrived at the temple. The royal entourage had retreated to guest quarters in the Peach Court to the south. The other disciples whispered that the tall fair man who led the procession was a eunuch, one Jade Tiger, advisor to the king of Quain. They speculated as to which of the king's eight sons had been sent to Dragon Temple.

I strained my neck to cast a furtive glance toward Jade Tiger and his charge, sensing that my fellows to either side did the same while attempting to retain the illusion of strict obeisance.

The eunuch stepped forward, fluttering a fan before his face. Upon its outward face was painted a trio of playful tiger cubs, their jaws open in comical smiles. I wondered at the coincidence of the image on the fan and our encounter outside the gates of the temple. It seemed unlikely that he would have seen our flight from the brigands, even less so that he would have conjured tigers to attack us.

Still . . .

"King Wen, by the Mandate of Heaven Monarch of all Quain, congratulates the new disciples of Dragon Temple," announced Jade Tiger. His voice was high and clear, yet not as fine as the voices of the celebrated castrati of the Chelish opera. He stepped forward, preceding his master in the inspection of our sweaty figures.

As the hem of the eunuch's robe passed inches from my head, I detected the strong odor of incense over the scent of road dust and cosmetic powder. Beneath it all, the eunuch's skin exuded a curious smell neither masculine nor feminine. It was an alien odor, and I wondered what Arnisant would make of it. Surely by now the hound had found Radovan. How much longer could it take them to follow my trail to Dragon Temple, allowing us to resume our journey to the capital of Quain?

The prince drifted past. I glimpsed a jeweled slipper beneath the hem of the embroidered silken robe. By some charm, the dust left no stain on the garment. A black scabbard chased in gold hung from an embroidered belt around the royal waist. Unlike the eunuch, the prince had not bathed in the smoke of incense, and I noted a wholly agreeable air of jasmine mingled with a surprisingly delicate scent of clean skin. Intrigued, I turned my head just enough to glimpse upward at the royal face.

From the low vantage, I peered beneath the veil that hung from the round brim of the hat. Within I spied dark eyes and a hint of perfect cheeks. I saw one other notable feature—or rather the lack of one—before Master Wu stamped the breath from my lungs.

"Eyes down," he hissed.

Stunned, I could barely muster the strength to return my palms to the ground beneath my forehead. Yet the punishment for sating my curiosity had almost been worth it.

The prince was possessed of the most supernal beauty I had ever been privileged to view, but I detected the absence of a key masculine feature: a prominent larynx. Combined with the intoxicating orchid fragrance of the royal skin, I could come to only one conclusion.

The prince was a princess.

Chapter Five
Judge Fang

In the land where I was born, Arnisant is the name of a great hero. My master gave me the same name to make me a good dog, so I would always do my best.

Master teaches me the rules and gives me jobs. When I do a job well, he gives me a reward, usually a piece of meat. Sometimes the reward is his praise, which I like almost as much. Praise means he is proud of me. It also means I'll probably get some more meat soon.

When the swordsmen surrounded us, Master sent me to fetch Radovan. I was glad to have another chance to do good after failing to fetch his horse. My master has often sent me to fetch Radovan, and it is a job I do well. I take Radovan's hand in my mouth and pull him to wherever my master is. I don't bite hard, because that's the rule.

Also, I don't bite hard because I am afraid to anger Radovan. I have seen his teeth.

Sometimes Master scolds Radovan for playing with me instead of giving me jobs. Also, Master does not like it when Radovan calls me "Arni" instead of by my full name. Radovan does not obey the rules. Sometimes he rewards me when I haven't done a job, but he does that only when Master is not present.

Radovan is not my master. He's my friend.

Fetching Radovan is easy because he has a strong smell, which is even stronger after he has caught on fire. Sometimes Master has offered to set him on fire, but Radovan doesn't like it. I understand, because I wouldn't like it either. Even without my master's help, Radovan manages to catch on fire. He catches on fire more than anyone.

I found Radovan's smell where we first fought the swordsmen. Long before I reached the spot, I could tell he had caught on fire again. I followed his fire-smell down from the hills and into the woods. It was hard to focus on his scent so close to the trees where there were so many other trails to follow. Some of the smells straightened my tail. I wanted to follow the path of the hare, but I am a good boy, so I followed Radovan's trail instead.

The trail led all through the forest. Radovan changed direction many times, usually beside a tree that had plenty of his smell on it. Some of the trees smelled like cats. The smell of what they had eaten and the heavy scratch marks high on the bark made me think these cats were too big to chase. I was glad my master had not sent me to fetch them.

Radovan's trail crossed the path of another man. The other man's smell was even stronger than Radovan's. I do not think my master would like the other man. He prefers people with weak smells.

The two trails came together in a clearing. They were strong there, so I knew that Radovan and the other man had stayed for a while. Now there was no one else in the clearing except some noisy birds. I told them to be quiet, and they flew away.

The two smells together left another trail out of the clearing. This one went back through the forest but without all the turns and twists of Radovan's path into the forest. I followed the smells back to where the swordsmen attacked us.

Radovan and a man with only one arm stood at the top of the nearest hill. If it had been Radovan alone, I would have greeted him, but my master taught me not to greet him or Radovan if someone is with them. Instead I ran toward him.

Before I reached Radovan, the one-armed man made a ball of fire around them both. This kind of thing happens to Radovan all the time, but it still made him angry. He called the other man Burning Cloud Devil.

The fireball moved off of the ground and flew away. I called out to Radovan, but the fireball did not stop. I chased after it, but it was too high and too fast to catch.

I was not going to be a good boy this time, either. I couldn't catch my master's horse, and now I couldn't fetch Radovan.

I searched the area and found my master's smell. It was surrounded by many other smells of men. They were mostly not the same men who came with us from the town beside the sea. Many of the smells were bad because the men were sick. Some were frightened, and those were the worst smells.

They were easy to follow, but sometimes they confused me. I could not always find my master's trail because it went in two different directions. Sometimes it smelled as if he were walking in two different places. I stopped often to make sure he was still with the other men. Checking made me slow, but I knew he was still with the other men. They all went together over the hills. Then they went along a road.

After dark, the bird sounds changed. When I had traveled long enough to feel thirsty, there were no bird sounds at all. I smelled the big cats again. The men had gone through their territory. I began to worry about my master. I didn't want a big cat to eat him.

It was late at night when I found the bones. Soon I also found pieces of his clothes, and I felt scared. I whimpered, but there was no one to hear me.

I noticed there was something wrong with the smell. The clothes were my master's, but the blood was not his. I kept searching.

All around the area I smelled the big cats. I smelled Radovan and Burning Cloud Devil, too, but no one was here anymore.

I searched all over the battleground before I found my master's smell. He was with another man who smelled frightened. They had moved away from all the other men, and a big cat went after them. The cat had eaten bears and horses. I did not want to fight a cat so big.

But for my master, I would fight one.

All three trails went through a big open doorway over the road. On either side of the doorway sat a big animal. The one on the right had a dog's face and a big cat's mane and the talons of a bird, and it smelled like stone. The other one had the horns and body of a stag, but the scales of a fish and the face of a lizard. It smelled like metal.

"Go away, dog," said the animal to my right. "You are not permitted through this gate."

"There is not even a door in the gate," I said.

The other one laughed. "Try to enter, if you dare."

"I dare!" I ran through the doorway. I saw nothing, but I felt a wall as hard as stone. A flash of green light stung me and threw me back.

"Not even an ordinary beast like you may pass the walls of Dragon Temple."

"There are no walls."

"Then try to enter, if you dare."

I did not dare again.

"My master's smell goes through this doorway."

"No master has passed through this gate since last autumn," said the animal on the left. "Only disciples and royal visitors have entered."

"I need to find my master."

"We were made to prevent all spirits and animals from entering the temple," said the one on the right. "I am Stone Guardian Chu, and this is my sister, Bronze Sentinel Wing. So long as we guard this gate, you will not pass."

"Tell my master I am here."

"We cannot leave our post," said Bronze Sentinel Wing.

"I must find my master. I cannot find my friend, and I smelled big cats!"

"It is not our concern," said her brother.

"You are useless," I said. "Who can help me find my master?"

"We serve the masters of Dragon Temple, not any stray dog that happens by," said Stone Guardian Chu. "Go away. No one will emerge from Dragon Temple until next spring."

"I pity the dog, brother," said Bronze Sentinel Wing. "Perhaps Judge Fang could help."

"Who is Judge Fang?"

"Sister," said Stone Guardian Chu. "There is no need to be cruel."

"I want Judge Fang to help me," I said. "Tell me where he is. Tell me now!"

"Look to that star that is twinkling," said Bronze Sentinel Wing. "Follow it into the woods and cry out Judge Fang's name. He will find you."

"Sister," said Stone Guardian Chu. "I do not think it wise to send this dog to Judge Fang."

"If Judge Fang will help me find my master, I want to find him."

I ran toward the woods. Behind me, Bronze Sentinel Wing laughed as Stone Guardian Chu scolded her. I didn't understand them, but I knew my job. I needed to find my master.

I ran into the woods and cried out Judge Fang's name.

The newborn crickets stopped singing. There were many smells among the trees. There were pigs and frogs and rats and birds and snakes and ferrets and all kinds of animals. Most of them fled or hid as I ran past. I wanted to eat some of them, but I had to do my job first. Still, I was thirsty. I stopped to drink from a pool. The water was cool and clean. I saw a tree branch reflected in the water. There were tiny lights above me, and something moved along the branch.

"Judge Fang! Judge Fang!"

"What is all this commotion?" called an old man's voice.

On the branch sat a man with the head and wings of a big cricket. He was so tiny that I could have eaten four of him in one bite. He wore a long robe and held a pipe like Radovan's but with a smaller bowl and a long stem as thin as a whisker. Beside him lay a bag, and across his knees lay a twig for a walking stick. "Who disturbs the Celestial Order today? Who cries out my name? For what calamity—?"

"Are you Judge Fang?"

"Interrupting is a sign of poor character, even in a dog. Who sent you here?"

"Bronze Sentinel Wing."

"Aha!" said the cricket man. He fluttered his wings and moved closer to the ground, but not close enough for me to eat him. I was not hungry, but I thought him wise to be cautious. He pointed his walking twig at me before leaning on it. "You must be a naughty dog."

"I am a good dog. I want to find my master."

"Is your master the one responsible for bringing the Jade Tiger into Dragon Temple? Is he the hero who flies on balls of fire through my sky?"

"No," I said, and it was true. My master did sometimes throw balls of fire, but he never flew on them. "The big cats chased my master. The fire came from Burning Cloud Devil."

"Both the Burning Cloud Devil and the Jade Tiger!" Judge Fang grabbed his chest and staggered. "Surely a great catastrophe is at hand."

"You must help me find my master. He fixes everything."

"Not so quickly," said Judge Fang. "If it is true that these twin dooms have come so close to Dragon Temple, it is my duty to restore the Celestial Order, the natural spring of virtue from which all rules of behavior fall like nourishing streams."

"I am good at rules."

"Perhaps so," said Judge Fang. "But one dog, however obedient, is insufficient for such an awful task. Jade Tiger and Burning Cloud Devil are powerful foes. They must have evil designs on the masters of Dragon Temple."

"My master is inside Dragon Temple."

"Then you cannot reach him. The temple is forbidden to our kind. However, next spring the masters and their students travel to Iron Mountain."

"I want to go to Iron Mountain!"

"And so you shall," said Judge Fang. He lifted his silk bag from the branch and began stuffing it with little items. I saw a mirror, some scrolls and yellow paper, lots of little jars, and a tiny dagger made of coins sewn tightly together with red cord. "But first you must perform some tasks for me."

"I am good at jobs." That was mostly true, even though I had failed my last two.

"Then it is settled," said Judge Fang. "Come with me, and to thwart the evil of Burning Cloud Devil and Jade Tiger, together we shall gather an army of beasts and kami."

Chapter Six
Eight-Figure Staff

Stand where you are, fiend!" The little guy thrust his finger at my face. If he'd been a few yards closer, I'd have bitten it off.

I was in no mood.

Truth was, I'd been in a foul temper since burying the boss's remains. I'd always figured I'd be the one to die on one of his screwy Pathfinder expeditions. It was a wonder I hadn't bought the acre a dozen times over just from our Egorian capers.

The worst part was that I spent the first few days hoping there was some crazy mix-up and the boss wasn't dead after all. I'd made that mistake before, and I wasn't in a hurry to make it again. The difference this time was that I found the body, or what was left of it.

Even burying him didn't spare me from daydreaming of improbable scenarios in which the boss had escaped the dragon. It took me days of tramping behind Burning Cloud Devil before I could finally get my hands around the throat of that son of a bitch Hope. A couple of good twists shut him up, and I stopped fantasizing escape scenarios that left the boss alive somewhere.

On that first night, I wanted to do the same to Burning Cloud Devil. If he hadn't lured me away, I could have gone after the boss. I thought about his guilt as I watched him snoring beside the fire he'd conjured. Did he need to speak to trigger his Quivering Palm whammy? A few days earlier, without warning, he'd hit me with it again.

Again I felt threads of energy streaming through my body from each point where his fingers had touched me. When I demanded, "What the hell?" he said it was an adjustment to be sure that I didn't die while he went off in search of wine and food. I got the feeling he was lying, or at least not telling me the whole truth.

Also, he had a neck thicker than a pig's. I'd need to strangle him if I couldn't break his spine with the first blow, and that could take a minute or longer. Plenty of time for him to kill me if it was as easy as he boasted.

Eventually I decided that if Burning Cloud Devil hadn't showed up, the Falcon-Head Sword Gang would have turned me into minced meat. I shuddered at the thought of ending up in those little dumplings we ate back at the last roadside inn we'd visited before the disaster.

No matter what the bandits would have done with me, I wouldn't have been free to go after the boss. When I thought about it that way, Burning Cloud Devil had saved my life. I should have thanked him, but I couldn't muster the gratitude. After all, if I didn't slay this dragon for him, he promised to kill me.

Before that, it turned out, he planned to spend a year torturing me.

After a couple of weeks, I'd had more than enough of his training exercises. They lasted from dawn until noon every day. They included strikes and kicks, not too different from the sort of thing I learned for myself on the streets of Egorian. The difference was that Burning Cloud Devil wanted them to look just so. He was more interested in my posture than in how hard I hit something. I explained my philosophy that what's good is what gets the job done. He didn't like that, and gave me one hell of a sermon about form and inner power.

I mostly ignored it, but that didn't stop him. He pushed and pulled and poked at me to stand exactly as he did, to raise my arm with my wrist bent for no obviously good reason. I began to think he was having fun with me, posing me this way and that as some sort of private joke. Still, he seemed deadly serious.

Eventually I focused on getting it right just to keep his mitts off me. It wasn't that I didn't get what he was saying. It's that when he wound himself up into a lecture he sounded a lot like the boss. I didn't want to think about that, but I couldn't help it.

Burning Cloud Devil's exercises looked a lot like the calisthenics I'd caught the boss performing before we'd embark on some footwork, back in the good days. The less-bad days. Whatever. Most of the postures and moves had poetic animal names like Horse Stance, Lazy Serpent, Crane Steps Forth, Monkey Plucks the Peaches.

That last one I'd known all my life. The first thing most street kids do in a fight is throw a punch or a knee at your gem bag. That's why I took to wearing a spiked leather cup. That was gone with the burned fragments of my clothes and whatever was left of my knives and break-in tools. Maybe some of our traveling gear was scattered among the bones where the boss had died, but I hadn't had the stomach to search the place. All I had anymore were my two knives, a copper, and a makeshift skirt made out of a banner.

It was that rag around my waist that had the little guy all up in my face.

"You disgrace my father's banner!"

The newcomer leaped off his dappled horse, which balked rather than approach me. I had yet to meet a draft animal who didn't get a whiff of me and either head for the hills or try to smash my skull. While the horse shied, its rider preferred the second approach.

He flourished his staff and held it perfectly horizontal behind his back with one hand. "How many of his men did you kill?"

As I opened my mouth to speak, my self-appointed tutor interrupted from his perch on a gnarled tree. I hadn't even heard him jump up there. He was a nimble old bastard.

"All of them, of course, Fong Jian, just as I slew your master when he dared challenge me."

"Burning Cloud Devil!"

The old man's laughter shook the leaves. "Hong Gau was no match for me. What makes you think his student stands a chance?"

Fong stabbed the butt of his staff into the dirt. He made a pretty picture of righteous indignation. "I do not challenge you but your demon."

"Devil," I corrected him.

In fact, I didn't know that for a fact. Most hellspawn where I grew up are descended from the infernal legions, literally from Hell. On the other hand, my mixed blood went way back to when my people lived in Ustalav, where they say my ancestors trucked with both devils from Hell and demons from the Abyss. The roots of my family tree ran deep.

Fong frowned, obviously unschooled in the language of Hell. Burning Cloud Devil translated.

"It doesn't matter," said Fong. His staff sprang to life, whirling invisibly until it snapped fast in his double grip. The weapon was dark red with a steel cap on either butt. It looked like the shaft was inlaid with real gold, but that was stupid. Something like that wouldn't last two good strikes—unless it was magical. I didn't like that idea. "I will send you back to the underworld and reclaim the banner you have disgraced."

I was tempted to whip the rag off and throw it at him, but I knew that wouldn't satisfy his pride. Anyway, no one wanted a look at what was under my skirt. I know I didn't.

"Hey, I took this from a gang of bandits." I looked to Burning Cloud Devil for a translation.

"My devil says he wipes his ass with your father's banner."

"Hey!"

Fong jutted his chin at the sorcerer. "You will not interfere in our duel?"

"I will not lay a hand upon you."

"Nor cast spells upon me?"

The old man leaped down from his branch and snarled. This Fong character was testing his patience. "I will cast no spell upon you." He stepped close behind me and plucked a hair from my neck.

"What the hell?" I rubbed the sting off the back of my neck.

Burning Cloud Devil dismissed my question with a shake of his head. He folded the thick bronze hair into a scrap of yellow paper on which he'd painted red characters. He waved his hand in a "carry-on" gesture as he walked away, murmuring.

Fong Jian thrust the butt of his staff square into my jaw. A hundred green stars exploded before my eyes. My teeth rattled in my head.

I raised my arms to guard my face. The next shot caught me hard in the belly, the third struck down below. That one didn't hurt nearly as much as I'd expected. The fact that it didn't reminded me of how inhuman my body had become.

By Fong's fourth strike I blocked his staff with my forearm. The wood cracked hard against it. The bony ridges running from my wrists to elbows were good for more than just show.

Pleased with myself, I grinned into his face.

Fong didn't even flinch. He was braver than he looked. Stronger, too. He beat my arms aside the way a swordsman parries a lighter blade before lunging for the kill. The butt of his staff struck me in the throat, in the eye, on the top of my skull.

"All right, all right!" I yelled. "That's enough."

Fong hesitated, unable to believe I was surrendering. That was fine, because I wasn't surrendering. I was asking for help.

I felt a little square of paper in my throat, even though I hadn't swallowed one. I tried to look back at Burning Cloud Devil, but my neck wouldn't turn. Instead, I assumed a lower stance. It felt correct, the way it never had when I'd been doing it. My left arm flashed forward and back with a flourish of the wrist.

None of this was my choice. Burning Cloud Devil was controlling me with his little paper pill.

The only part of me still obeying my thoughts was my right arm. That made sense, since Burning Cloud Devil didn't have one. I made a fist and held it up to protect my face.

"No, you idiot," said Burning Cloud Devil. "Tip the Leaf, not Scorpion Pincer."

I corrected my arm, extending it palm-up as if to tap a drop of dew out of a leaf, but I felt ridiculous. This was no way to defend myself, posing with both arms open like some sort of ballet dancer. Back on Eel Street, standing like this would have been a better way to get into a fight than to win one.

"You swore not to interfere!" cried Fong.

"I promised not to cast a spell on *you*."

The sorcerer moved me forward, shifting my body to lead with my left, which he controlled. It took me a second to follow what he was doing, and I raised my right hand to assume the trailing position.

He grunted approval of my stance. "Summon your ki!"

"Devils have no ki," said Fong.

All the same, he retreated, raising his staff high for a powerful counterstrike.

"This minion is no common devil."

"Hey," I said. "I'm not your damned minion."

All the same, I tried to do what he told me.

Burning Cloud Devil's ki business was another lesson I hadn't really understood. It started with breathing. That part I got. There was more to it, though, some vague summoning of power from my soul or my spirit or—the part that bothered me—my ancestors. The boss had described the concept during our Minkai caper, but the only skill I mastered from his Tian Xia lectures was pretending to listen.

Ki wasn't really my kind of thing, but there had to be something to it. I took a deep belly breath and held it. For an instant I imagined a stream of energy between the center of my body and the heel of my hand, which I planned to plant in Fong's chin.

My body trembled. I lunged forward. As Fong's staff swept down at my skull, I tumbled past its arc and came up beside his knees—not where I'd wanted to be. Before I could growl a curse about the way Burning Cloud Devil was moving me around, my left hand shot up and clutched Fong hard between the thighs.

Monkey Plucks the Peaches.

Fong's face twisted in a silent scream that made me wince for him even as Burning Cloud Devil tightened my grip.

His knee shot into my throat so hard I felt like my head had come off. He kicked again and knocked me back. He leaped away, howling and clutching his parts with both hands.

As I shook off the ringing in my skull, I felt a lump in my fist. With some reluctance, I opened my hand to see a hank of fabric. Desna smiled upon Fong, because that was all I'd torn off.

"That's dirty mean," I said. "Let go of me. I can take this chump."

"Good," said Burning Cloud Devil. "Because I have a better use for my magic." He coughed, and I felt the little magic pill come up as if it were in my own throat. Burning Cloud Devil spat it on the ground like a cat hacking up a hairball. My body relaxed for a second, and I felt my limbs come back under my control.

Fong snatched up his staff and gripped it with two hands. He glowered at me, eyes glistening from the pain. I thought of a jibe to make him lose his temper, but I knew he wouldn't understand.

On the other hand, he felt the breeze through the hole in his trousers, and he saw me smirk.

Worked like a charm.

He came on like a windmill in a storm. The steel-capped butts of his staff struck divots on the trail, sparking on flint once or twice. For a second I regretted pissing him off.

I stepped quickly to the side and threw a knuckle shot at his throat. He was too mad to anticipate the move, but he was still quick enough to lean back out of the way. He kicked at my crotch, but I caught the blow with a knee. He shouted as the spike on my kneecap pierced his foot.

My new bone structure had that going for it. Who needed a cup?

He battered me with either side of the staff, but the strikes came from the obvious four quarters. I caught them all with my bony elbows and knees. Just before I saw the flicker of sanity return to his face, I caught the staff with both hands and did what I hate most.

I bit.

Even before my "episodes," as the boss called them, my smile would send the barber running from a block away. After the fire, my jaws were more like a rusty bear trap.

Luckily for Fong, I didn't go for his face. Instead, I clamped my teeth on the staff. It split with a satisfying crunch. A yellow flash dazed me for a second, but it sent Fong flying back a good four yards. Spitting out the splinters, I tasted enamel and fragments of gold.

Fong gaped in disbelief, but it was Burning Cloud Devil who cried out, "Impossible!"

"What?" I said, dusting myself off an arm at a time. "I told you I could take him."

"The Eight-Figured Staff," wailed Fong. "Monster, you have destroyed the sacred weapon of my house!"

"If you liked it so much, you shouldn't have stuck it in my face." He still didn't understand a word, but that didn't matter. He rushed me.

His anger dulled his vision, not to mention his good sense. I stepped left as he came into range, and I caught him in the gut with the heel of my palm.

The blow threw Fong up and back, much farther than I'd expected. If the strike didn't kill him, the fall might.

But I was worried more about myself.

The instant my hand struck his torso, my blood turned to fire. I felt it surging through my veins before bursting out through the skin of my hands. Behind me, Burning Cloud Devil intoned arcane words. He was casting another spell on me.

"What do you think you're doing?"

Burning Cloud Devil spoke a few more syllables and sighed like a porter setting down a heavy load. "I have sealed the lesson into your body."

Looking down at my fists, I saw they glowed with tiny Tien characters. They ran across my wrists and halfway up my forearms, flared bright, and vanished.

Burning Cloud Devil knelt, exhausted. He picked up a fragment of the shattered staff and squinted at it. "Only another great magic should have the power to destroy such a weapon."

"You wanted his ass beat," I said. "I beat his ass."

Twenty feet away, Fong moaned.

"You have not just defeated him," said Burning Cloud Devil. "You have broken his honor." He shook his head as if I were too stupid to understand his point. He pointed the staff fragment at Fong. "Finish him off."

"Why bother?"

"Because I am your master, and you are sworn to do my bidding."

"Our deal is I kill this dragon. Anything else is just to get me ready for that."

Burning Cloud Devil looked ready to argue, but he opened and shut his mouth twice before rummaging in his bag. He selected a yellow scroll from a bundle of dozens and glowered down at it. Beneath the Tien characters, I recognized my signature and wished I'd had someone to translate the terms before I'd signed. I knew better than that, but I'd been distracted at the time.

The boss could have done it. But if he were still alive, I wouldn't have had to make the bargain.

Burning Cloud Devil grunted. "I should have worded our compact more carefully. Very well, devil. Do as you will."

I stood up and shooed Fong away, but he just lay there staring at the sky. A sliver of guilt nibbled at me. I whipped off his house banner, tied it around the broken pieces of his staff, and threw the bundle at him. "Go on. Get out of here."

Fong barely grimaced when he saw the worst parts of my inhuman anatomy. His face was a caricature of mourning as he gazed down at the ruins of his family banner and weapon. He clutched them to his chest and limped back to his waiting horse. I watched him ride away until I felt Burning Cloud Devil watching me with an expression of disbelief.

"And you think *me* cruel."

Chapter Seven
Enchanting Lyre

On the twenty-seventh day of my captivity, I resolved to escape Dragon Temple.

I had remained so long as I had not for fear of Master Wu's vivid descriptions of the punishment for leaving but rather because I had discovered the singular purpose of the order intersected perfectly with my original goal in traveling to Tian Xia.

I joined the Pathfinder Society in my youth, and in recent decades I served as one of the organization's many venture-captains. It fell to me and my peers to communicate with a number of field agents, guiding and supporting their efforts to uncover lost civilizations, to unravel ancient mysteries and—yes, from time to time—to retrieve buried treasure.

It was the Decemvirate who charted the course of the organization as a whole, and to them I submitted the summation of my own agents' reports. Those the Decemvirate deemed worthy became part of the *Pathfinder Chronicles*, an ever-expanding archive of investigations across Golarion. My own accounts had occasionally been deemed worthy enough to join the storied annals of our society.

When dispatched to collect the husk of a Celestial Pearl, its magic expended, it was only natural that I felt curious as to the reason. Thus I inquired of the masked member of the Decemvirate who had given me my orders.

To my eternal vexation, my anonymous superior explained nothing more before dispatching me to the other side of Golarion. When my initial efforts to fetch the husk failed, I took the initiative in traveling to the mainland in hopes of acquiring one of the hundreds of identical shells residing in the capital of Quain, largest of the sixteen Successor States of Imperial Lung Wa.

Yet those husks were delivered to the royal vaults by the monks of Dragon Temple.

Once every twelve years, the disciples of Dragon Temple enjoyed the honor of escorting an embassy past the fabled Flying Mountains to the base of Iron Mountain and thence to the Court of Heaven and Hell and its fabled gates. There a representative of the royal family summoned the Celestial Dragon and offered the immortal creature a mortal heart in exchange for its own, a great magic pearl whose contents bestowed upon the supplicant both longevity and a powerful wish. Afterward, the husk of the dragon's heart, its wish expended, was conveyed to the royal vaults within the capital city of Lanming.

If ever there was an opportunity to negotiate for the husk of the dragon's pearl, I had found it. Armed with the favor of the Pathfinder Society, a certain amount of diplomatic experience, and—if it came to that—a considerable personal fortune, I would appeal to the king to let me return with the object.

Had I simply traveled to the capital and acquired King Wen's permission, I should have joined the monks some months from now at this very site—albeit without the arduous and demeaning trials I had endured. Yet how much more persuasive would his majesty find my voice upon learning that I had personally accompanied his embassy to the Gates of Heaven and Hell?

The irony troubled my imagination. Not for the first time, I pondered the question of fate as a power greater than mortal will and chance.

More troubling was the weeks-long absence of Radovan and Arnisant. The temple's barrier against spirits and beasts might have prevented the hound from entering, but even with his Hell-tainted blood, Radovan remained essentially a mortal man. That is, I had no conclusive evidence to believe otherwise, despite his reticence to allow me to perform a few simple, if uncomfortable, experiments to determine the nature of his atypical transformations. He should have been able to enter the temple grounds or at least approach close enough to hail someone inside the first gate.

On the other hand, even one of the enormous tigers was capable of slaying one or both of my lost companions.

I banished the thought. In the past I had allowed cloudy circumstances to persuade me of Radovan's death without conclusive evidence. Never again would I presume my bodyguard dead without proof, yet I remained at a loss to explain why he had not yet found me. Even without the benefit of the hound's keen nose, Radovan was resourceful enough to discover my trail and follow it to Dragon Temple.

If not, then I knew he must await me at our rendezvous, the Inn of Forty-Four Delights in Lanming, which—despite its fanciful name and Radovan's great disappointment—was not a brothel but a famed restaurant. Bereft of my spellbook, I had no means of contacting Radovan from afar, and Master Li had flatly refused my request to send a message to Lanming. When I protested, the old man closed his rheumy eyes and counseled me to set aside my worldly concerns. Upon entering the temple as an aspirant, he said, I had pledged obedience and loyalty to the temple masters, forsaking any previous bonds of fidelity. Before I could argue that I had made no such vow, at least not explicitly, he took up his fishing pole and strolled out the inner gate.

Perhaps I should have spent more effort thanking the gods for sparing my life. It was no small miracle that I had survived the first weeks of training. As the least among the new brothers, it fell to me to rise an hour earlier than the other disciples. Each morning, rather than the gentle murmur of a servant bearing a fragrant tisane to ease me out of slumber, a sharp blow to the sole of my foot jolted me awake. When I did not immediately arise, a barrage of kicks traveled up my leg until I leaped up to stand before Master Wu.

"How dare you assault me in such a manner?" I demanded upon the first such waking.

He lifted one bushy black eyebrow at my umbrage.

"In Cheliax, I should have you thrashed for such—"

Before I could complete my threat, Wu blasted the air from my lungs with a punch to my sternum. My lips moved, but I could produce no sound. My silent complaint only intensified Wu's castigation until at last I bowed before him. He placed his foot upon my head to remind me of our relative positions, so unnatural to my custom. I seethed at the affront, but never again did I fail to rise at the first strike upon my soles.

Beyond the humiliation of menial labor, kitchen duty deprived me of an hour's exercise each morning and again before the evening meal. Thus it followed that I fell further and further behind the skills of my fellow "novices," although the term was a gross misnomer. None of the new brothers of Dragon Temple could truly be called a neophyte. Even to present oneself at the famous center of martial and spiritual study, one required previous distinction somewhere among the Successor States of Lung Wa. Kwan, for instance, had come from the Condor Fist Society in Lingshen to the north, while Karfai was celebrated as the most recent Hero of the Green Marsh in the south of Quain. Even Mon Choi had defeated a celebrated local champion who dared all comers to wrestle him in the square of his little village in Po Li, to the east.

No matter their origin, all of the disciples were now dedicated to serve the masters of Dragon Temple. Nationalism and familial loyalty dissolved upon passing through each of the four gates. By the time one entered the inner courtyards, only devotion to Dragon Temple remained.

I could have informed my fellow disciples of my service in the wars of colonial secession, or of my youthful triumph on the cliffs of Lepidstadt, or of my fatal duel on the roof of the Grand Opera with the thief known only as the Blue Gloaming. Yet no one asked for my pedigree, and I found no subtle moment in which to mention my achievements.

That I had been defeated not by peasants but by local heroes soothed the sting of my failure, or would have done so if not for the daily reminder of my kitchen labor on their behalf. Worse was the frequent use of the hated appellation "Younger Brother," which was both insulting and chronologically preposterous. None of my "brothers" had more than one-quarter of my years.

I had begun to feel old.

More than that, I felt perpetually exhausted. Even before joining the morning lessons, my limbs were limp after a frantic hour gathering eggs, fetching water, soaking rice, and chopping roots and preserved vegetables for the steam baskets. I was not unaccustomed to cooking in the field on those occasions when adversity deprived me of a servant, but it was another matter entirely to prepare meals in quantity and while striving to avoid the attention of Lo Gau, the dread master of Dragon Temple kitchen.

The man was once a master of instruction, but the gradual onset of cataract blindness had relegated him to the lesser role. Nevertheless, his sight—or rather, I surmised, his power of deduction—was keen enough to discern my slightest error in form. He demanded that I employ the proper grip on every tool from spoon to chopsticks to the various knives, each of which required a different technique.

Worse than Lo Gau's exacting standards for precision was that the slightest delay invoked his wrath. What his rebukes lacked in Master Wu's accuracy, they more than compensated for in proximity to knives and heavy kettles. Lo Gau went so far as to harry me with darts aimed generally at my feet as I returned with the firewood, costing me precious time as I gathered the wood I had spilled. More and more often, I avoided serious injury or death only by taking shelter behind a chopping block or dodging a ladle of hot oil. Too frequently, I suffered the impact or the scalding.

On those days when I arrived after Master Wu began leading the brothers in the Thirty-Six Forms, he invariably selected me as the example on which to present the day's lesson. Several times his demonstration rendered me insensible, after which I awoke to his peculiar version of healing, which was as agonizing as it was effective. The only happy side effect was that I soon became the foremost student in the art of the battle scream, or so my elder brothers joked.

I hoped to find respite in the meditation hall, where we assembled to contemplate the enormous scroll that contained Irori's sacred scriptures, *Unbinding the Fetters*. While Venerable Master Li sat in placid meditation before the scroll, exemplar to us all, Scrupulous Master Wu patrolled the ranks of students seeking flaws in posture and thought. He most often found the latter in me, for I found it impossible to meditate upon the wisdom of the god of self-perfection when my body had been rendered so utterly imperfect.

Only once did I commit the error of demanding to know how Master Wu could perceive that my thoughts had wandered from the prescribed subjects. At a nod of consent from the sagacious Master Li, Wu's succinct reply rendered me unable to complete the rest of the day's exercises. I resumed my meditations in the infirmary.

It was there that I first plotted escape. Yet several obstacles prevented me from immediately leaving Dragon Temple.

The most imminent problem was the knowledge that the tigers Mon Choi and I had narrowly escaped were not the only predators claiming the region as their territory. After weeks of labor and injuries in Dragon Temple, I was much less capable of outrunning the beasts.

Even more dreadful was the warning Master Wu had given us the day after our arrival. He promised to track down any novice who dared forswear his vow to the temple masters. After so much indelible instruction at his hands, I knew I would prefer to face one of the tigers.

For a time, I justified my reticence to leave by satisfying my curiosity about the temple grounds. Unfortunately, I soon exhausted the grounds of the only area we new students were permitted to explore, the so-called Cherry Court. In that district lay our dormitory, the meditation hall, a privy, the kitchen, a refectory, a scriptorium, four practice yards of different configurations, and an armory. The latter building housed rattan armor and shields as well as wooden versions of the Sacred Weapons of Irori.

To the north lay vegetable and herb gardens irrigated by a stream passing through a grate in the Plum Court wall. So early in the year, few of the plants were ready for harvest, but it was among my endless obligations to nurture the seedlings. Tending the garden provided solace, if also a painful reminder of how long it had been since I last enjoyed my hothouse in Greensteeples. No one intruded upon my solitude except Master Li, who occasionally inspected the garden, murmuring as he strolled its lanes.

From over the Plum Court wall I heard the voices of our elder brothers drilling with the weapons and techniques we would learn only after the second trial. I was not the only new disciple who was curious about them, but those who lifted their heads above the walls for a better look soon regretted their disobedience. Master Wu had a knack for being everywhere at once, and no infraction was too small to escape his wrath.

During our exercises on the pillars resembling a cluster of dock pilings, I could barely glimpse the interior of a garden nestled between the walls of the Cherry and Peach Courts. Except for the daily ministrations of an ancient gardener who also tended the koi pond, it appeared abandoned. I imagined it would become a lovely retreat in the full blush of spring.

It also appeared to be the most advantageous avenue for an escape.

The wall dividing the Cherry Court from the garden was five yards high and bereft of spikes, shards of glass, or other obvious deterrents to climbing. Its sheer faces offered no hand- or footholds, but someone reaching the top should have no difficulty dropping safely to the other side. Its height was greater than even Kwan's prodigious leaps could attain.

Yet the cherry trees stood enticingly near to the wall.

Musing on this data, I shuffled out of the kitchen long after nightfall, my body, mind, and spirit equally defeated by the day's exertions and dishonors. I imagined I heard faerie music in the distance, calling me out of this harsh refuge and back to my originally intended path to Lanming and the Royal Court of Quain. Above the Cherry Court wall I glimpsed the first peach buds of spring illuminated by paper lanterns suspended in the tree branches. In the warm hues of the light I saw the promise of freedom.

Against all likelihood, I had gained a few pounds over the past month, yet I estimated I was still light enough to scale a tree and leap onto the high outer wall on the southern border of the garden. Entering the garden itself was child's play. Although the gate was locked, the interior wall was no more than eight feet tall. I barely had to jump to lift myself up to the top, where I crouched and listened for any sound of approaching feet.

I froze as still as a gargoyle. The music I thought I heard emanated not from my imagination but from within the garden walls.

From closer vantage, the refuge was even more alluring than I had realized. Inside the outer ring of trees and walls, a gravel path wound through six or seven grassy hillocks. On each knoll stood a lighted peach tree attended by an ornamental shrub, a flower bed, a stone statue or bench, or some combination thereof. Near the center lay the black face of the koi pond.

Beside the pool knelt the princess. The lacquered scabbard lay on the grass nearby, the pool's reflected moonlight glimmering over its gold chasing. She had abandoned her masculine garb for an elegant robe of imperial yellow, the specific shade claimed by royal families among the Successor States. For anyone else to wear the color was punishable by torture and death.

Upon her knees the princess held a guqin, a distant cousin to the lyre. I had in the past desired to study Tian music, which differs so dramatically in tone and structure from the classical Taldan forms, but the loveliness of both the music and the player quite banished my academic thoughts.

She plucked the strings with gentle fingers, singly and in chords strange to my Chelish ear, yet the song itself was not unfamiliar. It was one of many I had enjoyed in the company of my old acquaintance, Song Chu-yu. I searched my memory library for the title, but the subtle contour of the princess's chin distracted my attention. The lute's music entranced me, drawing my gaze inexorably to her face. Her jet eyes—

A dissonant note dispelled my reverie, but the discord originated not from the guqin but from my reflexive refusal to be lulled into torpor. I feared I had

DAVE GROSS

been about to succumb not to the woman's natural charms but to some magical effect of her instrument. Without a riffle scroll at hand—indeed, without even a spellbook from which I could create one—I had no means of testing my suspicion.

Had I seen any indication of guile upon the placid countenance of the princess, I would have assumed the worst and hated her for daring to enslave my mind. In the absence of even such slight evidence, I was left jolted by my own susceptibility to both enchantment and cynicism.

It is a point of pride that I have constantly developed my intellectual acumen throughout my considerable lifetime. Constant exercise of my rational faculties, coupled with the mental fortitude bestowed by my half-elven heritage, normally makes me nigh invulnerable to charms. And yet only months earlier I had succumbed to an enchantment with revolting consequences.

Could it be that I was slipping into an early dotage?

I shook my head to clear my mind. Simultaneously, the princess began to sing, and two revelations blossomed in my mind.

First, I now remembered the name of the song as "The Laughing Carp," which, despite its lighthearted name, was in fact sacred to the worshipers of Sarenrae.

Second, I comprehended with an almost spiritual disappointment the singular flaw in the princess's otherwise peerless beauty. No courtly means of describing the defect came to mind, and instead I recalled one of Radovan's colloquialisms.

The princess could not carry a tune in a bucket.

There is an elemental difference between Eastern and Western music, and yet I felt assured that I could recognize a talented Tian singer as readily as I could evaluate a Chelish soprano. The voice of the princess was utterly without charm or skill. It was in fact the dissonance of her voice that shook me from the enchantment, natural or magical. If there was an arcane power affecting my mind, it came from the guqin, not the princess herself.

A vague movement in the shadows of the outer wall attracted my attention. Half-hidden by the gloom, Jade Tiger stalked the perimeter, one hand on the hilt of his sword, the other clutching his folded fan to his chest. By his erect posture and the constant turning of his head, I knew he safeguarded the princess against any intrusion into the garden while leaving her a modicum of privacy by the pond. The eunuch continued his circuit, vanishing once more into the shadows between the trees.

The sight of the princess had arrested my breathing, on which I had spent the past weeks focusing. Her beauty had also dulled the other senses Master Li had encouraged me to hone, for my usually keen hearing had detected nothing before another figure appeared beside me on the wall.

"What are you doing?" Kwan hissed in my ear.

Before I could reply, he spied the princess and quite forgot me.

"What is it?" gasped Mon Choi. While he landed beside me with the grace of a cat, I had detected his unmistakable aroma an instant earlier. The masters permitted us to bathe and wash our brown-and-tan robes in the stream running through the temple grounds once each week. While I supplemented this ration with a furtive toilet while fetching water each morning, my fellows seemed impervious to the miasma that threatened to suffocate me as bath day approached.

It was a marvel, I thought, that the princess had not smelled us already.

A rustling in the nearest boughs was our only warning of attack.

Kwan pushed me hard in the chest. I struck Mon Choi as I fell backward, and we both crashed to the hard earth inside the Cherry Court. An instant later, Kwan landed in a neat tripod, poised on the balls of his feet and three fingers of one hand. Between the knuckles of his other hand he held three long, slender darts. He gripped a fourth in his mouth. A stream of blood trickled over his lip and down his chin.

He dropped the darts. "Hurry. We must not be found outside the dormitory."

It was already too late.

The first strike sent Mon Choi tumbling across the courtyard. I turned just in time to receive a foot in the chest. The powerful blow flung me against the garden wall in a puff of masonry dust. I shook my head to clear my vision and saw Kwan kowtowing to Master Wu.

"The responsibility is mine, Master," he said. "I misled my brothers."

"No," cried Mon Choi, throwing himself down beside Kwan. "It is my fault. Punish me."

Master Wu scoffed at them. He paced back and forth and glared down at the offenders.

How simple it would have been to let my brothers take the blame. No doubt I would also endure punishment, but the instigator of our infraction would certainly suffer the most. I had endured so much already. It seemed only prudent that I should accept any buffer, however unexpected, between my body and the wrath of Master Wu.

And yet my silence would be a falsehood, and thus beneath the dignity of a count of Cheliax.

"My brothers protect me, Master Wu." I kowtowed beside them. "They sought only to prevent me from breaking curfew. I beg you to spare them."

I felt the leaden foot of Master Wu upon my neck, pressing down with such inexorable force that I sprawled helpless, unable to maintain even the groveling posture of a supplicant.

"Master Wu, please," said Mon Choi. "Be merciful. His mind is clouded with exhaustion from his extra duties."

I heard but could not see Wu's bone-crunching response. In whatever manner he struck Mon Choi, it did not require him to remove his foot from my neck.

"Master, you have lost your temper," said Kwan.

Such a direct challenge to a master of the temple was forbidden, and no one knew that better than Kwan. Wu stepped away from me, and only the power of gravity allowed my head to turn so that I could witness the beating that made all my previous castigations seem little more than a slap upon the wrist.

Chapter Eight
Drunken Boxer

After pissing on me for weeks, the clouds finally gave up. The sun on my neck cheered me almost as much as Burning Cloud Devil's absence, but the feeling lasted only until I saw my shadow on the road.

So far I'd avoided catching my reflection when I drank from a stream or puddle. Even without Burning Cloud Devil's magical "sealing" characters, my hands alone showed me how different I looked. The tiny nubs on my knuckles had grown into thorny spikes a couple inches long. I could feel those all over my body, on practically every joint and in ragged lines on my shins and forearms.

The spikes weren't the worst of it. I'd made the mistake of examining the whorls on my fingertips. Not only were they different, they weren't even remotely human. Instead of the usual irregular ovals, I had perfect pentagons spiraling down into infinity. They looked like something by one of those pesh-smoking painters the boss used to patronize.

I turned my attention to the scenery. I'd been trudging along the riverside road for three days, and this was the first time I'd had a good look at the surrounding valley.

The terraced fields were full of water that would have drained away except for the raised lips bordering each plot. Here and there were irrigation gates, little more than wooden planks in frames. A brown Tian man waded through the paddies to open one for a few minutes before closing it again.

A few tiers below, another man drove a plow-ox ahead of peasants who squatted to plant stalks of rice. The water already harbored some kind of floating plant. It looked like someone had scattered clover there. If the boss had been there, he'd have stopped to quiz the peasants about the stuff, taken home a sample.

But the boss wasn't here.

When the farmers spied me on the road, they bobbed their conical rice hats before returning to their work. I guessed I didn't look so scary from a distance.

My own wide hat and rain cape helped. Both were accidental gifts from a peddler I'd surprised a couple of weeks earlier.

I'd just settled down for my morning squat when I heard the rattle of wooden wheels. I finished my business and climbed back up onto the road for a look. The poor wretch leaped a foot off the ground when he saw me, leaving his hat and cape as he sprinted away. Since my spoken words still came out in Hell-speech and Burning Cloud Devil wasn't around to translate, I couldn't explain that I hadn't come for his soul.

Still, it was good for a chuckle. I took the peddler's abandoned hat and cape and helped myself to the contents of his abandoned cart. After eating most of a sack of turniplike roots, I wrapped the bag around my waist. It was a poor substitute for the leathers I'd picked up in Caliphas, but at least there was no one around to see me. No one I knew, anyway.

I was on the wrong side of the world, alone until I caught up with Burning Cloud Devil. He'd been wandering off more and more often since my battle with Fong. We'd encountered a few travelers on the road, most of them harmless.

Twice we'd run into gangs brave enough to have a go at me. The first was led by a man who'd lost his legs, but some sorcerous blacksmith had built him a new pair. Burning Cloud Devil made me fight him only with kicks, which is a lot harder than it sounds, especially when the guy kicking back has iron legs. I ached for days after that fight, and the sorcerer's skill-sealing spell did nothing to soothe the bruises.

The second gang was a band of deserters turned to robbery. I fought them knife against swords, but that wasn't good enough for Burning Cloud Devil. He wanted me to wear a blindfold. After a hot argument, he conjured spider-silk webs over my face and promised the men a purse of gold if they could take me. In the end it still wasn't much of a fair fight, since they liked to scream as they attacked, making finding them easy even while blind. I ended up with a few nasty cuts, but by the end my ears tingled with the sorcerer's spell, and I knew fighting blind was no longer a problem.

I was pleased with myself. "Not too bad, huh?"

Burning Cloud Devil wasn't satisfied. He grumbled that we were too far from any town likely to attract a hero strong enough to challenge me. He told me to meet him at a roadside inn to the east and paused with a look of concentration, like he was counting. I started to ask what he was doing when his hand shot out and struck me with that damned Quivering Palm again.

Tired as I was from the recent fight, I was ready to kick his ass right then and there. Before I could cock a fist, he flew off in his ball of fire.

That was two days ago. My anger had cooled, but I was getting hungry.

I considered snatching a goat from one of the nearby farms and decided against it. In daylight, I doubted I could get away without a fight. I had no qualms about the theft, but the idea of some farmer putting up enough of a fight to make me kill him rubbed me wrong. There was only one thing I wanted to kill, and that was this Burning Cloud Devil's dragon.

By the time the sun turned the Wall of Heaven Mountains purple, I began to regret not going for that goat. Before I could turn back, I spied colored lanterns on a simple gate at the crest of the next hill. Once I reached them, I saw the roadside inn.

This was the place. It was just one story tall, with a little orchard to one side and a well on the other. A hitching rail ran along a wooden porch, but the only trace of horses was a fading tattoo of hoof beats on the road.

Three men and a woman crouched behind the rail. The woman rose a few inches to peer in through the window, but the man beside her pulled her back down. I stood behind them and had a look inside.

The light of a dozen or so lamps flickered around the carnage. Shattered pottery and furniture littered the floor. A man dressed in plain servant's clothes lay unmoving on the bar. Another limp form was crumpled on the floor beneath him, probably a traveling merchant judging from his fine silk robes and the loop of gold coins on his belt. In one corner lay a pile of empty wine jugs, stacked like the skulls of a defeated army.

Only one undamaged table and chair remained. There sat a young man whose open vest showed off impressive muscles. Behind him an iron-ringed staff leaned against the wall. He had the surviving jugs of wine on the table, along with a soup bowl that he used as a wine cup. If his flushed face weren't evidence enough that he'd had plenty to drink, I could almost make out the character for "wine" in the fumes of his belch.

At that moment, the woman noticed me standing behind her and let out a little shriek. The man beside her covered her mouth without taking his eyes off the drunk inside. He hissed, "No, my plum. He'll hear you!"

The others saw me then, slapping their hands over their mouths to contain their own screams. I stepped back, hoping some shadows would make me look less frightening.

The man who'd silenced the woman noticed me. Rather than scream, he threw himself into the dirt at my feet, groveling.

"Hero, please save us! The boxer has driven off all of our other customers. If he is not stopped, he will drink all of our wine."

I liked the sound of "hero," even though I was starting to think it meant something different in these parts, especially if Burning Cloud Devil was telling the truth about being the King of Heroes. I decided I wouldn't mind a cup of wine, but what grabbed my attention was the smell of roasting pork.

There was no point talking to the guy until I got my own voice back, so I pointed to him, mimed slicing a roast pig, and rubbed my belly.

He got it. "Yes, you will be our honored guest, at our expense, if only you can make the boxer leave."

That was good enough for me. I stepped into the inn and tossed aside my rain cape and hat.

The souse squinted and smiled at me, his nose and cheeks round and rosy. He was cute as a cherub.

"Closing time," I said. It didn't matter whether he could understand my words. He couldn't have been drunk enough to mistake my tone.

"What a strange devil you are!" His face brightened, and he peered into his wine jug as if to see whether that's where I'd come from.

"Nice." I jerked a thumb toward the door. "Now beat it."

"Join me!" He filled the big bowl and pushed it across the table. He raised the jug above his beaming face. "To the exiles of Heaven and Hell!"

I couldn't tell whether he was toasting or mocking me, but either way I didn't like it. I moved forward to strike the jug out of his hand, but he slid off his chair and rolled backward. He kept the jug balanced on his palm throughout the fall, twisting his wrist to keep it upright all the way. He didn't spill a drop until he tipped it over his mouth. Then he let as much wine run down his chin as into his throat.

"You're a nimble little lush," I said. "I'll give you that."

"You should give me face, brother."

"I ain't your goddamned brother."

He laughed. The sound shook the thatched roof and exploded in my ears. "That is exactly what you are. That is perfect. You are my goddamned little brother!"

That's when I realized that he understood my infernal speech. I was too annoyed to give it a second thought. I couldn't say why, but the sound of his voice, the way he called me his brother, that big white smile, his baby face, the smell of wine on his breath—all of it pricked my neck. I wanted to kick his ass out the window and eat my supper.

I jumped across the table. His mouth opened in clownish surprise as my shadow covered him. He rolled away an instant before I landed.

His foot touched my back, and with the slightest shove he redirected my momentum.

A second later, I was spitting out splinters and blinking at the inn's yard. In front of me, the staff wailed and fell back from the hitching rail. To them, I must have looked like a mounted devil's head kept alive on some paladin's trophy wall.

I felt a furnace blaze in my belly.

Jerking back from the wall, I only succeeded in driving splinters deep into the back of my head. Just what my new look needed—more spikes. I cursed, and the innkeepers shrieked and leaped up from their hiding place. They retreated to the cover of the well.

Behind me, the boxer laughed at my struggles. He paused only to chug another drink from his jug before tossing it away. I heard it clink against the pile I'd seen earlier.

The angle was all wrong, so I changed tack. Pushing forward with all my strength, I bent the wall outward. There wasn't enough room for leverage, so I brought only a fraction of my strength to bear. The hole wouldn't widen. The wall wouldn't break. I pounded at it on either side, but just left scratches in the wood.

"Let me help, little brother," said the boxer. I felt him grab my ankle and pull. I cursed and kicked, but he laughed and slapped away my foot. The force of his "help" drove the splinters deeper into my neck. I twisted and strained my head, finally fitting the unfamiliar shape of my skull back through the hole it had made.

He swung me all the way around, hooting and laughing. After one circuit, he let go. I flew across the inn.

It couldn't have taken more than a second, but it felt like a cool minute as I sailed across the restaurant. I could almost count the empty wine jugs, adding them to the two whose paper seals were still unbroken on the boxer's table. The stunned merchant on the floor shook his head and looked up in wonder as I soared past and crashed into the kitchen.

The roasting pig flew away as I smashed through a shelf and landed in the fire pit. Hot water and oil splashed over me. It was almost hot enough to feel uncomfortable, but apart from the embarrassment, the only serious injury was from a kitchen knife that pierced my cheek. Blood began to fill my mouth. I liked the taste.

I knew I'd like the taste of the boxer's blood even more.

My roar shook the house harder than his madcap laugh. I burst out of the kitchen and leaped over the still-unconscious servant on the bar.

The mirth drained from the boxer's face when he saw me, but only for a second. He still wobbled like a dockside boozer, but there was something canny in his eyes. I'd spent years dealing with belligerent drunks, and some who only played the part to gull a fool.

I pulled up short. The boxer nodded approval. Ignoring the staff that stood within his reach, he snatched up another jug of wine and rolled it down his arm, across his back, and up into the crook of his wrist. He struck open the seal with a snake-head knuckle shot and offered it to me.

"Calm down," he said. "Have a drink. The wine is not so good, but it is strong."

That gave me an idea.

I accepted the wine and made as if to drink. The boxer smiled, but his good mood vanished when I hurled the jug to the floor. Clay shards scattered everywhere, and the wine seeped into the boards.

"What a waste!" Real grief contorted his face.

I reached for the remaining jug, but he was quicker. He grasped it in both hands and turned away, hugging it to his chest.

I threw a hard punch into his kidney.

He cried out and spun away. The jug leaped out of his arms, but he caught it on his foot and sent it back up under a protective arm. He bobbed and weaved, always protecting the jug with his body.

I followed, kicking and punching every time he left a target exposed. Each time, he dipped or faded just enough to avoid my spiky fists and clawed feet.

My hackles rose, scorching my neck like a hundred hot pins. For a few seconds, I forgot I had a plan. Screaming, I cocked a fist and glowered at the boxer's crotch.

Drunk as he was, he hadn't taken his gaze off my eyes. He threw the jug high in the air and shimmied back out of reach. But I wasn't really punching for him. I sprang up and swung for the wine jug.

"No!" He leaped right after me. His hands gripped my arm, and he swung from it like a monkey on a branch. The weight was just enough to pull my fist out of line. My knuckle spikes barely squeaked against the glazed surface of the jug.

He pulled himself up on my arm and tapped the jug with one finger, sending it once more toward the rafters. We fell together, backs against the wall, side by side.

That's where you don't want to be when fighting me.

I gave him an elbow to the chest. A square shot from one of my spurs was enough to stun most anyone. They hurt like hell, but they were too short to reach the heart—

That is, they used to be too short.

I jerked my elbow away. A stream of blood followed.

The boxer choked and reached for the falling jug. It slipped through his feeble hands toward the floor.

I reached out my foot and caught it in the nook of my ankle with a few inches to spare. I lowered it gently to the floor.

The boxer gazed at me in astonishment. He tried to speak but produced only a bloody bubble that broke upon his lips. The strength drained from him, and I lowered him to the floor.

"I'm sorry," I said. "I didn't mean . . ."

To what? I wondered. How did I expect to keep fighting in this infernal body without killing? I knew perfectly well that my spurs had grown longer. That's not the sort of thing I'd forget, not ever.

I'd just been so angry.

The boxer burbled some more. I wiped the blood from his mouth.

"Wine," he said. "One last sip . . ."

Still cradling his head, I broke the seal with my ragged fingers and poured a stream of wine into his mouth. His hands came up to tilt the jug, overflowing his mouth and splashing wine over the seeping wound over his heart.

"It is not such bad wine after all. Thank you, my goddamned brother." He smiled up at my face, but I don't think he saw me. He was having his first glimpse of someplace else.

I prayed to Pharasma, goddess of death, that they had good wine waiting for him.

The fight had spoiled my appetite, but I knew it'd be back. I went to the kitchen and cut a ham off the roast pig.

As I went to leave, I caught a last look at the boxer. The staff he'd never touched during the fight slid off the wall and onto his body. As it rolled along his arm and onto the floor, I couldn't help feeling his ghost was offering it to me. Was it my spoils for defeating him? Did he want it delivered to an heir? A hundred other spooky possibilities fluttered in my brain. I should have left it there on the floor.

Instead, I took it with me.

Chapter Nine
Flying Scroll

How swift your brush."

I muted my utterance of surprise at the unexpected voice so close behind me. Despite the susurrus of the late spring shower, I should have detected even the most careful footstep upon the rice mats of the scriptorium. The intruder moved with uncanny, perhaps even magical stealth. Once I heard the silken voice and discerned the rain-dampened scent of his favored incense, I recognized Jade Tiger.

There was no time to hide the results of my labor, which the eunuch might well have observed for minutes before speaking. It had been more than two weeks since the incident, yet I considered the possibility that he had come to investigate my disturbance of the princess's privacy, since surely they were his darts that had so narrowly missed us. It occurred to me that they would not have missed me if not for the fortuitous presence of First Brother Kwan.

No matter the reason for Jade Tiger's visit, I was intrigued by the eunuch, and by the princess. Surely Jade Tiger was similarly curious about the presence of a foreign half-elf in Dragon Temple. Preparing myself for a subtle interrogation, I turned and bowed.

"Noble Counselor, you honor me with your attention."

He smiled, perhaps disarmed by my use of the submissive tone I had finally, reluctantly adopted. As Song Chu-yu had counseled me years ago, the bureaucrats of Tian Xia were keen to perceive the most minute variances in demeanor, and quicker still to avenge slights and the pretentions of those of lesser status.

"I have been admiring these foreign characters," said Jade Tiger. "They are words of magic, are they not?"

And thus I was at his mercy.

While not specifically forbidden to write in my native Taldane, or in this case in the spidery characters of the arcane, I had been tasked with copying local histories in the Tien language. In themselves, the chronicles were educational, but they were not my true interest.

In fact, I had already copied something more than the minimum number of pages demanded by Master Li. After observing the speed with which I copied the sutras in our midday meditations, the wizened temple leader had permitted me to serve in the scriptorium during my convalescence, for Master Wu's latest chastisement had rendered me unfit for physical exercise.

Kwan had returned to the training grounds within a day of our punishment. To show his courage, Mon Choi had limped out of the dormitory to join his brothers two days later, despite his inability to raise his bruised arms above his head. It was another week before I was able to join them, but by then Master Li insisted I continue to devote two hours to the scriptorium each day. Unfortunately, he did not demand that Master Wu reduce my other obligations. Thus was I deprived of another two hours' sleep each night.

Secretly I was grateful for the chore. Not only did it spare me the glares of my fellow students, who reviled me all the more for leading Kwan astray, but it also allowed me to attempt a reconstruction of my lost spellbook.

Alas, it was a futile endeavor.

If not for my peculiar handicap, I might have inscribed any spell that lingered in my memory, yet I depended upon riffle scrolls rather than the ability to set spells in my mind, awaiting only a triggering word or gesture. While I comprehended the theories of magic with ease, fixing even the pettiest spell in mind sickened me. Two or three spells of any power wracked me with spasms. Actually triggering a spell caused an immediate and appalling reflex.

Casting spells made me vomit.

Of late I had discovered a means by which to inscribe magic directly onto a peculiar form of scroll composed of bound strips of paper. With the proper division of characters from one strip to the next, I could discharge a spell by riffling the pages beneath my thumb. While the method did not permit me to prepare more spells than a normal wizard of my own skill level, using a riffle scroll caused me no ill effect.

If I could create even one riffle scroll, I could cast a spell to deliver a message that would reach Radovan no matter where he had gone. I was so desperate that I would have stooped to casting a divination simply to learn his location. Yet without my spellbook for reference, I could not recreate so much as a cantrip.

I bowed to Jade Tiger, acknowledging that the writing was arcane.

"Then it is as I guessed. You are a wizard."

"Of a sort."

"Why do you conceal such powers? A wizard would make a formidable escort for the princess."

I felt no desire to explain my disability, but his question surprised me. "Does Dragon Temple teach magic as well as fighting?"

"Well, no, not for many years," he said. He tilted his head at a sly angle. "But I do."

His statement galvanized me. I kowtowed at once. "Master, teach me a spell for the sending of messages."

He stepped away, but I kept my forehead pressed against the rice mat. I calculated that only complete obeisance might sway a man himself bound within in a many-tiered bureaucracy. His fan snapped open, and I felt the reflected breeze as he cooled himself. I did not imagine he was weighing his decision so much as testing my composure. Even understanding his likely motive did not lend me the patience commensurate to the task. He said nothing for such an interminable period that at last I peered up.

With his lower face obscured by the image of frolicking tiger cubs, I saw only his emerald eyes gazing down at me. His lashes were as white as his long hair, although his skin appeared smooth and youthful.

"You must prove yourself worthy of my patronage."

"Yes, honored sir." I bowed again. It rankled, but if it would achieve my aims, I should endure the debasement.

"Furthermore, you must not reveal my tutelage to the temple masters."

This stricture gave me an instant's pause as I considered its implications. Just as he offered me something that I desired, so too did Jade Tiger expect some service in return. Before he could reconsider the offer, I bowed again.

"Very well," said Jade Tiger. "I shall return tomorrow. Prepare red ink and yellow paper."

For an hour each day over the next two weeks, my enthusiasm for Jade Tiger's arcane teachings ameliorated the fatigue of my kitchen labor and the requisite dodging and defending against Lo Gau's surprise attacks, followed by another hour devoted to transcribing chronicles of Imperial Lung Wa and its Successor States. Not even the twelve hours all Dragon Temple students dedicated to physical and spiritual perfection could quash my spirits, though I was grateful for the respite of purely intellectual exercise.

The first task Jade Tiger set me was to demonstrate my proficiency in writing arcane characters. Dubious of my claim of fluency, Jade Tiger demanded I demonstrate a Tian cantrip for which he provided a sample to study.

"Perhaps I could demonstrate on a scroll," I suggested. Even before his offer of instruction, I had prepared blank sheaves of paper cut into strips approximately the width of my thumb. Thirty-two or sixty-four pages thick, they were bored through at the end of each strip and bound tight with green cord.

When Jade Tiger saw the blank riffle scroll, curiosity spread over his face. "Is that some foreign version of a flying scroll?"

A long lifetime among the scheming nobility of Cheliax allowed me to mask my stupefaction, or so I flattered myself.

"Please, master, illuminate me."

Jade Tiger swept away my blank riffle pages and fetched a sheet of the precious yellow paper I had removed, without permission, from Master Li's calligraphy cabinet. He flung the sheet above his head and swept his fan from his sash. With five quick strokes, he divided the sheet into six perfect strips. They floated down to land upon my writing desk.

"Add this to your red ink." He opened his fan and held it out to me like a salver. Upon it was the shriveled body of a firefly. With the ink pestle, I crushed the insect's body into one of the reservoirs on the tray before me before adding a few drops of precious red ink—another theft for which I hoped to repay Master Li later. I dipped my brush into the ink.

"Now," commanded Jade Tiger. "Fix the spell into the paper."

To most wizards, his command would have seemed nonsensical. I grasped it immediately. With Jade Tiger's scroll of cantrips before me, I arranged the arcane words in my mind. Rather than let the filaments of their power set upon the walls of my subconscious, however, I imbued them into the paper with every stroke of my brush. With every character I wrote from the top to the bottom of the yellow strip, I felt the magic coursing out of my mind, down through my chest and arm, out through my fingers, into the brush and the ink, and onto the page itself.

An instant of nausea passed through me, and I knew the yellow strip contained the spell. I reached for the paper, but Jade Tiger snatched it up between two folds of his fan. His precision with the implement was breathtaking.

Observing my work, he hummed approval before returning it to me. Taking one of the blank strips, he held it between his second and third fingers and flicked it away with a snap of his wrist. The paper shot forth like a dart before fluttering to the floor.

"Just so," he explained. He indicated a target with his folded fan.

I flung the inscribed strip as he had demonstrated, but this time the paper blazed with white light and floated to the top of Master Li's calligraphy cabinet, where it came to rest on a tiny idol of Abbot Chin-hwa.

"Perfect," declared Jade Tiger.

"This practice is common among Tian wizards?"

"It is known," he said. "But no, it is not common. For most wizards, the scrolls are a mere novelty."

I understood. Because they were substitutes for, rather than additions to, the spells other wizards prepared, a disabled wizard like me was the only one to whom they were an advantage. For others they were an unnecessary expense. And, I realized, they offered more opportunities to "disarm" me magically. Rain, fire, and even a common pickpocket were threats that could deprive me of my magic. It was even possible that one could use them without my knowledge, as Radovan had once demonstrated with a riffle scroll.

Jade Tiger produced an ivory scroll case from his sleeve. He thumbed open a catch and pulled out a long string of spells he had copied from his own cache.

"Choose one."

Recognition of the Tian versions of spells I knew quickened my pulse. I called upon my lessons to control my breathing.

On the pages were eight spells, one from each school of magic. The first was an effective if distasteful necromantic spell for drawing the life out of an opponent. The next two were warding spells I had once longed to master for the purposes of proofing my library against uninvited browsers. So was the fourth, although its explosive effects threatened to bloody the very books it might safeguard. The fifth would produce a noisome miasma, effective in combat if distasteful to employ.

The sixth was one of my favored spells, but a fireball was a clumsy weapon for my present circumstances.

Only two spells remained, and I disdained both of those schools of magic.

Most spells dealing with prophecy and information-gathering are miraculously useful, even to one who has made study his life's principal passion. Yet employing them has always seemed a dangerous shortcut to knowledge, which is far surer when earned than when stolen. The true danger is in those spells that violate the sanctity of the sentient mind. In Cheliax, the revelation of private thoughts often leads down a short path to the gallows, if one can afford to purchase leniency, or the tines, if one cannot. In any event, I foresaw no immediate need for this particular spell, meant to detect the presence of the undead.

Yet even more than these voyeuristic spells, I dislike those charms capable of usurping one's will. From insidious love spells to direct and brutal manipulations, they are the most terrible of magics—assassins of the soul.

And yet the spell Jade Tiger offered me from the last school was the only one I could imagine useful in my present circumstance. It would not harm an opponent directly, yet it could prove effective in both offensive and defensive situations.

My hesitation brought a faint smile to Jade Tiger's lips. I suspected that his offering was a test. Did he mean to discover my preferences and specialties? Did some enmity among the ancient schools of arcane magic exist in Tian culture?

I discarded that notion. Jade Tiger carried all of these spells himself, suggesting that he was, like me, a student of all schools. In that case, was this a test of character? If I chose the necromantic spell, would he be pleased or horrified?

I indicated the final spell.

Jade Tiger nodded, but his expression remained neutral. "You may copy it on—"

At the sound of a footfall outside the scriptorium, the eunuch dispelled my light cantrip with a quick utterance. One look at it would be all the evidence Master Wu required to prove that I had spent my time in the scriptorium doing something other than my assigned task.

One of the elderly temple servants appeared in the open doorway. I leaned over the transcription I had set aside, pretending I had been at work all along. The eunuch craned his neck to peer over my shoulder, as he had done on previous days. The old man bowed to the eunuch and gathered the scrolls I had completed for delivery to Master Li.

When he had departed, Jade Tiger favored me with a conspirator's smile. Together we had narrowly avoided discovery of my disobedience and of his interference with the authority of the temple masters. From that moment forth our conspiracy bound us as inexorably as fate.

Chapter Ten
The Goblin Who Swallowed the Wind

While perched on my shoulders, Judge Fang scratched out a spark in his firepot. I set my paws firm on the ground and stopped. The cricket-headed man flew off my back and tumbled to the ground. His pipe and tobacco case rolled away.

"Impudent dog! We will never catch her in time."

Judge Fang knew I did not like him to smoke on my back. I told him so many times, and he was wise enough to remember that the strong smell made it hard to follow the trail. One time he tapped the ash onto my shoulder. That stung so much I almost bit him before stopping myself. Worse, it made a bad smell for days, and I couldn't get away from it.

Judge Fang gathered his things and flew back onto my shoulders. His transparent wings were strong enough to lift his little body a short distance, but he could not keep up when I ran.

"Go!" he said. "Hurry!"

I ran. It felt good to run, because I was on a job.

We were tracking a kami Judge Fang had sensed while meditating on a lily pad in a holy pond. He decided he needed to do that after we searched for two full moons and most of a third. In all that time, he had failed to persuade any of the beasts we met to join us. Some promised they would join us later, but now it was time for raising their offspring.

Judge Fang said we would have better luck among the kami, but we had not seen any yet. Having never seen one, I asked what they look like.

"There are nine thousand nine-hundred and ninety-nine sorts of spirits," he said, "all of them different. Some of them are oni, wicked spirits that have no natural bodies, but form new ones from pure magic in order to carry out their evil. Kami are guardian spirits, bound by the Celestial Bureaucracy to protect the natural order of things."

"So you are one sort of kami?"

Judge Fang grunted and fiddled with his divining tools. "According to these star charts and the motion of my lodestone, a powerful spirit is nearby."

"Is it a kami or an oni?"

"It is hard to know, but it is powerful."

We followed the direction of his lodestone for two more days and nights. When Judge Fang saw a rustling in the trees on a still day, he leaped up and told me to follow the wind.

"It is Gust!" he cried. "What good fortune! She was born when the Monkey King caused the Empress Dowager to laugh while eating her prosperity rice ball on her one hundredth birthday. The old woman choked, thus ending the Mu Dynasty and provoking the War of Four Brothers. This was long ago, mind you, three thousand years before Rovagug stirred in his prison and moved the Golden River to its present course."

He continued his story. What he said did not sound important to my job, and he hated to be interrupted, so

I kept my nose to the ground and learned more about our quarry.

Gust was made of wind and clouds. I still had not seen the kami, but her path smelled like the breeze just before a storm. Sometimes she left a path of clear ground where she had blown the leaves away. Sometimes she left piles of blossoms or leaves under the trees she had shaken as she passed. Always she left a trail of sweet air.

For two days we followed Gust's path through wheat fields and farm yards, but we could not catch up. Her trail was fresh enough that I could follow it even without Judge Fang's magic, so while I ran he clutched my coat and told me more stories of demigods and heroes.

When I felt too hungry to keep running, I caught a chicken near a house and carried it off before a woman ran out to shout at me. Judge Fang chuckled at her red face. The woman turned her anger toward the rooster who had failed to protect the hens. Judge Fang did not call me a good boy, but he also did not call me a naughty dog. It didn't matter, because he wasn't the one who decided whether I was good or bad.

I missed my master.

On the morning of the third day, I smelled a new scent following Gust's trail. It reminded me of a trail I had smelled a few times when I was a pup. It belonged to a creature my parents' master called a goblin.

I had never seen one, but Judge Fang told me that this goblin was different.

"One morning the Goblin made a great yawn," he said. "A great wind kami—like Gust, but even more powerful—flew right into its mouth and became lost inside the labyrinth of its belly. It nearly escaped by pushing out in all directions, but it could not match the strength of the Goblin's stomach. All it managed to do was to blow long spines out of the Goblin's back, forming a cloak of quills.

"From that day, the Goblin was no longer a normal goblin, but rather something else entirely. It caused nothing but trouble for its fellows. Every time it caught a cold, its sneezes blew out cooking fires and scattered the tribe's treasure. The kami in its belly swelled up to protest whenever it ate meat, releasing poisonous farts on the Goblin's tribe. When it knocked the goblin leader off his mound of pelts with a giant belch, the chief exiled this Goblin Who Swallowed the Wind.

"The Goblin soon learned it had to eat more wind to survive and keep its captive kami happy," said Judge Fang. "If it catches Gust before we do, it will devour her. We need her help, so we must stop him."

I liked Judge Fang's stories. They were easier to understand than the ones I overheard my master telling Radovan. All of Judge Fang's words made sense the first time he said them, but not because he was smarter than my master. His cricket head just knew how to talk with beasts and kami.

Gust's trail led up out of the farmlands and onto a rocky ridge. At the top was a grassy plateau with a few waving trees on top. Pebbles rattled out of the dirt as I ran up the incline. I jumped over tangles of roots and weeds sticking out of the ground. Judge Fang clutched my fur and screeched until we reached the top.

"There!" He pointed along the ridge, but I had already spotted the Goblin.

He was shaped like a man, only half as a big and with moss-colored skin. His chest was wide but thin, and his arms were long enough that he could scratch his knees without bending. A thick layer of porcupine quills covered his back.

The Goblin ran up the ridge toward a giant gray statue of a robed man looking out over the farmland. Behind the statue was a line of trees standing in pairs, like the soldiers we had seen in the big city. The smell of fresh air made me feel strong, even after running all day. At last I saw Gust.

She was a white cloud the size of a lamb, but she moved as fast as steam from a kettle. Wherever she touched the trees and bushes, they shook and dropped their leaves. She left a glistening trail on the ground behind her. The Goblin lunged toward her but slipped on the wet grass and cursed.

Gust laughed with the sound of a dozen little drums. Veins of lightning flashed inside her body.

"I'll suck you down and fart you out!" the Goblin squealed.

"Such a noisy little brute," said Judge Fang. "Catch him before he does what he promises. We need Gust."

I shouted at the Goblin. He turned to me and screamed, "Get back, you nasty dog!" I smelled the stink of fear all over him. He puffed up his chest and kept on inhaling. Soon, his body grew so big that his arms and legs looked like twigs poking out of a rain barrel.

When he looked ready to burst, he blew out a stinking gale. We flew off the ground and tumbled through the air. We struck tree limbs and fell back to the dirt, still choking on his foul breath. Broken twigs and leaves rained down on us, and the sun shone through the naked branches.

Judge Fang's muffled voice pleaded beneath me. I rolled away, and the cricket-headed kami struggled back up to his feet. He gaped at his bent wings and shook his walking stick at me.

"Clumsy dog! You gave him too much warning."

I ran up the hill, this time without shouting. At the top, Gust floated beside the statue's head. Beneath her, the Goblin climbed up its stony body. As he grabbed the stone beads around the statue's arm, Gust trembled and wept. Her tears slicked the statue, and the Goblin slipped down a few feet. He cursed and shook his fists at Gust.

He was so angry at her that he did not see me coming.

I leaped and caught the leg of the Goblin's pants in my teeth. My weight did the rest, pulling down hard. The flimsy cloth tore away, leaving the Goblin with one bare leg. He shrieked as he clutched the slippery statue.

"Get away, get away, get away!" He gulped and gave himself the hiccups. He was too frightened to puff himself up. Above him, Gust chortled and sparked.

"Leave . . . the cloud . . . alone," Judge Fang wheezed. The little kami puffed as he ran up behind me. "I require her help. There is a . . . disturbance of the . . . Celestial Order."

The Goblin climbed higher, thrusting his elbows over the statue's arm. "There is a disturbance in my belly."

"There are many rats in the canyons behind us. You need only—"

"I don't want a rat! I want the tasty little cloud. She is so sweet and moist. Besides, she laughs at me!"

Judge Fang glared at the Goblin for interrupting. A tiny rumble of thunder rolled down from the little cloud. Her wispy body turned dark gray, even though the sky above was clear and blue.

"You must do as I command," said Judge Fang. "You are barely more than a common goblin, while I am appointed magistrate of this region by the Red Crowned

Crane, August Overseer of Natural Beasts and Minor Kami within the Cradle of the Wall of Heaven Mountains, South of the Golden River and North of the Green Marshes, and All Mortal Lands Contained Therein, Wild and Settled, beneath Heaven and above Hell."

The Goblin blinked. "You call me a minor kami? *Minor?!*"

Judge Fang stroked his ruffled wings the way my master smoothes the tail of his coat before sitting in a chair. "Perhaps it is not evident to one who has not passed the Imperial Exam, as I did in my mortal life, and the Trials of the Celestial Bureaucracy, as I have done in my current—and no doubt temporary—existence among you lesser kami."

"'Temporary' sounds right," said the Goblin. He inhaled, but this time it was his back instead of his belly that expanded. All the quills lifted up and trembled. "Prepare for your next life, you pompous bug!"

Judge Fang screamed when he saw me leap. I shielded his body as the quills rained down. They were longer than thorns, and they burned like hot coals. A whimper slipped out before I could turn it into a growl.

Above me, the Goblin capered on the statue's arm. He hooted and pointed down at Judge Fang, who lay still on the ground where I'd landed. He was so small that I hoped I hadn't crushed him. The quills hurt so much that I wanted to bite the Goblin.

I leaped up. My jaws did not reach the Goblin, but the statue rocked on its base. The Goblin yelped and clutched the carved beard to keep from falling.

"Stupid dog! You can't touch me."

I jumped again, this time with all my weight against the statue. It moved a little more, but not enough to throw down the Goblin.

The Goblin whooped and hollered. He shrugged his shoulders to show off the quills he had remaining. There were many.

A crooked white spark shot out from Gust. It struck the Goblin in mid-leap. His legs splayed out like a frog's, and he fell hard onto the statue's arm, landing on his exposed crotch. The Goblin's pupils rolled back into his eye sockets, and he slid off the statue to fall onto the damp ground.

I stood over him, my jaws inches from his face. With one bite, I could snap his thin neck.

"Wait," cried Judge Fang. He rocked from side to side for a moment before pushing himself to his feet. "This Goblin is more formidable than I realized. It is possible his is the spirit I sensed."

Gust let out a tinny sound of thunder, and I knew she wanted the Goblin killed. She did not speak as other creatures do, but her electric smell and the changing air pressure were all she needed to convey her thoughts.

"No," said Judge Fang. "There is a kami within him. I must meditate on this problem. It could be that—"

The cloud kami repeated her demand that we kill the Goblin. She emphasized her thunder with a crackle of lightning.

"I shall do nothing of the sort, especially if you keep interrupting me, you impudent little vapor."

The Goblin stirred beneath me. His eyes flickered open, and he cringed when he saw my teeth so close to his face.

Judge Fang snapped his fingers. "We must take them both!"

"What?" said the Goblin. "I'm going nowhere with you. Definitely not with this . . . this . . . *dog*!"

"Yes, you will!" I told him.

The Goblin curled his arms and legs close to his body. I smelled his fear.

Gust began to float away.

"Come back," said Judge Fang. "We need your help, and it is your duty to obey the Mandate of Heaven."

Gust laughed, her body roiling like wind on the water.

"You must," I said. "Or I will carry this Goblin anywhere you go until he eats you."

A flash of lightning lit Gust from within. She was threatening us.

I remembered what my friend Radovan does when talking to someone who does not wish to do as he asks. I gave Gust the big smile.

She gasped and released a light rain. I knew she had agreed at last.

I looked at Judge Fang to see what he wanted to do next. As he looked back at me, his mandibles twitched. Just as I began to think he was displeased with me, he said, "What a good dog."

Chapter Eleven
Silk Sisters

Burning Cloud Devil caught up with me the morning after the killing. Right away he demanded to know why I hadn't waited at the inn. He shoved me before I could answer. I was in no mood for horseplay. I raised the ringed staff to crack him on the head, and he froze.

"Where did you find that?"

"Just some drunk. Things got a little rough, so he didn't need it anymore."

"You fool, he was a priest!" He pointed at the rings. "Those rings chime as he walks, warning beasts and kami not to attack his holy person."

"This guy was no priest." Not unless he was a worshiper of Cayden Cailean, I thought. I doubted they knew of the Lucky Drunk this far from Absalom.

"There are usually three rings on such a staff. They represent the mind, the body, and the spirit," said Burning Cloud Devil. "A master who has transcended his desires may add a fourth. Only the greatest prophet would dare add a fifth."

There were seven rings on this staff. The hairs on my neck prickled.

I offered the weapon to Burning Cloud Devil. "All right, you take it."

He shied away, a shadow of fear on his face.

"Fine." I raised it like a javelin and aimed for the tall weeds.

"No! The moment you touched the staff, you were bound to it. To discard it now would be more dangerous."

"You just made that shit up."

He shook his head.

After that we walked for days without speaking more than a few words outside of our morning practice. He'd been drilling me in his Quivering Palm technique. I liked that, and had half a mind to use it on him.

But I knew better. Burning Cloud Devil was no dummy. He wouldn't teach me something I could turn against him. Either he had made himself invulnerable to the attack, or he knew how to stop it. Still, it was tempting. I kept the thought in the back of my mind.

We'd been traveling north, passing fewer cultivated fields and more forests. As we approached the Golden River, we came across more towns. Before we showed ourselves, Burning Cloud Devil paused to cast a spell disguising our appearances. Me he made appear like a gangly Tian youth, complete with a real wicker backpack in which I carried enough food to get me through a week or so without resorting to raiding farms or killing drunks. Burning Cloud Devil turned himself into a different one-armed man.

"What are we supposed to be?"

"You are a young tax collector," he said. "No one will bother you, hoping to avoid your attention."

"And you?"

"Your bodyguard."

"How come you don't give yourself back your arm?"

"Because it would be only the image of an arm. Should someone offer me a bowl of wine . . ." He shrugged away the rest of his answer.

I smelled bullshit, and he sensed my doubt.

"Because I don't deserve it. Not while Snow suffers in Hell."

That sounded more like it, but it made me wonder again why he wore an empty scabbard at his waist. It was too slender for a weapon I could imagine Burning Cloud Devil using. The green floral pattern didn't suit him, nor did the delicate gold chasing at mouth and butt. Was the scabbard also a remembrance of Snow?

It was good to eat at a table, sitting in a chair, served by a pair of pretty girls, each of them plump as a ripe peach. I considered coaxing one of them up to my room, but knowing what lay beneath my magical disguise quashed that thought.

Burning Cloud Devil and I had that much in common. In failing to save those closest to us, he'd lost his arm, I'd lost my whole body.

Maybe neither one of us deserved them back.

We got away from the inn before Burning Cloud Devil's illusion evaporated. Less than an hour later, we were back to our usual selves. One look at us scared most travelers off the road. Those bold enough to pass within a few feet of us bowed low, or else they kept their gazes locked on the dirt road.

We turned west, then north at the next village and traveled undisguised for days. The sorcerer cloaked us in the same illusion whenever we came to an inn or a village. Sometimes he'd drink more than a few catties of wine, and he'd end up singing old songs. The man could carry a tune, I gave him that.

During his hangover the next morning, I'd ask him to translate the songs for me. My favorite was "The Proud, Happy Wanderer," but he also taught me "Two Peach Blossoms," "The Monkey and the Rat," "Five Silver Bells," and a few more. He hassled me about my fiendish words when I tried singing them, but eventually I learned to understand another hundred or so Tien words, even though I couldn't speak them with my devil mouth.

When we weren't singing, we walked in silence. Burning Cloud Devil seemed more interested in selecting pebbles from the road. He chose one every mile or so. If it was just the right weight and size, he added it to a little bag with a smile that invited me to ask him what he was doing.

I didn't give him the satisfaction.

A hundred times I considered slipping away while he slept and finding my way back to Cheliax, and damn our revenge. I'd take my chances that Burning Cloud Devil couldn't kill me if I got far enough away. Still, whenever I thought of the tiny bits that were left of the boss, I thought how much I wanted to tear out that dragon's heart.

My mind kept returning to the danger of carrying the stolen staff. I held the thing so as not to let the rings jangle. Burning Cloud Devil paused long enough to notice my caution. I caught him smiling.

"You can kiss my bare copper-colored ass."

That translated just fine, but it didn't rile him.

"Speaking of your bare ass—"

"I know, I know." My makeshift clothes wouldn't hold up much longer. I still got an unwelcome thrill now and then when the summer breeze hit me in the right spot. I'd wanted to buy a new getup in the last town, but Burning Cloud Devil pointed out the obvious problem:

the tailors couldn't fit me without seeing my real form, and one look would send them running.

"Leave it to me," he said. "I know a pair of seamstresses."

He refused to elaborate until a few days later, after we'd secured a ride downstream.

Bales of leaves and wrapped bolts of raw silk filled the center of the river barge. Four guards sat atop the cargo.

The bargeman had been too frightened to refuse Burning Cloud Devil's request for passage. With us aboard he'd probably never had a safer trip. Still, he sang out prayers for protection as he leaned into the pole that propelled us downstream.

Burning Cloud Devil sat on the edge of the barge and let his bare feet cool in the water, so I did the same. A dozen tiny fish gathered to suck at his feet. One came over for a taste of mine. The instant its mouth touched my heel, the whole school turned and fled.

Burning Cloud Devil let out a half-hearted huff of amusement. It was too hot for a proper laugh, especially with the sun reflecting off the river's surface. I didn't mind the heat so much as the glare. I kept my eyes on the banks.

Thick, green mulberry trees bowed their heads over the water. The locals had planted the trees everywhere that wasn't a road or a house. Burning Cloud Devil explained that white mulberry leaves were the only food for the region's silkworms. This close to the river, they reminded me of the willows of Ustalav and some of the secrets I'd left in their shadows.

"We go to the House of a Thousand Silks," said Burning Cloud Devil. He pointed downstream and recited a story.

For years, this couple of sisters owned a big dyeing house known for its many colors. Eventually they became so famous that they were the only ones allowed to produce the royal yellow cloth. Since the king chose them, everyone from lords to merchants took their business to the sisters.

That lasted until a rival silk dyer cursed them, or spread nasty lies, or nasty truths, or something like that. The rumors spread, and eventually cost the sisters the royal monopoly. For a while it cost them a lot of money, too. Everyone wanted to buy from those who made the royal yellow silk.

Rather than close shop, the sisters began selling their clothes at a premium and calling them magical. They produced a hundred shades of every color, and every color produced a different charm. They had colors for attracting a husband, colors for getting rich, colors for winning a fight. They had so many colors they had to invent new names for them.

The hell of it was these magic clothes were the genuine article. Some eccentric gambler was their first customer. He had them dye a lucky green sash for him, and he broke the bank at a half-dozen crooked gambling houses. When the gangsters tried to put an end to him, they all fell into a trap set by the local magistrate, and the gambler got a fat reward.

People came from all over the province to pay fortunes for a robe, a cloak, or a pair of slippers. Rich men sent emissaries bearing a prince's ransom for wedding clothes or funeral garb. Nobody gave a damn about the royal yellow anymore.

The silk makers who held the royal monopoly were unhappy. That meant the bureaucracy was unhappy, and eventually some court eunuch saw an opportunity for glory. He accused the sisters of witchcraft and sedition. When he showed up with twenty soldiers, the sisters kicked their asses all the way back to Lanming.

Just the two of them.

The story of the eunuch's defeat prevented anyone else from bothering the sisters. The prospect of a humiliating whooping was worse than that of disappointing the royal silk dyers, who couldn't afford much in the way of a bribe these days, with all the big money going to the House of a Thousand Silks.

"I'm starting to like these girls," I said.

Burning Cloud Devil turned his face toward the bright mirror of the river.

We arrived an hour or so before dusk. I knew it was the right place by the pungent smell of whatever stuff it is they use for dyeing. With that keen nose of his, the boss could have identified every flower and bug it came from.

The bargeman docked at a pier with a couple of skiffs attached. He raised a flag at the head of the dock while his guards unloaded the silk. Five servants with dye-stained arms arrived to take delivery. The bargeman poled his vessel back into the middle of the river and continued downstream to the eastern markets.

The servants led us through a small wood. On the other side was a brook that joined the river a few hundred yards farther on.

The House of Silks crouched over the stream. It was big as a barn. Age and rain had grayed its timbers. In contrast, long strips of bright silk draped over drying racks in the yard. Today's work was all in peony red and dandelion gold. Workers wound the dried silk onto spindles and covered them in paper.

A servant led us through the big building. From the rafters hung bolts of freshly dyed silk, still dripping red and yellow tears onto the floor. We passed enormous vats, their interiors stained dark from the touch of hundreds of different colors. A waterwheel in the center of the room filled a trough which in turn filled one of the vats with clear water.

We came to a room decorated with screens and lanterns. A tall silver mirror stood in each of the four corners. The servant invited us to make ourselves comfortable in the padded chairs and left us to fetch his mistresses.

Along one wall was a quilt of hundreds of swatches, each a different shade from the ones on either side. On each swatch someone had painted a character or two. I could read only a few: "Cherry Blossom Pink," "Peacock Blue," "Scholar's Slate," and so on.

Burning Cloud Devil chuckled and pointed to one of the colored patches. "Devil's Blood."

"You're hilarious."

He pinched the quilt to put the red next to a black swatch. "Breath of Hell."

I framed a reply involving his halitosis, but I liked the combination. It reminded me of my long-lost red jacket.

"Perhaps not for such a sallow complexion," said a woman at the door.

The seamstresses weren't so alike that you'd mistake them for twins, but they were definitely sisters. One wore her hair twisted in a coil held by pearl-clustered pins. The other wore her hair loose and looked younger, despite the gray streaks on either side.

I gave them the little smile. In Cheliax, older women always fancied me. If they were lucky—or rich—I fancied them back.

They returned my smile with a gentle bob of their heads that reminded me of the geisha back in Minkai. A moment later, their smiles died. The older one's lip curled, as if she'd smelled something repugnant.

"You see the challenge," Burning Cloud Devil said. He was still disguised in his illusion, but he'd dispelled mine without warning me.

Cautious, the seamstresses approached. Their hands felt my arms, touched the long spurs on my elbows and knees. Reassured that I would not bite, they produced measuring strings and encircled my waist, my chest, my neck, my arms and legs.

"What magic?" asked the elder sister.

Burning Cloud Devil indicated the colors he had selected.

"Can you afford the price?" asked the younger.

Burning Cloud Devil showed them one of those trade bars that looks like a little canoe and is worth about fifty coins. This one was platinum, ten times more valuable than gold. He dropped it into his fat purse, which he set on a chair.

"The Resplendent Goddess of Fortune favors you," said the younger sister. "We happen to have a bolt of each color prepared."

I left my pack and weapons in the fitting room and scrubbed up in a tub in the yard. The servants burned my rags as I lathered up. Even with the tingling lye soap, I couldn't quite manage to feel clean.

When I was done and dried, the servants gave me a simple white gown with cloth buttons running down the right breast. It made me look like a choirboy from Hell.

The seamstresses were ready when I returned to the fitting room. They had already cut out templates for three robes in black and red silk.

The elder sister took charge of fitting, cutting holes for my many spikes and marking them for her sister to reinforce with a layer of the black silk. "Breath of Hell," I reminded myself. Her fingers moved everywhere, tightening the initial cut around my waist, neck, and wrists, marking places with a piece of chalk for her sister to reinforce with a second layer of cloth.

The warmth of her tiny hands on my body reminded me of things I hadn't had for a while, pleasures I'd never know again if I didn't get back into my real body. I shoved that thought out of my mind, but every time she touched me, it nosed its way back in.

They moved with such speed that I knew they were working magic. It wasn't even dark before they had produced an inner, a middle, and an outer robe, along with pants and soft boots with openings for my claws and the spurs on my ankles. Servants entered to light candles beside the four mirrors. The sisters stood back to admire their work.

"Finished?" I asked.

Burning Cloud Devil shook his head at me. I figured the sisters didn't understand my words, but they frowned.

"Sorry."

The younger one conjured a short sword in one hand and what looked like a war razor in the other. The elder's fingers bristled with long needles.

"I said sorry!" I knew the Tien word, but it came out fiendish.

The swordswoman slashed at my arm. I was too slow to retreat, and a slender strip of fabric drifted to the floor.

"Be still!" shouted Burning Cloud Devil.

Despite his assurance, I flinched when the elder sister threw her darts. They struck everywhere, but they pierced only the clothes. Thread trailed behind every dart, and the seamstress plucked them like a harp. Black and crimson stitches secured the fabric, and heavy gold thread embroidered the black trim.

In their wake, the younger sister swept in with her blades, cutting threads and trimming cloth. I shuddered like the harvest wheat, but they never nicked me.

The assault lasted until the moon rose and the loons called to each other along the river. It subsided as the sisters plucked a thread or fiddled with some detail of embroidery here and there. When they stepped away to observe their work, I checked out my image in a mirror.

I looked like some Tian scholar's depiction of a devil, but I liked the clothes. Plenty of black trim kept the red from looking too garish, and the flared shoulders showed off my muscles, which are pretty good even when I haven't gone full fiendish. The thick black sash had hooks for my weapons and little pouches for my coins. The whole kit was fancy but comfortable.

I threw a few punches at my image in the mirror. None of my spikes ripped through their slits. A few kicks, same result.

"Good job," I said, hoping they'd understand my tone.

The younger sister held out her empty palm.

"Sure, sure," I said, indicating the fat purse Burning Cloud Devil had left on the chair.

She opened the bag and looked inside. Frowning, she removed a pebble.

"I don't understand—"

But then I did. Just as he'd disguised our appearance, Burning Cloud Devil had cast an illusion over the stones he'd gathered on the road.

The sorcerer's laugh echoed throughout the dye house, but he had vanished from sight.

The sisters turned toward me.

"Now, ladies, let's be reasonable."

I was watching for a blade, so the younger sister's invisibly swift kick surprised me. It knocked me through the wall and into the dyeing room. My body crashed into one of the empty vats. For a second or two I rolled around like a die in a cup.

The sound of the waterwheel covered their approach, but with my infernal vision I saw the elder sister leap above me, all black and gray like a charcoal sketch in the darkness. Her robes flared out like wings as she flicked her wrists. There was no room to dodge, but I hugged my shins to make myself smaller. My reward was that only two or three of her heavy darts burrowed into my neck and shoulder.

The seamstress flew past the open top of the vat. I knew where she'd gone, but I had no idea where her sister was. The rafters from which the silk hung were a good eight feet or more above me. I could never jump so far.

Not in my real body.

Kicking off from the floor of the vat, I leaped up just as a sword blade penetrated the wall and the space where my spine had just been. The rafter cracked under my weight but held just long enough for me to pull myself higher. I snagged a beam with my other hand.

A clammy tentacle gripped my ankle.

Below me, the elder sister held the other end of a damp length of silk. In her hands it came alive, whipping my leg back and forth. I twirled my foot in the opposite direction, but the silk was too heavy for me to escape before another length of wet cloth gripped my other leg.

"Pull him down," cried the younger sister. "Let me trim him into the shape of a man."

My claws tore into the beam, which uttered its last agonized sigh. I pushed away just as it broke.

I fell toward the waterwheel, hoping to trap the silk in its spokes. My weight was too much for its wooden frame to bear, and I went down in a tangle of strangling cloth and splinters.

The wreckage of the waterwheel caught in the trough, but I went through. I swallowed a big mouthful of water as I hit the surface of the brook. It was deeper than I'd guessed. My body sank until the weeds added their choking fingers to the throttling silk.

I reached for the big knife before remembering my weapons were back in the fitting room. My spurs couldn't catch the silk. My struggles only bound me tighter. I'd swallowed too much water, some of it into my lungs. Bright spots danced in my vision. Drums pounded in my skull.

I was drowning.

The realization calmed me. I could never unravel the heavy silk in time to escape, but maybe struggling wasn't how I ought to spend my last moments of life. Never mind that the only living souls I really knew were on the other side of the world. I needed a clearheaded moment to say goodbye.

A pale face framed in flowing black hair appeared before me. It wasn't one of the sisters, but a much younger Tian woman. A much prettier one, I thought. She smiled, revealing an overlapping incisor. The small defect made her prettier still.

Her name was Spring Snow. I don't know how, but I knew.

She nodded as the thought formed in my mind.

Years before I met Black Mountain, she said, *I fought the sisters to test my skill. When they captured my sword in their silks, I withdrew.*

Her lips didn't move, but I heard her voice as clearly as if I weren't drowning.

Do not allow my husband to follow me into Hell. Turn him back to a righteous path.

My face betrayed my immediate thought: Why should I give a damn about him?

Because you walk behind him.

It didn't matter. I was seconds away from taking my first step on the long stairs down to Hell.

Reach, said Spring Snow. *It is within your grasp.*

My thoughts balked, but my hand moved. It stretched out through the fronds and searched through the cool dark until my fingers closed around a sword grip.

Silver light filled the brook from bank to bank. The sword moved faster than I could have swung it, its blade slicing the cloth that bound me. I kicked down and flew up.

The remains of the waterwheel exploded into splinters. The sisters reeled away. I landed on the edge of a vat, my clawed toes gripping the wood like a bird's talons. My lungs ached as I gulped air.

The sisters snapped to. In unison, they swept their hands back like dancers. A pair of fat spindles spun on the shelves, and torrents of blue and orange silk poured out at me.

I leaped, Snow's silver blade held out before me. My wrist turned its edge, but the sword needed no urging. With each stroke, it cut away another yard of silk.

The sisters cried out with every stroke, like I was cutting them instead of their cloth. Their hands and arms moved in unison, tracing mystic symbols in the air. They summoned their ki and redoubled their attack. A half-dozen bolts of silk unspooled on the shelves and shot down at me.

Thick silk tendrils grasped my arms and legs, two more smothering the silver sword too quickly for its keen edge to cut itself free.

The sisters weren't the only ones with strong ki. My body was restrained, but my thoughts and desires were still free.

Burning Cloud Devil had shown me a lot of tricks leading up to his deadly Quivering Palm. One of them in particular had eluded me in practice, but then he'd squeezed another little scroll into a pill and walked me through it. I recalled his lesson on picturing not where I was but where I wanted to be. In my mind, I leaped across the room, away from where I was bound. In my heart—if the hot engine I felt pounding inside was still a heart—and in my mind, I believed it.

Bound in silk, I couldn't move an inch. But my thoughts and desire were free.

The silk bonds fell empty to the floor. I'd stepped away, but not through space. Instead I'd moved through that crossroad of mind, spirit, and body. One second I was smothering. The next I reclined on a high rafter.

The sisters looked around, stumped for a moment. I whistled and waved. Threw them the big smile.

The elder threw two handfuls of darts at me. I swatted them away with the silver sword. The younger flew across the room, her sword and razor twirling in a deadly cyclone. I struck them out of her hands and she fell to the floor, sucking on the bloody heel of her palm.

The elder moved to her sister, saw that her wound was not serious, and helped her to stand.

From the rafters above, I heard Burning Cloud Devil's voice chanting. My legs and spine grew warm with the magic of his "attunement."

The seamstresses kept their eyes on me, and I wondered whether they had even heard the battle wizard's chant. For a second I considered revealing him to see whether they could take their revenge while he was exhausted from the spell.

Instead I thought of Spring Snow and drew their attention back to me.

"Sorry, ladies." Despite the language barrier, the sisters could see I was done playing patty-cakes. I pointed Snow's sword at each of their throats. They bowed their surrender as I retrieved a swath of blue silk from the floor and wrapped it around the silver blade. As an afterthought, I collected a handful of darts from the floor and walls. They'd come in handy.

Considering that the sisters were the ones who put me in the drink, I didn't feel too broken up about leaving a wet trail on their carpet as I fetched my gear from the fitting room and walked out into the night.

Chapter Twelve
Red Brush

Your calligraphy must be flawless," said Master Li. "Just as you seek to perfect your martial skills by repetition, so must you write each character many times to unfold its essential nature. To create a single sheet useful to the mystics may require dozens of copies before you achieve perfection. Thus, most of you will write the lesser characters in common black ink on plain rice paper."

I dreaded the next words the old man would utter, but secretly I also relished them. Brush technique was the only skill taught at Dragon Temple in which I exceeded all the other students. If only it counted as one of the initial trials, I would not have been deemed Least Brother and relegated to the kitchens.

Perhaps the masters would also have admired my unorthodox spellcasting, but thus far I had successfully concealed Jade Tiger's tutelage from them. To reveal it now would constitute an admission of my own disobedience, for which I could expect no lesser rebuke than I had witnessed Master Wu inflict on Brother Kwan the previous month.

"Brother Jeggare shall inscribe the large scrolls," said Master Li. "Brothers Karfai and Runme shall provide him with red ink."

Karfai fixed his gaze upon the ground, but Runme glared at me until Master Wu rapped him on the skull. Among the students, these were the two who most often incited scorn at my expense. Runme had the motive of having now lost to me at least once in every contest except wrestling. While Karfai rarely suffered at my hand except in sword practice, he wore his disdain for "the foreign devil" as a badge of national honor.

No one would have been pleased to be assigned the chore of supplying the red ink, even if it were for Kwan, who remained the darling of the temple among masters and students alike. Crushing the red pigment and adding the precise amount of clear water for mixing was hardly an opportunity to distinguish oneself. Every student was striving harder than ever in the knowledge that the second trials approached, and with them an opportunity to advance in honor and prestige.

No one doubted that Kwan would once again win the distinction of First Brother, but no one wished to exchange his place with mine. Kitchen duty was disgrace enough, but now all of the students feared for their lives should they take my place. Lo Gau was in an especially poor temper.

One morning the previous week, I had avoided the kitchen master's sneak attack while bearing a yoke of water buckets. That would have been nothing, but in a moment of pique, I hurled the turnip that served as my hasty breakfast. The wily master of the kitchen gaped as the root bounced off his forehead.

Even that indignity might have been forgiven if Mon Choi had not witnessed the event and shared the anecdote with the other students. Whispers spread throughout the temple complex, and soon Lo Gau found himself the butt of jokes.

The kitchen master had enjoyed his revenge every day since, as my many cuts and bruises attested. I avoided more blows than I received, however, and at last I began to appreciate the silver lining of my kitchen drudgery. In dodging for my life, I had learned at least as much of defense in the kitchen as I had on the proving ground. Mon Choi noticed my unorthodox dodging and praised my "Kitchen-Style Evasion." I discerned no trace of mockery from him, but there was nothing but ridicule in the voices of those who overheard and repeated his praise.

Brother Kwan indicated the blank pages on the easel before him. "When will you judge the quality of the work?"

Master Li squinted. "After I have caught my fish."

A collective sigh escaped from the students. Not once all summer had anyone seen Master Li return from the pond with anything he had not brought with him.

The old master placed his bamboo pole upon his shoulder and strolled off toward the pond.

Master Wu remained to supervise our preparations.

Had it not usurped the time normally dedicated to my scroll inscription, I might have enjoyed the day's task. My assistants and I enjoyed a sunny spot near the scriptorium, while the other students were relegated to the central courtyard. They stood in pairs before each easel. One inscribed the character for each of the four hundred and forty-four beasts inhabiting the vast lands of Tian Xia, while the other removed each completed page and lay it aside to dry. Every ten minutes or so, scribe and assistant exchanged roles.

I enjoyed no such relief, but both Karfai and Runme were at my service, at least ostensibly. They performed their duties diligently enough, providing me with a bucket of red ink and fixing each thick yellow page to a four-foot-square plank leaning upon the Cherry Court wall. I wet my mop-sized brush with red ink and inscribed the arcane character for each of the eighty-eight common restless spirits.

Once we had finished, visiting mystics would use the five hundred and thirty-two pages as the material component in renewing the ward surrounding the outer walls and gates of Dragon Temple.

While I had come to appreciate the purpose of the temple and wished no harm to befall its inhabitants—excepting occasionally Karfai and Runme—I would have preferred to spend my time learning more of the spells that Jade Tiger doled out with such frugality. He had not even shown me as many as I could maintain simultaneously, much less the spells that would allow me to escape Dragon Temple or contact Radovan, who no doubt luxuriated in the fleshpots of Lanming while I labored in this prison camp.

My patience with Jade Tiger's tutelage had lapsed a few days earlier, and I demanded he show me a scroll of message sending. The instant the words had left my mouth, I knew I had overstepped our relationship. Happily, the eunuch replied mildly.

"Why is this spell so desirable?"

Despite our conspiratorial relationship, I did not trust Jade Tiger, yet I had no other choice. I had no other confidant within Dragon Temple. Mon Choi continued to treat me sympathetically, but after the incident at the garden wall he had been more circumspect in chatting with me within the hearing of the other disciples. Kwan was courteous but clearly focused on his personal advancement. Among the masters, only Li seemed mild enough to entertain my entreaties, but he would rather go fishing than humor a student.

And so I confided in Jade Tiger that I had been separated from a companion on the way to Dragon Temple and that I hoped to deliver him a message. I dared not admit that my intention was anything other than to remain and complete my training, for the masters reminded us daily of the punishment for desertion: pursuit, capture, and—if there were any mercy—death rather than punishment at the hands of Master Wu.

To his credit and my infinite relief, Jade Tiger only smiled when he might have pressed for further information.

"If you wish only to send a message, you may leave it to me. I have occasion to dispatch communiqués to the king. It would be a small matter to include a separate letter to your friend. Give me your message tomorrow, and I will see that it is delivered."

Despite my misgivings, I did as he bade, writing a short note in a simple Pathfinder cipher I had taught Radovan. Upon surrendering the note to Jade Tiger, I considered the more delicate challenge of entrusting my bodyguard's true nature to the eunuch. Radovan would be more difficult to locate by name than by description.

"A devil?" said Jade Tiger.

"Not precisely. In my homeland, some call them hellspawn, yet they are no less human than—"

"A half-elf?"

I responded with a civil if insincere smile. Every time I began to warm to Jade Tiger, the eunuch dispelled my ease with a subtle insult.

Contemplation of his condescension would not improve my calligraphy, so I focused on the effort at hand. The character for "ghost" was deceptively simple. It would have been a shame for me to waste one of the large yellow sheets by failing to capture it on the first effort. I stretched my back, took up the brush, and envisioned the character in my mind. Within a minute it was perfected in thought. I drenched the brush in ink and with five deft strokes rendered the thought incarnate.

Runme scoffed, but Karfai stared with admiration at the result. When he realized I was regarding him, he sneered, but I noticed the care with which he removed the page. I harbored a fleeting hope that he might learn to treat me with the respect he showed the other disciples.

We continued in this vein for more than an hour before Master Wu banged a miniature gong to herald the midday meal. Karfai and Runme bolted, leaving me to clean up before joining them in the refectory.

While my belly was empty, I felt a greater hunger for solitude after enduring their hostile glances while I labored. I took my great brush and the ink bucket to the stream running beside the Peach Court wall. As I passed the proving grounds, I saw that many of my fellows had left their brushes dirty, so I collected those as well. I reached the stream with two ink buckets and half a dozen brushes to clean.

Bending to my work, I felt a sort of peace I had rarely enjoyed. It was the calm that accompanied a simple task undertaken in serenity. So often in my life I have sought the thrill of uncertainty and danger, but never without the trepidation they breed. Soon I perceived little more than the burbling of the brook and the birdsong from the garden trees.

Somehow it was no surprise when I detected the delicate fragrance of the princess. In my tranquil state, it did not seem strange that she would tread so close to the labors of a lowly student. Not that I was truly lowly, but it was a pleasure to think of myself as a carefree student rather than a prisoner of circumstance.

Protocol demanded that I kowtow at once, but instead I squeezed the last of the moisture from the red brush and pretended not to notice her presence.

"Your calligraphy is beautiful."

At the sound of her voice, I turned and bowed in the dignified Tian fashion rather than kowtowing, heedless of the consequences of presuming above my apparent station.

She stood unveiled, but a silk-covered rice hat sheltered her face from the midday sun. Her garb was of a manly cut, but it was insufficient to the task of disguising her feminine shape. From her hip hung the black and gold scabbard I had observed earlier, the legend of which I had learned a great deal more while copying the historical chronicles.

If I were not mistaken—and I seldom am—the scabbard contained the fabled Shadowless Sword, a magic blade of surpassing strength and swiftness. It was one of a rare few swords powerful enough to open the breast of the Celestial Dragon at the penultimate moment of the Dragon Ceremony.

"Nothing under Heaven may be deemed beautiful in the presence of Princess Lanfen."

She did not blush, as is the custom of young Chelish noblewomen. Nor did she pale with anger, which was the privilege of her station. Her expression spoke only of curiosity.

I bowed again, this time in the Chelish manner. "Your highness, allow me to present myself properly. I am Count Varian Jeggare of Cheliax."

"A foreign lord knows my identity?"

"In truth, before misadventure led me to this refuge, I was on an embassy to your father's court." It occurred to me that Jade Tiger should be nearby, but I did not detect the scent of incense that followed him everywhere. I wondered that he would allow the princess to go anywhere unescorted by her guards. Her presence here suggested that she had eluded them. I felt a throb of admiration for her independence.

"My father has fourteen daughters. How is it you identified me?"

It would have been both true and obvious to mention the legend of her beauty, but I had gleaned another fact about the royal family during my labors in the scriptorium. "Among the daughters of King Wen, the youngest is distinguished by her talent for music."

The shadow of a smile touched her lips, but she mastered her expression. "Among the brothers of Dragon Temple, the outlander is distinguished for both his calligraphy and his talent for swordplay."

I felt more than the sun's warmth upon my face. It was proper to bow, but instead I smiled as I have so rarely done since the twilight of my youth. "Among the brothers, I do not disgrace myself, but Brother Kwan is first in sword."

"Then surely he will win the honor of bearing the Shadowless Sword." She touched the hilt of the blade on her hip.

Nothing I had read suggested that anyone but one of the royal family was permitted to wield the legendary weapon, so swift that the sun itself was too sluggish to lay a shadow beneath its blade.

"It is our custom to bestow the royal weapon upon the foremost swordsman of Dragon Temple for the pilgrimage to the Gates of Heaven and Hell," she continued.

From my reading, I knew that after summoning the Celestial Dragon, the royal representative opened her heart and offered it in exchange for a fraction of the dragon's immortal spirit, as embodied in an enormous pearl—its heart. Afterward, the dragon granted its supplicants a wish. In ancient years, imperial embassies used the wish to grant prosperity throughout the Empire of Lung Wa. Since the fracturing of the empire into the Successor States, however, the embassy from Quain had bent the dragon's wish to maintaining the tenuous balance of power between the warring kingdoms.

I had not realized that the honor of bearing the Shadowless Sword in the ceremony fell to the monk who distinguished himself as First Brother of Sword. Defeating Kwan was not required to escape my kitchen duties, nor had I felt an especial jealousy until I looked into the dark eyes of Princess Lanfen.

Petty rivalry aside, the favor of Princess Lanfen could prove crucial to my initial purpose in visiting Tian Xia. As the one destined to exchange her heart with that of the Celestial Dragon, it was within her power to grant the request for which the Decemvirate had sent me to the extremity of the world. Once she made her wish, the princess could dispose of the pearl's husk as she chose. Surely she would not refuse the request of one who safeguarded her passage to the Gate.

Especially not the bearer of the Shadowless Sword.

The thought perished the moment I applied reason to the situation. Even at my best, I had little hope of defeating Kwan. Our first contest had appeared close only because he had toyed with me. Since our initial trials, his sword skill had only improved, while I had neglected mine in favor of boiling congee and copying chronicles.

"Tell me of your country," said the princess. "And of the reason you traveled so far."

My consternation evaporated under the warmth of her regard. "While I have had the honor to represent Cheliax in past diplomatic missions, it is for another cause that I embarked upon this journey. Perhaps you have heard of the Pathfinder Society. Among them I hold the rank of venture-captain, a sort of—"

The princess looked past my shoulder. I heard the approach of my fellow students. I turned to see Karfai, Runme, Mon Choi, and two of the others departing the refectory. Silently I lamented the speed with which the disciples devoured their meals, and I wondered why they had not remained to gossip as was their custom. Runme pointed through the intervening trees toward the stream where I stood with the princess. For an instant Mon Choi protested, but the others scoffed at his caution.

I turned to warn the princess, but with a rustle of silk she was gone. A few mature samara fell from the nearby gutta-percha trees, but I could not spy her among the branches.

How light her step, I thought. She flies as gently as an angel.

"Leave it to Brother Brush to miss dinner and still not finish his chores," said Runme. He displayed his yellow teeth.

I ignored his jibe and bent to gather the black brushes.

Brother Lu Bai, a hairy fellow who vied with Mon Choi for the honor of Second Brother in wrestling, kicked the stream to splash me.

The others laughed, but I maintained my temper. It was especially difficult knowing that the princess might remain nearby to witness the derision of my "brothers." I filled the bucket with water for the black ink brushes, but before I could dip them, Lu Bai stepped forward.

I turned, hoisting the bucket out of range of his kick. On a whim, I reached out with one of the brushes to paint the character for "wet" upon his brow.

The others gaped. A guffaw escaped Mon Choi before he could clap his hand over his mouth.

"What?" demanded Runme, frowning at the word I had drawn. He was among the least literate of the disciples. "What does that mean?"

I demonstrated its meaning by throwing the contents of the bucket full into Lu Bai's face. "Wet" dissolved upon his forehead and ran down either side of his nose.

Mon Choi lost his remaining composure, and pock-faced Yingjie joined his laughter. The others were not so amused. Karfai struck at my head, but I deflected the blow with the bucket. As he shook the pain from his knuckles, I reached out and painted "fool" on his cheek. Shock froze him for an instant. Before he recovered, I slapped the inverted bucket over his head.

My opponents' skin was simply another form of scroll. With that realization, I decided to test an outrageous theory. If it succeeded, I prayed that the princess was our unseen witness.

Lu Bai looked at his brothers before assuming a ready stance and stepping toward me. Summoning to mind the characters of the first enchantment Jade Tiger had taught me, I held the brush behind me to disguise my grip. The ploy succeeded. Lu Bai's gaze dropped from my face to my shoulder. I shrugged a feint and stepped outside his advance. As he lunged past me, I wrote the characters for "hold" and "man" upon his back.

Lu Bai froze in place, paralyzed.

I could hardly believe my eyes. While clearly not impossible, successfully casting a spell in such a manner was not only unorthodox but highly unlikely to succeed. Otherwise, how could this method have gone so long undiscovered? Was it possible, I wondered, that the very defect that made me incapable of casting spells in the traditional manner somehow allowed me—

The bucket shattered over my head, scattering my thoughts and driving me down to one knee. I had allowed my astonishment to distract me from Karfai. I dropped the brush and rolled away, but a flurry of kicks followed me every inch of my retreat. I tried to rise, but he swept my legs. As from a distance, Mon Choi's voice implored them to stop, but the beating only increased as Runme and Yingjie joined in.

My last conscious thought was a prayer that the princess was, in fact, not witness to my latest humiliation.

Chapter Thirteen
Moon Blade

The night we left the House of Silks, Burning Cloud Devil limped down the road beside me. The spell he cast to imbue my infernal body with martial power really took it out of him. I decided to let him get a night's rest before telling him about the little chat I'd had with his dead wife.

When morning came, I couldn't think of a way to raise the subject. Hunched over the fire he'd conjured to boil water, he didn't look just weary. He looked bereft.

We sat there drinking tea while I thought of a way to break the ice. He'd gotten up to start the sword-catching exercise he'd been teaching me. He drew the sword he kept on the hip below his remaining arm. It should have been an awkward gesture, but he'd had thirty-five years to practice it. I didn't ask why he didn't just wear the sword on the other side, swapping its position with the empty scabbard he always wore as well. I knew the answer.

It was another remembrance of Spring Snow.

It was just as well. He hadn't sharpened the sword in years, maybe not since he'd lost his arm. That made it a better weapon for practice. He'd make an obvious slashing attack, and I'd try to catch the blade between my palms. While I didn't expect that trick to work in a real fight, I caught it more often than not. The trick was timing.

Whenever I screwed up and cut my hands, I'd lay them on the coals of the fire. In my devil form, the heat barely warmed me. A few minutes later, I was good as new.

I got an idea, what the boss might have called a "provocation."

"That blade has seen better days," I said. "I got a new one for you."

I removed the silver sword from my pack. It seemed about the right size to fit in the constantly empty scabbard, but the angle of the guard was the wrong shape. Besides, the scabbard was gilded, while the sword's pommel and crosspiece were untarnished silver. They weren't a match.

"You found that in the river?" Burning Cloud Devil's tone gave nothing away, but he was a sorcerer after all. Sorcerers make great liars.

"Don't act so cute," I said. "You knew I'd find it."

"Why do you say that?"

"How were you planning to kill this dragon of yours if those sisters had drowned me?"

He shrugged. "If you could not defeat them, you surely could not learn the Twin White Palms technique. You would be useless to me."

I watched his face to see whether he was joking. He wasn't.

"Son of a bitch."

He didn't rise to the insult, which I knew he hated. Calling anyone a dog in this country was a shortcut to a fight.

"Tell the truth," I said. "You wanted me to find that sword."

"I had no idea it was there."

"You'd fought those sisters before, hadn't you?"

"I had never even seen them." He straightened his back and lifted his chin. At last my accusations were getting to his pride.

"Then how did you know about them?"

"Everyone knows their legend. Many young heroes seek them out to try their skill."

"Young heroes like Spring Snow?"

"What?"

"This is her sword, isn't it?"

His hand went to the golden scabbard. Scowling, he shook his head. "Snow had a golden blade when I met her. She left it in the throat of the dragon."

"But she'd fought the sisters before she met you. They defeated her and kept her silver sword."

He peered at the weapon, his thick eyebrows forming an angry V above his black eyes. "Give it to me," he said.

I stopped myself from tossing it to him. Instead I stood and offered it with both hands, not for his sake but out of respect for Snow. Maybe I have a soft spot for the ladies, but she seemed like a swell kid. Spirit. Ghost. Whatever.

Burning Cloud Devil grunted as he balanced the blade on his finger, two inches above the guard. "It is the correct balance for Snow. Still, I cannot imagine the sisters could defeat her and not you."

"She fought them a long time ago," I said. "Long before she met you."

"How can you know?"

I told him what I'd seen on death's doorstep. "She said to tell you to give up your revenge and return to, I don't know, a virtuous path or something."

Burning Cloud Devil had become as still as one of those stone idols we passed along the road now and then. He thought a long while, then raised a suspicious eyebrow.

"You wish only to be released from our bargain." His voice sounded like a distant warning of thunder. "You dare to invoke my wife's name in such a ploy?"

"It's no picnic tramping the countryside with you," I said. "But I saw her. She spoke to me."

"You lie. Only a dishonorable wretch would give up the revenge of his dead master."

"He was my friend." My palms itched to encircle his throat.

"A friend! Only a coward would tell such lies. If you care so little for his memory, you must have been no more than his slave."

I felt the heat of a furnace rising in my chest. "Don't you talk about the boss. Don't you call me a slave."

"You dare to speak of Snow."

"Yeah, but I—" I tamped down the heat before it hit my brain. "Fine."

I'd said my piece. I stood up and collected my pack. When he saw me stamping down the road, Burning Cloud Devil followed. If he wanted to walk a path to Hell, I decided, that was fine with me.

I'd hold the door for him.

Weeks later, we were back in the western provinces, a hundred miles south of the Golden River. It was mining territory, with dozens of little towns devoted to cutting stone and scraping copper and gold from the guts of the Wall of Heaven Mountains.

The region was lousy with soldiers. We ran into a security company on a road through a bamboo forest.

Before we came within shouting distance, the guards had already braced for an attack. Spearmen stood before swordsmen, and in the rear stood archers with crossbows. One look at the firepots on their hips disturbed an angry snake that had been living in my belly since we ran across the Falcon-Head Sword Gang.

We weren't traveling in disguise, so they recognized the sorcerer at once. My looks didn't help matters much, despite my fine new clothes. In the end, Burning Cloud Devil and the chief of security approached each other. They exchanged a little news of the road before we continued on our separate ways.

"Did you hear that?" Burning Cloud Devil slapped his thigh and grinned.

I shrugged. There was this one swordswoman on the security team with dimpled cheeks and a stray lock of hair she kept blowing off the tip of her nose. I wasn't paying much attention to the conversation.

"The Green Marsh Wrestler is nearby! It is time to put the Quivering Palm to practice." The sorcerer sounded as happy as a child expecting a puppy. For the first time all summer, I realized what Burning Cloud Devil had done.

He'd appointed himself my manager.

Years ago, when I first left the Goatherds and before I officially joined up with the boss, I had a hard time making ends meet. My old crew spread the word that no one was to let me freelance, and I wasn't interested in joining another gang. I couldn't get a tip to save my life, and no one would so much as sit lookout for me on a second-story job. Somebody even tipped off the city guard, and they'd passed my description to the goddamned Hellknights. It got so bad I couldn't even pick a pocket in the Plaza of Flowers on Judgment Day.

All I had left was my fists and a skull thicker than most. So I did a little fighting.

My first bout was against a stevedore a foot taller than me, champion of the Eel Street Docks, backed by my old gang boss, Zandros the Fair. It took the better part of half an hour, but I got him down on the street and beat his head until his dwarven handler threw in the towel. Nobody cared that I was seconds away from dropping down beside him. Afterward, his manager wanted to be my manager.

That lasted only a few months before something better came along, but I remember how the dwarf hustled to set up fights with every neighborhood champion and kept half my winnings—more than that if I didn't keep an eye on him.

That's pretty much what Burning Cloud Devil had been doing for me. The only difference was that he didn't care about any short-term payoff. He only wanted to get me to that championship bout.

Each morning for the next few days, Burning Cloud Devil spent a couple of hours lecturing me on wrestling technique. What he had in mind was more about throws and evasion than the sort of wrestling I knew, but the end result was the same. One fellow was going to end up on his back with the other one's hands around his throat.

We had a look at the prisoners working in four different mines and quarries before a stonecutter directed us to a granite quarry a few miles beyond the forest. We walked beneath stalks of bamboo taller than oak trees. Their enormous fronds shaded us from the hot summer sun.

A few miles from the forest's edge, we stopped at an open-air tea house to eat pork buns while the owner's teenaged sons slapped at flies with horsehair whips.

Between bites, Burning Cloud Devil filled me in on the Green Marsh Wrestler's story.

"His technique is impeccable, his strength legendary," said Burning Cloud Devil. "It is said he strangled two of his neighbors' oxen at the age of sixteen. The village elders sent him to Dragon Temple to save the remaining livestock. After leaving the temple, he bested the royal executioner in a dispute over a courtesan, and just two years ago he defeated the Eight Stone-Faced Brothers of Wailan Mansion simultaneously."

"Sounds like some mean customer."

"It is a shame you have learned so few of the rudiments of the Quivering Palm."

I waved away his criticism. He'd been lecturing me about internal energy, ki flow, and a bunch of other mumbo jumbo. It wasn't so hard to understand.

"It would be easier to teach a dog," he continued.

"I've heard that before."

Burning Cloud Devil said so many things that reminded me of the boss that they didn't make me angry anymore. They just highlighted the differences between the men, and Burning Cloud Devil came up short. He made me appreciate how good I'd had it before. That trail of thought led down a dark hollow, so I changed the subject.

"How did the wrestler end up on a chain gang?"

"He killed a magistrate's son in Lanming. The judge sentenced him to ten years of hard labor."

"I'd like to have seen the fight at that hearing."

"There was no fight. Like all disciples of Dragon Temple, the Green Marsh Wrestler respects authority. Once judged, he obeyed the sentence."

I pressed for more details, but that's all he had. Burning Cloud Devil had never seen the guy fight, so I could only imagine what he had in store for me. Probably he'd have a hard time getting a good grip on me, with all my spikes. The trick was to find a way to use more than my elbow spurs, which I'd put to good use in scraps since I was a tyke.

After our rest, we walked a few miles through the forest to the base of the mountains. There we found the quarry. Beside the road leading down into the rock pit, a severed head was stuck on a bamboo shaft. Below it someone had fixed a board with a name written in dried blood. Burning Cloud Devil translated it, and I knew we'd found our guy, or what was left of him. Flies formed a black halo around his rotting brow. My stomach is cast iron, but I had to cover my face at the stench.

Burning Cloud Devil went livid. Without waiting for me, he flew to the headman's office, his smoking fireball setting fire to the nearby tents. He dispatched the guards with a few casual slaps and pulled the man from his shack.

By the time I reached them, Burning Cloud Devil had his hand raised as if to strike a mortal blow to the official, who kowtowed over and over fast enough to start a breeze.

"I swear, dread sorcerer," he blubbered. "We did not execute him. It was the Moon Blade Killer."

The name cooled Burning Cloud Devil's fury. He lowered his fist and stroked his chin until he seemed to pull the amazement off of his face. He lifted his beard on his wrist, considering what he had heard.

"How long ago did this happen?"

The official raised his head only long enough to reply. "Four days."

The wrestler's head looked pretty ripe for being only four days old, but on the other hand, it was hot.

Burning Cloud Devil turned to me. "Go, bury the remains. Such a great hero deserves better."

"But—" The overseer swallowed his words when Burning Cloud Devil raised his hand.

It had become clear that "hero" meant something different to Burning Cloud Devil than it did back home. Still, four days with your head on a stick seemed plenty to me. I climbed back up to the edge of the quarry and grabbed a shovel from the nearest prisoner. He scuttled away, forcing his nearest companions on the chain to do the same. They cast sidelong glances at me as I dug a little grave. When I pulled the bamboo pole from the ground and tipped the stinking head into the hole, they cried out prayers to Pharasma and ran away as fast as their shackles allowed.

By the time I tamped down the last of the grave, Burning Cloud Devil rejoined me, an annoying little smirk on his face.

"I'm going to go out on a limb and assume this Moon Blade guy is my next opponent."

He nodded, but his smile still mocked me with a secret.

"How're we going to track him down?"

"There is no need," he said. "He will surely find you."

The wind picked up as we returned to the tea house. On its breath came the warmth of late summer and a scent of lightning.

The owner had lit green and blue lamps around the outdoor tables. They bobbed like buoys in the evening tide. The rising moon set the clouds to glowing silver through the black stalks of bamboo, which bent their heads toward each other to gossip. In better company, it would have made one hell of a romantic setting.

The shop owner promised us roast duck and carp before retreating into his covered kitchen. Meanwhile two of his boys brought us out little bowls of rice and dishes of steamed vegetables, most of which looked almost but not quite like the ones back home. The carrots tasted more or less like carrots, only they were purple.

There were also these thin white slices of something one of the boys kept telling me were shoots from bamboo, but not the nearby kind, which were apparently poisonous. Not that I'd felt any compulsion to start gnawing on the trees, but that was good to know. It was also good to know my grasp of Tien was improving even though I couldn't practice speaking it myself.

With his chopsticks, Burning Cloud Devil pinched a green stalk of something like leafy broccoli and gestured for emphasis. "No one remembers the Moon Blade Killer's true name, but forty years ago, he too was a disciple of Dragon Temple."

"Forty years?" I whistled low. "Guy must be decrepit."

I covered my smile by concentrating on using my own chopsticks. After months of practice, it was getting easier, but I still had to focus on getting the food from the plate and into my mouth without any sudden detours across the table.

Burning Cloud Devil snarled at my jibe. He wouldn't tell me his age, but my guesses were getting closer. His thick dark hair threw me off. I bet he used a spell to keep it black.

"He was peerless among the students and soon became First Brother in each of the Eighteen Weapons of Irori. Yet the masters of the temple deemed him too cruel. They cast him out of the temple.

"Ever since then he has wandered across Tian Xia, seeking out former disciples of Dragon Temple to prove that he alone remains worthy of the title First Brother. With his moon blade, he beheads every foe."

Even at only a few fights a year, over forty years, I reckoned that was a big pile of heads. I liked mine where it was, even though it wasn't its usual pretty self.

"Too bad I never went to this Dragon Temple. This Moon Blade Killer's got no reason to fight me."

Burning Cloud Devil chortled. "Ah, but you have given him one. He also slays those who disturb the remains of his victims."

Terrific, I thought. This chopper guy was probably looking for me already, ready to turn me into one of these headless stalks of the local broccoli. The thought chased off my appetite. I looked around to see whether the next dish was on its way.

In the kitchen doorway stood one of the serving boys, his mouth open in a perfect O. I followed the line of his gaze to the fallen body of his brother.

The headless body of his brother.

Before anyone could react, the surprised boy's head flew off his body. I looked in the direction it moved, but all I could see was a brief flash of silver.

I rolled away from the table and hunched my head down as close as I could to my shoulders. "I can't see a damned thing."

Burning Cloud Devil didn't reply. He'd vanished again.

The tea house owner came outside, calling his sons' names.

"Get down!"

He didn't understand a word I said, but as he looked toward me he saw the corpses of his sons on the ground. As his mouth contorted in anguish, a moon-white ring of metal encircled his neck. His blood left a black trail in the moonlight as his head vanished into the sky.

There was no sense in that. Those boys and their father hadn't gone anywhere near the Moon Blade Killer's prize. I bellowed what I thought of that, not caring whether the killer understood me.

All of a sudden my neck itched. I shrugged on my wicker pack. It rose up behind my head, making a target wider than the beheading ring.

At least, that was my working theory, as the boss might have said.

The bamboo whispered above me. I looked up to see the silhouette of a man standing on one of the high fronds. He was thin as a switch, with a smoky halo of hair and beard whipping about his head. He held a staff, its head an irregular circle within a circle. An eclipsed moon.

His eyes were lost in shadow, but I knew he was staring an accusation into my face. I shot it right back at him, along with the tines. He shook his staff toward me, and I heard the skirling passage of his moon blade.

I dropped to the ground. A metallic chime sounded beside my ear, and I felt an impact just behind my neck. The staff I'd taken from the drunken boxer saved my neck, but the top twelve inches of my wicker pack were gone, despite being twice as wide as the loop of the man's blade. The outer edge of that moon blade was as sharp as the inner.

Looking back up, I saw the Moon Blade Killer catch the razor circle on the top of his staff. For the first time I glimpsed the slender chain that drew it back into place. It was finer than rope, barely visible in the moonlight.

The branch on which he'd stood swayed back up. I didn't see him move, but he was gone.

"After him," hissed Burning Cloud Devil. He was nearby but still invisible.

I dropped my pack and ran toward the base of one of the giant bamboo trees.

"No, you fool. Have you learned nothing? Use what you won from the sisters. Leap!"

A terrific report cracked beside me. Before it flew away, I glimpsed the moon blade cutting through the edge of a giant bamboo, returning on a sharp arc to slice through the other half. The enormous trunk slid down toward me.

I tumbled forward and kept rolling to avoid the massive weight, but it didn't fall the way I'd expected. The giant bamboo slid down and plunged into the soil beside its own base. It stood there without so much as a quiver, as if it had just decided to step a little closer to its neighbor.

I heard the metallic song of the moon blade as it flew out again. Without waiting to see it, I kicked off from the ground and flew up into the fronds. It was terrifying but strangely easy, not much different from bounding around the rafters at the House of a Thousand Silks.

About three-quarters of the way up the giant bamboo, the fronds and sprouts formed a dense cover. There was much more moonlight, but it spilled across such a tangle of green that I had no idea where the Moon Blade Killer had gone.

That was until I heard the blade flying through the trees. Leaves fell in its wake as it closed.

I leaped to the next bough. It bent under my weight, just as the first had done. As it began to lift me back up, I bent my knees and pushed off in another direction. I heard the path of the moon blade a few feet below me, farther away than the earlier throws.

I was getting the hang of this flying business.

Within a few jumps, I sensed the general location of the Moon Blade Killer. He reacted to each of my moves with a brief pause and a leap of his own. I snapped a few darts after him to raise the stakes, but he was quicker. A couple of seconds after he reached the next branch, the blade came whirring toward me.

Thinking of Burning Cloud Devil's sword-capture technique, I lifted my hands to clap them shut on the moon blade, but at the last moment I thought better of it. The disc wasn't even a blur. It moved so fast it was invisible.

The next time the disc zipped out toward me, I pretended to leap but hung on to the upper fronds of the bamboo. My weight slowed its return motion just enough for the trunk to catch a glancing blow from the moon blade. The blade cut the wood but kept flying, slightly off course. When the chain pulled taut, it snapped back around the shaft of the next bamboo.

I jumped over to pin the chain between the bamboo and my chest. When the disc came near, I leaned back to avoid its razor edge and stabbed my knife through its hole.

It held fast, but only for a second before the inner ring cut through the steel. The handle of my favorite knife fell away, leaving the blade in the bamboo.

"Son of a bitch!"

The moon blade snapped back into place on the Moon Blade Killer's staff. A second later it sang out again. I dropped to the ground and ran back to where I'd dropped the pack.

And the boxer's staff.

That guy was quick with the blade, throwing it out and pulling it back as if it were a fishing pole. The second throw brushed my scalp. I barely felt the incision, it was so sharp, but seconds later my neck was hot with blood.

I felt the shadow of the blade on the back of my neck as I ran the last few yards toward the pack. The Moon Blade Killer knew where I was headed. The trick was for me to get there first.

Still pumping my legs, I sped myself with mind and spirit, striving to remember Burning Cloud Devil's lessons. One second I was yards away, the next I had the ringed staff in hand, raising it up to where my head should be.

I caught the moon blade on the staff. Its inner edge squealed and caught on the staff's ringed head.

A few trunks away, I heard the grunt of the Moon Blade Killer as he pulled on the staff. It was no use. The staff held the ring in place. I stabbed its butt deep into the ground.

Before he could wise up and leap around for a better angle, I jumped onto the chain and ran up at him. He hesitated a moment, deciding whether to drop the weapon and let me fall.

A moment was all I needed to get my fingers around his neck.

Up close I didn't need the moonlight to see his features contort as I squeezed his windpipe shut.

Somewhere in the dark below us, Burning Cloud Devil chanted his spell. I felt it tingling in my hands and in my belly.

All I could think about were the dead boys and their father. They wouldn't be bringing us roast duck later. Instead, I'd be digging their graves.

The Moon Blade Killer scratched my face, but I didn't care about my looks anymore. He kneed me in the soft spot, but that wasn't what it used to be either. I opened

Chapter Fourteen
Assassin's Chain

The injuries I suffered at the hands of my fellow students paled in comparison to the threat of Master Wu's inquisition as to the instigation of our fracas.

Despite his aggressive and brutal tactics, a portion of my sympathies lay with Master Wu. It was his duty to preserve order in the temple and administer discipline whenever and wherever it was required. The brawny master of martial instruction was as feared for his ability to root out the perpetrators of mischief as he was for the swift and brutal justice he meted out. This time, however, he made it clear to all of us disciples that a beating was the least we could expect. He promised that those who had beaten me faced expulsion for delaying the completion of the warding scrolls.

A wicked temptation urged me to name my attackers, but I refused to indulge it. While I would not lament the expulsion of Karfai, Runme, or the other brutes, I wished no harm to Mon Choi. Crude and simple though he was, he remained the closest thing I had to a friend within the temple walls.

Even if I could point the finger at the others without implicating him, still I hesitated to testify against the bullies. No matter that I would report only the truth; turning against them would only further diminish my reputation among the disciples. Moreover, surrendering my personal revenge to the machinery of authority would leave an indelible stain on my honor as a count of Cheliax, a Jeggare, and a venture-captain of the Pathfinder Society.

For now, I would keep silent, and I would abide.

I harbored no hope that my silence would earn me appreciation from the other disciples. Yet despite my disdain for my so-called brothers, I felt perversely disappointed in that prediction. No matter how long I lived aloof from my peers at home, it was no pleasure to remain the outsider. It was, alas, my fate.

Through the hot summer days, none of the other students offered me so much as a nod in recognition of my silence. Their hazing waned, but not out of respect for me; rather, they feared to attract the suspicions of Master Wu.

Mon Choi was once more the exception to the silent wall of ingratitude. He insisted on trading places with those who had been assigned to mix the red ink for my scrolls. When he volunteered to take my place in the kitchen, he attracted Master Wu's suspicious eye. He added half of his supper to my bowl when he thought others would not notice and constantly offered folksy advice on herbs and isometric exercises to speed my recovery. Much of the latter was surprisingly accurate, and I once again reevaluated my earlier appraisals of his knowledge and intellect.

While he never gave Master Wu enough cause to accuse him, Mon Choi's fawning over me earned the resentment of the belligerents. Karfai, Runme, Lu Bai, and Yingjie exhibited no fear that I might identify them to Master Wu. Indeed, they were safe, even the two principals of my assault. All other factors being equal, a sudden vengeance would leave me unsatisfied. I had no taste for petty revenge.

My revenge, when its time came, would be grand.

Despite my best efforts to achieve serenity during combat, my desire for retribution smoldered during our drills. The angry emotion interfered with my training, and that I could not allow. Of the Six Sacred Weapons of Irori, I was adept at only the sword. Setting aside my spite as best I could, I concentrated my energies on mastering the other five: fist, staff, knife, spear, and wrestling.

I most detested wrestling, which placed me in intimate contact with these sweaty brutes. The other disciples soon recognized my aversion to physical contact and used it to their advantage. A smack on the buttocks or a pinch of my nipple was a sure route to vexing my concentration, whereupon I soon found myself flat on my back, the bout decided.

I fared better in staff and spear, which at least conformed in general to the tactics of swordplay. Fist and knife were more difficult, but I had a hundred times observed Radovan dispatch street thugs. Thus had he indirectly taught me a few techniques unknown to my rivals.

More and more often I found myself on the brink of victory in our sparring sessions. Sometimes I relished the surprised disbelief on my opponent's face as I placed the tip of my weapon at his throat. Afterward I would bow with a mask of humility upon my face. After the third or fourth time, I felt I had perfected the illusion of calm indifference.

More often, especially when facing my most hated rivals, I allowed my opponent to prevail, concealing my ability. Far better, I thought, to reinforce the impression that I remained a feeble old foreign devil. Overconfidence in my rivals could prove the most potent weapon of all.

Still I could not achieve the serene detachment that Master Wu demanded in physical exercise and Master Li described during our meditations. Only in the scriptorium could I achieve the tranquility that we sought in martial and spiritual exercise. In the realm of the intellect, I was at home. My most perfect mantras were the acts of reading and writing. Serenity fell upon my shoulders as my hand lifted the brush.

Yet even in the haven of knowledge, distractions rooted me out.

Chief among them was Jade Tiger's absence. At first I imagined the eunuch avoided my company because I had attracted the displeasure of Master Wu. Objectively, I could only approve of his caution, for he had both his own and the princess's reputations to guard. Yet every day he failed to visit me was another lost opportunity to learn a spell enabling me to contact Radovan.

Since learning the tricks to overcome my disability, my command of magic had improved dramatically, yet Jade Tiger had shared far fewer spells than I could prepare as flying scrolls. I suppressed the impulse to seek him out, instead creating and re-creating flying scrolls to the limit of my abilities. Some ineffable premonition caused me to conceal a few of them on my person before hiding the rest within the scriptorium.

When separated from the solace of my studies, I turned to Master Li's mantras for help clearing my mind. Far more than our martial training, his guided meditations complemented my efforts both in the scriptorium and outside in the Cherry Court, where I resumed my writing of the major scrolls for the temple wards. Typically I turned to silent recitation of passages from *Unbinding the Fetters* after glimpsing a sneer of contempt from one of my tormentors. My natural inclination was to rise to the affront and challenge the jackanapes. Instead, I turned my focus inward and recited a sutra on emptiness. It helped to soothe my ire, but I did not expect it would bring me a shadow of transcendence.

Yet then it did.

My brief transportation occurred not during a moment of conscious meditation, but while I copied the mystic characters in red upon yellow paper. A sound stirred me from a trance, and I realized that Mon Choi had been calling to me for some time. I was surprised to see dozens of dry pages beside the easel, the fruits of over an hour's labor.

I thought only a few minutes had passed.

"Brother, Master Li summons you."

I did not wonder what the venerable master might want of me. I simply set aside my brush and moved to obey. "Very well."

Mon Choi appeared nonplussed. "He summons you to the Persimmon Court."

Only after the second trials would we novices be permitted into the Plum Court, where our elders trained and resided, much less the mysterious Persimmon Court. When we asked about the western quarter, whose persimmon trees we glimpsed above the highest walls on the mountain, the masters shook their heads. The Persimmon Court was forbidden to students. Only masters and their invited guests were welcome there.

Overhearing Mon Choi's message, Kwan and Lu Bai collected my work and lingered to hear more. Lu Bai turned away a guilty expression, but Kwan regarded me with astonished envy.

Mon Choi led me to the Plum Court gate. There Lo Gau awaited us. The kitchen master whirled his hand in a hurry-up gesture I had seen all too often while chopping carrots and taro root. When the other students attempted to follow me through the door, he blocked the way.

"I'll take those." He nodded at my yellow scrolls. Kwan and Lu Bai surrendered the pages.

As I passed through the gate, Mon Choi bowed solemnly before a loutish smile creased his face and he waved like a child saying farewell to an elder brother leaving home. Beyond his beefy shoulder, I caught a glimpse of Jade Tiger for the first time in weeks. The eunuch furrowed his brow as he saw where I was going. Rather than return my inquiring gaze, however, he summoned Kwan to his side and whispered to him. I desired to observe their exchange, but my ability to read lips was poor in any language but Taldane. Before I could guess the shape of a single word, Lo Gau closed the door.

We ascended a narrow, twisting stairway to the higher court, where once again a gatekeeper stood waiting for us, keys in hand. He opened the portal, and we stepped through onto a grand plaza paved in blue-green river stones. Behind rows of manicured plum trees stood ancient stone buildings similar to those in our dormitories, but of a finer quality.

Through open panels in one such structure I heard the rhythmic shouts of two dozen of our elder brothers as they drilled with three-section staves. None appeared to be above the age of thirty, and the youngest were barely older than the novices, myself excepted. Such was their discipline that none glanced in my direction as I followed Lo Gau through the compound to the western gate. Once more we ascended a winding stair and came to a second portal, where he handed over my pages to an aged servant who led me inside.

The walls of the Persimmon Court were carved in reliefs of fabulous scenes, some of which I recognized from my reading of the chronicles of Lung Wa. Prominent among them were depictions of the Dragon Ceremony, in which the dragon's heart appeared as a pearl the size of a cannonball.

One look at the image reminded me of my original goal in traveling to Tian Xia. How strange that I should forget it, I thought. I had to acquire the husk, locate Radovan and Arnisant, and return to Absalom.

But foremost in my thought was the sense that my duty was to protect the princess and follow my masters to the Dragon Ceremony. That obligation discharged, then I could attend to my personal desires.

Through a dragon-faced iron grate in the western wall, a mountain stream entered the inner compound and flowed around a tiny island. To my left jutted the lowest roof of the Temple of Irori, whose entrances opened into the lesser three courts. On the whole, the Persimmon Court resembled a public park, although like none in my native Cheliax. The flora appeared at first glance to grow naturally between the walls and the waterway, yet careful observation proved every detail was cultivated and maintained. Even the stones lying upon the stream bed appeared in perfect, if asymmetrical, order.

Beneath the many trees—and indeed the persimmons were dominant—a number of modest structures lay in no obvious pattern. I found the marriage of nature and construction in this area far more agreeable than the regimented order of the Cherry and Plum Courts.

Lo Gau led me to a small wooden house on the island. To reach it we crossed one of three small bridges connecting the island to the north, east, and south banks. As we approached the round door, we heard the conversation within.

"When you return to Iron Mountain, Brother Su Chau, please inform my brother that we shall bring him fifty-four guardians in spring."

At a small tea table, Master Li sat beside a pair of men wearing the dusty saffron robes of traveling monks. Each man carried a tome upon his hip suspended from a wide leather belt. One glance at the arcane characters on the bindings told me these men were not just monks but also wizards, no doubt the mystics we had been expecting to renew the temple wards. Around their necks hung strings of prayer beads ranging in size from apple to melon. Lesser men might have bowed under such a weight, but not these two. Robust of belly and limb, they resembled brawlers who had won monks' garb in a game of Fortune Tiles. They might have been brothers by blood as well as sect, so alike were their chubby faces. One was slightly larger and wore a thin beard around his mouth.

"So few?" The smaller exclaimed with clownish surprise.

His bearded companion laid a hand on his arm and smiled. "If they are from Dragon Temple, Wen Zhao, it shall be enough."

"But, Elder Brother, if the reports are true, surely Burning Cloud Devil intends—"

Su Chau lifted a finger to silence his companion as he noticed my arrival.

I bowed to all present.

Master Li indicated my person with a gesture. "This is Brother Jeggare, the student who prepared the red glyphs."

Neither of the monk-mystics could conceal his surprise at my foreign appearance. Wen Zhao stared at my Avistani features and half-elven ears, but Su Chau laughed aloud. He continued to laugh as he looked me up and down. I stiffened at the affront, but the unconstrained jocularity of his tone somehow blunted the offense.

"A foreign spirit," he said. "I think it a good omen."

Su Chau trod perilously close to the pejorative "foreign devil," but instead he used a term that indicated a benign entity. Lest I embarrass Master Li, I bowed as if receiving a compliment.

The servant who had delivered me presented my latest glyphs to Master Li, who passed them to the monks. Su Chau nodded and hummed approval as he examined the yellow sheets. Wen Zhao barely glanced at them. He walked around me for a closer examination of my foreign features.

"Now I understand how such a talented hand avoided a position in the Royal Court," said Su Chau. "You are cunning, Master Li, to import a scribe to improve the temple's reputation."

Master Li offered him a polite smile, but I detected discomfort in his eyes. Su Chau's boisterous personality disarmed even the sage of Dragon Temple.

"And our good fortune as well," said Wen Zhao. "We need not waste time rewriting the glyphs. Your students are renowned for their fighting skill, not their calligraphy."

Su Chau once more deafened us with his laughter.

Master Li winced. I sensed he had heard the criticism before, and I felt a pang of pride in my precise hand, which I had taken for granted since I was a child.

"Nor are they usually known for their magical skill," said Wen Zhao. He unfurled one of my flying scrolls. I had not even felt his touch upon my sash.

"What is this, Brother Jeggare?" said Master Li.

I bowed, but my indignation at Wen Zhao's liberty stopped me short of kowtowing. "Forgive me, Venerable Master Li. I have been restoring the spells I lost while traveling to Dragon Temple. Only after I finish copying the chronicles, I promise you."

Wen Zhao eyed me with suspicion, but Su Chau patted his belly and beamed as if delighted by a precocious child who had delivered an improbable excuse when discovered stealing treats. "Perhaps we should return to Lanming," he said. "They train their own wizards at Dragon Temple these days."

Master Li's reaction was more difficult to discern. He took the flying scroll from Wen Zhao and squinted at it. He passed it to me. "Demonstrate."

The scroll was an evocation of disruptive bolts of energy, useful in a fight but problematic to demonstrate in the master's tea room. I removed another scroll from my sash, causing the eyebrows of all three men to rise. "Perhaps a less destructive spell."

I flicked the scroll to the tip of an unlighted candle. The strip of yellow paper flew, disintegrating as it released the cantrip that ignited the wick.

Master Li frowned. "You had no spellbook when you arrived."

Despite his distracted demeanor, there was nothing slow about Master Li's mind. He had only to ask one question to put me in an impossible position. I struggled to control my breathing.

Master Li's lips tightened. "I see that this is not your first visit to the Persimmon Court. I should not be surprised, considering your inability to respect the boundaries set for novices."

It was logical, if incorrect, for Master Li to assume I had learned my spells by stealing in to peruse tomes hidden within this forbidden district. Either Master Li was unaware that Jade Tiger was a wizard, or else he could not imagine the eunuch's sharing knowledge with a temple novice.

If I remained silent and accepted the punishment for trespassing, I need not betray my co-conspirator. Even if Jade Tiger failed to resume our tutorials, now I knew there were other spells within the temple grounds. Surely one of them would allow me to contact Radovan. My sense of relief tempered my anticipation of punishment for my imagined offense.

"You have frightened half the life out of him, Master Li." Su Chau mistook my expression for simple fear. "Let his penance be to assist us in the ritual. As a favor to me, do not let Wu chop him up as firewood."

Master Li frowned more deeply than ever, the corners of his mouth threatening to separate his chin from the rest of his face. I wondered what he was thinking but immediately decided it was better not to know.

"It is settled, then," said Su Chau. He stood and slapped me on the back, a vulgar and unwelcome gesture of camaraderie. "Come, Brother Jeggare. Let us disturb Master Li no longer. He must contemplate your atonement, and I foresee many copied pages in your future. Has he yet given you the *Record of the Four Regents*? If you have trouble sleeping, I can recommend no more potent remedy. It is said that the Monkey King once read a page by mistake and slept for eighty-eight years."

I eluded Su Chau's grasp long enough to bow to Master Li and back out of the room. Once outside, I joined the mystics as they strolled across a little bridge to the west bank.

I interrupted Su Chau before his next opus could gain momentum. The suspicion that Jade Tiger had not fulfilled his promise to contact Radovan had been growing in my mind.

"Pardon me, Elder Brother, did you say you are traveling through Lanming?"

He nodded.

"On my journey to Dragon Temple, I was separated from a traveling companion. We agreed to meet in Lanming in such an event, but my vow to the temple masters prevents me from leaving the grounds."

"Yet it did not prevent you from sneaking into the Persimmon Court and stealing a peek at the arcane scrolls?"

I gazed at the ground in hopes that he would leap to the wrong conclusion. "Let go of your worldly concerns, Little Brother. If your friend is half as resourceful as you, rest assured that he is cheerfully breaking the rules of some other master."

I wished to protest, but it was futile. Su Chau had already done me a kindness, and he meant to collect the return by quizzing me about my life in Avistan. It fell to me to oblige as the three of us strolled along the shade of the western wall.

We paused from time to time beside some legendary or historical image graven into the wall. Wen Zhao made a study of each, pretending to ignore us as Su Chau unleashed a barrage of questions, each time interrupting my answers with a laugh and an anecdote of his own, often based on the subject of a nearby carving. Wen Zhao cast his gaze to heaven, as if he had heard all of his companion's tales a hundred times before.

No doubt he had.

Su Chau held forth for hours, until the dusk became dark. At last, Wen Zhao interceded.

"Brother Jeggare will miss his curfew."

Su Chau sighed, reluctant to release me. "Very well. Let us return to our quarters."

He led the way to the Peach Court gate and opened it with a key. We descended to the southernmost quarter of Dragon Temple. Its walls contained six houses standing independent of the walls, each a miniature manor fit for a noble. The royal spearmen stood before the largest. By the lantern light I saw their eyes follow our movements as we walked to the small house set aside for the visiting monks.

"I trust you can find your way through to the Cherry Court," said Su Chau. He nodded toward the walled garden that separated the visitors' quarters from the novices' court. "I understand you are quite the climber."

Despite his patronizing tone, I could not help but feel affection for this gregarious wizard-monk. In some ways he reminded me of Radovan. I bowed my thanks in the Chelish fashion, an oddity that delighted Su Chau and left his junior shaking his head in wonderment.

I hoped that a shortcut through the garden would afford me another glimpse of the princess. There was no sound of her lute, but as I vaulted the southern wall onto the nearest tree branches—a feat I could not have imagined performing just a few months earlier—I detected low voices. They quieted at my approach, and I heard a disturbance of branches on the opposite side of the garden. I dropped from the peach tree and surveyed the area.

The princess sat beside the pond. Her fingers arched over the strings of her guqin, but I sensed pretense in her posture. She had not been playing a moment earlier. Her sword lay beside the instrument, but there was no sign of the person with whom she had been speaking. I imagined they had heard my approach and separated, she feigning that she had been alone all the while.

There was no sign of Jade Tiger. It seemed prudent to warn him of Master Li's discovery of my flying scrolls and his mistaken assumption of my source for the magic. I could not think of a reason why the eunuch would conceal himself from me—not unless he wished to avoid perpetuating our relationship. Yet I knew a man of his station had only to command me to cease imposing my company upon him. There was no reason for evasion.

Unless he had laid a trap for me.

I granted myself one minute to consider the possibility, controlling my breathing as I imagined scenarios in which my apprehension or death could benefit Jade Tiger. The last time I had seen him, he ignored me in favor of Kwan. Both men had proven themselves to be subtle, yet I was at a loss to envision a motive for my destruction. If Jade Tiger had indeed withdrawn at my approach, then Princess Lanfen had to be aware of his stratagem.

My minute expired, I deferred my misgivings for later contemplation.

Despite my certainty that she was aware of my presence, I emerged from the shadows and approached Princess Lanfen openly so as not to startle her. The tune she played faltered as she saw me, but again I detected art in the gesture. She had known I was there from the moment I set foot upon a branch. No matter. I smiled and bowed once more in my native style, then again in the local manner, down to the ground as befits a disciple of Dragon Temple greeting the royal presence.

"You are brave to risk the wrath of Master Wu again." Her tone was light. I could not tell whether she was mocking me.

"The lure of your music is irresistible."

"You must be a great lover of music."

"And of beauty." If I had gone too far, she made no sign of it. If anything, she appeared impatient or bored. I took her indifference as a challenge. "In my country, there is no more glorious expression of emotion than the opera."

"I have been to the opera. It is a fine amusement for the lower classes."

"In Cheliax, the opera is first performed for the pleasure of the queen. Entire palaces are devoted to the art, and the singing is . . ." I almost said that the singing was far superior to that which I had heard in Tian Xia. It was true, yet it was impolitic to make such a comparison to a princess of Quain.

"Demonstrate," she said.

For the third time that day, I felt I had walked into a trap.

"Your highness, mine is not an operatic voice. I can barely—"

She struck a discordant note on her guquin. "You refuse?"

"No, of course not. Yet—"

"Excellent," she said. She began to play a tune I barely recognized. It might have been something I heard during our all-too-brief stay in Bosan, but I could not name it.

I gestured to her instrument. "If I may, your highness."

She barely moved, but she nodded at the guqin. Her remaining so close was an invitation or a dare. Either way, I accepted, reaching across her shoulder to pluck the strings. She turned her head, and her breath warmed my cheek. I reached around the other side to fret the strings and began to play.

The result was an approximation of the opening strains of the lover's regret from *The Lay of Gundra and Her Defender*. So close to the princess, I sang softly in my native tongue.

> *Under the moon I sang the nightingale's promise,*
> *Never to leave you, never to leave,*
> *Yet morning's choir sings to me of duty,*
> *And I must return, I must return.*
> *So give me the sword that I lay by your bed,*
> *And kiss me, my love, kiss me for love.*
> *Cover the mirror and pray to Shelyn,*
> *And kiss me again, kiss me goodbye.*

"How strange," said the princess.

I felt a pang of shame. "My apologies, your highness. The original language—"

"No," she said. "I do not understand the words, but I feel great sorrow in them."

"Yes, that is it exactly. Many operas are performed in languages foreign to much of the audience, but it does not matter. A great singer conveys the meaning without words."

"Then you are a great singer."

Heat surged into my cheeks. There was no danger of mistaking her compliment for an informed opinion, but I felt foolish and tongue-tied. I babbled some feeble protest but stopped as I heard leaves stir in a nearby branch.

There had been no breeze this evening.

I interposed myself between the sound and the princess. "Your highness, you must withdraw."

She did not retreat. Instead, she grasped her sword and stood behind me. A whisper of steel told me the blade was in her hand.

I held a flying scroll between my fingers. As I reached for another, my moonlight vision perceived a black-swathed figure dropping from the nearest peach tree. A chain-knife in his hands, he ran directly toward us.

I sent a volley of force bolts hissing toward the attacker. They struck the four quarters of his torso but barely slowed him. Rather than await his charge, I stepped forward to intercept him.

He thrust the blade at my heart, but I stepped inside his guard and caught his wrist. He wrapped the chain around my throat and drew it tight. I choked as he turned the dart at the other end of the chain toward my face.

The princess leveled her sword at the attacker's eye. I could barely see the blade. Even motionless, it was a blur, like a smudge of pigment on a hasty sketch. The princess spoke with the voice of royal authority. "Release him and surrender. Otherwise, you die."

The assassin hesitated for an instant, all the time I needed to fling my flying scroll and clutch his free arm.

Lightning crackled through his flesh. The current lashed back at me through the chain around my neck. My head jerked, serendipitously smashing his nose with the back of my skull. I was dazed as much from the force of the blow as from the surge of electricity, but the chain that choked me fell slack.

The attacker staggered a few steps away, his limbs jerking involuntarily. My body sympathized with his convulsions.

The princess stepped past me, her sword aimed at the assassin's throat.

"Who sent you?" she demanded.

Before the man could speak, darts flew past the princess and sank into the assassin's throat. The man fell to the ground and released a final breath.

The eunuch moved with uncanny speed. One moment he was across the pond, the next he had run over its surface and stood beside her. He took another step to interpose himself between us.

"I am well, but I wished to question the assassin," she said. "You have made that impossible."

Jade Tiger bowed to the ground. "Your highness, I did not—"

The princess gestured to me. "If not for Brother Jeggare—"

"Brother Jeggare must return to the dormitory at once." Jade Tiger spoke without looking at me. "The alarm will sound at any moment. If he is found here, I doubt Master Wu will be lenient."

"Yes." The princess spoke only to Jade Tiger. To her I had become invisible. "Of course, you are right. He must go."

Jade Tiger turned his gaze upon me. He snapped open his fan to cover his mouth with the side I had not previously seen. Upon it was the snarling visage of a ferocious tiger.

Without further protest I ran across the garden and scaled a tree near the wall. Moments later, I slipped quietly into the dormitory and sought my pallet. As I went, however, some sixth sense caused me to pause as

I passed Kwan's pallet. His breathing was steady, but too measured for genuine sleep. I took a moment to inhale deeply before laying my body down in my own place.

It took me almost an hour to fall asleep. During that time, I pondered the implications of the scent of peach blossoms emanating from First Brother Kwan.

Chapter Fifteen
Whispering Spider

We ran through the forest until Judge Fang stood on my back, pulled on my ear, and pointed out our destination.

It was a ruined temple covered in flowering vines. The fat moon chased us through the trees. Sometimes it winked through a sheet of gossamer hanging between the branches.

Fireflies danced all around, but there was something strange about the big ones near the temple. They moved too fast, and they changed colors as they chased each other through the stones. There was a strange song near the temple, but I couldn't hear it in my ears. I felt it buzz in my bones.

I began to think the fireflies weren't really fireflies. The fur on my neck rose, and Judge Fang fussed when it got into his mandibles.

"Slow down, you stubborn wolf!" cried the Goblin Who Swallowed the Wind. He had been running behind me since we picked up the trail. He could not keep up when I ran. I didn't like his calling me a wolf, so I did not slow down.

Just behind the Goblin were the nine little foxes that had joined us when the moon was dark.

At first it was only one big fox who agreed to Judge Fang's invitation to join us. She did so in exchange for our help slaying the ogre that had killed her mate.

Judge Fang devised a scheme. I would lure the tattooed ogre out of its cave. Gust would shock it to make it run in the right direction, and the Goblin would blow it into a pit of spikes.

It would have worked, but despite Judge Fang's careful plan, the Fox could not resist running in to bite the ogre once. Before it fell into the pit, it struck her with its great mace of skulls. The blow smashed the Fox into nine pieces.

I howled my despair. Gust wept, and the Goblin cursed. We had lost the ally we hoped to gain.

Judge Fang just lit his pipe and sat on a big yellow toadstool to wait. "Look," he said. "There is no blood."

He was right. The nine pieces of the Fox each looked like nothing more than a piece of her bushy tail. As we watched, the nine fuzzy patches began to stir. Each was a tiny baby fox, blinking in the sunlight as if just born. An hour later they were big enough to hunt mice. The next morning, their legs were long enough for travel.

As we approached the temple, the foxes nipped at the Goblin's heels, urging him to run faster.

Above us, Gust laughed. I liked the way Gust smelled when she laughed. She smelled like spring, even in summer.

The Goblin did not like Gust's crackling laugh. He stopped shouting at me and cursed his nemesis. I felt bad for Gust, but I was glad the Goblin forgot about me. He had been shouting at me all day.

He was angry that I would not let him ride on my back, and he kept calling me a wolf. I didn't like that because my parents taught me to hate wolves. I was a dog. It made no sense to call me a wolf.

Judge Fang told me goblins do not fear wolves as they do dogs and horses, who live with men. The Goblin would never ride a dog, but he would ride a wolf. He was tired of running, so he pretended I was a wolf.

Judge Fang said I should refuse because the Goblin could not be trusted. I was not afraid of the Goblin, but I did not want him on me because he smelled worse than Judge Fang's pipe. Besides, if I carried both Judge Fang and the Goblin, we could never catch up with the Hopper.

The Hopper was the reason we traveled to this forest full of streams and cobwebs. Somewhere among the trees we would find a kami who could see through illusions. Judge Fang said we would need its help in gathering the rest of our army. When we had gathered enough kami and beasts, we could finally go to my master in Iron Mountain.

The only other things I knew about the Hopper were its smell and its footprint.

Its scent was different from any I'd smelled before. It was like a chicken without dander, but also it was like a snake, so I had no idea what it would look like. It left no droppings behind, so I couldn't even tell what it ate.

Its footprint didn't help me know how it looked. It was round, like a hoof, but the edges were not so sharp. Also, there was only one print, always the same.

The Hopper had only one leg.

Ahead of us, something leaped over a puddle and vanished inside the temple walls. I barely saw it. It had a body as round and orange as a pumpkin. Its fur was as thin and puffy as a dandelion's head just before the wind blows it off.

"The temple wards have faded," said Judge Fang. "Follow it inside."

I leaped over a hollow log and landed covered in gossamer. It was invisible in the air, but on my fur it was white and sticky.

Behind us, the Goblin jumped up on the log. He pointed at us and laughed. He slapped his rump and stamped on the log until his foot went through the rotten bark. He disappeared with a puff of mushroom dust.

The fox cubs yipped and ran over the log. They had grown no bigger since the day after we met them, so they were too light to fall into the crumbling log.

Judge Fang jumped off my back to tear off the gauze. I rolled on the grass. Most of it rubbed off.

"Watch where you're going!" said Judge Fang. He jabbed his walking twig at more sheets of gossamer hanging from tree branches and the stones of the temple. "There are webs everywhere."

After he got the shouting out of his cricket head, Judge Fang realized that he could not see the webs except in direct moonlight. In the shadows, they were invisible. "Hm," he said. "Our quarry will have the advantage here. Stay close."

He flew back onto my shoulders. The Goblin moved toward me, but I gave him the big smile. He sulked and walked behind me.

Whatever had broken the temple left piles of rocks and decaying timber everywhere. They blocked the trails and made new ones with holes in the walls. I smelled rat and insect dung, and the strong smell of dead bodies. The Hopper's trail was fresher. I followed it through a few more rooms and into the center of the ruin.

Shafts of light slanted through the broken roof into a big room. The light turned everything the color of the moon, except for one dark corner littered with the bones of three or four men. There a sinkhole had eaten up much of the wooden floor and drank up a stream that poured through the broken wall.

Something with large teeth had gnawed the bones many times. I smelled the trail of the Hopper and of big rats, but also I smelled something else. It was like the odor of a nest of insects, but not exactly the same. Whatever it was, it ate big rats.

It ate many big rats.

My growl came up, and my hackles rose. Judge Fang flew up from my shoulders, sputtering at the fur in his cricket face.

The Goblin ran up beside me and kicked dust over my paws. "What's the matter? Are you afraid of the dark?"

It was what might be in the dark that worried me. "The Hopper went this way, but I can't see in there."

Behind me, the fox kits mewed. They didn't want to go in the hole either.

"We need a light," said Judge Fang. He fussed with his firepot. "Goblin, fetch me some wood, and I'll make you a torch."

"Fetch it yourself, bug-head. I don't need a torch to see." The Goblin walked into the sinkhole before anyone could say another word.

A few seconds later, we heard him fall and slide down the wet passage. He whooped and cursed.

Gust filled the room with her giggles. Judge Fang hissed as the sudden breeze caused him to burn his fingers while lighting his tiny lamp.

Down in the tunnel, something made a sound like a goose that had just run into a dog. The Goblin screamed and cursed. The kits crowded beneath me as if I were their mother. Gust stopped giggling, and a few drops of rain fell on my back.

"Hurry!" Judge Fang flew up to my shoulders, holding his lamp above his head. I didn't like the fire so close to my fur, but the Goblin was in trouble. He smelled bad, but he was our ally. It was my job to protect him.

I padded down the sinkhole. The bottom was wet, but my claws kept me from slipping down after the Goblin. We heard the sound of struggles beneath the Goblin's curses. Under the strong smell of wet earth, I could smell both him and our quarry.

"Hurry, you stupid beasts! I've got—ugh! As soon as I get my hands—ow!"

We came around a bend in the tunnel and saw them. The Goblin clung to what looked like a hairy pumpkin on a crooked pony's leg. Instead of a hoof, it had a round, toeless foot with skin as thick as ox hide.

The Hopper leaped up and down, trying to shake off the Goblin, who wrapped his arms and legs tight around the kami's leg. With each jump, the Hopper's big eye blinked, and the Goblin slid a few inches closer to the floor.

I growled a warning. The Hopper's eye opened wide. That was good. If it feared me, it would obey and calm down.

But it did not calm down. Instead, it jumped more furiously than ever.

"Careful," warned Judge Fang. "The tunnel . . ."

The Goblin slipped off the Hopper's leg. Instead of escaping, the Hopper honked and jumped straight over the Goblin's body. The Goblin threw his arms over his face and squealed, but when the Hopper landed, it pushed them both through the soft floor.

The Goblin shrieked and the Hopper honked as they fell through the hole.

The dirt beneath me slid toward the widening gap.

I scrambled backward, but the kits crowded my steps. My front paws slipped over the edge of the hole, and the wet tunnel soil poured forward, taking us down into the dark.

For a second we were falling. Something broke beneath my weight before a spongy surface caught and held us. Judge Fang tumbled from my back, but I saw his lamp hanging in the air nearby. It was stuck against a shivering white line as thick as one of my claws. All around us were similar lines intersecting in a familiar pattern.

It was a giant web. But it wasn't like the ones I'd seen high in the corner of the stable where I was born. There was something different about it.

It was too perfect.

Every strand lined up perfectly with the one next to it, and not in a spiral but in perfect rings, each slightly larger than the next. Except for the segments broken when the Hopper, the Goblin, and I fell through, there were no accidental gaps.

The kits cried as they dangled from the sticky lines just above me. Judge Fang clutched at my ear, but he was too weak to pull himself up onto my shoulder. His lantern twisted on a loose string a few feet above the kits.

The turning of the lantern cast eerie shadows of us and the web all around. We were in the middle of a ruined cellar. Gnarled roots reached toward us from the dirt walls. Apart from the hole we had fallen through, two more dark gaps hinted at a way out.

But we couldn't go anywhere while we were stuck in the web.

Below us, the Goblin hung limp on the strands that had caught him after the higher ones broke but slowed his fall. Near him dangled the Hopper, thrashing so much that it wound itself up in a thick blanket of white fibers. With only the tip of its foot and the upper half of its huge eye visible, it looked like a shrouded corpse I had seen my master and Radovan bury.

"Who disturbs the serenity of my meditations?" It was the soft voice of a woman. I couldn't tell where it came from. It seemed to come from everywhere at once, or from inside my head.

The kits quieted their whimpering, but through the web I could feel their tiny hearts racing.

Judge Fang's voice creaked with terror. "Scare her away, Arnisant."

I filled the chamber with my most fearsome shouts.

"Such commotion," whispered the stern voice. She did not sound even a little bit afraid. "I will not tolerate it."

From out of one of the dark gaps in the wall emerged a pair of long limbs. They were pale as grubs but long and slim as snakes. They gripped either side of the entrance and pulled.

Two more limbs appeared, and the face of a young woman followed. White hair flowed behind her head, but her face was different from that of other women. Her nose was normal, and so were her cheeks and chin. Mandibles emerged from her swollen human lips, and eight unblinking eyes lay across her wide brow. Our reflections appeared upside-down in each glassy blue orb.

"Has half the forest found its way into my lair? You are spoiling my beautiful home."

The Goblin moaned. He blinked at the spider. His eyes opened wide and he began screaming again. "Help! Don't let that ugly thing touch me!"

The Goblin's panic frightened the kits. They scratched and bit at the webs, but their teeth were too small to cut through.

"Ugly, am I?" The spider sounded sad. She squeezed the rest of her body into the cellar. The opening was big enough that I could have walked through it.

Through the hole above came a white thread of lightning. Its tingle raised the fur all over my body and popped the kits off the web. They tumbled into a damp, roiling pile of fur on the cellar floor.

Wind blew rain down from the upper tunnel, extinguishing Judge Fang's tiny lantern. Gust glared down, sparks for eyes. The spider crept toward the Goblin.

For what felt like a long time, there was only darkness and a flickering from Gust's anger. Then a pale blue beam of light emerged from the Hopper's wide eye. The lower half was smothered by spider silk, but half a beam was enough to shine over the spider's face. In the light of the Hopper's eye, she looked like a young woman without any spider parts.

The light of the Hopper's eye shone through the spider kami's body and spread throughout the cave. Everything was white and blue and black, but we could see.

The Goblin grimaced and shut his eyes as the spider's face moved close to his.

Before she could tear his head from his body, Judge Fang spoke. His tone reminded me of the way the master spoke to women when he wished to please them. "How lovely thou art."

The spider whirled toward him. "Do not dare to mock me!"

"I do not," said Judge Fang. I could smell his fear, but he kept his cricket head held high. "Under the Hopper's flawless gaze, all truths are revealed, and in your face I see a perfect beauty."

The spider raised the tip of one leg to her face. Under the direct gaze of the Hopper, it became a delicate human hand. She gasped at the sight.

"When I look at you," she said to Judge Fang, "I see a pot-bellied old man who dyes his hair and wears a—"

"Yes, yes, and so I appeared in my previous life," he said hastily. "But a man of my station is held to a high standard, and so for a few minor infractions it was determined that I was to be indentured for a period to serve the Celestial Order in my current state."

The spider hummed her doubt.

"Forgive the wretched Goblin, gentle kami," begged Judge Fang. "He is a coarse thing, but he came here for a good purpose."

"Good? You have broken my house. Now your cloud kami is flooding it!"

"Indeed, we have been clumsy in discharging our duty," said Judge Fang. "Please, imagine that I kowtow to thee, as I surely would were I not constrained by these magnificent strands thou hast woven in—if I may be permitted to offer a compliment—the most symmetrical web it has ever been my honor to look upon. My shame would fill the seas, yet my need would cover the sky. It is my duty as a duly appointed functionary of the Celestial Order to gather all virtuous beasts and kami in defense of the Dragon Ceremony, which even now is threatened by the schemes of the wicked Burning Cloud Devil and the subtle Jade Tiger."

The spider looked back at the Goblin. Her half-human mouth was too small to devour him in a single bite. Two, maybe.

She did not see, as I did, the restored mother fox crouching below her, teeth bared, ready to leap.

The spider shook her head and turned back to observe Judge Fang. "Who could have imagined so many words could fit in so small a head?"

Her tone was friendly. She reached out with her foreleg and tapped Judge Fang above his mandibles, where his nose might once have been. Whenever the Hopper's gaze caught her face full-on, I saw the spider's human mouth smiling. Judge Fang's words had worked their magic.

Behind her, the Goblin released a sigh of relief.

"Tell me more," said the spider. "But first, make your cloud stop wetting my web. And you there beneath me, nine-tailed fox, do not think you escaped my notice. Remove this noisome little Goblin from my web, and we shall discuss the matter further."

Chapter Sixteen
Phoenix Warrior

The basilisk slithered through the streets of Khitai. Now and then it lunged, always at a child or a pretty girl who froze in place. The monster's orange eyes bore down until its victim shrieked. Then it shook green and yellow scales out of its mane and danced away.

Children gathered the scale-shaped leaf wrappers and ate the sweet bean cakes inside. The eight-legged basilisk moved along to the next throng of children, its painted silk skin rippling at every turn. The bare feet of the men inside the monster slapped the pavement in time with the festival drums.

I was the opposite of the basilisk, a monster hidden beneath the silk cover of a man.

Even without Burning Cloud Devil's magic, it was a good enough disguise. Unless someone got close, I could have been another of the big northern barbarians who'd come south looking for mercenary work. I was glad I'd picked up a black rice hat with a brim so low it had an eye slit in the front. I felt like a kid playing at knights in armor, but at least no one had run screaming when I came into town.

Burning Cloud Devil was still holed up at the inn. I'd wandered off to find a smith to repair my big knife. As an afterthought I asked him to make a new one just like it, only big enough for my devil hands. We negotiated until I got tired of pantomime. I showed him the big smile, and we had a deal.

The rest of the day I figured I'd take in the sights. There was no point telling Burning Cloud Devil where I was going. After our long journey back from the western mountains, and a hundred failed attempts to teach me his Quivering Palm technique, he said he needed to catch up on his sleep.

After the business with the Moon Blade Killer, we'd both had some rough nights. More than once I'd woken from nightmares of the boss writhing inside a dragon's belly. Across the fire, Burning Cloud Devil twitched in his sleep, soaked with night sweat. I figured he dreamed of Spring Snow in the same damned place.

Despite the nightmares, I wasn't buying his "need some sleep" excuse. He'd been wound up tight since I showed him the silver sword. He said he didn't believe I'd seen Spring Snow, but I could tell it was gnawing at him. I'd seen it a thousand times before with the boss.

Burning Cloud Devil wasn't slipping away to rest. He was off to get stinking drunk.

Weeks ago I'd figured out that most of the joints he called "tea houses" were really taverns. Let him drink, I figured. At least it spared me more lessons on clarifying my soul or maintaining the perfect nature of my body or some other airy stuff. When he wasn't full of wine, he was full of bad poetry.

Since I'd seen her face, I had a hard time picturing Spring Snow with this guy. She struck me as a good kid, full of life at one time. She had to have been a lot more fun than he was. Burning Cloud Devil didn't deserve someone like her.

The way I saw it, he was responsible for the deaths of the family back at the restaurant. Sure, it was me the Moon Blade Killer had come to kill, but Burning Cloud Devil knew it would happen. He'd tricked me into burying the wrestler's head. He might as well have murdered those boys and their father himself.

Anyway, it had to be his fault. Otherwise, it was mine.

I couldn't stand to think that.

Among the festival crowd, a woman dressed as a warrior caught my eye. Her golden scale armor glittered in the sun. She held one of those long-bladed glaives, sort of halfway between a spear and a sword. Where its grip met the blade twined a golden phoenix.

Something told me she hadn't dressed up for the festival.

Most people in town hadn't given me a second glance, but this woman stared in a way that made me think she could see through the brim of my hat. In other circumstances, I'd tip her a wink, but she was the one who threw me a fetching smile.

Normally, that's all the encouragement I need. Instead of taking her up on the invitation, I walked away.

Until Burning Cloud Devil released my body, I was in no fit shape for a cuddle. And yeah, I knew that probably wasn't what her smile meant, but it was what it made me think about.

Likely she wanted a whole different kind of trouble. Without Burning Cloud Devil around to slap me up with the fight whammy, there was nothing in it for me.

She called after me in Tien. "Face me, devil."

I kept walking. A few steps later, a wave of nausea rolled through me. She'd thrown a spell on me.

I ran down a narrow lane between a block of townhouses and a spice shop. Waiting for me at the other end was a woman dressed identically to the first, except she held a scepter with a golden phoenix on its head. She looked exactly like the other woman.

Twins, of course.

Under other circumstances, I'd have been tickled. With their thick jaws and thin noses, they were no beauties, but they were all right. Later there'd be time to imagine the scenarios that could have been, assuming I survived this little tryst.

She pointed the scepter at me. Its wings began to move, its feathered breast glowing red.

I didn't wait to see the result. I pulled a little juice from inside the core of my spirit and jumped from the ground to land on the roof of the spice shop.

No matter how many times I did that trick, "flying" never got old. Burning Cloud Devil said it came easily to me because of my abundant ki. Sometimes I wondered whether I'd still be able to do it when I got back to my regular body. It'd be a useful trick, not to mention one hell of a lot of fun.

My first step crunched through the roof tile. I weighed a lot more these days, so I stuck to running along the beam lines. A few more tiles clattered away behind me, but I made it to the other side without falling through. I leaped down onto the next lane, heard a cry, and looked around to see who I'd startled.

There was no one in the street except the armored woman. She lunged, twirled the glaive, and stepped back. I realized she'd already hit me only when the front of my rice hat fell off, revealing my face.

She gave me a smug smile and turned her blade so the reflected sunlight light dazzled me. I shaded my eyes until she turned the blade again, showing me the opposite side.

On the metal was etched a familiar symbol. I'd seen it in Minkai. It was the mark of Shizuru, goddess of ancestors and honor. This woman wasn't just a warrior.

She was a paladin.

Her smile vanished as she advanced, whirling the long blade. I turned to run, but there she was on the other side, this time with the golden scepter.

"Xifeng." The one with the scepter saluted her sister. "The honor of first attack is yours. Smite the evil beast!"

Xifeng returned the salute. "I thank you, Dongmei. I accept your charge and—"

"Listen, ladies, thanks all the same, but no smiting today. Despite my looks, I'm not actually evil."

Hey, I'm entitled to my opinion.

"It says it is not evil," said Dongmei, translating my devil-speech to Tien. Good for her, I thought. Know your enemy. Speak the language. Maybe we'll have a drink later.

"Impossible," said Xifeng. "I see its aura. It is a fiend from Hell."

"Cheliax, actually," I said. Dongmei's face remained blank, so I did boat-on-the-wave with my hand. "Far across the sea, on the other side of the world."

Dongmei showed me her palm, two fingers up, thumb nestled to the side. She said a few words in the language of angels, which I never learned because it's got no decent curses. A pale golden circle formed around us. Motes of holy light danced in the alley like dust under a bright window.

"Say it again," demanded Dongmei. "Tell us you are not truly evil."

"I'm not— I'm actually a perfectly— The thing is—"

I couldn't say the words. Her magic turned them to dust in my mouth.

"You condemn yourself!" cried Dongmei. "Not even a devil can tell a lie within the Circle of Truth."

Xifeng's slipper scuffed the ground behind me. Even in armor, the woman was quick. She damned near succeeded where the Moon Blade Killer failed. I moved just in time to make sure it was only the rest of my hat that fell onto the street.

I jumped back to the roof. Xifeng vaulted up behind me. I let her chase me across a couple more buildings while I searched for an escape route.

No dice. Dongmei had already cut me off, running up steps of air on the other side. I'd seen that trick before. It meant a god was listening to her prayers.

I was fighting both a paladin and a priest. If there'd ever before been a question of my going to Hell, it was answered now.

I tossed a handful of darts to keep her occupied. She covered her face with her arm, but the little blades glanced off an invisible barrier a few inches from her skin.

A crunch on the roof tiles warned me of Xifeng's attack. To make sure I knew it was coming, she added a battle cry. "Shizuru, guide my hand!"

I leaped away. The roof exploded in yellow light inches away from me. Sharp tile fragments bit into my face and neck.

Xifeng's battle cry was mighty.

I feinted a forward roll and swept her legs with a kick. Xifeng fell for it, and then she fell for it—right off the side of the roof.

It's always funnier when something like that happens to a paladin.

I grinned as I turned to face Dongmei. She had just finished calling down a spell, her arms raised to heaven to receive it.

It landed on me, a pillar of roaring flames. I threw back my head to laugh—fire doesn't bother me when I'm cloaked in Hell—but out of my mouth came a howl of pain.

The holy fire was hot and cold and something else I can't explain. It hurt far more than the burning I feel just before fire turns me big. My hair floated up like I was underwater. My clothes rustled but didn't so much as smoke.

My grin turned into a snarl.

"All right, sister, you got my attention."

Dongmei's eyes widened. She ran and leaped to the next building, once more walking on an invisible stair. I sent a pair of darts after her, putting one just above her shoulder blade. She faltered but didn't fall.

The gap was wider than those I'd jumped before. I pumped my legs, my clawed toes tearing divots in the burning roof. I threw myself across the street and landed hard on the opposite roof, leaving the burning building behind me.

Dongmei's fingers sketched another spell. She babbled holy words.

I charged across the tiles, diving into a tumble to come at her from below. My palm caught her on the breastbone. I let my fingers do the spider-crawl strike Burning Cloud Devil taught me. I sealed them with the final blow.

Dongmei recognized the attack. Her face paled. She slapped at her sternum, gasping as I raised my fist and squeezed it tight.

I felt no invisible strings between my fingers and her heart. I still hadn't got the knack.

Her color returned. She raised her scepter.

I shot her a fast one in the breadbasket. My knuckle spurs pierced her armor.

She pressed her hand against my forehead. I felt her pulse fluttering through her palm. The last few syllables of her spell came out in blood, but she pronounced them well enough for her goddess to hear.

The goddess replied.

Holy fire erupted out of my brain. Hot tears poured down my face, so thick I feared they might be my melted eyeballs. Dongmei showed me a pained smile of triumph as her face blurred from my vision.

My thoughts melted away next. All I had left inside my head was hatred. My hand found the grip of the big knife. I brought it up hard and low, through Dongmei's belly and up into her chest.

She didn't scream. The only sound was the scrape of my blade across her metal armor and the bone beneath. I lifted her up, twisting and jerking the blade to tear her heart to pieces. The cloud over my vision drifted away.

"Sister!" Xifeng screamed from the edge of the roof.

I turned to show the paladin what I'd done with her sister. Dongmei's blood was on my face, running down my lips and across the long, ragged teeth of my big smile.

Across my shoulder, Dongmei stretched a feeble arm toward Xifeng. For an instant, the gesture plucked at something that had slipped down deep inside me. It was something important, something I used to value. I couldn't think of its name.

Whatever it was, I didn't need it anymore.

Xifeng stood at the edge of the roof. She raised her hand toward her sister's.

Dongmei's weight lifted off of me. Her body faded away, but the ghost of it floated toward her sister. As their outstretched hands touched, the image of

Dongmei vanished. Xifeng stood alone, her sword-glaive in one hand, the phoenix scepter in the other.

She tucked her sister's weapon inside her belt and assumed a fighting stance.

"You want some of the same?" I said.

There was no one to translate, but she was done talking. She came on like a storm.

I drifted back and tried another kick, but she set the butt of her weapon into the tile and blocked me. The dark wood was hard as steel. There'd be one hell of a bruise on my instep.

She attacked with both the blade and the spiked butt of the glaive. She was strong as a bull, and fast. It was all I could do to bring up my arms to protect my body. The blade hit hard, but it couldn't cut the sleeves of my enchanted robes. Xifeng noticed and redirected her blows to my hands, face, and feet.

Her limited targets gave me breathing room. With the big knife I gave her a good shot in the shoulder, hard enough to bloody her golden scales. The wound barely slowed her.

I followed up with a knee to the belly, but she faded back and stepped to my right. She'd gulled me!

The blade creased the back of my skull. The bone cracked, and I felt a cool rush of air slip inside. I rolled away, expecting a finishing shot to land where my head had been.

Xifeng anticipated that, too. The butt of her glaive slammed into my mouth. I choked on blood and the shards of my teeth.

Something came apart inside me. It felt as though some enormous hand had grasped my spine and cracked it like a whip. Everything I saw turned the color of blood. I clutched and clawed, kicked and raked, snarling and spitting like an animal.

It didn't matter what I touched. I ripped it in my hands, shredded it in my ruined teeth. Shattered tile, metal, and flesh filled my mouth. At last I felt a hard kick on my ass, and I fell off the roof and face-first onto the pavement.

I came up spitting fragments of paving stones.

Mocking laughter rained down from another roof across the street.

"The gods punish you for starting another fight without me," said Burning Cloud Devil. His voice was equal parts amusement, irritation, and wine.

He sat cross-legged on the edge of a bakery roof. Cradled in his legs were a steam basket and a wine jug. He'd brought refreshments for the show.

The sun exploded behind me. That's how it felt, anyway.

I turned, shielding my eyes from the radiance. On the roof stood the silhouettes of both sisters, each holding her weapon. They stepped forward. Each was bloodied, but Dongmei's wound now appeared little more than a deep cut.

They hesitated at the sight of Burning Cloud Devil. He laughed at their reaction.

"The Phoenix Warrior! I meant to seek her out, but only after you had mastered the Quivering Palm."

"Maybe you can give me a hand," I said. Even in devil-speech, my words came out a mushy mumble through my broken teeth. "Which sister you want?"

"Which sister?" He juggled a hot dumpling one-handed. "There is but one Phoenix Warrior."

I figured he meant Dongmei, then, since she carried the phoenix scepter. I pointed at her. "Almost got that one."

Dongmei scoffed. "Burning Cloud Devil, let us see what fiend you have summoned to plague our town."

She touched the butt of Xifeng's glaive to wet her fingers with blood.

My blood.

She blew it like a kiss onto a strip of white parchment and read the words that formed there. "Radovan Virholt Norge kel Zogreb Dokange the Flaying Tongue Fell Viridio . . . This is not a name!"

In her hands, the blood turned her parchment completely red before trickling down her fingers. She cast it away like a filthy thing.

Burning Cloud Devil choked on his dumpling. "So many!"

Dongmei and Xifeng raised their arms to the sky and bathed in healing radiance. I'd have to start all over.

"Bitches cheat," I said. "Come on, Lefty. You can take the little one."

Burning Cloud Devil lost his smirk and glared at me. All right, I admitted. That was a little mean. But if he hadn't come to fight, he could use all the encouragement I had to offer.

Dongmei ran down her steps of air to stand twenty feet away to my left. Xifeng hit the ground on the right. They raised their weapons and closed in toward me.

"It is a pity you were not a more diligent student," said Burning Cloud Devil.

Before I could ask what he meant by 'were,' Xifeng made a flourish with her glaive. Despite my tough robes, I was shy of that blade, but I was tired of running. I sidestepped, but her attack was only a feint. On the ground between us, Dongmei's shadow swallowed up mine and kept growing.

I leaped aside just in time to avoid her massive fist. It struck the ground like a boulder, and I kept rolling away. She'd grown taller than me, bigger than an ogre.

On the roof, Burning Cloud Devil laughed. His voice echoed through the streets and shook the shutters. He wrote on a sheet of paper on his knee.

"Take your notes later!" I shouted.

Xifeng came for me in earnest. Her glaive smashed a hitching post where my legs had been an instant earlier.

It was time to get away. I ran up the street and skidded to a halt. The city guard had arrived. They formed a barricade of pikes and shields. I turned to run down the street, dodging the giant Dongmei and her smaller but still vicious paladin double. Beyond them, another phalanx of guards appeared.

I looked around, but every path was closed. There were archers on the rooftops, and every door and window had shut.

"A little help!"

Burning Cloud Devil washed down the last of his dumplings with a huge swig of wine. "Very well," he said. "But only if you use the Quivering Palm."

"I can't—" What the hell. I could give it a go. "Fine!"

"Put them close together." Burning Cloud Devil's voice whispered in my ear. I heard it as clearly as if he'd stood behind me, but he remained on the rooftop. He dropped the empty jug and steam basket and assumed a horse stance.

He let the giant kick me around a little while I focused on keeping Xifeng's blade from my neck. At last, the spell that made Dongmei big wore off. I rolled toward a wall, ran three steps up the side, and flipped back to kick her in the face.

It was a heavy blow made worse by the claws on my toes. Four deep grooves cut across her face, and for a second I thought I'd taken out an eye. In an instant, the wound faded to half its depth. She whipped around to strike me with her glowing scepter. I leaped out of the way.

From the other side, Xifeng screamed as she lunged for me. I twisted aside and felt her blade slide across my shoulder blades. One glimpse of her angry face showed me she'd suffered half the kick I gave Dongmei.

"Now," whispered Burning Cloud Devil. "Strike both at once."

I crouched low and struck both women at once. My palms hit just below the breastbone. The fingers of my left hand traced out the pattern of a cage, or a net. I'd never thought of it that way before, but I knew it could capture a life.

Xifeng gasped.

The fingers of my right hand moved also, but too slow.

Dongmei slapped my hand away.

"Do as I do," hissed Burning Cloud Devil.

For another second I tried to remember the moves he had made through my left hand. Then I gave up and just tried to *feel* them.

I struck again, hitting both women in the same place. My fingers moved, this time faster than Burning Cloud Devil could command them. They formed the same patterns, built the same cages. Xifeng and Dongmei cried out as one. Their bodies trembled and became translucent. They moved together, forming a single person holding Xifeng and Dongmei's weapons in either hand. She fell to her knees.

I rolled back and stood. A cool calm washed over me, but underneath I felt the heat of anger. They—she—had meant to kill me, but now I was the one who held her life in my palm. I felt it trembling there, like a hummingbird.

"Mercy," moaned the Phoenix Warrior. "Spare me."

"Crush her," whispered Burning Cloud Devil. "Prove what you have learned."

"I didn't come after you," I told her. "You came after me."

"Please."

I needed another reason. "You broke my teeth."

She opened her mouth, but before she could plead again, her courage returned to clamp her jaw shut.

"You have this coming," I told her. I wanted to believe it, too.

I closed my hand. A bird-shaped flame leaped from her chest and flew away. In its wake, the buildings caught fire as the woman's corpse fell onto the dusty street.

Chapter Seventeen
Magic Fist

The morning after the night of the assassin, the residents of Dragon Temple rose to assume their duty as if an attack on the royal visitor had never occurred. The masters made no announcement of an intrusion, nor did they deviate from the routine to which we had become accustomed. We disciples trained and meditated as usual, and for three days I assisted the mystic monks Su Chau and Wen Zhao in replenishing the wards against beasts and kami.

Combining arcane and divine magic, the particulars of the ritual often eluded me, although I grasped its basic function. We posted the scrolls I had prepared facing the four winds and their twelve ancestors, linking them with the lesser scrolls prepared by the other students. The ceremony involved more sacrament than arcane crafting, so my part was little more than that of an apprentice observing the work of two masters. By the time Wen Zhao sealed the final link of the expansive ward, I realized I had learned far more than I had contributed.

After the mystic monks departed Dragon Temple, Master Wu woke me at dawn the next morning and led me to an empty room adjoining the armory. Certain I was about to enter a chamber of pain I had not yet visited, I followed with all the stoicism I could muster. Instead, Master Wu relayed Master Li's instructions that I was to be allotted two candles each evening to continue my studies in the arcane library of the Persimmon Court.

Elation filled my heart. From that moment, my kitchen duty became an exercise in tempering impatience. As when I first began studying with Jade Tiger, the chores I once considered drudgery again became effortless, and my preparations were completed with time to spare. I used the time saved to add a few fresh ingredients to a soup of rice and preserved vegetables. Slivers of salamander peppers and diced green onions would enliven the familiar meal. I left it covered near the fire to remain warm while joining my fellow students for our morning exercise.

By the time we broke our fasts, my thoughts were bent to speculation on what spells I might find in the temple's arcane library. If only a communication spell—

"Something is wrong with the soup." Runme scowled at his bowl. He looked around, seeking support for his complaint.

Before anyone could agree, Lu Bai licked his bowl. "It reminds me of my grandmother's congee."

"It is good," said Mon Choi. He raised his bowl to toast me. "Brother Jeggare has cooking skill!"

Runme stuck out his tongue as if sickened, but the others murmured agreement with Mon Choi.

"It must have been an accident," suggested Karfai. It was a feeble defense, but I admired loyalty to a friend, even when it was misplaced.

"May Brother Jeggare have the same accident again tomorrow," Kwan said. He stacked his empty bowl on the others before leaving for the shrine.

For nearly a century I had devoted my life to mastering disciplines ranging from botany to the grammar of ancient Thassilonian, but never a chore so mean as cooking. By grace of my noble upbringing, I could identify wines from every vineyard from Varisia to Taldor, and I had sampled the rarest delicacies from Ustalav to Qadira. And yet even the greatest chefs were slaves or servants, so I had never considered their craft worth pursuing.

That morning, I took pride in my soup.

During our unarmed sparring, my mind racing ahead to the afternoon's studies, I found myself subconsciously incorporating arcane gestures into my strikes. When I realized what I was doing, I felt a momentary fear of Master Wu's ungentle correction. In the earliest weeks of our training, the master of combat was quick to correct the slightest deviation from basic form. Yet in recent months, Wu had gradually relaxed his grip, allowing each student to begin to develop an individual style.

Brother Kwan, for example, was unusually vocal. One could track his fights from the opposite side of a wall merely by listening to the piercing cries and whoops that, like his talon tattoos, evoked the image of a diving bird of prey. Yingjie fought silently, yet with every retreat he flourished the tip of his staff like a scorpion's tail to distract his opponent. Mon Choi's prominent idiosyncrasy was a wide variety of terrifying facial expressions as he charged forward or heaved an opponent above his head.

Except in sword, I struggled to master even the rudiments of each weapon technique. My only previous indulgence of personal style was an unconscious return to the Chelish sword techniques I favored. Now I felt a curious urge to incorporate more arcane gestures into our sparring bouts.

After delivering a credible strike to Karfai's chest, I added a feeble finger-strike to his throat. It startled but did not harm him, yet somehow it felt correct, or close to some improvement in my technique. I flattered myself that I was on the verge of a revelation concerning the art of hand-to-hand combat.

My experiments continued with a light press of my thumb against a pressure point on Mon Choi's wrist as I escaped an arm lock. Once more my effort was distracting but ultimately ineffective. The gesture was too light to stun a nerve and provide a tangible advantage, and yet again it felt near to some previously undiscovered *correctness* related to my recently reawakened spellcasting.

After the unarmed exercises, my opponent in sword was Harbin, who still far exceeded me in knives but had not significantly improved his swordplay over the summer. While I kept his sword at bay with a series of parries and feints, my thoughts drifted to the somatic ritual of one of the spells I had reclaimed. While parrying another of Harbin's aggressive but obvious thrusts, I subconsciously performed the gestures with my left hand.

One of my flying scrolls exploded inside my sash. Simultaneously, my hands crackled with electricity.

I retreated, relinquishing the advantage of position to Harbin. He heard the sudden crackling at my hip, but also saw that I was open to attack.

"No!" I said.

He ignored my warning and lunged.

I threw myself to the side and dropped my wooden sword. Pressing my hands to the ground, I discharged the shock charge harmlessly into the earth.

Harbin rapped me smartly on the back. He repeated the blow twice to ensure that everyone had seen his victory.

"Brother Jeggare must have traded his sword skill for cooking skill," suggested Runme. The resulting laughter restored the mocking leer he had lost since breakfast. Fortunately, it also distracted everyone from what had truly happened.

I was learning to combine my swordplay with wizardry.

Weeks later, the arcane library of the Persimmon Court became the locus of my despair.

Virtually all of the spells contained within the dusty scrolls were dedicated to combat. In other circumstances, I should have been delighted, for I have always favored evocations and conjurations, whose applications are best demonstrated in battle. Yet the spell I most desired was absent.

Only once did I dare inquire of Master Li for assistance with the arcane library, but his only answer was a withering glare before he walked away to resume his fishing. I could not reconcile his hostile disposition with the mercy he showed after the discovery of my flying scrolls. Why did he allow me to continue these studies if he disapproved? He must have felt that Su Chau's generous plea had forced him to act as he had.

The master's displeasure only added to the anxiety I felt as I continued my studies. As the summer waned, I compiled an arsenal of spells to inspire lust in the black hearts of the arcane assassins of Her Infernal Majestrix, Abrogail II. Inscribing the spells contained within the library increased my practical skill along with my repertoire.

And yet within the library I found no magical means of communicating with Radovan.

It was all but inconceivable that an otherwise comprehensive collection should lack such a spell. I scoured the chamber for a misplaced scroll or hidden cache. The library was a small building, barely larger than one of my wardrobes at Greensteeples, with scrolls resting in narrow racks not unlike those lining my wine cellars. The outer wall was filled with shelves except for the large circular entrances on the northern and southern walls. I hopefully pored over their contents.

My most promising discovery was of a long-neglected cabinet containing the materials required for the spells I had already discovered. Within the dozens of tiny compartments I found the preserved legs of grasshoppers, scales of various reptiles, drops of bat guano, sulfur rocks, and dozens of other ingredients.

I cursed every bare compartment and empty spot on the shelves. My intuition told me that there should have been more scrolls and books than currently remained, but in the dust I could discern no trace of any recent disturbance. Indeed, with the exception of a few corners, the entire chamber was unexpectedly clean for a place left so long in disuse.

That fact was in itself intriguing.

When I beckoned a servant to the library, he paused at the threshold and glanced warily at the floor. His hesitation suggested to me that the chamber was secured against unauthorized intrusion, yet I had entered without triggering a magical defense. The library contained a spell for inscribing runes that would blast anyone crossing them—and indeed, I had already added that particular weapon to my arsenal—yet I saw no such runes at either entrance.

On the other hand, I knew of at least two common spells that could remove or disable such wards.

After Wen Zhao revealed my flying scrolls, Master Li had been quick to assume I had stolen into the arcane library and bypassed the magical ward. That was a logical deduction if he knew, as I did, how easily a wizard or sorcerer could bypass the explosive sigils. Unlike Master Li, however, I knew I had not entered the library.

I also knew I was not the only practitioner of the arcane arts in Dragon Temple.

The obvious suspect was Jade Tiger. There was no question of accusing the eunuch of the theft, or even of inquiring of him directly. Clearly he had been avoiding me since the night of the assassin, and his interest in Kwan made me suspicious of his motives. Had Jade Tiger stolen into the arcane library and removed the one spell he knew I desired? To what end? What was his interest in Kwan, who smelled of peach blossoms after the night of the attack on the princess?

If only I could speak to her again. Unfortunately, she was farther out of reach than ever. Despite my newfound privileges in the Persimmon Court, I felt the eyes of the servants and my fellow disciples on me at all times. I had no doubt that one or both of the temple masters had ordered a general surveillance of my activities.

Only during training on the high posts had I glimpsed the princess's veiled hat as she descended the stairs from the Peach Court to the garden one afternoon. Noticing the object of my attention, Kwan took advantage of my distraction and knocked me from the poles. When my battered head cleared, I looked up from the sand to see him staring in the same direction with a fierce look on his face.

Was it mere rivalry, I wondered, or some other secret that fired his heart?

The waning moon illuminated the paper windows of the library. An autumn breeze set the panes to trembling as leaves skittered across the roof. I had just lit my second candle with a spark cantrip. It was a waste of paper for the flying scroll, but it pleased me to practice even the most trifling of spells. For so long I had been unable to do so without regrettable consequences, and I meant to make up for my years of abstinence.

After learning or setting aside all of the spells available in the library, I turned my efforts to innovation. From my earliest days at the Acadamae in Korvosa, my interests inclined toward the means of altering and enhancing standard spells: the field of metamagic. Alas, my disability had always limited my studies to the theoretical. With the advantage of riffle and flying scrolls, I hoped to at last turn theory into practice.

Unfortunately, the principals of metamagic that I had learned applied only to preparing a spell in the traditional manner. It was left to me to discover how to apply them to my particular means of casting spells.

I closed my eyes to peruse my memory library. It was a trick I'd mastered early on in my schooling: the art of imagining every new fact or concept I learned as a book, which I then shelved according to its subject. Now I used it to browse my volumes on theoretical magic. Owing to my wealth and longevity, the number of such tomes was considerable, most of them direct transcriptions of actual books I had read over the course of my studies. Though I could recount every chapter title and many of the authors' arguments verbatim, they contained little in the way of guidance and nothing in the way of revelation.

My powers of recall are great but finite. No doubt there are a few wizened sages throughout Golarion whose capabilities rival mine, yet I found myself wishing for a moment's use of the boundless knowledge of Nethys, or even one glance inside the god's *Book of Magic*. The All-Seeing Eye is notoriously indifferent to the practitioners of his art, so I was unsurprised that no vision came upon me.

However, an unexpected sort of messenger did arrive.

"You have ingratiated yourself with Master Li."

I turned toward Jade Tiger's voice and bowed without opening my eyes. He had interrupted my perusing a mental copy of Khaled Mumata's treatise *On the Contraction of Perceived Time in Abjuration and Evocation*. I hesitated long enough to finish the paragraph before responding.

"I cannot claim so, Your Excellency."

I opened my eyes. The eunuch wore a splendid green robe with gold embroidery. On one side the garment depicted a phoenix, complete with peacock feathers sewn in to form a tail; on the other side, a sinuous serpent wound around his sleeve and down to his hem. Besides Jade Tiger's omnipresent fan, he carried not one but two slender swords in his sash. More than ever before, I sensed an aura of danger about the man.

"It is strange that he grants privileges for your mischief."

"Master Li is wise. Perhaps he sees a lesson in assigning me this duty."

"Perhaps," said Jade Tiger. "But a lesson to whom?"

If I understood the eunuch's insinuation, I had underestimated Master Li. Perhaps the venerable monk only appeared uninterested in the day-to-day affairs of the temple. It was absurd to think that Jade Tiger's visits to me in the scriptorium had gone unnoticed by the servants. Likewise, it was equally tenuous to assume that the monk remained unaware of the eunuch's wizardry; I discarded the foolish notion. Master Li must have assigned me to the arcane library not to reward me but to remove my dependency on Jade Tiger.

The eunuch removed a scroll from his sash and held it before me. I saw at once that it was different from the spells he had shared from his personal spellbook. The parchment on which it was written was similar to that of the scrolls in the Persimmon Court library.

No, not similar. Identical.

"The subtleties of this illusion might remain beyond your understanding," he said. "But if you can master it, the spell allows you to communicate with a dreamer, no matter the distance."

I bowed, suspicious but grateful for this unexpected boon. "Your generosity quite overwhelms—"

"It is not a gift." Jade Tiger returned the scroll to his sash. "If you wish it, you must take it from me."

"But Your Excellency—"

He threw me one of his swords and drew the other before the first had touched my hand.

"Defend your life."

He attacked, moving faster than Kwan. Retreating, I parried his thrust with the four inches of blade I could draw from the scabbard before my back struck the wall. Pushing him away, I shifted to the side and drew the blade fully.

"Why—?"

He attacked again.

I concentrated on my defense. His swordsmanship was admirable, but I sensed mine was superior. The challenge was to defeat him without causing injury. Even defending oneself against a member of the royal court risked a judgment of instant death. To wound him would surely invoke a far more lingering punishment.

"You insult me by concealing your true talent," said Jade Tiger. "Fight with all your skill, or I will leave your body on this floor."

Often have I faced a foe with a flair for the dramatic. Some had nothing but bluff behind their words. Others were perfectly capable of executing their threats, no matter how bombastic.

I sensed Jade Tiger was one of the latter sort.

While I held his sword at bay with a simple variation on the Lepidstadt defense, I plucked a flying scroll from my sash. It was the spell he had first taught me, an enchantment capable of paralyzing him in an instant.

Smiling, Jade Tiger snapped open his fan. With a wave he dispelled my magic. Normally invisible, the spell dissipated in a thin pink smoke. Jade Tiger snapped shut both the fan and his smile.

I marveled at the magic of his fan. I wondered how many secret properties it held.

Jade Tiger obliged my unspoken question by binding my blade to the outside and whirling in to graze the tip of my nose with the razor-sharp tip of the fan.

It was an insolent, mocking strike. In an instant it dispelled all deference with which I viewed the court eunuch. No one may insult a Jeggare with impunity.

I pressed him with a swift attack, driving him to defend his leading shoulder. It was child's play to draw his guard open. Rather than execute the mortal strike, I tested his vanity with a feint toward his face. He overcompensated, drawing his defense too close. I swept his legs with a low kick.

He rolled over the strike and resumed a balanced stance. A flicker of doubt crossed his face. I was almost satisfied to have placed him on the defensive, but only almost. The eunuch required a lesson in mutual courtesy.

Before I could administer the instruction, I glimpsed a motion from his hand and parried the darts he flung from his fan's hollow spine. One cut the shoulder of my robe, but the others glanced off my blade.

He made a grudging nod. "You emulate Kwan, but you lack his strength."

A few apt taunts about what Jade Tiger lacked came to mind, none of them worthy of a count of Cheliax.

I discharged another flying scroll. My eyes blazed with arcane fire. I directed their heat onto the eunuch, but once more he dispelled my magic. I could not touch him with a spell. He was far too quick with the fan.

No, I realized. I was too slow. More precisely, my spells were too slow.

I plucked the scrolls for two of my meanest spells from my sash. Neither was apt to kill Jade Tiger, but one might repay him for the slight of my nose.

Maintaining my guard, I recalled certain metamagical principals and adopted an unorthodox stance, gesturing with my free hand as though I were modifying the spell I had already inscribed. If I had paused to consider what I was attempting, I should have abandoned the effort as preposterous. There was no reason to believe it would have an effect.

And yet I did not pause, and I did not think. I acted on impulse.

The first scroll caused frost to radiate from my finger. Jade Tiger swept it away, but before he could close his fan, four gray bolts of energy leaped from my hand and struck his torso.

He gasped and felt his body where the bolts had struck. At each point a neat round hole penetrated the cloth. Blood seeped from the wounds.

I knew I should throw myself at his feet and beg that he spare my life, yet I could not bear to do so. Instead I sheathed the sword he had given me and laid it at his feet.

Jade Tiger studied his stained fingertips with an astonished expression. A long moment later, his gaze returned to my face. His fine lips began to twist, and his fan snapped up to conceal whatever emotion they might betray.

On the side facing me, three smiling cubs tumbled upon each other.

Jade Tiger retrieved the sword and swept out of the library. In his wake lay the scroll with which he had tempted me. I seized it at once, examining it for any sign of defect. My beating heart slowed as anxiety released its grip. The spell upon the scroll was exactly as it appeared at first glance.

At last, I had a means of contacting Radovan. Now the question was whether my bodyguard could reach me before the eunuch's inevitable revenge.

Chapter Eighteen
Necromancer

I knelt by the grave and stroked the granite face of a dead girl.

For some reason I couldn't pin down, her carved face attracted me to the stone. Sure, she was pretty, but there was something more to it than that. Maybe it was her sad expression. The words beneath her image meant little to me. I could read the numbers, but I never learned how they count years in Tian Xia. It didn't matter. The face carved into the stone told me more than words could have. The artist had given the image all the life its subject had lost, maybe more.

It wasn't just the woman's beauty, and it wasn't her fetching pout as she played on a bamboo flute. It was more about what the artist hadn't carved. Her long straight hair hid half her face, giving her a mystery.

A few stones down, Burning Cloud Devil offered incense and a bowl of wine at the grave of an old master of his. While he bowed and chanted prayers, it was a cinch to steal the rest of the wine, an empty bowl, and three sticks of incense. I took them back to the pretty girl's grave.

Lighting them was no problem. I'd figured out weeks earlier that popping my fingers could produce a little flame. There was a time when that would have amused me.

I stuck the smoking incense into the ground beside the headstone. It occurred to me then that I didn't need to read the headstone to guess the girl's age. Rain and the seasons had softened the chiseled edges, so I figured it to be fifty or so years old. If the girl hadn't died, she'd be a crone by now. Back in Ustalav they'd call her "baba." I wondered what the Tien word for "granny" was.

"Sweet dreams, kid," I mumbled through the ruin of my mouth. My smashed teeth were growing back in rows, like a shark's. They were so sharp I could barely speak without slicing my lips. It was worth the risk to offer up a little prayer for the girl whose face had made me forget my troubles for a moment.

I thought for a while before I realized I didn't have any prayers left in me. I sat there anyway, half-wishing I could trade places with the departed.

The stone relief pushed the hair back from her face and smiled at me.

I blinked, but it was no trick of the gloom. Not only was the image moving, it wasn't the same girl anymore. It was Spring Snow.

You are leading him down the wrong path.

"I'm not the one leading, sweetheart." I immediately regretted my tone. Spring Snow didn't deserve my disrespect.

If it bothered her, she didn't let on. *Give up your revenge. Help him to give up his.*

"He's doing it out of love for you."

No, she said. *He is doing it out of hatred for himself.*

That sounded fair enough to me. I thought of the people who'd lost their lives—or their souls—on account of Burning Cloud Devil's desire for revenge. I couldn't stop thinking about the Phoenix Warrior, who'd died on account of mine.

You must turn away from the path of vengeance. It leads only to . . .

I put my hand over her face to shut her up.

Five notes from a flute drifted away on the breeze. I looked up but saw nothing but the moon leering down through her veils. When I lifted my hand again, there was only smooth stone beneath. I heard the same five notes again, farther away. Spring Snow was gone, and she'd taken the mysterious beauty with her.

"Hell," I growled. For an instant I wondered whether I was completing Snow's prediction or stating my philosophy in a nutshell.

There was no point making myself sick with this introspective bullshit. I got up and paced behind Burning Cloud Devil while he finished his prayers. I wondered why Spring Snow didn't talk to him directly. Why did she bother me instead?

We were somewhere in northeastern Quain. I didn't know exactly. After we made our departure from the town where we'd left the corpse of the Phoenix Warrior, I stopped paying attention. We fell into the usual routine of training and travel. Burning Cloud Devil was pleased I'd finally learned the Quivering Palm.

He rewarded me by renewing the one he'd hit me with each month since we met. Next, he promised, I would learn his ultimate technique, the Twin White Palms. After a few weeks listening to his mystical mumbo-jumbo about it, I no longer thought the Quivering Palm was all that complicated.

The novelty of the foreign country was wearing off. All I could see anymore was how Tian Xia was no different from Cheliax, or anywhere else in Avistan. Hungry farmers harvested their crops. Greedy bandits swept in to steal them. Indifferent soldiers marched home from their annual patrols. Everyone braced for winter.

An early frost turned the grass brittle, but there was as much green as brown on the nine hills that formed the cemetery above the city of Nanzhu. Burning Cloud Devil insisted on arriving here on the last day of Lamashan, or whatever they called the harvest month in these parts. It was the anniversary of his old master's death, and he had a promise to keep.

Before the sun set, I'd been curious about the dead guy. Burning Cloud Devil explained that his teacher's will demanded an annual service from his last pupil. Briefly I wondered how they'd met, what the old fellow had taught Burning Cloud Devil, what kind of food they liked to eat— the sort of thing ordinary people talk about.

The feeling passed.

In the cool autumn night, I was more interested in finding out when we were going to move along. It was cold for Lamashan, but it felt even colder among the headstones. There was something unsettled living here—or not living, as the case might be. I felt it in my spurs. We needed to find an inn that served something hot and strong.

Burning Cloud Devil rose from his prayers. He paused and turned his head to the side. I heard nothing.

It must have been something other than a sound that disturbed him. He knelt and placed his palm upon the earth. I did the same. A faint tremor pulsed through my hand, and after a few seconds I was sure it wasn't my own pulse.

"What is it?"

He didn't answer. Instead he removed an octagonal mirror from his bag and held it up to the moon. A beam of light shone on its surface for a moment. He flipped the mirror as if catching the moon ray inside.

Then he flipped it back and placed a queer dagger on top. It wasn't a weapon but a string of coins laid in a cross shape and tied tight together with red cord, a red tassel dangling from its butt. The trapped moonbeams lifted the coin dagger from the mirror's surface. It turned like the needle of a compass.

Burning Cloud Devil studied the light as it darkened to purple. He glared in the direction the coin-dagger pointed.

"Someone disturbs the dead in my master's cemetery."

I followed when he leaped into the trees.

A pair of phantoms passed us in the boughs. One was a grimacing old man with an odd little mortarboard hat tilted on his head. The other was a portly woman whose hands kept wringing an apron not included with her funereal dress. Lotus coffins lay shattered and empty between the churned graves. Brittle limbs scattered in the lanes told me we were getting closer to the cause of the disturbance.

We came to the highest hill on the cemetery, where balding oak trees mourned around a shrine. A yellow nimbus licked at the upturned corners of the building's three roofs, and shadows slithered on the ground. A halo flickered in and out at the spire on top, uncertain whether it wanted to be party to what was happening below.

Burning Cloud Devil flew toward the base of the hill, and I followed. We made less noise than the wind through the leaves. We crouched on the nearest thick branch and observed the necromancer mustering his troops.

The yellow light gave the man a waxy pallor. His sunken chest and potbelly reminded me of a pear. Around his scrawny neck curled a black torc in the shape of a serpent's skeleton. Behind him stood a tall scroll stand, a long blank sheet of paper hanging from its crown. Despite the chill, he'd peeled down the chest of his robe to display dozens of red Tien characters on his skin. I saw the bloody knife at his feet and realized he hadn't used a brush.

His lieutenants were four bald women wearing only iron torcs like their master's. Between their bare breasts they had painted snake skulls in ash. The women threw back their bald heads and babbled curses at the sky. Shadows of snakes slithered out of their blackened fingers to desecrate the ground.

Above the murmur of his acolytes, the necromancer sang an eerie song in an ancient tongue. With each phrase he jangled a big brass bell. With his other hand he flicked strips of yellow paper into the air. Rather than fall, they squirmed like minnows in a current. Each one sought out a grave.

Two squads of dead stood four by four beside the shrine. In life they'd have made an unlikely mob of merchants and porters, ladies and prostitutes, children and crones. Their clothes were all different, the last outfits they'd ever wear. Their only uniform was a strip of yellow paper hanging down their faces from a dark spot on their brows.

A third squad came up a winding lane, clods of earth falling away from their hems. They didn't shuffle the way you figure the dead would do, or maybe these ones were different. They hopped in unison up the lane, leaping each time the necromancer shook his brass bell.

The parade should have looked ridiculous. Instead, their halting jumps gave me the shudders. I knew the smell of the restless dead, the touch of their putrid fingers on my skin. No matter how they moved, there was nothing funny about them.

"How dare he conjure minions from this sacred place!" I had a feeling Burning Cloud Devil's outrage had more to do with the presence of his master's grave than with a sense of civic duty. He made arcane gestures and intoned a spell. The magic glimmered and sank into his body. He cast another on me, another on himself. I got bored of it.

I watched the undead army grow. Considering how many yellow strips the necromancer had thrown, he'd have an army soon.

"There is no time to waste." Burning Cloud Devil drew the silver sword and flew at the necromancer.

He moved so fast that I expected him to impale the man, but the sword was just a prop for his grand entrance. He floated to a stop ten feet from the shrine.

"Who dares—?" The necromancer held the bell and another handful of papers above his head, like a housewife who'd spied a mouse. Half a dozen emotions wrestled for control of his face until an awed smile won out. "Burning Cloud Devil! You honor me with your presence."

The necromancer dropped the yellow paper to press an open hand against the fist gripping the bell. It rang again as he bowed. The approaching dead leaped another step closer.

Burning Cloud Devil tilted his head. Maybe he was surprised by the compliment. He lowered his blade and waited to hear more.

"Have you come to join your infernal legions to my undying army? Tonight I shall have enough to conquer

Nanzhu. If you will open the gates of Hell to muster an army of devils, we can rule Quain by spring."

Burning Cloud Devil sheathed his sword. He brushed an errant leaf from his shoulder.

I considered leaping down to join him, but I was tired of straight-up fights against sorcerers and priests, not to mention paladins and magic seamstresses. Instead I shrugged off my pack and crept around toward the back of the shrine, careful to stay in the shadows that didn't look like snakes. The priestesses kept chanting, oblivious as I moved past them.

The long silence finally prompted the necromancer to speak.

"Forgive me, King of Heroes. I am rude. Of course you do not remember me from our brief encounter in Fuchuan, but I could never forget the sight of your battle against the Six Peerless Sons of Wo Han at the Gate of the Alabaster Unicorn, nor the spectacular duel against the eunuch sorcerer who sought to avenge their deaths. I am Bingwen of the White Branch School, formerly Court Conjuror and now Summoner of the Undead. In the south I am known as Foul-Eye Bingwen, and the oni of the Salt Desert call me Master of Agonies."

I slipped into the shrine while Foul-Eye listed all his names. I crouched behind one of eight thick pillars carved in the shape of entwined constrictors. They looked new compared to the rest of the monuments in the cemetery, and felt warm under my hand. I pulled it away.

Burning Cloud Devil lifted his beard on his wrist as he considered the introduction. "You disturb these honored ancestors for revenge?"

"To overthrow a despot who has no appreciation for the true power of sorcery!"

"Ah," said Burning Cloud Devil. He shook his head, disappointed at the answer. He turned in the direction where he thought I still was. "You may kill him now."

"What treach—?"

I shoved the big knife through Foul-Eye's spine. It was a neat cut, right between two of his vertebrae, maybe the best I'd ever done. Not that I'd made so many like it. Not as many as people thought back home.

The bald women screamed, feeling their master's pain. Foul-Eye slumped forward, but he kept standing. Unbelievable for anyone but a necromancer.

I shoved the knife to the left, twisted, and shoved it back in the other direction. The women screamed again, their arms flailing as the shadowy snakes fled their fingers. Bingwen's heavy torso leaned farther, but still he refused to fall.

He didn't bleed so much as he oozed. The orange-colored blood—or ichor, or goo, or whatever it was—had the thickness and stench of hot tar. Thick, snotty ropes of the stuff stuck to the big knife.

Foul-Eye turned to face me. He twisted at the waist, detaching the rest of his torso from his legs, which flopped to the ground as the remainder of his body hovered above. His eyes blazed and darkened. He leaned forward, grasped my shoulder in his fat, sweaty hand, and sprayed my face with steaming whispers.

Blasts of fire erupted all around the shrine as Burning Cloud Devil began incinerating Foul-Eye's troops, but I couldn't look away from the necromancer's sunken eyes. They had been dead for decades, disguised by an illusion of life. All the weight came off my body. I fell forward, into those black pits.

"Resist." Burning Cloud Devil's magic whisper breathed in my ear. "Do not let him dominate your mind."

Easier said than done, but the encouragement snapped me out of my daze. I shoved Foul-Eye and shook the confusion from my head.

By the time I was ready for another go at him, yellow-green vapor poured out of the necromancer's mouth. His skin blistered as the fumes rolled down his naked chest and spread in all directions.

I fell back to roll out of the shrine before the stuff touched me. The priestesses clutched at me despite their sightless eyes. I kicked one back into the green cloud. The poisonous fog stifled her screams.

Shaking off the other three took a moment. Their hands were weirdly strong, but a good crack on the noggin laid each of them out. For a second I considered cutting their throats, but I had a feeling they weren't volunteers. Foul-Eye's dead gaze had almost done a number on me, a street-raised hellspawn. These girls wouldn't have stood a chance against his magic charms.

A strong gust blew away the noxious fog. Burning Cloud Devil hovered above a pile of smoldering corpses, a triumphant smile creasing his face. The smile vanished when he saw what the wind revealed.

In his own blood, Foul-Eye had drawn a symbol on the giant scroll. When Burning Cloud Devil saw it, he choked and writhed in the air. The necromancer turned it toward me. I closed my eyes and threw myself to the ground, but it didn't matter.

Pain screamed into my body, twisting my limbs and shriveling my guts. Pain had come before, so often it didn't even knock anymore. I opened my eyes and screamed back at it with all the hell I'd been saving for the dragon. I stared the bastard down. And you know what?

Pain blinked.

Whatever magic Foul-Eye set off got one taste of me and had enough.

While the necromancer worked his next spell, I rushed him, dropping the useless knife. Instead, I moved in for Burning Cloud Devil's favorite strike.

Even with my eyes closed, it was a perfect shot. My hand struck the necromancer dead between the nipples. My fingers spidered out to touch the Seven Margins of the Soul, then back to bind them all to my command.

It was perfect. After I'd killed the Phoenix Warrior, I felt exactly how it was done. The strings of Foul-Eye's soul should have been tied to my will. But I felt nothing.

"The Quivering Palm!" Foul-Eye's raspy voice was full of admiration. With his yellow nails he slit open his chest and pulled open his ribcage. Where a heart should be lay a gore-slicked stone. "Your skill is impressive, but it is useless against one who has entered the Ninety-Ninth Chamber of Undying—"

I crushed his larynx to spare myself the boredom of hearing his story.

Apparently he'd skipped the chamber that puts a stone in your throat. His limp hands slapped uselessly against his neck.

"Twin White Palms!" shouted Burning Cloud Devil.

What the hell? I gave it my all. Knuckle shot to either side of the stone heart, cupped palms to receive the Immortal Essence . . . and there was nothing. I hit the necromancer anyway. The force of my open hands upon his chest knocked him back a few feet, but that was it.

No instant death. No fireworks. Not even a good yelp. I was disappointed.

A fireball exploded inside the shrine. Fire washed over me. The blast sucked the breath out of my lungs, but otherwise it barely mussed my hair. I glared at Burning Cloud Devil.

He nodded with satisfaction at the sizzling corpse of Bingwen Foul-Eye and the flaming remains of the scroll stand.

"A little warning next time." Still, there was no harm done. Not even a thread of my magic robes got singed. In fact, I felt pretty good after the bath of flame. Even my teeth stopped hurting. I realized they'd grown back completely the instant the fire caressed me.

The cheer lasted only until I saw the smoking remains of the priestesses I thought I'd spared. It would have been nice to end the night with a little bit of a rescue to take the edge off.

I sank to the ground, too exhausted to work up a good mad. It wasn't my fault those girls were dead. It wasn't Burning Cloud Devil's, either. It was the necromancer who'd made them come here to call up the dead, which they had no business doing. Or else they were as twisted as he was and chose to come along of their own free will. I hadn't seen a thing to tell me different.

That's what I kept telling myself as I followed Burning Cloud Devil out of the cemetery and down into the city of Nanzhu.

Chapter Nineteen
Shadowless Sword

Even after mastering the spell Jade Tiger gave me, I remained unable to reach Radovan through his dreams. Night after night I made the attempt, only to wake exhausted and with nothing to show for my efforts.

The most likely cause was that he was not asleep when I cast the spell. Under other circumstances, I would simply have cast the spell earlier or later, but I required the privacy of the arcane library lest a servant or one of my brothers overhear me speaking while entranced by the spell. Communication with anyone outside the temple was among the hundred behaviors forbidden to first-year disciples. One whisper that I was using the magic of the Persimmon Court to violate temple rules could deprive me of my library privilege.

My window of opportunity was both narrow and immovable, for I dared not linger in the Persimmon Court beyond curfew. Since Master Li granted me access to the Persimmon Court, I sensed intensified resentment not only from the servants and my fellow disciples, but also from the master of combat.

As my fruitless attempts continued, I prayed for guidance from Desna, Tender of Dreams. In Cheliax, I reserved my public homage for the devil-god Asmodeus, Prince of Law. In private, however, I worshiped the Song of the Spheres before any other deity. Radovan shared my secret veneration, although his informal—and arguably sacrilegious—invocations called upon her as Lady Luck. In that aspect, she appeared to favor the hellspawn rogue above her other worshipers. I would not entertain any notion of his death as a cause for my spell's failure because Radovan had escaped from more seemingly impossible catastrophes than anyone I had ever known.

In his succinct vernacular, Desna smiled on him.

One chilly autumn night, perhaps more for Radovan's sake than mine, the Tender of Dreams rewarded my efforts to contact him. Just as I had done so often on previous nights, I intoned the arcane syllables and performed the mystic gestures. The magic lulled me into a trance.

My mind lifted away from my body and traveled to the dream realm, searching the chaotic void briefly before speeding toward my intended goal. Intuition and a nebulous sense of familiar territory assured me that I had at last contacted Radovan's dreaming mind. While I expected a fantastic interpretation of the seraglios of Qadira or perhaps the squalor of a Trick Alley brothel, what I found instead was a series of battlegrounds.

Bodies of men and women lay knee-deep in a tumble of different landscapes. I stepped over the splintered timbers of a ruined waterwheel, climbed the rugged slope of a quarry pit, and struggled through the corpse-cluttered alleys of a town. Everywhere I went lay murdered heroes, their shattered weapons the only monument to their lives.

In the distant gloom I heard voices hissing accusations: "Bastard . . . monster . . . devil . . . *thing!*"

I fought down a powerful urge to flee before realizing they did not speak to me. These voices tormented the dreamer, not the intruder. To make myself heard over their recriminations, I had to find Radovan where he lay within this nightmare.

I called his name. The sound of my voice hushed the whisperers, but only for a moment. When I called out again, they raised such a clamor that I could barely hear myself.

"Radovan, if you can hear my voice, come to Dragon Temple!"

The cacophony grew louder each time I shouted. Yet somewhere behind those damned voices I felt another intruding presence directing the whisperers. It remained invisible, but I felt a great hot mass looming just behind me. Whatever it was, it did not welcome my intrusion into the nightmare.

"Radovan, can you hear me?" Through magic of his own, my hidden adversary changed my words. *"Radovan, I burn in the dragon's pit. Avenge me!"*

After several more futile attempts to relay my own words, I canceled the spell rather than repeat the false message. Regaining consciousness in the arcane library, I found myself sweating and shivering. Who was this interloper who interfered with my message?

Jade Tiger was the logical suspect. Yet something about the hidden presence within the nightmare seemed wholly different from the court eunuch. Despite the inherent subtlety of illusion magic, it was a far more aggressive and masculine presence.

I had another arcane foe to consider, and I did not know his identity.

The question worried at me for days after the event. With trepidation, I attempted the dream spell again each night, but I failed even to reach Radovan's nightmare visions. No amount of perusing the Persimmon Court library or my own recollections of magical theory provided an insight into the problem. Yet nothing could distract me from pondering the issue until Master Wu announced the impending second trials.

Anxiety permeated the Cherry Court. Every disciple hoped to improve his standing since the first trials, none more than I, who had the least to lose and the most to gain.

My martial skill was now such that I had little fear of retaining the shameful appellation "Least Brother," but placing higher than least was no longer satisfactory. To start, I would have my revenge on Runme, Karfai, and the others who bullied me. Yet shaming my adversaries was no longer my principal ambition.

I intended to defeat Kwan at sword.

The morning of the second trials, we woke to the sound of singing and the smell of hot noodles. The cool of early winter had made us huddle under our covers, and a blast of cold air sent a wave of complaints through the dormitory. Mon Choi held open the door, allowing fat flakes of snow to drift in. His enthusiastic whoop brought us all out of our pallets before I had time to realize that Master Wu had not awakened me for kitchen duty.

"Look!" Mon Choi pointed out the door. "Our elder brothers greet us."

A parade of gray-clad monks hurried toward the refectory from the Plum Court gate. They ranged in age from barely older than the novices to ten or more years older. The foremost bore heavy pots and stacks of steam baskets. Others carried bundles of the gray robes we would wear upon completing the second trials, while those bringing up the rear carried racks of steel swords, knives, and spears to the practice yard.

We donned our brown novice robes and emerged from the dormitory to join the elder brothers. They responded with friendly greetings until we reached the shelter of the refectory, where they laid down the feast and opened the lids to a general gasp of delight. Not only did the feast smell delicious, but my first taste contained a startling discovery.

I would have testified to the severest Egorian judge that the meal contained meat, but the elder brothers assured me it was all bean curd prepared via a culinary secret. With a wink, Elder Brother Deming said he looked forward to sharing recipes with the latest First Brother of kitchen.

The food was so delicious and plentiful that most of my fellow novices returned for second helpings. Kwan caught me observing the phenomenon and offered a conspiratorial nod when he saw that I too resisted the bounty and ate sparingly. The trials would be more difficult for those who overindulged. In a moment of gratitude for his friendship, I lay a hand on Mon Choi's arm as he reached for his bowl again.

A glance at our elder brothers' expressions confirmed my suspicion that the generous feast was a trap. Some could barely conceal their smirks, while two that I presumed to be the First Brothers of their cohorts exchanged furtive whispers as they observed our behavior. The second trials had begun.

Once all the new students had an opportunity to overindulge, our seniors led us outside. Brother Deming gestured toward the gate leading to the Plum

Court. "After today, you shall don the gray robes of our order, and that door will remain open to you."

While we dined, the elders swept the snow from the central training ground and erected racks of staves, spears, knives, and swords around the perimeter. Beneath a canopy on the southern edge of the courtyard sat Princess Lanfen and Jade Tiger. No longer disguised as a man, the princess wore a gown of royal yellow, while Jade Tiger favored a robe of deep crimson. To either side of the pavilion stood their guards, the tassels of their spears gradually accumulating caps of snow.

Masters Li and Wu sat on unsheltered mats to the north. The elder students took their places on the east and west. Their Eldest Brother, a muscular man of perhaps thirty years, led them in a brief cheer for us juniors. We novices took out places in the center, four ranks of four. We bowed to the royal entourage, then to our elders on the east and west, and finally toward our masters.

Master Wu stood to address us.

"You came to Dragon Temple as heroes of many towns and distant provinces."

"Some more distant than others," added Brother Deming. The elder monks laughed, but none of my fellow aspirants reacted. Master Wu's eyes remained upon us, but he did not so much as glower at Deming for his interjection. I sensed they had choreographed the outburst to test our discipline. Another trifling test passed.

"Upon acceptance as disciples, you became brothers dedicated to perfecting your bodies, minds, and spirits. Today you shall demonstrate how well you have learned."

Master Wu sat, and Master Li led us in eighteen prayers to Irori. Afterward, he quizzed us on the history of Dragon Temple and its mission to safeguard the royal embassy to the Gates of Heaven and Hell every twelve years. After our repeated recitations throughout the year, Master Li's questions posed no challenge, even to the uncultivated minds of Runme and Lu Bai. In less than an hour's time, it was clear that even the masters were ready to dispense with the trials of mind and spirit and move on to the trials of the body.

Master Wu announced the first martial trial: fist. Eight of the elder brothers stood to act as judges, with at least one watching over each of the bouts. Unlike the first trials, a single blow was insufficient for victory. To prevent mortal injuries, the elder students would declare a victor when it became obvious to them that one had gained a decisive advantage.

My first opponent was Yingjie, the pock-faced youth who had twice defeated Kwan in staff. His unarmed skill was also formidable, but he favored long foot strikes and showed little talent for innovation. I blocked three kicks before catching his ankle and twisting him to the ground. Two firm strikes to the back, and our judge declared him defeated. Surprised, Yingjie bowed and accepted his defeat.

I struggled to demonstrate the same grace after I faced Kwan in the second round. The bout lasted less than ten seconds before his fist snaked through my defense to leave the impression of his knuckles on my chest. Three more such blows, and the judges deemed me the loser.

Mon Choi defeated me in the first round of wrestling, pinning me so quickly that I heard the judge's decision in the same breath with which he had signaled the contest begun. Mon Choi resisted his natural urge to apologize, and I endeavored not to thank him for a quick end to that hated contest.

The next contest was in staff, leaving the bladed weapons for last. The only two I had never defeated in staff were Kwan and Yingjie. Not only was I spared facing either of them in the first round, but they were pitted against each other. This good fortune reinforced my determination to win, and I surprised even myself by rendering my opponent unconscious with my first thrust.

Kwan required a few minutes to defeat Yingjie before he was paired against Karfai and I with Runme. Within a minute, Kwan prevailed. Moments later, so did I.

Certain that my streak of good fortune would soon end, I made a silent prayer of thanks to Desna when I faced Harbin. The carpenter had proven one of the more skilled fighters generally, but staff was not his strength.

Harbin took the initiative. His attacks were firm but cautious. The rhythm of our strikes accelerated, but Harbin maintained a balanced defense, intending to weary me. A few months ago, his strategy would have prevailed, but I had grown strong. I feigned a grunt of exertion and exaggerated two parries. On the third I rolled low and struck his inner thigh, an inch below disaster. When he flinched from the blow, I reversed the staff and rapped his head. He wobbled and fell to one knee. The judge's hand rose to indicate my victory.

For the honor of First Brother in Staff, I faced Kwan.

No sooner had I heard our elder signal the start of our fight than Kwan pushed me back with dizzying ferocity, his staff appearing like a dozen stalks of bamboo flying at me. The moment I stood to repel his advance, he beat my staff aside and struck me five or six times with the butt before I fell onto the courtyard floor.

The astonishing speed of his victory dispelled my hope of defeating him in sword. The best outcome I could now imagine was victory over anyone I faced before Kwan.

To heap despair on my loss, my first bout in spear paired me with Yingjie.

Only Kwan regularly defeated Yingjie in spear. I imagined the First Brother's face in place of Yingjie's and considered how I might have blunted Kwan's overwhelming assault with the staff.

Immediately I discarded the thought as a mistake. Yingjie favored a long stance and point attack, completely unlike Kwan's Forest Storm style. Instead I imagined myself above the Moutray River of my youth, my heels upon the cliff, my target Yingjie's right cheek.

At the signal, I acted first. No feints this time. I struck at his face. Yingjie parried, twirling his weapon to trap my spear with his tassel. I cut below to evade the bind and thrust again at his cheek. His head drew back to avoid the point of my spear, lowering his own point. I cut above his guard and attacked the other cheek.

Mindful of his eyes, Yingjie retreated. I followed, pressing, binding, cutting above his weapon, encircling his guard, drawing a relentless spiral toward his face until the point of my spear licked in to cut his cheek.

Yingjie hesitated in anticipation of the call, but the judge said nothing. In that moment, I turned the point and bloodied his other cheek.

The judge raised his hand in my favor, but he stared at me. Whether his gaze held accusation or disbelief, I could not tell. He had to wonder at the ferocity of my attack. In Ustalav, Yingjie would now be considered a more marriageable man with the Lepidstadt scars upon his face. But of course here my tactic appeared merely cruel.

Perhaps it was cruel. I felt the disapproval of our audience but looked away. To defeat my rivals, I might require more cruelty yet.

The next two bouts were briefer still. After cowing him with feints to the face, I pinked Karfai on the arm and shoulder before he conceded defeat. In the next contest I threatened the same to Mon Choi before chasing him out of bounds. My heart sank as he bowed and praised my victory, offering thanks that I had not disfigured him.

Again I faced Kwan, but this time I was prepared to repel his first attack.

Yet it did not come.

Instead Kwan moved to outflank me. Once more he had me on the defensive from the start. I gave ground as he stepped to the side. He shrugged a feint that should not have gulled me yet did. Each time I launched the high attack, he retreated beyond reach. He kept me at bay, forcing me to dance to his tune.

I changed tactics and lowered my spear—too soon! Kwan beat my point to the ground and ran forward, stepping on my spear as he beat my head on either side. With a whoop, he set his foot upon my chest and drove me to the ground. The tip of his spear hovered above my eye, and I heard the unrestrained cheers of the other monks, even the elders.

Even, to my regret and shame, Mon Choi.

My face burned with multiple shames. My loss to Kwan was the least of them. Worse was the knowledge that my brothers—no longer so-called, but my only current peers here or anywhere the world—found such common joy in my defeat.

Worst of all was my growing suspicion that I deserved no better than their disapprobation. All could witness how I had let my arrogance exceed my ability. And yet I could not quench my desire to defeat Kwan, no matter the cost.

I could not reach him at knives. Harbin slipped a blade under my guard and creased my belly with the edge of his butterfly blade. For an instant he appeared almost as surprised as I at his sudden victory. While I withdrew to bind my wound, he raised his weapons in triumph at the call. Shortly thereafter, he slunk away from defeat after Kwan gently pressed his blades against Harbin's throat.

The first three bouts in sword were over in moments. Inevitably, Kwan and I faced each other at the end. He had come through the first five challenges unscathed. My wounds were largely superficial, but I could still hear the echo of his staff upon my skull.

From the moment our duel began, we moved as through a shared dream. Kwan did not repeat his ruse of the dragging foot, and I abandoned the aggression of my spear attack. Instead, we assayed each other's minutest defenses with every gambit in our respective repertoires.

Kwan leaped and flew, whooping like a crane, screeching like an owl. I was the serpent to his bird, evading his strikes with precise economy. The edge of his blade caressed the fabric of my robe but never cut it.

A hundred times the judges witnessed glancing strikes, but they checked their eager hands as they saw the hits caused bare scratches. They awaited a more substantial blow to declare a victor.

I did not consciously employ Avistani forms, but rather blended the Dragon Temple style with tactics from fencing schools in Cheliax, Andoran, Taldor, Ustalav, and half a dozen other lands. Kwan did not need such knowledge, for his was a natural skill, innovating and adapting to every change of attack. Later I would sit and contemplate in awe the manner in which he appeared to invent an entirely original form of swordplay as we fought.

We dueled until the morning shadows shrank beneath us. Our sweat dripped pink upon the ground, the frost long since thawed by our ten thousand steps. We had cut each other's sleeves to ribbons. Kwan ripped away his tunic, revealing the perfect bronze muscles of his arms and torso. The sight of a dozen shallow scratches my sword had left on his skin inspired a new attack, one of my own extemporaneous device.

Dodging sideways, I moved to outflank him. Kwan matched my movement. I reversed it, and in the instant before he reacted, the point of my blade inscribed two faint lines upon his shoulder.

The cost to me was a similar scratch, but neither of us landed a blow sufficient to prevail.

I let my eyes slide slightly out of focus, envisioning the characters I had studied only last night in the Persimmon Court library. What I was about to attempt would seem preposterous to any wizard who had not encountered the mysteries of the riffle and flying scrolls as well as the promise of the metamagical gestures I used against Jade Tiger.

What I was about to attempt was improbable at best. Under the gaze of the princess and all of Dragon Temple, I dispensed with probabilities. I *could* succeed because the past year had been only one of many I had spent training my mind and body for this moment, never before realizing when this moment would come. And I *would* succeed because, in this moment, I willed it.

Also because, folded in a scrap of yellow paper within my sash, I had a drop of molasses.

On our second clash I added two more lines to the scratch on Kwan's shoulder, and he pinked the flesh above my right eye. Kwan's eyes narrowed in suspicion, but before he could guess my scheme, I completed the character I was drawing upon his skin.

Slow.

The released enchantment tingled on my fingers before gripping Kwan's body. His feet hit the ground in a perfect landing, but his blade lagged as he returned it to the defensive.

I beat it aside and pinked him on the breast.

The judges failed to react.

I struck again.

Slowly, Kwan lowered his weapon and stepped back, conceding my victory. Still the judges did not move. They turned to Master Wu for direction.

Wu turned his reddened face to Master Li, whose venerable eyes were fixed on Jade Tiger. The eunuch returned the gaze with a mild, unreadable smile.

That smile told Master Li what I only now understood: I had been a pawn in a game I had never perceived.

Kwan bowed to me and then to the masters. "I am defeated."

One of the judges knelt and bowed before Masters Wu and Li. "Masters, Brother Jeggare employed magic in a contest of swords."

Brother Deming came from the stands to kneel before the masters. "Masters, in the second trials, students are encouraged to display their unique styles of combat."

"Masters," said the first judge. "It would be right to declare Jeggare First Brother in Magic, but surely not in Sword."

Master Wu's lips twitched. He wanted to speak, but he waited for the decision of his senior. Master Li remained quiet and introspective. A hush fell over the Cherry Court.

Behind his open fan, on which we saw the mischievous cubs, Jade Tiger whispered to the princess. At her solemn nod, he rose and broke the silence.

"Since Princess Lanfen shall bestow the Shadowless Sword upon the victor, it is appropriate that she decide."

There could be no disputing the suggestion. Not even Master Li would desire to offend the daughter of the king. Following his lead, we all kowtowed before the princess.

She walked to the center of the courtyard and stood before me and Kwan. At her gesture, we raised our heads but remained on our knees.

"Brother Kwan," she said. "Your courage and honor are unmatched."

She turned to me. "Brother Jeggare, I declare you First Brother of Spell and Sword."

Beside me, I felt an almost imperceptible slump in Brother Kwan's posture. He was not truly defeated until that moment. But as I bowed to the princess and received the Shadowless Sword from her perfect hand, I glanced past her toward Jade Tiger. There was no mistaking the expression of surprise and anger on his face before he concealed it with his fan.

The ferocious face of a tiger stared back at me.

Chapter Twenty
Phantom Virgin

Judge Fang said I should go into Nanzhu while the others waited beside the cemetery.

The sad little Phoenix smoothed her feathers and stared at the sky. She hadn't spoken since she landed on a fence the Goblin leaned on while we all watched smoke rise from a town Judge Fang called Khitai. The sight of the Phoenix's beautiful cream and crimson plumage awed the rest of us to silence. When the Goblin saw we were staring above his head, he looked up, yelped and farted at the same time, and fled almost out of sight before returning in a sulk.

Judge Fang declared the Phoenix a good omen. He bowed to her and recited a speech about the importance of our mission. His speech grew longer every time he repeated it, and he enjoyed it more than anyone listening did.

Most of the beasts and kami he had approached turned down his request to join us in our march toward Iron Mountain for the Dragon Ceremony in spring. As winter approached, more and more did not even listen to the whole speech. The Phoenix listened to it all but said nothing.

Afterward, she followed wherever we went. She covered her head with a wing at the first snow. I think she missed the summer.

"Find out what has happened here," Judge Fang told me. "No one in Nanzhu will mind a dog. The others would frighten the human beings."

The Goblin puffed out his chest and stuck his thumbs under his arms. "One look at me, and they would evacuate the whole miserable town."

Behind him, the Hopper squeaked. I still could not understand him, but Gust and the Whispering Spider laughed until the Goblin stomped off. Even the Phoenix raised her head at his remark.

The Fox brushed against me and whispered, "The Hopper is funny. Don't you agree?"

The feel of her shoulder against my leg made me nervous. There was no reason to fear her. Even if we weren't friends, I was bigger, even when she was one grown fox instead of nine little ones. She was the kind of animal smaller dogs might chase for their master. But when she lay beside me at night or put her muzzle close to mine, I was the one who felt like running away.

It was a relief to go into the town, but we had come for the cemetery. Judge Fang wanted to find three kami called the Dancing Courtesans who lived here.

When we reached the cemetery, however, the gate was shut. Judge Fang read a sign stating that the cemetery was closed until further notice. There was a ward on the sign, and we could not enter the grounds. Judge Fang said it was a weak magic. He could open the gate with the magic inside his bag, but it would take all day. In the meantime, he wanted me to find out what had happened.

There were other dogs in the town. Most of them walked beside their masters, but others roamed in small packs. They greeted me, and I greeted them. One strong-chested dog with a short coat and erect ears told me he was in charge of me. I gave him the big smile so he knew he was wrong.

I missed my friend Radovan. Outside the cemetery I caught a scent that reminded me of him after he'd caught on fire. I called out until workmen came and Judge Fang begged me to be quiet.

Even more than Radovan, I missed my master. It was taking a long time to gather our army, but Judge Fang said we could not go to Iron Mountain until spring. Judge Fang was wise, but he wasn't as wise as my master.

There were many people in the streets of the town. Some of them cooked on fires beside the street. I took a big piece of hot goat meat from a spit, and the cook chased me until he saw two other dogs moving in to steal the rest.

Most of the people ignored me. I listened to their talk, but I could barely understand it. I knew who was angry or sad or sick, but their words did not make sense. Even though I understood more of what Judge Fang and the kami said, I preferred the way my master gave me jobs with a few words or hand signs.

Even if I didn't understand it, I had a job now, so I tried to do it. I greeted people everywhere I went. Most of them were tired or hungry, and many were afraid, but their smells told me nothing about the cemetery.

I found a pair of dogs with thick manes sitting beside their master as he listened to a man wearing his arm in a sling and talking fast. Another man drew a picture while he talked.

"What has happened?" I asked after they greeted me.

"A one-armed sorcerer came to town, challenging heroes to fight his devil. He offered gold to anyone who would try.

They heard his devil had killed many heroes, so no one dared face the fiend. The one-armed man became angry and beat the men when they tried to chase him away."

Burning Cloud Devil was a one-armed man. I had heard people call Radovan a devil.

"Where did the one-armed man go?"

"He turned into fire and flew away."

Before leaving the market, I stole a plucked goose for the Fox. I wondered why I did that, because she could easily catch her own goose. What would she think if I brought it to her? Since I had the goose, I decided I might as well share it with everyone.

Judge Fang made a fire with magic and roasted the goose legs for the Goblin, but he took only a few blades of grass for himself. The Hopper ate only insects, and Gust ate nothing at all. The Fox and the Whispering Spider shared the rest of the goose. The Phoenix smoothed her feathers and settled down on the embers of the fire, soaking in their heat.

Judge Fang had already broken the wards. Even I could feel the absence of the magic, which had lifted my hackles earlier. The Hopper bounced impatiently beside the gate.

"The Dancing Courtesans are good kami who watch over the graves at night," said Judge Fang. "They soothe the souls of the recently departed and leech away the sorrow of their mourners."

"But they aren't dangerous to us, right?" The Goblin tried to sound brave, but he was not the only one who was afraid of the cemetery. Gust kept still. The Spider pretended to be busy weaving a cloth out of her own silk, but her legs trembled.

"Not if we approach with respect. Leave it to me to present our plea."

"Don't worry," said the Goblin. He grabbed the second goose leg and waved it. "You can recite your speech until the sun comes up for all I care."

Judge Fang clicked his mandibles while he considered the Goblin's tone.

"Very well." Judge Fang flew up onto my shoulders and pointed through the gate with his tiny walking stick. "Let us seek the Dancing Courtesans."

I went through the cemetery gate. The remains of the ward tickled my skin. Judge Fang spat as my fur went into his face again.

Inside was a little forest on a series of steep hills. The stones that had looked gray in the sunlight were blue and white under the quarter moon. Some had carvings of human faces, but most just had writing. Old sticks of incense jutted out of the ground near the stones, still pungent long after they had burned to the stem.

"How do the Dancing Courtesans appear?" asked the Whispering Spider. "Are they pretty?"

"They are supremely beautiful," said Judge Fang. He sensed, as I did, that the Spider did not like this answer. "Their loveliness cannot compare with yours, however. They have shed their human features and appear now as bright lanterns, guiding the souls of the dead toward Pharasma's Spire."

"How virtuous." The Spider made a sour face.

Gust swept through the trees above us, sending down a shower of brown leaves. There were few left in the branches. The Phoenix flew from tree to tree, moving ahead of us but never going out of sight.

The burning smell I noticed earlier was stronger inside the cemetery, but it was still faint. Whatever had made the smell was no longer here. As we moved deeper into the cemetery, I picked up other scents.

Most were like the smell of many dead bodies, only weaker. Another was stronger but much worse. It stung my nose and made me blink my eyes.

"What is that stench?" The Goblin pinched his nose and looked around with suspicion.

The Hopper bounced up to the Goblin, snuffled, and leaped away with an alarmed squeak.

Gust laughed, but the others only smiled. I felt Judge Fang's tiny hands grip my coat tighter.

I stopped. From somewhere near the center of the cemetery came a musical sound. Ahead of us, the Phoenix became still upon her branch. She lowered her head to listen. It was a melancholy sound that made me feel alone and afraid. Beside me, the Fox moved close, and I felt her shivering.

"Someone plays the flute," said Judge Fang. "Let us see who."

In the center of the cemetery stood a shrine with eight big pillars shaped like snakes. The lower parts of the pillars were scrubbed clean and white, but the higher parts and the roof had been burned black. On the floor of the shrine, light gray bricks contrasted with the darker old ones. The workmen had left a stack of bricks beside the path, and on it sat a ghost in a gown as fine and white as the Spider's silk.

In her hands she held the flute we had heard. Her head leaned to the side as she played, so she did not notice us. Moments after we arrived, three glowing lanterns bobbed through the trees to hover above us. One glowed yellow, the next blue, and the third green. Their lights dimmed as their movement slowed, and I could tell they also were listening to the song.

The ghost continued to play, and we listened in silence. The Fox lay down beside me, her russet head on her black paws. The Goblin hugged my shoulder and wept into my fur until I shrugged him off. No matter how often Judge Fang insisted the Goblin wade through a river or stand in the rain, he smelled bad.

Soon the Hopper was weeping too, and the sound of his squeaking sobs caused the ghost to raise her lips from the flute. The music stopped, I felt as if I had just woken from a long nap.

The ghost looked at us. Half of her face was hidden behind her long, black hair. The side we could see was as smooth and blue as a statue in the moonlight.

"A phantom virgin!" whispered Judge Fang. "The poor child died before she married."

Despite his quiet voice, the woman heard his words and gasped in indignation.

"How dare you speak to me of such things, insect!"

"Please do not be affronted," said the tiny magistrate. "Despite the sorrow of your life, you will hold a high place in Heaven. Those who perish of this world before knowing the pleasures of the marriage bed—"

"You know nothing! As you can see, I am not in Heaven. I am trapped here in the world, like you."

"Harrumph!" Judge Fang cleared his throat, tried to speak, and instead cleared his throat again.

He leaped down to rummage in his bag for objects which he then set on the ground. He lit three red candles and placed them on his little mirror. He shook a cup of sticks, removed the one that rose to the top, and observed it in the reflected candlelight.

"You made a vow," he said. "There is a task you must complete before your soul may rejoin the Celestial Wheel."

"How can you—?" The ghost paused and nodded. "It is true."

"It is possible that your path to Pharasma's Spire may be straightened if you were to aid the Celestial Bureaucracy in another significant matter. We are gathering an army to oppose the mischief plotted by the Burning Cloud Devil and the Jade Tiger. It is for the help of these delightful Courtesans that we came, but perhaps you too could join us."

"These names mean nothing to me," said the ghost. "I will remain here until . . . until the return of the one I must face."

"Alas," sighed Judge Fang. He turned to the Dancing Courtesans and began his speech.

Something about the ghost's sad face reminded me of my master when he had been sitting alone too long. He was not so sad when he was with Radovan, or when he was talking with other people. Wherever he was, I hoped he was not alone.

I went to the ghost and sat at her feet. She lifted her hand to pat my head, and I let her. I could not feel the weight of her hand, but my fur tingled where her hand touched me. We sat for a while as Judge Fang spoke to the Dancing Courtesans. They quietly agreed to come with us, but that did not stop him. He wanted to finish his plea.

The Spider joined the Phoenix in a nearby tree and watched Judge Fang swing his arms and clench his fists for emphasis. Soon the Hopper and the Goblin grew restless and began bumping each other. The Goblin pinched the Hopper hard beneath its round body until it screamed. Gust flashed a spark to chastise the Goblin, who rubbed his burned buttocks and leaped in time beside the agitated Hopper.

The wind from Gust's laughter blew back the ghost's hair. That surprised me because I thought nothing could touch the ghost, but also because of what I saw beneath her hair. Her skin was patchy and ridged like a dry ravine. Someone had burned her with fire or acid.

The Virgin gasped and smoothed her hair back down over her face. No one else saw the hidden side of her face. The way she looked down at me, I knew she wished I had not seen it either. I lay my head on the bricks beside her lap, and she stroked my head some more.

Judge Fang had barely noticed the quarrel between the Goblin and the Hopper. He continued his speech without pausing. ". . . after we seek more help in Shanxin Province, we shall convey our forces west to Iron Mountain and support the monks of Dragon Temple as they defend the Gates of Heaven and Hell during—"

"What did you say?" said the ghost.

Judge Fang straightened his robe and stood as tall as he could. "I said we must travel to Iron Mountain to join the monks of Dragon Temple—"

"I will go with you."

"Are you certain?" said Judge Fang. "It seemed that you were compelled to remain—"

"This place is no longer safe. Devils and necromancers fought here not long ago."

The Dancing Courtesans bobbed in agreement. Their lights glowed red and orange in alarm.

"Still, your sudden change of heart surprises me. Is it something I said? Did my presentation move you to join us?"

"That is exactly it," said the ghost. She placed her flute in the sleeve of her gown and stood. The Courtesans fell in behind her, and we turned back to the gate from which we had entered.

Oblivious to the Goblin capering behind him and making rude gestures, Judge Fang polished his fingernails on the breast of his robe as he walked beside the Phantom Virgin. "Tell me, lady, which part of my oration did you find most persuasive? Was it the epigram by General Gar-Sung? At first I thought that might be a trifle too grand, but then I recalled the adage made famous by the Imperial poet . . ."

The Fox brushed against me and tossed her head in amusement. The other kami exchanged looks and flashes, but no one interrupted until we were miles away.

Chapter Twenty-One
Three Grandfathers

The cold didn't bother me. What I hated was all the white.

Most of it was snow, which is pretty much all you find halfway up a winter mountain. Even when the blizzard paused to catch its breath, the sun was a silver coin on a white sheet. The snow glare was worse than the direct light. If I hadn't been walking close behind Burning Cloud Devil, I would have lost the path in a minute.

My claws gave me a decent grip on the frozen ground, but kicking through knee-high drifts was exhausting. I leaned on the ringed staff I'd taken from the drunken boxer. With every step, the bronze rings chimed: *Beasts and kami, watch your ass. Here comes an unholy person.*

"Tell me again why we aren't flying."

Burning Cloud Devil trudged on without so much as a glance back. He'd heard me all right. He just didn't care to answer.

I figured he was spent. He'd been casting plenty of spells lately. Sometimes it was another illusion to let us walk into a town without a fuss. When the night terrors woke me with visions of the boss in a dragon's gut, Burning Cloud Devil would be nearby sitting lotus style, murmuring arcane words. His thumb moved from finger to finger, as if he was counting verses. It was no louder than his snoring, so I left him alone, poked the fire, and tried to get back to sleep.

He'd taken to casting a bunch of spells each morning, and one on each of us morning and night. When I demanded to know what it was, he said he'd warded us against the scrying of other sorcerers.

"Somebody coming after us?" I said. "I thought we were looking for a fight."

"We want only worthy challengers," he said, "not every ambitious disciple fresh out of training. And you have yet to perform the Twin White Palms strike."

He made a couple of good points. Since the business in the cemetery, I hadn't had a fight lasting more than a few swings.

Twice the local governors had sent their armies after us. Burning Cloud Devil had no patience for that. He set me loose to scatter the cavalry, while he called up his devils. Some were man-sized white tumors. Others were made of chains and malice. They tore into the soldiers with a passion that made my giant blade look like a breadknife. By the time Burning Cloud Devil unleashed his hell hounds, the survivors were in full retreat.

The second time, we followed the fleeing soldiers back to their post. Burning Cloud Devil set fire to their headquarters. When the men fled the burning watchtower, he froze them with a blast of frost. At last, the commander staggered forward to challenge him to a duel. Burning Cloud Devil laughed, the power of his voice buffeting the man until blood ran from his eyes and he died on his feet.

That kind of thing used to bother me. Now it wasn't even interesting, except as a warning not to make a move against the sorcerer. I'd have better luck against his dragon.

On the snowy path ahead of me, Burning Cloud Devil stopped. I moved beside him, and he pointed ahead.

"There."

He cast another spell while I squinted into the white abyss. Rising above the mountain's shoulder was a cloud of white smoke against the slightly whiter sky. Beneath it I saw the regular curve of a domed roof and a chubby little chimney.

Burning Cloud Devil shook his hand as if he were about to throw dice. Instead, he opened his fingers, and a bunch of tiny balls floated up. Each swelled until it was about the size of one of the little oranges we'd enjoyed a few months earlier, only faint as gauze and with a blemish on one side.

One of them winked at me.

With a few words and a gesture, Burning Cloud Devil sent them gliding ahead.

"I thought you knew these guys."

"I do," said Burning Cloud Devil. "That is why I am cautious."

We'd climbed halfway up the side of the world to see the Three Grandfathers. They were masters of criminal gangs throughout Quain. All winter they holed up in this hideout to settle disputes from the previous year and negotiate territory for the next. Until spring, they were sworn to a truce among themselves. To keep them safe from outsiders, they'd brought their strongest bodyguards.

It was one of those guys Burning Cloud Devil wanted me to fight. But first we had to ask permission from their bosses.

The Grandfathers hadn't always been so peaceable. Years ago they had a terrific war. Two of them called Burning Cloud Devil in to settle matters, but he didn't like their offer of money. It offended him to be treated as a paid assassin. Instead of killing the third Grandfather as they'd asked, he forced all three to make peace, promising to destroy the first to break the truce. If they were angry with him, they didn't show it. Instead they bowed down and thanked him for his wisdom, promising to repay his favor whenever he asked.

He'd come to collect.

"You're thinking maybe they've got short memories?"

Burning Cloud Devil shrugged. "The only reason they do not betray each other is that they swore an oath in front of their men. They have sworn no oath to me, except in front of each other. No one alone would betray me. But all three together . . ."

"Got it."

We built a windbreak out of snow and hunkered down beside the last of our firewood, which the sorcerer ignited by wiggling his finger. Before the warmth reached our bones, his magic eyes returned. He gathered them in his palm and squeezed them tight, closing his eyes in concentration.

His expression changed and kept changing. I saw surprise, confusion, anger, and then something like terror. Burning Cloud Devil clutched his beard and pulled. Slowly, his fearful expression melted into a hopeful smile.

"What is it?"

"A most unexpected opportunity."

He didn't elaborate, so I said, "Spill."

He furrowed his brow. Even after the better part of a year, the fiendish language we shared didn't always translate. Sure, I understood a couple hundred more

Tien words, but no matter how hard I focused, I couldn't say them. My tongue belonged to Hell.

"Tell me."

"They have a visitor," said Burning Cloud Devil. "A most potent visitor. Forget the bodyguards. It is he you must challenge."

"Won't that cause trouble with your pals?"

Burning Cloud Devil smiled. "No, I can assure you it will not."

"You'll smooth it over with them?"

He shook his head. "You must go alone. I will send my eyes to watch for me."

"How will I know which guy to fight?"

"You will know."

It smelled like bullshit, but there was no point arguing. All this intrigue was wasted on me, anyway. All I wanted was to get back into my old body and out of this damned country.

I pushed through the drifts toward the hideout, pausing only to run my scarf through the jangling rings of the staff. No sense ringing the bell.

Even without the cover of snow, the place was hard to see. It looked like the mountain had devoured a little temple. Its domed roof was the same color as the mountain stone, rough blocks of which formed the foundation. The irregular columns flanking the main entrance might have been natural formations, the round door itself a cave mouth.

From a distance, I couldn't be sure whether the dark creases in the face of the building were defensive slits. The cold was settling in again, and I wasn't feeling nimble enough to do the arrow dance.

Maybe the chill I felt had more to do with my knowing that something inside that lair was what Burning Cloud

Devil figured to be a worthy opponent. Sure, I'd been stirring my pity pot. But the truth was, despite what I'd done and what I'd become, in the end I was a lot less keen on dying than I was fussy about killing.

Putting on my business face, I veered off from the main door. Like a mole burrowing through the garden, I plowed my way over for a better look at the sides of the buildings. There was nothing between the corners and the mountain face. If there was a side entrance, it was well hidden.

I crept back to the front to check out the openings I'd seen earlier. They were arrow slits, all right. But I didn't sense anyone moving on the other side. If there were guards, they had some stealth in them. I kept my head down and listened at each one.

From deep within the building I heard a god-awful racket. Either someone had finally had it with the cat, or else the singer was an old man who'd never hit a note in his life. Accompanying his wailing was some kind of lyre and a drum, both out of sync.

> *Little brothers cheer our elder.*
> *His wisdom guides our steps.*
> *Teach us, show us, Elder Brother,*
> *Lead us to the golden path.*

No wonder these guys met in the mountains. If they made a noise like that in the city, they'd be run out of town.

I moved closer to the main door and stopped when I saw it was hanging open. A few feet away I spied a man-sized tunnel in the snow and a pair of slippers disappearing into the blue gloom.

I reached in and grabbed a scrawny ankle. The snow muffled a few startled cries before I pulled out a skinny old man in the plain robes of a servant. He had a big red circle painted on the top of his bald head. I clapped a hand over his mouth to give him time to calm down. That took longer than it did back when I had a prettier face.

"What's going on in there?" I knew he couldn't understand my words, but I was betting my tone was enough.

"He will kill us all when he grows bored." He looked past my shoulder, and his face wrinkled into a mask of fear.

"Who?"

"The Monkey King."

The Tian and their crazy names. I released Baldy. He wormed back down his escape tunnel and resumed his excavation.

I peered through the open door. There was no one nearby, so I brushed off the snow and stepped inside.

The air was warm and full of good smells. There was lamb roasting in the kitchen, and somewhere were enough spices to open a market. I could also smell perfume, and not the cheap stuff. Beneath it I detected my favorite scent of all.

Women, and plenty of them.

For half a second I mused on the gratitude of rescued women, but it was no good even thinking about it until I was my old self again.

Beyond the front entrance was an antechamber with thick furs on the floor and heavy tapestries on the wall. Ahead of me was another big round door. To either side was a narrow hall full of sunlight from the arrow slits. There was nothing in them but a few abandoned crossbows and stools covered with lynx pelts.

Through the round door I found a couple of salons. They must have been nice little rooms once, filled with stained wood carvings, painted silk panels, vases, and statues. Now they were littered with rubble and the bodies of five guards.

Not all of them were corpses, I realized. At least two were still breathing, but neither was getting up soon. One was definitely dead, unless he had a knack for turning his head all the way around.

I followed the trail of destruction. No surprise, it led toward the horrible music. I peeked around the corner for a look.

The survivors of the attack had gathered in a banquet hall. Lining the walls were red silk tapestries embroidered in gem- and metal-colored thread. On mounts of pillows on either side of the hall sat eleven old servants like the one I'd seen outside. Their miserable expressions told me they weren't happy to sit in the places reserved for their betters.

Wide braziers had been dragged into the center of the room, forming a line of blazing coals. To either side of the fiery path lay half a dozen brutal-looking men and the burliest woman I had yet seen in Tian Xia. Most of them looked unconscious or dead. The others groaned as if they wished they were dead or unconscious. I saw no wounds on them except for deep burns on the soles of their bare feet. So much for the bodyguards I was supposed to challenge.

Or maybe not. Two more knelt at the end of the line of braziers. One was a lean woman clad in little more than a dozen leather straps, each bearing two or three sharp throwing knives. The other was a bare-chested man with a colorful lion tattooed on his chest. Iron claws dangled from his wrists. The woman and the man held their slippers in their hands and exchanged you-next glowers.

At the foot of the dais, three old men capered while singing and playing the instruments I'd heard earlier. It was no mean trick, since all three were bound with yokes tied ankle-to-wrist, forcing them to crouch. Two wore expensive clothes, while the drummer had been stripped to his loincloth. Despite their predicament, I took them for the Three Grandfathers.

Sitting above them on a mound of pillows and furs, surrounded by the doting courtesans, sat the Monkey King.

He must have escaped halfway through receiving a curse, because he was only half-transformed. His body looked human enough except for the tail, but his face was all monkey. He wore silk trousers, velvet slippers with the toes curled up, and an open vest that revealed a wide expanse of golden brown hair.

The six consorts surrounding him each offered him a bowl of wine. They gazed into his monkey face with naked adoration as he drank them down. When he drained the last one, he smashed the bowl at the feet of his musicians.

"Another song," he demanded. "In honor of our uninvited guest!"

And here I thought I'd been careful.

As I stepped out from hiding, the Monkey King plucked at the air and one of Burning Cloud Devil's spying eyes appeared between his fingers. At the same moment, more than a dozen others became visible throughout the hall. With a gesture, the Monkey King summoned them all to a bowl, where they shrank down to the size of grapes. He ate them one by one, smacking his simian lips with relish.

The Three Grandfathers hopped and plucked and banged and warbled. Fear and shame wrestled in their faces.

The courtesans laughed and stroked the golden fur of the Monkey King's arms. Alone among those in the hall, they appeared unafraid. I felt a pang of admiration for the guy. Unless he was using magic—and somehow I didn't think he was—a guy who looked like that and could still make the ladies swoon was all right in my books.

Obviously this Monkey King was the guy I was meant to fight, but something about him bothered me. The way he cocked his head when the musicians played a rancid note, the way he poured as much wine down his chin as into his mouth, all seemed familiar. Even the name I thought I'd heard in passing, maybe in one of Burning Cloud Devil's stories or at a festival.

"Who would like to try to kill me next?" The Monkey King beckoned to one of the remaining bodyguards. "You with the knives. It is your turn to tread the Glorious Path."

Lion sighed in relief. Knives scowled and filled her hands. She threw the first blade as she leaped onto the coals.

The Monkey King plucked the knife out of the air and used it to pick his teeth. "You must reach me first."

The woman drew another knife as she ran. Sizzling coals clung to her feet. With every other step she threw a knife. The Monkey King caught them all.

She faltered on the fourth step and tumbled to the floor on the sixth. There was more pain than fury in her shout as she fell beside the others who'd failed.

At the other end of the braziers, Lion kowtowed to the Monkey King. "All praise to the Fearless Son of Heaven and his mercy."

"It is true I said I would spare the last challenger," said the Monkey King. He looked straight at me and winked. "But you are not yet the last."

Lion's shoulders slumped as he turned to face me.

I brushed him aside. "Don't worry, pal. You can still be last. I want a shot next."

He didn't understand my words, but Lion was only too eager to step aside.

The Monkey King hooted and replied to me in Tien. "Brave words for a foreign devil."

At least he understood me. Why was I not surprised? "Let me get this straight: Whoever runs down these coals to reach you gets a free shot?"

He smiled, parting his vest to show off his chest. Again, something about his manner was familiar. He pointed at the boxer's staff. "Will you kill me with that weapon?"

I felt a guilty lump in my throat for no good reason. I swallowed it and tugged the scarf out of the rings. "Maybe."

I slowed my breathing and concentrated my thoughts. From what I'd seen of this Monkey King, this was definitely a job for Burning Cloud Devil's Twin White Palms.

Assuming I could finally throw it right.

I pulled off my slippers and hopped onto the first brazier. The heat of the coals was nice and toasty after the blizzard. I strolled toward the dais, twirling the staff to let the rings chime. Maybe I could rattle him.

The Monkey King threw back his head and whooped. I'd heard that boyish laugh before. "The first trial is no challenge for a devil who has come in from the snow so long before the spring thaw."

"What do you mean, the first trial?"

Lion leaped on my back, his iron claws tearing into the back of my head. His attack surprised me so much that I nearly fell off the braziers, which I figured would queer the deal. Holding the staff for balance in one hand, I gave him the short elbow. Lion's weight slid off me. He screamed as he hit the coals and rolled away beside his defeated predecessors.

"Too easy," cried the Monkey King. He rolled his hands around each other as his consorts poured more wine into his upraised mouth. The dais rose twenty feet higher, the ceiling rushing ahead to make room. "This is more fun. Come on up."

"You're a rotten cheat."

"Perhaps a ladder will help."

The knife-woman's blades flew from their sheaths, their butts sinking into the front of the platform. Their blades formed a deadly ladder from the ground to the lip of the dais. The Monkey King blew a spray of wine down upon them, and their edges gleamed with magical sharpness.

Climbing those blades was going to be a lot harder than walking coals.

I covered my hand with the sleeve of my robe and touched the first knife. Even under gentle pressure, the blade cut through the enchanted cloth and slit my palm.

Giving up on protecting my hands, I pinched the blade from below. My fingers were inhumanly strong in devil form, but I weighed a lot more than usual, too. Seemed like a bad bet to put my hands and feet on those knives. They'd be calling me Stumpy.

Then I thought of Burning Cloud Devil's sword-capturing move.

I stuck the staff through my sash and slapped my palms on either side of a knife. Bracing my feet to either side of the "ladder," I pulled myself up one knife at a time before reaching up to slap my hands around the next.

Above me, the Monkey King slapped his knee and barked out a laugh. He drank a toast at every rung.

It was hard to appreciate the encouragement. I tried not to look down. It was enough to know that if I lost my grip even once, I'd fall on every blade beneath me. They'd be calling me Mincemeat.

I focused all my strength on the task at hand, but my thoughts returned to the Monkey King's words. He'd pronounced the words "snow" and "spring" with unusual emphasis.

Somebody'd been talking about me. But how would some monkey-faced tough guy end up talking with the ghost of Burning Cloud Devil's wife? And why?

The thought distracted me from my task. My hands slipped, and the sharp blade cut an inch-long slice off my palm.

The why could wait. I concentrated all my effort on clapping the knives tight. It got harder with every rung, especially since the Monkey King kept dribbling wine down on me, making the blades as slippery as they were sharp.

At last I threw an arm over the edge of the dais and pulled myself up. The consorts recoiled as I drew the staff from my robe and struck the floor to make the rings chime.

The Monkey King grinned and offered me the bowl of wine he'd been about to drink. My impulse was to dash it from his hands, but I'd come here for a reason. No amount of hospitality was going to make me forget it.

I let the staff fall to the floor of the dais and focused my thoughts. I sketched the mystic gestures to summon ki into my hands, and I put my heart into it. The power surged through my body. It felt delirious and calming at the same time. It would work, I could feel it. I only had to reach out and press the unraveling energy into the Monkey King's heart, and he would die.

He sat there, smiling placid as a prophet, holding the bowl of wine in one hand while he tugged open his vest with the other, letting me have my shot. He was really going to take it. I could see it in his eyes.

I knew those eyes. I'd seen them close for what I thought was the last time at a roadside inn last spring.

I lowered my hands.

"The righteous path is difficult," he said. "But those who falter suffer far more than those who reach the end."

I took the wine and drank it in one gulp. I threw the empty bowl over my shoulder and was somehow not surprised when it shattered on the floor only a few feet below the dais.

"I guess this is yours." I picked up the ringed staff and offered it to him.

He let it fall casually into the crook of his elbow, as if it had always belonged there. Still he held his vest open, inviting me to hit him.

I shook my head. I'd murdered the guy once before, by accident. After all the blood I'd spilled since then, more than anything else I wished I could take back that killing.

"I'm sorry about before."

The Monkey King's grin softened, and I saw the boyish features of the Drunken Boxer plain on his face.

"Forget it," he said, patting a spot beside him. "Have another drink, my goddamned little brother."

Chapter Twenty-Two
Red-Tasseled Spears

The moment our seniors opened the gate to the Persimmon Court, my brothers raced to the two great armories in the eastern quarter: one for the Six Martial Weapons of Irori, another for the Six Subtle weapons.

Some of the weapons were enchanted or otherwise fabled by virtue of their presence at the massacre at the Gates of Heaven and Hell thirty-six years earlier. Everyone wished to distinguish himself in an advanced weapon technique and win the honor of wielding one. Most had already been claimed by senior students, but in the imaginations of the new disciples those that remained were equally glorious.

None was so fine as the Shadowless Sword. After my use of magic to defeat Kwan and the decision of the princess to declare me the victor, apparently against her eunuch's advice, I felt little pride in wearing the royal blade. Fortunately, the masters left us no time for ruminations. After a quick ritual bath in the winter-cool stream, we donned the gray robes of our elders and immediately resumed our martial training.

With the assistance of the seniors, Master Wu first instructed us in the Six Martial Weapons: the battleaxe, hammer, snake halberd, glaive, tiger fork, and monk's spade. The strongest brothers favored these heavier weapons. Mon Choi demonstrated an immediate affinity for the double hammer technique, sweeping the field of as many as four opponents at once. Lu Bai proved just as formidable with the battleaxe, reducing practice dummies to sawdust so quickly that he was required to dedicate hours of his practice time to constructing replacements to obliterate the next day.

Others were attracted to the Six Subtle Weapons: the rope dart, double crutches, three-section staff, chain whip, and tiger hook swords. In our enthusiasm over our new privileges, none of us thought to ask: What is the sixth subtle weapon?

It was days before I realized that, alone among all the disciples of Dragon Temple, I knew the answer.

In the meantime, Runme proved adept with the rope dart, finally exceeding all other students in one style. Soon he abandoned all effort to develop the other advanced techniques, and pride in his accomplishment smoothed his rough demeanor. Harbin learned to combine the chain whip with a single butterfly knife, giving his attacks a reach they had previously lacked.

Yingjie expanded his repertoire to include the snake halberd and spear, as well as his favored staff. Soon he could sometimes defeat even Kwan with the new weapons.

Kwan took easily to the double-crutches and three-section staff, but he focused more and more of his energies on his Condor Fist style. Not even the senior students could defeat him in an unarmed contest. In fourteen of the remaining sixteen techniques, even against the seniors, Kwan prevailed in every bout.

Only in sword did he fall short. He could no longer defeat me, even without my use of spells.

The Shadowless Sword made the difference. Holding it, my hand became precise enough to divide a falling snowflake, steady enough to catch it on the point of the blade. Even my vision felt sharper, and the elation I felt in wielding the fabled weapon consumed none of my stamina. Aside from any martial advantage the sword lent me, its most miraculous effect was one I had long since thought impossible.

It made me feel young.

The enormity of the blessing was not lost on me. The joy I felt while using the sword diminished even my painful regret at further alienating my brothers by winning it. Without the full heat of my resentment to muddle my thoughts, I gradually began to appreciate the perspective of my rival disciples—even those who had tormented me.

With an eye toward vengeance, Karfai dedicated himself to the tiger hook swords. I admired his tactic, simplistic though it was. With curved blades designed to capture an opponent's sword, the tiger hook swords were the logical antidote to a sword-wielding opponent. Karfai trained so intently that within two weeks he could defeat any other brother wielding a single sword.

With my own thirst to vanquish Kwan so freshly slaked, I felt a surprising sympathy for Karfai's desire to defeat me—not enough to yield a match to him, certainly, but enough to add a few complimentary words after evading the trap of his hooks and tapping the point of the Shadowless Sword on either side of his neck.

"Excellent technique, Brother Karfai."

He sought any trace of insult in my voice or gaze. There was none to find, and at last the muscles in his neck relaxed. He bowed with something approaching respect.

The youthful feeling bestowed by the Shadowless Sword soon turned my thoughts away from martial matters. Within the bounds of the Cherry, Plum, and Persimmon Courts, I sought every excuse to catch a glimpse of the princess when she strayed from the visitors' quarters.

Alas, after the second trial she retired to the Peach Court and had not since emerged. Jade Tiger's reaction to her awarding me the royal weapon all but proved that she had defied his advice. I wondered why she had done so. The most reasonable if unsatisfactory of my speculations were of some courtly intrigue whose clues lay far from Dragon Temple. And yet I could not help wishing the princess were motivated not by guile but rather by affection.

Perhaps even desire.

"There is no fool like an old fool." How often had I seen men forty years my junior demonstrate the truth of that axiom? Invariably the cause of the proof was a woman. Invariably she was young. Invariably she was beautiful. I comprehended the full absurdity of my wistful thought. And yet . . .

Surely I did not appear so old as a human even half my age. Without benefit of a proper mirror, I could not say whether the traces of gray at my temples had grown wider. I fancied they had vanished altogether as a result of the taxing but healthy regimen I had enjoyed at Dragon Temple. Certainly I was more fit of limb than I had been in many decades.

Princess Lanfen's manner betrayed no recognition of the disparity in our ages. She called me brother, not uncle. She had smiled, laughed, leaned toward me as we sat beside her guqin. Against all objective margins of taste, she praised my singing voice. Our conversations, while brief, evinced a promise of friendship, even intimacy.

And she had granted me the honor of bearing the Shadowless Sword.

Upon such slender evidence I lay my doubts and smiled.

Twice I spied the princess, both times in the company of her advisor.

The first time, Jade Tiger turned a baleful gaze upon me and hastened their return to the Peach Court, the one location within Dragon Temple that remained forbidden to me.

On the second occasion, Elder Brother Deming observed my disappointment at their similar retreat. He approached me with a grin too open to harbor hidden mockery.

"Do you know the tale of Chuntau and the fisherman's son?"

He needed say no more. I knew the tale of caste-crossed romance. I knew a hundred more from the countries of my native Avistan, although their outcomes occasionally favored the lovers. Such was never the case in the stories of Tian Xia.

Deming leaned on his monk's spade. His weapon of choice was a polearm with the eponymous blade on one end, a crescent moon on the other. He leaned back on the nearby wall and said, "The princess is far from home, where she never spent an hour beyond the company of her sisters."

This too I understood, but I saw no reason to utter the thought.

At last he clapped me on the shoulder, a gesture that no longer offended me. "Come, Brother," he said.

"Show me more of your sword and spell skill. My father always wished I had a talent for wizardry."

"You are a wizard in the kitchen."

He shot a playful punch to my arm. "You mock me!"

"No, it is true," I said. What little pride I felt in my meager success near the end of my tenure as "First Brother of Kitchen" evaporated when Deming took over. His skill was such that even the fearsome Lo Gau deferred to his authority.

Despite my best efforts to escape, Deming clung to me until I agreed to show him a cantrip. We went to the arcane library in the Persimmon Court, leaving the wall panels open to enjoy the fresh air of a sunny winter day.

There I explained the elements of wizardry, and Deming listened in perfect stillness. Distilling the dreary lectures I had endured at Korvosa's Acadamae into the briefest possible summation, I described the verbal and somatic components of evoking a spark. To demonstrate, I threw a flying scroll to light a candle.

Deming nodded at the effect. "Do you need the scroll?"

His perceptive question surprised me. "You have studied arcana?"

"No," he said without a trace of guile. "It just seems superfluous to the process you described."

"And so it is," I said. Reluctant to describe yet again the nature of my special dysfunction, I changed tack. "Forget the scroll. Show me how you would cast the spell."

He smiled, embarrassed. "Brother, I have no magic."

"No wizard does before casting the first spell."

Immediately I regretted my words. Learning to cast even the minutest spells required weeks if not months of theoretical study, and success required both knowledge and a modicum of natural talent.

Before I could stop him, Deming imitated the gestures I had showed him. He uttered the syllable of fire.

"Ah!" I recoiled as a spark burned my neck. "How—? I can't believe—"

"Forgive me, Brother," said Deming, bowing. "I missed the candle."

"Never mind that," I said. "I am unharmed. It is simply that . . ."

"What is it, Brother Jeggare?"

"You have spell skill, Brother Deming."

The next morning, Master Li announced that any disciple wishing to study the Sixth Subtle Weapon of Irori would report to me for the two hours before sunset. All fifty-three of my brothers joined me beside the arcane library that afternoon. Most found my instruction tedious and soon returned their attentions to mastering their chosen weapons.

On the following day, fifteen students sat at my feet and tried to light candles.

Four succeeded.

The next evening, eight more returned to hear my tutelage. In the days that followed, more and more demonstrated a basic aptitude for magic before some inevitably gave up in frustration.

After two weeks, I had nine dedicated students, each able to ignite the wick of a candle with arcane magic.

Deming was one of the more adept students, but I was dumbfounded to watch the honor of "First Brother of Cantrips" go to Karfai. Alone among the junior students, he had persevered through my arcane instruction. Even before his seniors, Karfai understood without instruction that he could cast the spark cantrip with either a gesture or a word alone. Respect for his aptitude, and pride for the role I had taken in unleashing it, banished the last remnant of vengeance lingering in my heart.

Karfai wasted no time basking in his accomplishment but went directly to Master Li with a plea to extend our lessons. When Master Wu approached me in the Persimmon Court, I winced in anticipation of his displeasure. Instead, he ordered me to forgo further martial training in favor of instructing the other adepts. He made a point of stating that I was not a master, merely First Brother of Spells. I should not presume more than that.

My gratification was countered by the knowledge that I would now be confined to the Persimmon Court all afternoon, preventing me from seeking out Princess Lanfen during the time she was most likely to emerge from the Peach Court. I tempered this disappointment with the hope that she would hear of my achievement and seek me out.

Yet for agonizing days she did not appear beyond the walls of the Peach Court, at least not while I was vigilant.

Only a few times did I spy her, always at a distance, always in the company of Jade Tiger, and always followed by her guardian spearmen. The heightened security was only prudent after the assassin's attack, but I could not help wishing her protectors were more lax in their duties. Only the masters of the temple dared approach as she strolled the compound.

And I was not a master.

One day in late winter, the setting sun cast a long purple shadow across the court and threw the silhouettes of the persimmons against the eastern wall. Kneeling on their rattan mats, my nine pupils copied the spell from the large scroll on the stand behind me. The Plum Court gate opened for the royal entourage. After the appearance of four guards, however, the next to emerge were Princess Lanfen and First Brother Kwan.

Jade Tiger appeared a few moments later, trailing at a discreet distance and followed by another quartet of guards. Kwan and the princess spoke too quietly for even my half-elven hearing to detect their words. I stood for a better vantage, stepping to the side as they passed behind the trees. Reading the lips of one speaking Tien was challenging enough, but their movement and the changing line of view rendered my effort futile.

"Master Jeggare?" said one of the students. He had asked a question I failed to hear.

Deming chucked him on the arm. "Do not call him 'Master.'"

"Indeed," I said, barely looking at them. Across the courtyard, the princess smiled at something Kwan said.

The student apologized and repeated his question, but I could spare him no further attention. The procession made its way to the Peach Court, where all entered except Kwan. He bowed low—not kowtowing, but offering the courtesy of a lord or emissary—and withdrew from the royal presence. Once the gate closed, he dashed back to the Plum Court, the buoyancy of his step confirming my fears that his had been a social encounter.

"Brother Jeggare?"

"Just copy it again. Your brush strokes are too heavy."

"But—"

"Just do it."

I met the murmur of my students with what I hoped was a forbidding glare. Their gazes returned to their pages.

Unable to contain my anxiety, I paced the length of the library steps. It was far too short a distance to sustain an illusion of serenity. I wished to get away, to contemplate the meaning of what I had just witnessed in solitude. But there was no way to depart without causing a greater stir.

A figure flew up from the direction of the Plum Court to scurry across the lower eaves of the Shrine of Irori. It was impossible to discern his identity once he entered the twilight shadows, but the muscular silhouette looked familiar. I caught only a glimpse of him as he dropped inside the walls of the Peach Court, but it was enough to confirm my suspicion that it was Kwan who invaded the royal refuge.

"Continue your exercises." I walked toward the Peach Court gate with as much nonchalance as I could feign.

"But Brother, we will be late—"

"Do not stop until I return." My patience dissolved. I dashed forward, hand on the hilt of the Shadowless Sword.

With the sword's invigoration, my step was lighter than a snowflake. I leaped to the top of the wall, crouched a moment, and leaped again to the edge of the shrine's roof. Beneath the point where Kwan had dropped stood a rectangular building. Passing it on my previous visit I had thought it abandoned. From within its walls I heard panel doors closing and voices rising in anger.

I dropped to the ground and knelt by the building, my ear against the wall. The first voice I recognized was that of the royal eunuch.

"—bold as to take the bait. The princess is beyond your reach. Not even Master Li will complain of your death when I reveal your true identity."

"I am no assassin," said Kwan.

Jade Tiger's fan popped. I wet my finger and pushed a hole through the paper window. One of the guards blocked my view of the proceedings, so I dared to cut a larger opening with the Shadowless Sword. The blade was so swift and keen that it was the work of a silent instant, and I returned the weapon to its sheath.

"In that case, you are a spy. You cannot deny that you have infiltrated Dragon Temple by deception." He moved beyond the obstructing shoulder of the guard, prowling back and forth on the far side of the room.

"Not to kill the princess."

"And yet you were present moments before the assassin arrived."

"I was there to stop him."

"So you knew there would be an attempt on her life."

"Of course," said Kwan. "For too long, Quain has kept the Dragon Ceremony for itself. It is only just that the Dragon's wish be shared among the Successor States."

"And if not shared, then stolen?"

"Not if that meant any harm should come to Princess Lanfen."

Jade Tiger scoffed. "I am to believe that a prince of Lingshen can be trusted to defend his enemy's daughter?"

"You are not a man. You understand nothing of such things."

The affront stirred a ripple across the faces of the guards. Tiger only smiled and fanned his face.

"I need not kill you. If I inform Master Li of your intrusion, he will cast you out."

"More likely he will assign me clerical duties in the Persimmon Court."

"Indeed," said Jade Tiger. He understood as well as I that Kwan referred to my earlier trespass and undeserved reward. The eunuch fluttered the fan, causing the image of the angry tiger to tremble as if with rage. "Dragon Temple teems with puzzles, and

I shall deal with each in turn. Your treachery stands revealed, Prince Tengfei. Defend your life!"

Jade Tiger pointed his fan at Kwan—I could not think of him as Prince Tengfei. The guards closed in, the points of their spears forming a contracting spiral. Unarmed, Kwan stood trapped in the middle.

The spearheads licked at his face. Kwan dropped to his knees, reaching up to grasp two spears. He pulled blades a few inches out of line and shoved the spears back at their attackers. Two of the guards released their weapons, clutching bloodied faces. Kwan tossed up the spears and caught them mid-shaft.

The guards attacked again. Kwan leaped high and dropped down on the necks of two spears, breaking off their heads. The guards cast down their broken weapons.

Jade Tiger snapped his fan and uttered a few harsh syllables: "Tiger Prowl, Crane Dive!"

The unarmed guards stepped forward in low stances, their hands curled for tiger strikes. Behind them, the spearmen held their blades over Kwan's head. He could not leap without throwing himself into their razor-sharp edges.

The unarmed guards attacked first. Kwan held the spears against his ribs, threatening the attackers in front and rear. He kicked to strike the prowling tigers.

The spearmen pressed down, lowering the ceiling of blades.

Kwan shifted his grip and thrust his spears, striking two of the guards in the thigh. He could as easily have gutted them both, but he held back, reluctant to slay royal guards. I knew just how he felt.

The guards drove Kwan lower with their spears. He flattened himself on the floor, turning his stolen spears parallel to his body, and rolled under their feet. Two leaped over him rather than be tripped, and Kwan escaped the deadly circle.

Behind Kwan, Jade Tiger slipped darts from his sleeve into a slot in his fan's frame.

"Kwan, beware!" I called out.

The eunuch turned to the aperture in the window. His green eyes locked with mine, and for an instant I felt a pulse of vertigo. I snapped out of his hypnotic gaze just in time to evade the darts that shot through the window and past the space my head had just occupied.

Through another window flew Kwan, spears in hand. Without hesitation, he let the weapons fall to the ground and leaped up to the roof. I followed his example.

As I lit upon the roof's edge, Kwan looked at me from the opposite end. His body glistened with the sweat of his recent triumph over half the royal guard, a reminder of how far he exceeded me in strength and vigor. If Jade Tiger's accusation were true, Kwan exceeded me in rank as well. Prince Tengfei: I recognized the name from the documents I had transcribed. It was that of the eighth son of the king of Lingshen, foremost rival to Quain among the Successor States.

There was a message in Kwan's stony expression: Tell no one.

If Kwan had lied to the eunuch—if he did intend to harm the princess—I decided I would spend my life to thwart him. I fixed that vow upon my face and returned his gaze.

Kwan's muscles coiled like those of a predator ready to pounce. Yet when he leaped, he leaped away. He took two steps upon the Peach Court wall and vanished to the south.

I heard the clamor of the guards emerging from the building below and fled in the opposite direction.

Chapter Twenty-Three
Five Nagas

Burning Cloud Devil waited for more than a day in the snow for me to return from the mountain hideout. He told me he'd sent more of his invisible eyeballs inside for a look, but I knew the Monkey King popped them into his mouth as soon as they arrived. The rest of the time the self-proclaimed demigod—it seemed the Monkey King had a pretty high opinion of himself—told tall tales as we drank the last of the gangsters' wine.

The more we drank, the more ridiculous his stories became, and the less I could be sure of what happened since I entered the mountain refuge. At the same time, I believed his crazy stories more and more.

For example, he claimed his staff could reach all the way to heaven. Once he'd used it to tip the world to create the seasons. He cheated demons at dice and released the Cloud Horses from their heavenly pastures. When the gods sent Irori to capture him, he slipped away and took a piss on the Gates of Heaven and Hell.

So maybe I didn't believe every word he said, but some of it sounded pretty good at the time. It was, after all, a lot of wine.

After a long delirium, I woke with what felt like the filth of a hundred summer sewers crammed into my skull. The Monkey King was gone, and the survivors of his visit treated me like unwelcome royalty. I waved off the supplicants, but they pressed packages of food and gold into my arms. I couldn't imagine ever eating again, but who doesn't like free gold? When I stumbled out into the blinding light, they kowtowed and thanked the gods as they saw the back of me.

Burning Cloud Devil hopped up the moment he heard me crunching through the snow.

"You live!"

"Not so loud." I cradled my head.

"The Twin White Palms," he whispered. "Did you—?"

"Yeah, yeah," I moaned. "Now shut up already. You'll start an avalanche."

Sure, I hadn't killed anyone, but I was certain that I now knew the Twin White Palms. We'd talked about it at some point, me and the Monkey King.

My goddamned big brother.

I chuckled at the thought. Gremlins pounded nails inside my skull, but my mirth unsettled Burning Cloud Devil. At least he stopped pestering me for the time it took us to climb down the mountain. Maybe he was getting a little scared of me. That could be useful, but I couldn't think of exactly how to use it just yet.

When I woke the next morning, the interrogation began with hot tea and an accusation.

"You did not kill the Monkey King."

"No," I admitted. "But I could have. He just sat there and let me have a shot."

"And you did not take it?"

"Nah. I could feel my ki, though, just the way you described. It would have killed him."

Burning Cloud Devil grumbled and lifted his beard on his wrist. "Perhaps it is just as well you did not try. Still, I need to know you have mastered the Twin White Palms. Only with my ultimate technique can you prevail against the Celestial Dragon."

"And then you'll let me back into my regular body."

"As agreed in our compact," he said.

I still couldn't look at food, but the hot tea was loosening the screws in my skull. "No demigods. No paladins or priests. Definitely no women. Whoever I fight, make sure he's got it coming. Give me a real son of a bitch."

"How about a son of a snake?"

"Go on."

It was his turn to be coy. Burning Cloud Devil spun out his story a little at a time. Over the next few weeks, he told me so many stories of the southern land of Nagajor that I suspected he'd invented half of them on the fly. Even if one in ten were true, he convinced me the world would be well rid of the snake goddesses and their fanatic worshipers.

Among the worst were a group of spies known as the Five Fangs.

Three of the gang were monks of an outfit called the Order of the Poisoned Fang. They were more or less human but still devoted to their naga matriarchs. Each took the name of a snake representing his variation on a serpentine fighting style called Ular Tangan.

Python was a wrestler known for strangling high mucky-mucks in foreign kingdoms. Adder concealed poisoned blades in his shoes, and his specialty was neutralizing guards. Viper was their kidnapper. His nerve strikes could paralyze or activate toxins in the body of his foe. From what Burning Cloud Devil had heard, these guys were all great fighters, but I wasn't worried about them.

The other two were another story. Cobra was some kind of half-human, half-serpent aberration. He was the most venomous of the gang. His double spears injected four different kinds of poison, and like me he had a reputation as a biter.

The real prize, the monster serpent who'd get my special whammy, had no name that Burning Cloud Devil had ever heard. What he did know was that she threw powerful magic. When he told me she was mother to the others, even though they were a bunch of snakes, I hoped he was speaking poetically.

We took our time walking along the base of the Wall of Heaven. Burning Cloud Devil didn't summon his flying fireball once. Instead he kept casting his bunch of spells every morning and night, most of them not on either of us. When I asked, he said he was consulting the local spirits, learning where to find the nagas, who moved from lair to lair as they perpetrated various intrigues against the Kingdom of Quain. Still, all the spells he was casting seemed a lot of work for that.

I had a feeling the real reason we dawdled was that Burning Cloud Devil enjoyed the first blush of spring. Snow still dusted the peaks, but the rivers overflowed and loosened the frozen soil. After a while, the smell of earth and fresh water finally cleared my head of the hangover from Hell.

Traffic returned along the roads and waterways, most of it military patrols and security caravans hoping to reach their destinations before the weather improved enough for the bandits to come out and play. We avoided the first few, but when the provisions ran out we traded a gold bar for as much food and wine as I could carry. These days, that was a lot.

Burning Cloud Devil grumbled that I'd paid too much. "Some thief you are, giving our money to soldiers."

I ignored the "our money" bit. I was surprised that he'd remembered how I got along before working for the boss. We traveled in silence so often that I forgot just how much idle chit-chat we exchanged in the drowsy hour before sleep.

Didn't matter. Burning Cloud Devil might think he knew everything, but he couldn't figure me out worth a damn. I explained it in simple terms.

"When I'm broke, I steal. When I'm flush, I spread the wealth. Back in Cheliax, that's what we call the economy."

"You speak like a eunuch."

While I wasn't proud of every nook and knob of my new shape, I hadn't lost the vital bits. I was still a man, and if Burning Cloud Devil wanted to make something of it—

The sorcerer saw my hackles rise and lifted his hand for peace. "You mentioned economy. In Quain, the eunuchs dispense the royal treasury. Only those with no hope of passing their wealth to a son can be trusted with the king's wealth. I meant nothing more than that."

I relaxed. "All right then."

"It is different in other countries. Most eunuchs in Lingshen work as prostitutes, and in Po Li they are known for their powerful magic. Certain sorcerers achieve their arcane power by self-castration, sacrificing their masculine essence to achieve balance between—"

I glanced down. "You didn't . . . ?"

"No! I bargained with the Ministers of Hell for my powers."

"You just seemed to know a lot about eunuchs."

He loosened his sash. "If you want to see—"

"I really don't. Hey! Hey! Don't do that. By the way, Spring Snow spoke to me again."

Burning Cloud Devil's face darkened. He re-tightened his sash—which is a good trick when you have only one arm—and hastened his pace.

"Third time, actually," I said. "I think she likes me."

He whirled to face me. "You said nothing of this earlier."

"What was the point? You didn't believe me the first time."

"I don't believe it this time, either." He turned away and resumed our march.

I hefted the overloaded pack on my shoulders and followed.

"I think she knows this Monkey character. He gave me the message this time."

"The Monkey King is a notorious trickster. You have been duped."

"Yeah, but before that I saw her at the cemetery. She looked the same as when I saw her at the House of Silks. She said—"

"It does not matter what she said. It was not her. Even if Spring Snow did wish to communicate with you, another entity could alter her message. You are beguiled by illusion. It is child's play to manipulate one such as you."

Digs like that were beginning to spoil my serenity. Maybe I'm not a wizard like the boss or a sorcerer like Burning Cloud Devil, but I'm no chump either. "Who'd want to do that?"

"The Celestial Dragon, obviously. It knows we are coming. It fears the Twin White Palms."

"All right, then why does it send me these visions? Why doesn't she go straight to you?"

"My mind is not as malleable as yours, devil. I am not deceived by illusions of my lost love."

Again with the digs, but I heard real sorrow in his voice. "So you *have* seen her?"

His step slowed for a few paces. "No."

After a few minutes, he picked up his feet and leaned into a good clip. Maybe compared to his, my mind was malleable. But I could still tell when he was lying.

By the time we reached the Seething Hills, Burning Cloud Devil regained his cheerful disposition. Somewhere nearby was a complex of caverns fed by hot streams. According to the spirits Burning Cloud Devil contacted, the cold-blooded naga had wintered there.

I followed the one-armed sorcerer all over the hills, which were already thick and green with new life. The plants grew fast so close to the warm caverns. Steam rose up from narrow ravines and sputtering blowholes. Now and then we stopped, and Burning Cloud Devil peered around to get his bearings.

"It has been so long," he said. "I don't remember which opening leads to the lair of the Four-Waters Turtle."

I gestured toward a jutting shelf of rock. "Why not take a peek?"

"We must not disturb the Turtle. He sleeps late into the spring and wakes with a great hunger. Not even the Five would dare intrude into his sunless lake."

"Big turtle, huh?"

He gave me a meaningful nod, and we kept up the search. At last he cast a spell near a slick granite chimney and said, "Aha!"

"What 'aha'?"

He didn't answer. Instead he sent his magic eyes down the hole. While they did our spying, we gathered material for rope.

"Why aren't we flying down?" I braided a few tough vines together.

"I preserve my magic for the fight."

"So you're taking a hand in it this time?"

"So close to the ceremony, I dare not risk your life."

"Getting sweet on me, are you?"

He shot me a warning glare, but it just made me laugh. Funny, I thought. Despite knowing he could end my life with a gesture, over the past year the one-armed bastard had grown on me. He wasn't what I'd call a good guy, but he had his moments. In the end, he wasn't half bad for an arrogant, drunken blowhard.

I thought of the boss. A lot of folks might have described him the way I saw Burning Cloud Devil, but it wasn't the same. I realized I couldn't picture how the boss's face looked the last time I saw him. Had he shaved that little stripe on his chin? I couldn't remember.

Anyway, despite sharing a few quirks, Burning Cloud Devil was nothing like my boss. No matter how chummy he got while singing or drinking, he was still the guy who smacked me in the chest once a month and promised to kill me if I didn't do as he said. There was no mistaking him for a friend.

Yet the sorcerer had his moments, and I had the feeling he used to have them a lot more often. Spring Snow had loved him. With a girl like that, he couldn't be all bad. Maybe things would have been different if she'd lived.

When the magic eyes returned, Burning Cloud Devil sat holding them one by one, nodding as he absorbed what they had seen. At last he said, "The nagas are here. I know the way."

We shimmied down the rope and rappelled down a steep incline. My devil eyes made out the outline of the place all right, but the shadows drank up all the color. At the base of the slope was plenty of grit. Everything smelled moist and rotten. I took a step and felt a spongy patch beneath my foot.

Burning Cloud Devil drew Snow's silver sword. He set the tip aglow and held it like a torch.

Pale roaches scattered at our feet. Burning Cloud Devil grimaced. "Filthy things."

"Don't be a baby."

The wall beside us was covered in fungus of every color. Blue-veined clusters of pink glistened like exposed brains among hundreds of pale brown lumps that might have been the backs of shorn sheep. A lacy fungus shrank away as I brushed by. I heard it breathing.

"All right, this is pretty nasty."

Following what he'd seen through his magic eyeballs, Burning Cloud Devil led the way down under stone waterfalls, over crumbling ridges, and across fields of white and yellow lime formations that looked like fried eggs. We leaped a narrow chasm, slid down a couple chimneys. We passed through pockets of cool air, only to feel a blast of steam from vents ahead. Where it was hot, green and purple slime thrived. Wherever it was cool, the fungus took over. The stuff grew bigger and weirder-looking the farther down we went.

A deafening screech sounded just around the bend.

The big knife in hand, I slid along the wall opposite the sound and peered across. At first I saw nothing move, but the sound came from a point only feet away. All I saw were a trio of fat mushrooms, each the size of a pig. Air shot out of a dozen fat sphincters across their bulging caps. The ear-splitting piping sliced into my brain.

"Hurry!" Burning Cloud Devil shouted and waved me forward.

I moved, cautious at first but faster as the floor leveled off. The cavern ceiling rose higher. Long black stalactites hung like fangs above us. There weren't any stalagmites below. Instead, the muddy floor looked as though a drunken ox had run a plow through it.

A snake slipped through the wet field. Not a snake but a man lying on his back, pushing himself along with incredibly swift kicks. Had to be Python. I tensed to leap over him as he closed.

Burning Cloud Devil shouted. I was already in the air by the time I made out his words over the noise of the shrieking fungus.

"Above you!"

The man on the ground was the one I was meant to see. Something else skittered across the ceiling.

I twisted in midair. A bladed toe swept past my cheek. It would have cut me, but a powerful grip pulled me down by the skirt of my robe.

Thick arms looped around my waist and squeezed out my breath. I shot back with my spurs, but they hit only the hard stone ridges through which Python slithered. His serpentine approach wasn't just eerie, it gave him good shelter.

Burning Cloud Devil shouted another word. Beneath me, Python's body shuddered and his grip relaxed.

I rolled away just in time to avoid another kick from above. Dark eyes glittered near the ceiling. Adder clung to the wet stone with iron claws on hands and heels. Dripping blades jutted from the toes of his slippers.

He kicked down at me, hanging from the claws of one hand. I blocked the first few shots before I got an idea.

I dropped the big knife. Instead of blocking the next kicks, I caught Adder by the ankles and pulled down hard. He hissed a warning to his brother, but Python lay dazed by Burning Cloud Devil's spell. He stared, horrified, as Adder's poisonous blades stabbed into his thigh and belly.

Adder tore into my head with his claws. I hoped they weren't poisoned.

I hoisted a low punch up into his vitals. That took the squeak out of him. He leaped back, toe-blades snickering back into his slippers.

Adder hit the ground in a roll. I grabbed the big knife. He took one look back at me and ran, taking to the wall and ceiling as he fled.

Beside me, Python moaned. His face contorted in such pain that I drew the wings of Desna over my heart in thanks that he'd taken the dose, not me. I covered his mouth and cut his throat to put him out of his misery. Because I'm a soft touch.

"Go!" Burning Cloud Devil shouted over the din of the shrieking fungus. "Catch him before he can join the others."

Keeping a sharp look ahead, I hustled across the wrinkled floor of the chamber and into another narrow passage. Two steps in, a blast of steam blew my robes up and drenched my trousers. Me it just tickled, but the heat stopped Burning Cloud Devil in his tracks.

I hesitated, unsure of whether to wait. Screw it, I decided. He was barely any help anyway.

The passage opened into a lopsided chamber full of mismatched furniture scattered among puddles and broken stalagmites. Not broken, I realized, but trimmed.

One large trunk of stone was hewed flat and covered with ledgers, scrolls, lighted candles, and a pyramid of human skulls. A tarnished throne, a moldy loveseat, and a stool made out of the foot of some enormous gray beast ringed the stone table. The rest were piled thick with carpets, furs, and tapestries probably meant to hang on a wall. Someone had built a cozy den in this cavern.

A drumroll distracted me for an instant, but I wasn't fooled this time. I rolled forward onto the carpets as Adder's blades swept through the space I'd just left.

Another man leaped out from behind one of the remaining stalagmites, not the direction of the drum. An oily sheen covered his skin. He reached toward me but paused when he saw the knife. The way he held his fingers closed in the shape of a snake's head, I figured him for the one with the nerve strikes, Viper. He moved to the side, trying to put me between him and Adder. I moved with him to keep that from happening.

A third man emerged from a side passage. "Man" was a charitable term, considering his scaled black-and-yellow skin. His neck looked like an ogre had given him a good throttling and left the flesh bulging to the sides. Cobra.

But the drum sound didn't come from him either. It grew louder.

Across the room, the body of an enormous snake emerged from a cloud of steam. Instead of a snake's head, the naga had the face of a deformed giantess. From her ears and one nostril dangled golden rings and jewels. Thick folds of flesh hung like damp hair from her head. They stiffened and rose up in a high collar as she spotted me. She kept coming, yards and yards of scaled flesh scraping against the stone wall. At last her tail came out of the murk, its tip twisting a hand drum to whip the wooden balls from head to head.

I felt woozy, maybe from some magic of the drum. Or maybe it was just the steam finally getting to me. More likely it was the stress of keeping two eyes on four snakes. I shook my head to put it back in the fight.

I heard Adder's claws scrape the ceiling. I snapped a couple of darts in his direction and heard them ping off the stone wall.

Viper took the cue to attack. He shrugged an arm at me. I stood my ground, since he was still ten or twelve steps away, but I felt a blow to my shoulder. My arm went limp. The big knife slipped out of my fingers.

Adder leaped down, but a fiery beam caught him on the way. He screamed and beat at his flaming clothes, missing me by inches as I stepped back. I dropped a heavy kick on the back of his neck. His body stopped flailing and just burned.

"Take Viper." Burning Cloud Devil stood behind me, already casting another spell. Cobra rushed toward him but stopped in the center of the room, mesmerized by the wavering sigil that trailed the sorcerer's fingers.

My arm still felt numb, so I hurled two more darts at Viper and ran after them. He bent like rubber, dodging the steel blades. He wasn't strong, but he deflected my strikes just enough to put them out of line.

Another fiery ray shot out, this time from the direction of the naga. She caught us both in the flame. She clearly didn't give a damn about Viper.

The fire didn't hurt me none. While the naga's minion howled, I tipped her a wink. "Thanks, sweetheart."

I spared a glance back at Burning Cloud Devil and Cobra. The sorcerer had his man locked up in some kind of charm. Cobra's neck swelled out in a brilliant yellow snake's hood, his fanged mouth open to reveal a flickering forked tongue. He swayed to the sorcerer's silent tune.

Viper and I kept trading shots. I caught his on my arms or shins. He dodged and deflected mine. I was stronger and a little faster, but he had both arms and would get past me soon. Before that happened, the naga blew us another deadly kiss. This one was made of lightning.

We both felt that one, our bodies wracked with spasms. All the hairs on my body sprang out in quivering needles. Viper felt it more than I did. I smelled his cooking flesh, its sizzle louder than his angry hiss. To speed him on his way, I whirled around and put a spur in his ear. His eyes filled with blood. Our dance was over, and he fell smoking to the damp cavern floor.

Desna smiled on me then, because the electric jolt brought my arm back to life. I flexed my arms and felt all the power of my infernal muscles return.

The naga uttered another spell. Behind me, Burning Cloud Devil repeated it. I'd heard the boss do the same thing months and months ago—he was countering her spell.

Sure enough, whatever magic she had on the tip of her tongue dribbled away.

That was my cue.

While the magicians babbled at each other, I dashed forward. By the time I reached the naga, I had summoned all my energy into the desire to strike her.

The blow was immense. A wave of soundless force washed over me. I perceived every scale upon the naga's body, smelled every subtlety of her reptile musk, felt every vein beneath her flesh, could even taste her sweat upon the steamy air.

The silence passed in an instant, and I heard her last breath rattle out. I withdrew my hands and saw their white imprints on her flesh. Her lifeless body collapsed to the cavern floor with a sound of so much chainmail.

The big smile creased my face so big it hurt. I turned to make some quip to Burning Cloud Devil, expecting to see him chanting away over the body of his foe.

Instead I saw the inflamed face and open hood of Cobra only a few feet away.

His spittle struck my face before I could even think to dodge. The venom seared my eyes, stabbing deep into my brain. I let out a hellish howl and threw myself to the floor.

"Watch out!" cried Burning Cloud Devil, far too late.

I thrashed and scraped at my eyes, trying to wash them in any poor puddle I could find on the floor. Water didn't help. It only made the pain worse.

A blast of fire burst over me, lifting me off the ground a few inches. Another followed before I could get up to my knees. With the second blast, hot gobbets of Cobra showered down on me.

The concussion scrambled my mind as the flames washed away the sting. For a long time I blinked and slapped myself, trying to bring the world back into focus, but it was no good.

I was blind as a mole.

Chapter Twenty-Four
Floating Mountains

In the light of dawn, I saw my own trepidation reflected on the faces of my companions. With each distant bird call and unexpected agitation of the hanging vines through which we forged, we knew the oni might attack.

Shadows concealed the floor of the narrow passage, but the cloud-reflected light colored the omnipresent mist and imbued the surrounding flora with a semblance of human flesh. The valley air was humid and startlingly warm for so early in the year. Despite our proximity to a complex of steam caverns beneath the Seething Hills, I suspected the uncanny climate to be another effect of the same strange power that held the Flying Mountains aloft.

From a distance, the tops of the titanic pillars appeared to be islands floating among the clouds. Their twisted fingers of quartz-sandstone defied the principles of geology and gravity, yet there they stood trailing thousand-yard lengths of vines teeming with pale flowers where no natural plant could eke out enough sunlight to survive.

Two days earlier, an herbalist and his son had warned us of a roaming band of oni-led monsters in the region. They had spied enormous footprints and found the remains of a camp they estimated included at least half a dozen of the grotesque oni sometimes mistakenly called ogres for their physical resemblance to those unintelligent brutes, as well as twice as many goblins and other fell creatures. The perspicacious herbalists abandoned their mission and turned back with empty baskets. Master Wu dispensed a few coins in thanks for their report.

As we entered the Valley of Flying Mountains, my companions gasped as they felt their weapons tremble. Master Li explained that the surrounding mountains radiated a magnetic force. Spread so widely, the invisible power served to stabilize the colossal pillars but was not so great as to steal away the weapon of an attentive monk.

Curiously, I felt no such drag upon the Shadowless Sword. Whatever rare metal formed its thin blade had to be nonferrous. An interesting quality, I decided, but not so urgent as to demand immediate study.

Master Li returned from a conference beside the royal palanquin, where I glimpsed the delicate hand of the princess upon the window curtain. Jade Tiger remained mounted upon his fabulous white steed, whose magical origin I had long suspected. While I too could conjure a steed, I knew better than to presume to ride while my brothers walked.

Day and night, the eunuch and the princess remained surrounded by their twenty royal guards. I noticed no sign of injury among them and imagined that Master Li had applied his healing touch to those injured in their confrontation with Prince Tengfei. If so, I wondered whether Jade Tiger had revealed the true identity of First Brother Kwan.

A return to the historical chronicle in the Cherry Court scriptorium confirmed that the name Tengfei was that of the eighth son of King Huang of Lingshen. Unfortunately, the only other information I could uncover about the prince concerned his birth and majority celebrations, the years of which coincided with Kwan's apparent age.

The record of his father, King Huang, was more extensive. Among the sixteen nations that once composed the vast empire of Lung Wa, Lingshen vied with Po Li and Quain for dominance. While these three had avoided full-scale war for over three decades, border skirmishes and intrigue were not exceptions but the rule.

Huang's generals regularly alleged that the eunuchs of Quain's King Wen plotted the assassinations of his sons. The princes stood accused of leading their troops into Quain territory under the guise of brigands. Their deaths caused only a brief lull in hostilities. After Huang returned the heads of King Wen's ambassadors, only an unprecedented diplomatic effort by Quain's eunuchs averted outright warfare.

None of these records mentioned the participation of Prince Tengfei in such actions, but the absence of his name did not imply a lack of ambition—nor a lack of desire to avenge his siblings. In the months we had spent as brothers and rivals, he had demonstrated a talent for both combat and guile. It required no great leap of imagination to see him as an agent dedicated to disrupting the Dragon Ceremony that enriched his nation's rival.

And yet I was now certain it was Kwan's voice I had overheard speaking with the princess before the assassination attempt in the Peach Court garden.

If Kwan—or rather Tengfei—meant to kill Princess Lanfen, then he had already enjoyed the opportunity. That she still lived suggested Kwan's true motive was to gain access to the Dragon Ceremony.

The music of Princess Lanfen's enchanted guqin came unbidden to my mind. I could not discount the possibility that Kwan had spoken the truth to Jade Tiger, that he would defend the princess with his life. Whether he did so of his own accord or as a result of the guqin's magic remained to be seen.

The same question applied to me. After stooping to the use of a few minor divinations, I felt sure that I was free of magical charms, but the nature of enchantment rendered me unable to diagnose my condition with surety. A powerful enchantment could cloud my mind into thinking I had cast spells that I had not, or into believing the results of my divinations were the opposite of the true findings.

No matter how I desired to see Kwan as a villain, it was equally likely we remained merely rivals, as we had been since the day we first met. Whether by magic or by nature, we both felt devotion to the same woman. Logically, he should be my ally, not my adversary. Nevertheless, the safety of the princess was in question. Both as a disciple of Dragon Temple and as a gentleman of Cheliax, I was bound to exhaust all avenues of defense—even if one of them amounted to betraying Brother Kwan's secret to our masters.

It was with that motive in my heart that I approached Master Li days before our departure from Dragon Temple.

The aged monk raised a silencing finger before I could speak. In his other hand he held the simple bamboo pole that I had seen him carry over his shoulder every day since we met at the outer gate to the temple. He sat upon a flat rock jutting over the edge of the pool that lay between the first and second gates.

I waited until he lifted the pole for another cast.

"Master—"

Again he gestured for silence. He motioned for me to sit beside him, and I obeyed.

So near to spring, the swallows had returned to rebuild their nests. The mated pairs called to each other as they took turns gathering twigs and dead grass before returning to their chosen tree.

I contemplated the pool. It was not truly a pond but a tiny lake fed by the same stream that ran through the temple grounds. The water was perfectly clear, the bottom clean and sandy. As if brought to life from a painting, it was the ideal of a tranquil pool. Yet there was something missing. With a start, I realized the omission.

"Master Li, there are no fish in the pool."

The old man made no indication that he had heard me. He cast his line again. There was no bait upon his hook.

A squabble broke out in the branches above us. A sparrow intruded upon another's territory, or perhaps two solitary birds quarreled over a mate.

"When I came to Dragon Temple, I thought myself quite old," said Master Li. "I was nearly twenty-three."

While I had yet to see an elf, much less another half-elf, since arriving in Tian Xia, I knew our kind were not unknown in these lands. Master Li had to understand that I was decades older than he, but I suspected my longevity was not the thrust of his argument.

"I became a monk because I quarreled with my brother over a woman. Only by forsaking our worldly passions could we find peace, he as a guardian of Iron Mountain, I as an instructor at Dragon Temple."

Silently I awaited further detail.

"A young man believes the Wheel of Heaven encircles his every desire. Whatever he perceives, he understands only in relation to how it flatters his vanity. To the young man, that which thwarts his desire is wicked. That which exceeds his understanding is a puzzle to be solved. A young man is not content until all the world is arrayed about his feet that he may look down upon it."

I contemplated his words as the Wheel of Heaven turned invisibly around us. Before I felt the slightest glimmer of enlightenment, Master Li rose and affixed the hook to the base of his fishing rod. Only then did I realize we had sat silently for hours, not the few minutes during which I had been aware of the outer world. I followed him back into the inner gate and bowed. As I turned to join my brothers at supper, Master Li spoke once more.

"We are all young men."

From that moment my need to share my suspicions with the masters waned.

Still, I considered confronting Kwan directly. His royal status did not awe me, not here in Dragon Temple, where princes and fishermen and brawlers and counts of Cheliax were brothers. And there was something meaningful to that leveling of status. If a "foreign devil" such as I felt it, how could Kwan, prince or peasant, not feel it too? Whatever differences lay between us, I had no fear of confronting them man to man. Yet beyond demanding an explanation I felt he would not yield, I could think of no effective method of interrogating my crafty peer.

Instead, I concentrated on instructing my brothers in the rudiments of wizardry. Through the early months of spring, they rewarded my efforts by proving apt pupils. Soon all nine were capable of casting the available cantrips and one or two spells of substance. We had even begun to discuss simple tactics for coordinated casting when Master Li announced it was time to depart for Iron Mountain.

We left Dragon Temple the next morning, pausing only to allow Master Wu to remove talismans from secret compartments on the sentinel statues flanking the outer gates. He placed one on a cord around his neck and gave the other to Master Li, who did the same. Much as I longed to know more about the amulets, I dared not disturb the equilibrium I had felt since my silent interview with Master Li.

We marched for ten days before reaching the Valley of the Flying Mountains, where the procession paused so the leaders might consult on the matter of the oni war band. After the discussion at the palanquin, Master Wu signaled the resumption of our march.

It was he who had organized us into nine groups of six. One group included the swiftest runners and the foremost practitioners of the Six Subtle Weapons of Irori. They were our scouts, shuttling back and forth with reports of what lay ahead.

Six other squads supplemented the twenty royal guards in defending the royal emissary. Secretly I wished to be among them, especially when Kwan enjoyed the honor of Elder Brother in his group. His proximity to the princess kept me ever aware of his location.

The remaining two squads were our reserve units, including all of my students of the arcane and two others. One of these was Mon Choi, who took it as small consolation that I treated him as my unofficial lieutenant. Like me, he gazed frequently at Kwan, although the nature of his longing could not have been more different from mine. Despite his many kindnesses to me, he longed to stand beside the great hero of Dragon Temple, not the foreign devil.

Brother Deming led the other group of wizard-monks. We consulted at every opportunity in deciding which spells were best suited to our mutual defense. While my preference was for the often spectacular evocations for which wizards are known and feared throughout Golarion, my students preferred spells allowing them to strike an unerring blow or to jump higher than even Brother Kwan. Heeding the advice of Brother Deming, I agreed that the others should be allowed to enhance their physical prowess at the expense of preparing a wider array of spells. It fell to me to prepare a variety of spells, and so I filled my sleeves and sash with flying scrolls.

A couple of hours before noon, the scouts reported an enormous animal carcass ahead. We did not vary course. A few dog-sized mammals fled as we approached the body.

The remains more resembled a rhinoceros, albeit a specimen closer to the size of an elephant. The other significant variance was a bifurcated horn at the end of its snout. The creature had died recently. Its wounds already teemed with carrion insects, but they were obviously the result of steel blades, not the teeth and claws of a rival predator. I turned to say as much to Master Wu, but I saw from his expression that he already comprehended the evidence.

A deep rumbling shook the ground. Previously silent birds cried out and flew east.

From the west I heard the sound of a man running through the forest. I signaled the direction to my brothers. A moment later, they heard it also.

As the royal guards closed ranks around the palanquin, Jade Tiger stood tall in his stirrups and peered into the distance. I signaled my men and cast the first of my preparatory spells, trusting that Deming had done the same.

The sound of approaching thunder increased. Far above, the treetops shook. Closer still, I heard the scout's body slapping fronds and branches as he ran toward us. He cried out a warning that only I could hear. I repeated it for the others. "The oni come!"

Everyone heard the scream that followed. Above the scout a dark shape leaped through the trees. Beside me, Mon Choi shifted as he saw movement from another direction. Then the trees began to fall toward us, and the first oni burst out of the forest.

Astride a gigantic two-horned rhinoceros, the leader raised a huge glaive above his head and bleated a challenge. Six more brutes with enormous maces ran beside him. They crashed through two squads before we reserves intercepted them. My brothers sweetened their weapons with spells and stabbed deep into the hide of the riding beast.

I loosed a beam of fire upon the rider. The oni bellowed and slapped the flames from his cloak, oblivious that seconds later he would feel the fiery candle of his greasy ponytail.

To either side of the leader, hulking oni swept into the defenders. Two monks wielding hammers stood fast against the charge. In an instant, the pendulum of an ogre-thing's mace lifted one and flung his ruined body into a tree. In the next, another oni trampled the second to moist pulp.

I set another scroll to fly above the oni. Its magic fell upon them like honey rain, stiffening their joints and slowing their charge.

A sharp cry drew my attention back to the palanquin. Still mounted, Jade Tiger snapped his fan. The royal guards returned their spears to point outward. Whatever they had struck fell in a dark clump of silk and black feathers. A glimpse of yellow talons and a long dark beak reminded me of tengus, the raven-headed assassins of Tian Xia.

All around, the unmistakable voices of goblins rose in ululating song. They scurried in after the oni-wreaked carnage. Most soon fell to the staves, fists, and other weapons of my brothers. One shrieked in crescendo as Yingjie hoisted him on the point of his snake halberd.

As my brothers pulled the oni from the dying rhinoceros, second and third waves of goblins and tengus ran howling into camp. Mon Choi roared as his hammers plunged down to pulverize the rider's head.

I threw a scroll to send a serpentine line of fire through the charging monsters. The goblins blackened and perished in an instant. A tengu leaped the barrier with a bark of triumph that soon turned to alarm when the rising flames ignited its feathers. It shrieked out its last moments thrashing on the ground.

A few swift attackers darted past the outer ring of defenders and rushed the royal palanquin. Flinging another scroll, I struck three goblins and a tengu with missiles of pure magic. All faltered, but none fell until they approached the circle of royal guards.

The goblins leaped in a vain attempt to climb the spear shafts. Despite their bravado, none had even a fraction of Kwan's alacrity. Only a few of their severed limbs made it past the barrier of blades.

A few timid goblins balked at the sight of their comrades' fate. The tengus paused long enough to hurl throwing stars at the guards. As the spearmen dodged, the bird-men dashed under their blades to stab with their daggers and sharp beaks.

The princess swung out of the palanquin window and onto its roof, the guqin in her arms. She sat in a perfect lotus posture, the instrument upon her lap.

"Your highness!" cried Jade Tiger. "I beg you to return to cover."

Lanfen ignored his plea. She struck a dissonant chord across the guqin strings, drawing the attention of every combatant, monk and monster alike.

The nearest tengus scrambled up the bodies of the royal guards, too close for the men to strike with their spears. They leaped above the palanquin, daggers poised.

Princess Lanfen's hands lashed the guqin, each stroke evoking a chord more terrible than the last. Witch-fire emanated from her fingers, and the strings flung the magic out in all directions. Where it struck the tengus, only black feathers floated down to the earth. The goblins it rendered into steaming piles of fat and bones.

I stared in awe of her power for only an instant, but an instant is all it took for the enemy to pounce.

A pair of goblins fell upon me, clawing and stabbing. I let myself fall under their weight, rolling as I kicked one away and struck the other a stunning blow to the throat. My momentum brought me back to my feet, where I grasped the Shadowless Sword, struck twice, shook off the blood, and returned the blade to its sheath.

The goblins clutched their throats, gurgled, and died.

The action was complete before it had formed in my mind. Some small portion of my heart wished to relish the moment, but instead I turned in a circle to evaluate the course of battle.

Master Wu fought a horned and painted oni clutching an iron scepter in one hand and a tattered scroll in the other. The surly monk calculated his strikes to stifle his foe's every utterance and arcane gesture. I took a step toward him, but then I saw Runme and three others run to his side to finish off the oni.

On another side of the field, six of my brothers defended Master Li as he pressed his healing hands against the bloodied neck of Lu Bai. Briefly I saw the translucent image of an enormous qilin surrounding Master Li. At that point I understood something of the nature of the talismans the masters had taken from the temple guardians.

The monks of Dragon Temple scattered the remaining attackers. Without exception, their discipline kept them from chasing the defeated foes. Instead they returned to defend the royal procession and tend the dying.

Two of the palanquin guards had fallen. The survivors closed ranks around the vehicle. Above them, Princess Lanfen stood upon the roof, her magic guqin at her feet.

"Help them." She pointed to a few groups of monks still fighting goblins.

The guards hesitated, looking to the eunuch for confirmation.

Jade Tiger shook his fan, indicated six of the guards, and sent them off to reinforce the monks. I began to follow, but out of the corner of my vision I saw Kwan sprinting toward the palanquin. He moved so swiftly that no one else had yet marked his approach.

"Princess!" I realized my mistake as soon as I cried out. She turned to me, away from Kwan, completely unaware of his charge.

I ran, knowing as I did that I would never reach her before Kwan. Unless, I realized, I spared a moment to enchant myself. I threw the scroll that gave me speed.

Combined with the spell that made steel coils of my legs, my magic let me fly far above the guards' spears. I drew the Shadowless Sword as I descended toward the palanquin. I reached the princess just as Kwan's shadow fell upon her face. She saw him then, turning with excruciating slowness as he thrust his staff like a spear.

In that final instant, I understood Kwan's true intention. I too saw the blurred image of a fat, orange oni descending toward the princess.

Jade Tiger snapped his fan toward us.

Kwan's staff deflected the monster's trident from its intended target, the princess.

With only the briefest thought, I moved the line of my blade away from Kwan's breast and pierced the oni's eye.

Both Kwan and I flew past the palanquin, landing outside the ring of guards. The oni fell heavily among the guards, who stepped back to plunge their spears into its body.

The last decisive blows fell upon the defeated oni, and silence blanketed the battlefield. Standing with my hand upon the sheathed Shadowless Sword, I felt all eyes turn toward me and Kwan. I looked to him and saw two wounds upon his torso. As I watched, blood streamed down his belly in a growing torrent.

Kwan seemed unaware of the injury. Instead, he stared at me, his eyes widening.

Only then did I feel the eunuch's darts within my own belly, their razor edges cutting deeper into my intestines with every breath.

Chapter Twenty-Five
The Hell of Dead Heroes

There he is." Judge Fang pointed his walking twig at a corpse hanging from the great black tree. Its noose had slipped down the branch, letting the body lie upon the trunk. Its flesh and clothing had melted together and tanned like a strip of rawhide. I couldn't tell the strips of shriveled meat from the scraps of moldering cloth, but I knew somehow that it was much older than it appeared. There should have been nothing left of it but bones.

It was one of many bodies hanging like rotten fruit.

Some had fallen apart, leaving bones and rusted weapons lying on the ground beneath their dangling skeletons. Others had vanished, leaving behind only frayed nooses of braided bark. Only a few still had meat on their bones. Dark fluid seeped out of their wounds and across the bark as the frost thawed.

The smell was too foul even for the carrion birds. The day before we had seen dozens of condors picking over the remains of a village that had been ravaged by an oni war band, but none dared follow us. Where we were going, Judge Fang said, there were much more dangerous things.

The rocky forest was different from the others we had traveled. It stretched along the base of mountains whose snowy tops had begun to melt. I thought of the cold water we had drunk from the many brooks we had passed. It tasted so sweet and clean.

Smelling the dead bodies made me want to run back and bathe my tongue in the streams, but I hid my fear. Judge Fang often told me I had to look brave to help the others find their courage.

They were all afraid. Even the mighty Four-Waters Turtle lowed like a nervous bull, even though alone he had nearly killed all the rest of us.

The Turtle had been reluctant to join our quest. After a long search in which Judge Fang read many maps to lead us across the land, we found a hilly island in a steaming lake. When the Hopper turned his all-revealing eye upon the island, we saw that what we had mistaken for a hill was really an enormous turtle shell atop a mound of coins.

Even though it had been springtime for weeks, it took hours to wake the gigantic creature from his hibernation. The grumpy Turtle told us to go away until summer, but I told him we needed to reach Iron Mountain in time for the Dragon Ceremony.

Judge Fang asked me to step aside as he filled his tiny lungs and began his recitation. His speech on the virtues of national service put the Turtle back to sleep. I shouted until he woke again, and we took turns persuading him to help us.

The Phantom Virgin played songs on her flute while the Hopper and Courtesans danced to amuse him. Still the Turtle would not stir from his hoard.

The Goblin spat and scooped handfuls of treasure into his pants. At the sound of jingling coins, the Turtle awoke in a fury. We had to fight back.

Gust made a typhoon in his cave, and the Phoenix boiled the underground lake. The Four-Waters Turtle slurped up the wind and the fire and spat it back as steam.

The Whispering Spider tried catching the Turtle in a web, but she could not spin fast enough to cover his cottage-sized shell.

The Fox and the Hopper distracted the Turtle while Judge Fang cast a spell to make me bigger than a horse. I leaped upon the Turtle's shell, took his neck in my jaws, and rode him three times across his underground lake. He bellowed and complained that the nearby snakes would steal his treasure, but at last he gave up.

Defeated, the Four-Waters Turtle agreed to join us. The Whispering Spider knitted a bandage for his neck. Judge Fang made a great show of casting another spell to prevent anyone from stealing the Turtle's gold while he was absent.

The Fox confided that she thought Judge Fang knew no such spell. I said that didn't matter. Snakes did not need treasure, only eggs or mice. As long as the greedy Goblin believed the treasure was protected, the reputation of the Four-Waters Turtle would keep it safe from other thieves. The Fox said I was as cunning as I was brave, which made me feel a little scared of her.

I tried to remember my bravery as we looked up at all the bodies of dead heroes.

Judge Fang lowered his walking stick and harrumphed at the corpse dangling against the tree trunk. "This poor hero has dangled here for more than three decades. He is the last survivor of the Dragon Ceremony Massacre."

The Goblin scratched his head. "If he's dead, how can he be a survivor?"

The Phantom Virgin covered a smile with her hand. Behind her the Dancing Courtesans bobbed and flashed. When the sun reappeared from behind the clouds, all four of the moonlight kami faded out of sight.

Judge Fang raised his head in a gesture I had learned meant a speech was coming.

"Don't be so indignant," said the Spider before he could speak. "The Goblin has a good point."

"The last victim, then." Judge Fang's mandibles twitched, but instead of saying more he filled his pipe and lit the tobacco. For once I did not mind the smell. It covered the stink of putrid flesh.

"I do not see the medallion," said the Fox.

I couldn't see it either. Maybe it had sunken into the dead man's rotting flesh. If so, I hoped someone else would have the job of digging it out. Maybe the Goblin, who already reeked again, even after the steam bath at the Turtle's lair.

We turned to Judge Fang for direction. For weeks he had been leading us to the Tree of Dead Heroes. Here we were to find a medallion that would allow beasts and kami to pass the gates of Iron Mountain and join the guardians of the Gates of Heaven and Hell.

Judge Fang removed the magical tools from his bag. He lit candles and burned incense. He crushed pigment and added water to make ink. He wrote words on a scroll barely wider than a string, crushed it into a tiny ball, and swallowed it. At last he burned a grain of rice and set it on a tiny dagger made of coins, which floated above the surface of his octagonal mirror. He clutched the mirror in his hands and walked in the direction the dagger pointed.

"Here there is plenty of magic," said Judge Fang. "We must search it all to find the talisman." He nodded at

a spot between two green-and-black roots that looked
less like wood than writhing snakes.

"Dig here."

The Goblin plunged into the dirt and scratched at
the damp soil.

At the next spot Judge Fang chose, I began to dig.
The soil was warmer the deeper I scraped. I did not
like the feeling.

Judge Fang walked on, nodding and indicating
more places to dig. As he moved, the clouds veiled the
sun again, and the Courtesans and Phantom Virgin
reappeared. No matter how far we traveled in daylight,
when the sun was hidden, they were still with us.

The Fox tried helping me, but Judge Fang called
her away to start another hole. The Hopper was no
use for such a chore. Neither were the Courtesans or
the Virgin, but the Four-Waters Turtle scooped up a
huge clod with his beak and hurled the crumbled soil
away.

The Goblin yawped and held up a ringed sword.
"Mine!"

Judge Fang opened his mouth to protest, but he
sighed and moved on to inspect the next hole.

We unearthed more scraps of armor and bones.
Judge Fang sent the Phoenix and the Spider up the
tree to retrieve bracers and a steel skullcap from two
of the hanging corpses. He walked the ground with his
mirror-compass until he was satisfied we had found all
of the magical objects in the graveyard.

Judge Fang lay them on a sheet of silk the Spider
had woven inch by inch whenever we stopped to rest.
Beside the sword, bracers, and skullcap lay a leather
jerkin studded with bronze discs, a rod with a twelve-
sided spinning wheel on top, and two jeweled rings.

The Four-Waters Turtle snorted at the loot. None of it was made of gold, the only kind of treasure he loved. Still it troubled him. "Who hung all these corpses here without taking their treasure?"

"The roots of this tree reach all the way to Hell," said Judge Fang. "Hanging from the boughs you see the remains of those who challenged the King of Heroes. He is the one who tried to slay the Celestial Dragon almost twelve years ago. Now he is known throughout Quain as Burning Cloud Devil."

"Burning Cloud Devil!" I remembered the name. "He is the one who took Radovan away in a ball of fire."

Judge Fang nodded. "After he fought the dragon, Burning Cloud Devil bargained with Hell to learn sorcery. Since then he has searched for an apprentice to teach his Twin White Palms technique. Many pledged themselves to him, but none could master his teachings. Here you see the bodies of those who failed him."

The Fox looked up at the meatiest corpse. "It appears he has had no recent disciples."

The Dancing Courtesans fluttered. The Virgin said, "My little sisters say that this Burning Cloud Devil has a new disciple, a powerful devil. It was they who harrowed the cemetery at Nanzhu. Together they travel the country, seeking challengers to test the disciple's skills. Many heroes have fallen to the fiend's powerful ki."

Beside the Virgin, the Phoenix shed a molten tear.

"The Twin White Palms is the only blow that can slay an immortal being," said Judge Fang. "If this new disciple has learned it . . ."

"Then I'll cut off his arm, too." The Goblin jangled the ringed sword. The weapon was so big in his hands that I thought he might fall over, but it looked as light as a switch.

Judge Fang let loose a little shriek. "What have you done?"

While the rest of us listened to Judge Fang and the Virgin, the Goblin had donned all of the magic armor. The skullcap, bracers, and belt had seemed far too big for him before, but now they fit perfectly. Only the breastplate was still comically large on his skinny frame.

"You fool!" said Judge Fang. "I have not had time to determine what magical properties these objects contain."

"Who else is going to wear them? Most of you don't even have hands!"

"You spindly . . . chinless . . . flatulent . . . bowlegged . . . idiotic—!"

"Chins are overrated."

"Don't interrupt!" Judge Fang snatched up the remaining items before the Goblin could touch them.

"Esteemed Judge," said the Whispering Spider. "I do not like to be the one to say so twice in one day, but once more the Goblin has a point. He is the only one among us who is both tangible and man-shaped."

Judge Fang gaped like a carp and stuck his pipe back in his mouth. He lit the tobacco and puffed a few times. "Fine," he said at last. "But no one takes the rest until I have a chance to study them."

"You're too small to carry that rod," said the Goblin. He kicked the dirt. "But I don't want it. It looks stupid."

"Didn't we come here for a medallion?" said the Fox. The Hopper peeped agreement.

"Indeed," said Judge Fang. "I detect no more magic nearby, except for the aura of this tree. I sense an ancient enchantment beneath its bark."

"I cannot hear the souls of these corpses," said the Phantom Virgin. "I should be able to speak with them, but they are hiding."

"Perhaps they appear only at night." The Spider lifted her head. The sun had disappeared behind the western mountains, but it would be light a little longer.

"Perhaps." The Virgin did not sound convinced. She put her ear to the gnarly bole of the tree to listen. "I hear weeping."

From out of the crevices in the bark, dark red strands oozed out of the tree. In an instant they took the shape of human hands and grasped the Virgin's arms and hair. Before she could scream, they pulled her into the tree.

I ran to her, but she was already gone. The Fox was beside me, and everyone shouted at once.

I pushed and scratched at the bark, but there was no opening big enough to force a paw through.

"Gust, Courtesans," snapped Judge Fang. "Can you follow her?"

Gust swept herself onto the tree, but her vapors spread over its surface instead of entering. She tossed the branches, but there weren't even buds to shake loose. The tiny cloud wept in frustration.

The Dancing Courtesans hesitated, their lights dimming to deep purple and blue. Then they brightened and flew into the tree. They vanished into the bark. We waited for them to emerge.

"Let's get out of here before it eats us, too," said the Goblin.

The Hopper honked in defiance. The weird kami threw itself against the tree over and over, but its hoof barely dented the bark.

"Cut it open with your sword." The Whispering Spider pushed the Goblin toward the tree.

"You do it!" The Goblin offered her the sword.

"You're the one with hands."

While they argued, the Four-Winds Turtle lumbered over to the tree. He placed his forefeet on the trunk and pushed his enormous weight against the tree. Roots erupted from the earth, and the ground tilted.

"Well done, Mighty Turtle!" Judge Fang leaped up and shook his fist. "Open that gate."

"A gate to Hell?" whispered the Spider. "Are you sure we should open such a—?"

A great crease opened in the side of the tree, unleashing light redder than the sunset. A hot blast threw us into the air. We floated helpless for a moment before the tree sucked us inside.

Hell was a lake of steaming blood under a black sky. The only light came from the Dancing Courtesans, who trembled above the surface of a dark red pool. All around us, the drowning corpses of heroes reached toward us. They moaned for help, but before we could answer they pulled us beneath the surface.

One clutched my fur hard. I bit his wrist and felt my teeth sink into flesh.

Did that mean he was alive?

Did it mean I was dead?

Beside me, the Fox yelped as more of the living or dead men pulled her under. I bit through their sinews and tore the fingers from their hands. I did not care if they sank to the bottom of the lake. They hurt my friend.

A blinding ray of light shot through the lake. It turned the dark liquid bright red, and I saw the Hopper's big eye blazing. Where it touched the corpses, I saw them as whole men and women.

"Come to me," said the Turtle. His deep voice sent waves through the sea of blood, forcing the dead away, if only for a moment. "Climb upon my shell."

The Fox and I gathered those who could not swim. I set Judge Fang upon the shell and went back for the Goblin. When we returned, everyone else was already safe on the island of the Turtle's back.

There was another island in the sea. It moved toward us, or we moved closer to it. In this strange Hell I could not tell the difference.

The other island had eight sides of eight steps each, and in the middle sat a pagoda. Beneath the pagoda stood a couch on which lay a human in red robes. I could smell the human's flesh, neither man nor woman. About its neck hung a silver medallion in the shape of a whiskered dragon.

When it spoke, we heard two voices. One was the voice of a frightened man. The other was that of an angry woman.

"How dare you trespass in my domain? Did you think your pathetic menagerie could steal from my spoils and escape?"

The Goblin leaped up and shook his sword. "Yeah!"

"Be silent, fool!" hissed Judge Fang.

"No hero that comes within my grasp has ever left."

"August Minister of Hell, we have entered your domain by mistake." Judge Fang kowtowed three times. "Please let us go. There are no heroes among us."

"No," said the Fox. "We do have a hero."

"Yeah," gulped the Goblin. He rattled his sword with a little less enthusiasm.

"Not you," whispered the Spider. "Arnisant."

I stood still, trying to remember where I had left my bravery. The Fox nuzzled my shoulder, and I found it.

"I am the hero!" squealed the Goblin. "I'm the one with the sword!"

"Give us the talisman," I told the Minister of Hell. "Or I will bite you deeper than your heart."

The Minister cackled and tittered in a woman's and a man's voice. She and he raised a hand with nails so long they curled three times. "Drag them down, my wretches!"

The dead heroes clambered up the edges of the shell. The Turtle drank up the blood-red water and turned his head. When he spat it out again, flames shot out, and the shell began to spin.

The Hopper leaped high and crashed down upon the head of a fat hero carrying a two-headed hammer. The dead man's skull collapsed, and his body fell back into the sea of blood.

The Goblin slashed and screamed, scaring his foes more than hurting them. Two tripped over each other and fell back, while the other slipped forward, right onto the ringed sword. As he died, he sighed, "I should have used a spear. I let him come too close . . ."

The Courtesans flew into the faces of the groaning dead. Behind them, the Phantom Virgin played her flute. Her fingers leaped like spring crickets upon the keys, and the heroes gaped and stared.

"My father wanted me to be a baker, like him," said one.

"Woodcutter," said the next. Together they slipped back into the endless pool of blood.

"No!" screamed the Minister of Hell. "They are mine, and so are you!"

The Fox ran beneath the legs of those who climbed higher onto the back of the Turtle. I followed, tearing the weapons from their grips. One left bloody palm prints on my fur after I tore the fingers from his hands.

"I had a dog once. I can't remember his name. Maybe it was . . ." He too slipped into oblivion.

Above us the Phoenix flared brightly, illuminating the cavern. It was smaller than it looked before, with slick walls and a domed ceiling. From the center hung a twitching lump of flesh.

"Strike there!" shouted Judge Fang. "It is the Minister's heart. She and he is the tree."

"No!" he and she cried.

The Spider shot a filament to the ceiling and pulled herself up. The Phoenix and the Virgin flew after her.

The bloody sea churned, and all the walls heaved.

"No, you must not. I command you!"

"This is not truly Hell," said Judge Fang. "By the Authority of the Celestial Bureaucracy, I order you to surrender your domain and all its inhabitants."

"I dare not," he and she howled. "It is our charge—" She and he screamed as the Spider tickled the heart with the tips of her legs.

"Surrender the talisman," said Judge Fang. "Release your dead."

The Minister protested again, but after the Phoenix and the Virgin blew upon the heart, he and she fell to the floor of the pagoda and kowtowed to Judge Fang.

"I and I submit to the will of Heaven and your judgment." The Minister removed the medallion and presented it to Judge Fang.

The tainted waters ran clear, and above us the bark of the black tree opened to reveal a starry sky. Below us, the bodies of the fallen heroes became moonlight.

"Come with us!" I shouted to them. "We go to Iron Mountain and the Gates of Heaven and Hell!"

The Spider returned, and the Turtle rose up through the open mouth of the tree. The Phoenix and the Virgin followed us, and behind them came a legion of fallen heroes.

The Goblin capered and waved his sword. Behind him, the heroes saluted.

"See?" The Goblin leaned upon his jangling sword. "I told you I was the hero."

Chapter Twenty-Six
Master of Devils

After a few flights in Burning Cloud Devil's fireball, we traveled the last few miles to Iron Mountain on foot.

All I could make out were blurs of green and black, leaves and tree trunks. I smelled the thick loam of the jungle floor and heard the distant call of birds. I tasted the skunky musk of some creature we startled, but I couldn't tell you what it looked like.

Burning Cloud Devil held out his golden scabbard, and I grasped the other end. It occurred to me that he pulled me like a cart, but I felt more like the ass.

He'd hoodwinked me again.

The pain had faded, but the venom ruined my sight. I could still make out rough shapes and colors, but everything was smeared like a chalk drawing in the rain. In the dark, I couldn't see a damned thing.

When I closed my eyes, though, my last unimpaired vision returned as clear as day, with details I knew I hadn't just imagined. I saw Cobra's enormous mouth opened wide to spew his poison in my face. Behind him, crouched on a mushroom-dotted ridge, was Burning Cloud Devil.

Smiling.

Once he was done incinerating everything in the cavern with his fireballs, the sorcerer made a fuss over my injury, leading me back to the surface and making a poultice for my eyes. At the time I thought nothing of it, but now it seemed odd that he had the fresh herbs on hand.

Since then he'd changed the bandages every morning. The injury wouldn't stop me from fulfilling my bargain, he said. He would direct me in the fight against the Celestial Dragon.

"It is just as well you cannot see the dragon," he said. "Its holy aura destroys the courage of all but the greatest heroes."

"But not yours."

"Am I not the King of Heroes?" He was silent long enough that I realized he was awaiting a reply.

"You're the king, all right." Of something else, I thought.

"Do not despair. Once you have fulfilled our compact and I release you from this infernal form, your mortal eyes may be undamaged."

"May be?"

"I have never met a hero with your particular qualities, but it seems probable—"

That was about as much as I could stand hearing. The more he went on about it, the more I was sure he had something to hide.

The crafty son of a bitch had set me up. I couldn't prove it, but I felt it in my spurs like a change in the weather. Burning Cloud Devil released Cobra from his charm on purpose. He couldn't have been sure that the snake would blind me, though. That meant he had to have told Cobra what to do and sicced him on me at just the right time. Or maybe he just dominated the snake and did it himself.

The scheming bastard had blinded me.

There was no point calling out the deception. That'd only put him on his guard. He could claim he'd been distracted while countering the naga's magic, or that Cobra's will was too great to keep him bound in the enchantment. Conveniently, Cobra was little more than snakeskin and ashes now, so I couldn't beat the truth out of him. That's one of the problems with wizards, sorcerers, all those types: they're ready with all the answers, all the angles, no matter whether they're made of truth or lies.

What I couldn't figure was the why. How come Burning Cloud Devil needed me blind? What was it he didn't want me to see? His line about the awesome sight of the dragon was so weak even he said it halfheartedly. There had to be something else.

I knew we had to kill our way past a bunch of guardians at Iron Mountain, and Burning Cloud Devil knew I wasn't too keen on wholesale slaughter. Still, I said I'd kill his dragon, and I meant to. Sure, I'd had some misgivings, but as long as he would hold up his end of the bargain, I'd do the same.

Besides, there was the compact he'd made me sign. He hadn't told me the details. Now I realized how he'd rushed over them, and how stupid I'd been to sign what I didn't understand. The only thing I knew, or believed anyway, was that I was in for real trouble if I broke the bargain.

My yellow scroll was one of many he kept in that grimy bag of his. He wouldn't carry them around if he didn't need them at some point. I had the feeling I'd find out sooner rather than later.

"The Gates of Iron Mountain, one of the most magnificent sights of ancient Lung Wa," said Burning

Cloud Devil. I heard the satisfaction in his voice, but he changed his tone. "You will see them soon, my disciple. Once your task is finished and we leave this place."

I showed him my teeth, but I didn't trust myself to speak. There was a powerful mad building up inside me. Best to keep it banked, I decided. Save it for the dragon. Any resolution between me and Burning Cloud Devil could wait until after I was my old self again. Maybe I wouldn't be so strong anymore, but I'd learned plenty of good tricks over the past year.

"The new disciples of Dragon Temple are still hours away," he said. "We have plenty of time to dispense with the present guardians. There are three of note, two of them wandering monks who arrived only a few days ago."

"Just point me at them."

"Do you not wish to hear of the history of the Brothers Li? They may now be masters of Dragon Temple and Iron Mountain, but there was a time when both were the sorts of 'sons of bitches,' as you say, that you would not mind killing."

"Do I look like I give a damn? Just get me to this dragon. I'll slap it up good, and you'll put me back in my body. That's the bargain, isn't it? That's our compact."

Burning Cloud Devil sighed, and for a second I thought I heard as much regret as impatience in the sound. "Yes, that is our compact."

He bolstered us with magic and bellowed out a mighty spell to open the doors. The cool subterranean air meeting the outside warmth made my skin damp and clammy.

I saw dozens of steely glints on the points of long weapons, but I couldn't make out the features of the men who bore them. They surged toward us with brave shouts.

The rest was flame and blood.

The sorcerer opened the way with his fireballs, and I waded in. Even in flames, the defenders were skilled enough to strike me a hundred times. The enchanted cloth of my robes blunted most of the blows to my body. I barely felt the shots to my head until the weight of blood soaking the bandages around my eyes made me rip them from my face. Someone screamed at the sight.

Burning Cloud Devil's arcane fire healed me faster than the men could wound me. Some bloody urgency tugged at my guts. It felt a little like guilt, a lot like pleasure. I was a dark demigod wading through the carnage.

Demigod was the wrong word. I was a devil among the damned.

Burning Cloud Devil's deafening laughter echoed in huge chambers whose borders I could barely see until his magical flames lit them up. That provided enough light to give me a feeling for the space. When one of the poor bastards defending the place put himself between me and the light, I killed his silhouette.

Others I found by following their screams and snuffing them out.

Only one gave me any trouble. Him I had to find by the path of the spells he stung me with. He cursed me in Tien, and I cursed him back in devil-speech. He had a flair for it, and something about his voice made me think he'd be a fun guy under other circumstances. When I caught a grip on his hair, we wrestled for a good five minutes before I got my arm under his chin and broke his neck.

In half an hour, it was all over but for the weeping. It's true what the veterans say about battlefields. Damned near everyone with breath left cried out for his mother. I mused for a second that they'd have felt different if they'd had my mother.

Or maybe they wouldn't.

I silenced a couple with as much mercy as I had left, which wasn't much. After a few I began to feel disgusted with myself, so I quit.

Burning Cloud Devil went from body to body, chanting. I heard him unrolling his scrolls and calling out unholy names. From each fallen defender emerged a flame so bright that even my ruined eyes could see them clearly.

No, it was more than that. The little things I couldn't see in the real world I saw just fine on these fiends. I could see the cracks on their claws and nails, the veins in their bloodshot eyes, every ridge on every boil and blister. All of it painted in fire.

I didn't want to think too hard about the why. Instead I watched as foul things crawled up out of the hearts of the dead.

Some of my infernal cousins were all grubs, chains, and bones. Others had the shape of angry winged women or horse-faced ogres. Still others looked so strange they defied description. Through my damaged vision, they all were made of blazing red fire. Brimstone and smoke stifled the air, and the wails of the damned souls echoed through the chambers they had died to protect.

The first fiends summoned joined Burning Cloud Devil in his rituals, their voices raised in depraved song. I felt the heat of their summoning behind me, and all the light they brought. I couldn't look back down. I climbed up, following the dark.

I couldn't stand it anymore. Feeling my way along the walls, I tripped at the base of a wide stairway. It was too much effort to stand, so I crawled step by step, trying to get away from the sounds and the smells and the greasy smoke licking at the back of my neck.

I found a rail and pulled myself to my feet. No one stopped me, so I kept walking, without any idea of where I was headed. It didn't matter, as long as it was away from the charnel pit below.

Eventually the rail turned, leading off to a side passage. Following the wall, I came to another large chamber. The cool air was a respite from the furnace we'd made below. A gentle tinkling greeted me from above. I lay down and looked up, pretending it was the night sky above me.

As if in answer to that image, motes of light twinkled down at me. I squinted at them a long time before I realized they were reflections off the surfaces of mirrors suspended from the ceiling. My entrance had disturbed the air in the room, and the mirrors swayed and turned on the chains that bound them to the ceiling.

One of the lights grew brighter. I stood to get a better look as the face of the mirror twisted away. I held its edge still and looked at it full-on.

There stood Spring Snow where my reflection should have been. Unlike the devils, she wasn't made of fire but of moonlight.

"Forget it," I told her. "Don't even start with me."

Even now, on the brink of catastrophe, it is not too late.

"I'd say we were pretty damned far past the brink. Do you know what your husband is doing down there?"

Your help made those atrocities possible. He could not have come if you had not sworn to be his hands.

"I seem to remember you came with him last time."

341

That too was wrong, and so my spirit is justly banished from the afterlife. I linger here until the day of my husband's final judgment.

"You should talk to him about that."

You know he will not heed me. Always he has believed it is he who must lead, all others who must follow him.

"If he won't listen to you, what made you think he'd listen to me?"

He won't. But if you refuse to slay the Celestial Dragon—

"He'll kill me."

Perhaps.

"Even if he doesn't kill me, he'll leave me stuck in this body."

Think of who you truly are. Think of what you want yourself to be. She dipped her fingers toward me, and the surface of the mirror rippled like a pool of water. As the ripples stilled, I saw an image of myself.

My real self.

Gone were the long spikes and the grotesque ridges. Gone too was my towering height and ogrish build. In the mirror I stood only a couple of inches taller than Spring Snow, but for once my own height didn't bother me. Still, I saw things I'd never noticed before.

The traces of Hell in my features were more obvious than I'd ever realized. I saw it in my tapering chin, the lines of my high cheekbones, the copper-colored skin and golden eyes. And there were the spurs on my elbows, barely visible through the slits in my sleeves.

Spring Snow smiled and placed her hands on the shoulders of my reflection. Even a loyal ghost wife couldn't keep her hands off of me. I was one handsome devil.

Grinning at the thought, I revealed my riot of teeth. Those give away my hellspawn heritage even in dim light. The sight of them snapped me out of my trance.

"That was the wrong thing to show me if you want me to renege on the compact, sweetheart. I can't take a chance of getting trapped in this body."

Perhaps if you could—

Before Spring Snow could complete her thought, a bright moonbeam shot through the hall. It ricocheted from mirror to mirror, finally settling into one that wavered back and forth, squeaking on its chains. I reached out to steady it. Inside I saw a familiar face.

It was the girl whose face I'd seen on her tombstone the last time Spring Snow appeared to me.

I'm not a big believer in coincidence.

"I can understand why she's here," I jerked my thumb at Spring Snow's mirror and pointed at the newcomer. "But why are you following me?"

I am not following you! the girl insisted. She beat her fist against the mirror's surface, but didn't so much as crack the glass. *I came for my revenge.*

"Get in line."

She tossed her head in a petulant gesture that might have been real cute if it hadn't revealed the horrible burn hidden by her hair.

"What the hell happened to you, kid?"

I am not a kid! I was old enough to be married, before . . .

She beat on the surface of her mirror some more, but she couldn't stir up so much as a ripple.

I glanced at Spring Snow, who shook her head in commiseration. *It is no use, little sister. These are ghost traps. We cannot escape until someone breaks them from the outside.*

343

Help me! cried the girl. *It was you who released me from my grave.*

Truly? said Spring Snow. *It must be that our fates are somehow entwined. Yet as you see, I am as helpless as you.*

Then you *must help me.* The ghost looked back at me. *It was to speak to you that she disturbed my gravestone.*

"What's your name, ki— That is, what's your name, miss?"

I was known as Shuchun. She stamped her foot and showed me a pretty little pout. *Release me from this trap.*

"I don't know," I said. "What are you going to do if I bust you out?"

I will torment a man. I will harrow him. I will drag his soul to Hell.

"Yeah? What did he do to you?"

Turns out young Shuchun had two suitors in life, a pair of brothers from the Li family. Both wanted to marry her, and she chose the younger. Jealous, the elder splashed her face with acid and fled the village to become a monk. The younger, disgusted by her ruined face, followed his brother to the monastery.

But not to punish him, said Shuchun. *They were reconciled and lived long, contented lives.*

"Figures. Only the good die young."

One brother is already damned, his soul sacrificed to summon a devil. The other will arrive soon, and must face me. I will make him pay!

"You make a good case."

No, said Spring Snow. *Iron Mountain is a place of tranquility, the balance between Heaven and Hell. It is not a place for vengeance but for redemption. In our pride, my husband and I disturbed the Celestial Order three cycles ago. All this time the monks have striven to restore tranquility between the gates. You must not tip the balance further.*

"Your husband is downstairs calling up a legion of devils," I said. To reinforce my argument, the footsteps of the damned echoed up from the stairway. "I think the balance is as tipped as it can get."

Please, speak to him. Persuade him. Turn him away from this path. If not—

"Sorry, Snow. It's too late for him." I smashed Shuchun's mirror. "It's too late for all of us."

The ghost cried out in delight, but the next trap swallowed her up. I smashed that one, too, and then the next. The Hall of Mirrors sang with shattered glass. Shards rained down on me until my face and arms ran hot with blood.

At last, Shuchun's ghost flew out of the last shattered mirror. Without a backward glance, she flew out of the room and up the staircase.

Only the mirror holding Spring Snow remained.

Please, she said. *Stop him.*

"Stop him yourself." I took her mirror down from its chains. Beyond its surface I could still see Spring Snow, but she turned her face away. "Yeah, that's what I figured."

The light of an inferno rose from the stairway.

"Come," Burning Cloud Devil called to me from the head of his army. "It is time."

The mirror trembled in my hands. I could have let it shatter on the floor, but on a whim I stuck it into my robe.

"Who were you talking to?" he asked.

"Nobody."

"Then what are you waiting for?"

"Not a damned thing." I fell in line with the other devils, and we marched up the stairs toward the Gates of Heaven and Hell.

Chapter Twenty-Seven
Broken Bastion

As one, Brother Kwan and I dropped to our knees. Blood streamed through our fingers where we pressed our hands to stanch the flow.

That we rivals should perish simultaneously and by the same hand was too much. My first laugh was a painful choke, the second a bloody gasp. All mirth died as my mind grasped the mortal consequences of such a wound. My body slumped to the ground, and I rolled onto my back to stare beyond the leafy canopy at the sky.

The faces of my brothers appeared above me. Foremost was Mon Choi's sweaty countenance, blood-flecked from the destruction his hammers had wreaked upon the oni band. Reading the Tien words from his lips required too much concentration. I favored him with a smile, grateful for his affection, however fickle. It was no fault that he admired Kwan more than me. He did not know the true intentions of the disguised prince, and now it no longer mattered.

In the distance I heard Jade Tiger's cool reply to angry words from Karfai. It was something about "protecting the princess" and "good reason to distrust both Kwan and the foreign devil."

Distantly I thought I should be analyzing the eunuch's tone for deception, but as I felt the world revolve behind me, I found I cared less for how our drama played out and more about seeing the face of Princess Lanfen one last time. If she but smiled down at me, I should gladly stand upon Pharasma's scale and pray my qualities outweighed my defects.

When an intruding presence dispersed the faces of my brothers, it was not Lanfen's gentle visage but the scowling face of Master Wu. He shook his head at my imminent demise. Rather than order me buried, however, he pushed up his sleeves, sketched a solemn design in the air, and struck me upon the chest.

The impact brought no pain. Rather, it divided my thoughts from my body. It seemed a small mercy until I felt his thick fingers rummage in my guts. Strangely, I felt less alarm than umbrage. How dare his rough digits intrude upon the person of a Count of Cheliax?

The absurdity of my ire—and my pathetic grasp for the niceties of status that I had long since lost—caused me to smile, but I heard a sound like weeping. It could only have been my own voice.

Wu removed one of the eunuch's long darts and thrust his fingers back inside my body. I protested the indignity, but my vocabulary had shrunk to a single syllable.

"Ah . . . ah . . . ah . . ."

Master Wu held up a dark red sliver in his bloody hand while someone else began sewing the flap of my belly closed. To escape the pain, I concentrated on the precision of the sutures. I could feel it was sloppy work and meant to say so, but even my lone syllable had vanished.

I wondered what had become of Radovan. My irritation at his failure to find me slipped away. I hoped he would find his way home and framed a prayer that Desna smile on him. And on Arnisant, too. He was a good dog and had been with me far too short a time.

Then I was calm. It was only a matter of waiting, and I was content to do so.

Master Li interrupted me. I heard his whisper as from across a domed chamber.

". . . all I have left. You must help. Join your thoughts to your . . ."

Such an annoyance.

I tried to ignore the warmth of his hands pressing down on my wound. Soon I would see my mother's face, and I had so much to tell her. I liked to think she would have been proud of some of my accomplishments, and only she might forgive my gravest failings.

The heat of Master Li's touch began to itch, and he would not stop his incessant babble. ". . . must not abandon your duty! Your oath is to serve the temple and defend the princess. If Kwan will not give up, how can you . . . ?"

Kwan must not survive, I thought. He was going to kill Princess Lanfen! No, I was confused. That was what Jade Tiger wanted me to think. Was that the reason he struck us both as we tried to protect her? I did not yet know the answer, but no one else knew of the eunuch's scheme.

I could not die before I had unraveled the mystery.

Master Li's voice grew louder and less comprehensible. It faded into the distance until I felt only the light of heaven suffusing my body, scattering my thoughts, and dissolving the last iota of my soul.

On blood-washed decks, I have ordered men to shove the ravaged bodies of their brothers into the sea. In Sargava

I stitched shut the open belly of my ensign to sustain the illusion that he might live without the viscera he'd left on the ground outside my tent. Trudging through the sucking mud of Isgeri battlefields, I searched for my commanding officer, finding only his insignia on a ragged shred of meat.

None of those scenes prepared me for the aftermath of the slaughter within Iron Mountain. The ruined remains of the red-robed guardians littered the inner court. Despite the different colors of our attire, I could not help feeling the loss as if I were gazing upon the bodies of Dragon Temple disciples.

Smoking tracks leading from the grand entrance hall hinted at the nature of the beings conjured from their mutilated bodies. Only black craters remained where their hearts had been.

My recent brush with death gave me some idea of how they must have felt in their final moments. The fissures cut by Jade Tiger's darts still ached within my belly. Only the combined ministrations of Masters Wu and Li had preserved my life—and that of my rival, Kwan.

Others had not been so fortunate. Sixteen of the original twenty royal guards had survived the oni attack, four of them wounded beyond Master Li's capacity to heal before our arrival at the gates of Iron Mountain. Of the fifty-four disciples who left Dragon Temple, forty-five remained.

Master Li knelt beside the body of his brother, the former Master of Iron Mountain. Death had not diminished the resemblance between them. The dead brother had Master Li's weathered skin, white hair and beard, and a familiar look of mild detachment, despite the grievous devastation of his body.

Master Wu dispatched groups of brothers to investigate the adjoining chambers. With Karfai and Deming at my side, I searched an empty armory and a meditation chamber before discovering Brother Wen Zhao slumped over a scroll stand in the scriptorium.

The traveling mystic-monk had been spared the physical debasement of his fellows, but he was no less dead. The brush at his feet was still wet. In one hand his corpse clutched a strip of parchment.

"Burning Cloud Devil has returned," I read. "He has summoned a terrible fiend. Su Chau sacrificed his life to stop it, but he failed. They have overwhelmed the bulwark. Soon I shall step out to face them, but first I must warn—"

Whatever else he wrote was drowned in blood.

"Check the other rooms." Deming and Karfai obeyed without question.

As I recalled the gregarious Su Chau, a cold shadow fell upon my heart. His boisterous familiarity, at first so offensive to my noble sensibilities, had left a void after his departure from Dragon Temple. I wished now that I had heard him tell another hundred stories last summer. Quain and all of Tian Xia shrank a little with his death.

Whatever else befell us at the Gates of Heaven and Hell, I swore in the name of Asmodeus that I would slay the fiend who had murdered him.

Searching the desk for further clues, I came upon an unsealed letter from Su Chau to Master Li. In it he praised the results of Master Wu's martial instruction and Master Li's indirect guidance in nurturing the talents of "a most unlikely foreign spirit." Perhaps, he wrote, this Brother Jeggare would one day prove himself an instructor of the Sixth Subtle Art of Irori.

Dragon Temple had been far too long without a master of the arcane.

The accuracy of Su Chau's prediction tightened my throat. Once I had calmed the unwelcome swell of sentiment, I realized that Master Li was both wiser and more subtle than I had estimated. How often had his frowns of displeasure propelled me toward the course he had secretly intended?

Further in his missive, Su Chau hinted that Jade Tiger was not to be trusted, but he did not elaborate on the reason. I scanned the rest of his letter but found no mention of Kwan, Prince Tengfei, or Lingshen. If Master Li's prescience served him as well in this matter as it had in developing my undisclosed talent for magic, he was already prepared.

The thought was not entirely comforting. I still did not know whether it would prove wise that I had not confided in Master Li what I had learned of Kwan. It is a rare intellect capable of manipulating me without arousing my suspicion. Yet in Dragon Temple both the masters and Jade Tiger had employed me as a pawn to some unknown end.

I considered whether Kwan was a player or another pawn. Perhaps he a was pawn who thought himself a player. The same could be true of me. For all that I had deduced, I still could not fathom the nature of the scheme about to unfold.

How much Princess Lanfen had been a party to the game, I could not know. In my vanity, I hoped she was innocent of intrigue. In my experience, I knew such a hope was foolishness.

None of the other materials in Su Chau's study appeared pertinent to our mission. I blotted the blood from his last note and gathered it with his unsent letter.

Perhaps they would be enough to arm Master Li against whichever royal scheme proved to be the true threat.

I turned to leave, but Kwan stood in my path.

Our gazes met, and we drew our swords with such synchronicity that I could not say who had moved first.

I sought some clue of his intent within his eyes. They revealed nothing but resolve. I strove to make my own eyes a mirror of his determination. At last Kwan spoke.

"What you know, you know. But how much can a foreigner understand?"

I dislike gambling, but it was time to throw the dice. Lowering the point of my blade, I said, "I understand that your mission is not one of assassination but of unauthorized diplomacy."

The infinitesimal widening of Kwan's eyes encouraged me to continue.

"You mean to thwart the plot of another during the Dragon Ceremony. Afterward, you will reveal yourself to the princess to prove your goodwill."

Kwan sheathed his sword. "Among her father's court, Princess Lanfen has long been a voice in support of peace. I would join my voice to hers."

I listened for any trace of deception in Kwan's voice but heard none. Still, I had not forgotten the lesson of his trailing foot. Like any prince, he was full of guile.

And I did not like his phrasing. I suspected there was much more of himself that he would like to join with Princess Lanfen.

I returned the Shadowless Sword to its scabbard. "You have not persuaded Jade Tiger of your good intentions. He meant to slay us both. The question is, why now? With a word he could have had either of us expelled from the temple."

"Not without explaining his reasons."

353

I considered that argument. "Do the temple masters know your true identity?"

"Master Li suspects. One day he took me aside and recited an aphorism about young men."

"I know the one."

"Why did you not confront me after I fought the guards?" said Kwan.

"To what end? Were you ready to confide in me?"

"No, not until I saw Jade Tiger was willing to sacrifice your life as well as mine. I have long suspected you were the eunuch's creature."

"He hoped to make me so." A revelation came to me. "No, he hoped to make me *appear* so to you and the other disciples."

"What did he promise you?"

"Spells," I said. "I lost my book before arriving at Dragon Temple. But that was before the incident of the assassin. Later, when Master Li granted me access to the Persimmon Court, Jade Tiger tested me much as he later tested you."

"You have come to steal the pearl." Kwan's accusation surprised me as much for its suddenness as for its accuracy.

"Not to steal it," I said. "I will beg the king to grant me its husk, after Princess Lanfen has made her wish."

As I had done earlier, Kwan searched my face for any trace of deception. He nodded, accepting my word. "What does Jade Tiger wish? As Lanfen's guardian, he has had a thousand opportunities to murder her."

"He seeks to usurp the ceremony and take the wish for himself." The answer seemed so obvious now.

"Impossible," said Kwan. "The King of Heroes himself tried to do the same, but his wife and he had already consummated their love. The Celestial Dragon offers its heart and grants its wish only to a mortal maiden."

"Perhaps Jade Tiger means to force the princess to make his wish for him?"

"Impossible. Princess Lanfen is as perfect in her courage as she is in beauty and wisdom."

Kwan could have made no clearer declaration of his admiration. I was more certain than ever that he hoped for more than diplomatic favor when he revealed his identity. But he had forgotten one important fact. "Princess Lanfen granted me the Shadowless Sword."

"Only to defy the eunuch. She must suspect his treachery."

"Jade Tiger promised you the sword, didn't he?"

Kwan's fierce reaction told me I was wrong. He lifted his chin in a gesture of affront so noble that I could not believe I had mistaken him for anything less than a prince. Nearly a century of courtly life took over. Before I could stop myself, I bowed.

"My apologies, Your Highness."

"You are not a man of Lingshen. I am not your prince."

"No," I agreed. "But at last I understand you are my brother."

He gripped my arm. "Brother Jeggare, help me safeguard the life of Princess Lanfen."

I returned his grip. "Brother Kwan, I swear upon my life."

We had only a moment to scheme before Master Wu's deep voice summoned us back to the bulwark. Those who remained in the great hall had covered the desecrated bodies of the Iron Mountain Guardians and moved them to a place of honor. Master Li stood beside the shrouded figure of his brother, his fingers working a string of prayer beads as his lips moved in prayer.

I left him to his mourning and delivered the papers I had found to Master Wu. He squinted to see Kwan standing beside me, but his eyes widened after a glance at the papers. Kwan and I bowed and withdrew as he read over them a second time.

Kwan approached the princess. Her remaining guards closed ranks before her, but she spoke a command and they allowed him to kneel at her feet. As Kwan spoke, the eunuch leaned forward to hear his every word.

Just as we had planned.

Far behind the royal entourage, I discreetly discharged a flying scroll. Its magic activated, a ghostly image of a hand appeared above my natural appendage. In a moment it vanished from sight, but I could feel its invisible digits. I willed them fly across the room to pluck the eunuch's fan from his sash.

Years of observing Radovan's pocket-picking technique guided my magic touch. The eunuch's fan glided gently to my hand. Quickly, I performed my intended task and sent the fan back to the eunuch's sash. He felt its return and stepped away from the guard he imagined had brushed against his hip.

I returned to the masters, my signal to Kwan that his diversion was no longer required.

Master Li was returning Wen Zhao's pages to Master Wu. "There is no time for accusations and examinations. We must ascend now to the Gates of Heaven and Hell."

Master Wu bowed. He turned to bellow out our orders. "Gather beside your brothers. Safeguard the princess at all costs. From any attack."

We formed ranks at the base of the ascending staircase. Mon Choi stood to my left, Kwan to my right.

Together we began the long march up toward the Gates of Heaven and Hell.

Chapter Twenty-Eight
Quivering Palm

Squatting on a stony ridge miles above the base of the Wall of Heaven Mountains, I looked down at the Court of Heaven and Hell.

My ruined eyes made out the blurry shape of three giant stone fingers jutting into the clouds. Between them they held a misty smear the size of an Egorian plaza. Along the edges stood statues of weird lions and some scaly cross between a dog and a stag. Those I could see as bright as moonlight. There was magic in them. I counted twenty-two of the things, plus a couple of empty spaces to either side. They hadn't stirred when we poured out of the archway in one of the three stone columns.

From above, the platform didn't look any more solid than the clouds. Fog ran across the surface to vanish over the edges. No matter how much poured off, it never cleared.

"Where are the gates?"

"Patience," said Burning Cloud Devil. "We wait for the princess to open them."

I stood to stretch my back. On either side of me crouched a dozen devils. Like the magic guardians below, they appeared bright and sharp to my damaged eyes. Only they weren't made out of moonlight. They were gargoyles carved out of fire.

A few of the fallen angels hid behind the rocky pillars. Before they went, one with a face that reminded me of a sweet-hearted Thuvian whore tipped me a wink. I knew better, but I almost smiled back until I noticed the grubby devil wriggling in her talons.

"Be still," said Burning Cloud Devil. "They come."

The last dark angel flew up from her position beside the door. Except for the mist-hushed beat of her wings, her retreat was silent.

Burning Cloud Devil did his magic. He'd told us to stay close so his spell would conceal us all, but the only effect I noticed was a slight dimming of the devils beside me. I looked back at the sorcerer and saw nothing. We were invisible.

"Remember," he whispered. "Stay with me until the guardians are scattered."

"Yeah, yeah." I'd heard it plenty of times on our long journey up the stairs. We passed eight radiant archways, and each time I got the same funny tickling sensation I felt when we were first teleported from the other side of Golarion to Tian Xia.

I heard the chime of a gong. It sounded at regular intervals, setting the pace for a march. After a while I smelled the incense. Soon, the first monks emerged from the arch and spread out across the platform.

Most of them were gray-and-white blurs, but some were red-capped black blurs carrying what had to be spears. They kept close to a couple of slender figures I took for women. One was a bit taller than the other, and pale as a ghost except for sparkling gems on her fingers.

They took a place near the center of the platform. Facing them, a couple of monks in white—one short and slim with a white beard, the other stocky and dark—stood with an honor guard of six of their lackeys.

The red and gray fellows looked in all directions. They had to know we were nearby after seeing Burning Cloud Devil's handiwork downstairs. Still, they didn't seem to see us.

The four figures in the center seemed to be the principals. I could hear their voices but couldn't make out what they were saying. Whatever it was, Burning Cloud Devil gripped my arm, muttering, "Good, good. They know the danger, but they choose to proceed."

The ones near the center moved back, leaving only the shorter woman and the white-robed monks near the middle. The white monks touched something at their chests. The moonlight outline of the missing statues appeared around them, trembling like a reflection on water. They growled, turned around a few times, and loped over to their spaces with the others. All the statues stirred, shrugging and stretching their backs: ready for action.

The white-haired monk sang out. I understood some of the words, but he must have been speaking some ancient version of Tien. To me, it was all opera.

The woman replied. Her voice was young and kind of sweet, but the poor kid couldn't carry a tune in a bucket. Whatever else happened, I hoped she had sense enough to run when it came down.

Thankfully, her solo was short. She produced some dark object, sat with it on her lap, and began to play. Unlike her singing, the music from her harp or lyre or whatever was gorgeous. It made me wish even more that I could see her face. There wasn't a melody, not like those I know from back home, but there was some kind of magic in those strings. I felt it sweep over me in relaxing waves. My eyelids felt heavy, but I shook my head to stay alert.

A harsh chord snapped me out of my little trance. Instead of the angelic tones she'd used to lure me in, now the musician tortured me with rank and jumbled notes. The sound made me want to jump down and smash her instrument, give her a smack across the face.

It was then that I noticed the red glow. It came from beneath the misty court, growing in power with every note of the song. I looked up to see a circle of blue radiance over the court. I had a hunch it was a door to Heaven, the other a portal to Hell.

Tien characters blazed in blue and red between the guardian statues. Once the perimeter filled, another ring filled inside, and another, and another, until all that was left was a hole maybe fifteen feet wide in the center. Below the platform I saw a glimmer of deep red.

The clouds thickened. Thunder echoed in the mountains.

Burning Cloud Devil's grip tightened on my arm. "He comes."

The air changed. Something vast moved outside the three stone fingers clutching the Court of Heaven and Hell. It circled us, coming closer with each circuit. Its mass pulled at me even before I saw the indistinct shadow of its body. At last its head curved above the surface of the court. In the reflected divine and hellish light, I saw the face of the dragon.

Its skin was the color of fire, earth, metal, wood, and water all at once. Its whiskers flowed like weeds in a deep current from a face like a child's memory of a lion, a snake, a man, and something from a forgotten nightmare. Tapered horns swept back on its skull, black as the space between the stars. The stars themselves were its eyes.

At first I didn't recognize its tiny limbs as arms, but then I saw the too-human thumbs opposite the claws. Its skin appeared as smooth as a silk gown made of equal parts fire and moonlight.

"Go!" shouted Burning Cloud Devil. I tensed to leap, but he held me back and whispered, "Not you. Not yet."

The other fiends leaped down from their perches. The fliers screamed as they soared out from their hiding places to drop their passengers on the ceremony.

Lightning licked up from the platform, one bolt and then another. The electricity in the air pricked up the hair on my arms. One of the fallen angels screamed and broke apart, the flaming outlines of her body fading as they plunged into the mist.

I whistled low. "They brought their own wizard."

"It doesn't matter."

A dozen eldritch bolts shot out from the ranks of gray-and-white defenders. The flames of four more devils died.

"Damn," I said. "They brought a whole army of wizards."

"Be silent."

All the moving humans were a blur, so I listened for their voices. Most hollered battle shouts as they grappled with the devils. Four or five human voices shouted commands repeatedly. They were the leaders, the ones who'd get in my way later.

One voice sounded familiar, but I couldn't place it. Maybe it was one of the heroes I'd fought, but that didn't seem right either. I blamed the language. Even after almost a year in this country, I hadn't heard anyone other than Burning Cloud Devil speak more than a few times. You walk ten miles, you find a different dialect.

The grublike devils were already gone. They were punks, shambling forward in fear of Burning Cloud Devil rather than under the power of their own malice. Even before the wretched shades reached the humans, the guardian statues leaped upon their tumorous bodies and snuffed out their flames.

The remaining dark angels did better. They kept above the fight, shooting their flaming arrows from a distance. They concentrated fire on the magic statues, sending a few over the edge. Now and then a tongue of lightning or a volley of magic bolts shot up to give the girls a good lashing, but they hadn't brought down another since the start of the fight.

The defenders' spells came from only two figures anymore. The others had to be apprentices to those two masters. I tried to keep track of their positions. They'd deserve my special attentions if they got between me and the dragon.

The craftier devils took on their opponents in groups. With hell hounds guarding their feet, they lashed out with their chains and barbed beards until they tore apart some poor bastard. Then the hounds wasted time squabbling over his entrails while their foes regrouped.

"Why doesn't the dragon help?"

"It has come to give its heart to the world between Heaven and Hell, not to determine the recipient."

"So I can just hit it? It won't fight back?"

"Oh, it will fight. Once it sees it is in peril of its life, it will fight."

"Maybe we should wait a little longer before I go in."

"Yes."

The devils wore away the human defenders. A fallen angel swept down and dragged one off the platform. Another followed her sister's example. The fading screams of their victims seemed like the right kind of music for this sort of fight.

"Do you feel that?" said Burning Cloud Devil.

I did feel something. My neck itched, and I had an urge to piss.

"Something is coming."

Out of the entrance ran a fox made all of starlight. Close behind came a tiny white figure riding a great dark blur of a steed.

A gigantic dragon-headed turtle rose above the edge of the platform, steam roiling beneath its flippers. It shell blazed brighter than the moon as it searched for a target.

Next came some weird one-legged monster, a blazing phoenix, and a giant spider with a woman's face. They brought a legion of ghosts of wounded warriors, no two dressed alike. They didn't advance in ranks. Instead, each one chose an opponent and charged in, crying out his name so it would be remembered after the fight. These guys weren't soldiers.

They were heroes.

The misfit army crashed into our legion.

Among them I saw the ghost who'd interrupted my chat with Spring Snow. She hesitated, gliding above the fray to search the mortal faces I couldn't see. The dark angels harried her with arrows, and she withdrew. Still she circled the battle, her eyes seeking something or someone she had not yet found.

The phoenix shot up to engulf a fallen angel. They clawed and pecked at each other's faces and dragged each other over the edge of the court.

The dragon turtle blasted another angel with steam. She screeched in outrage and sent flaming arrows at her foe. The dragon turtle pulled back its head. The arrows glanced off its shell.

On the platform, the fox and the little man tore through the legion. Wherever they went, they knocked the legs from beneath their foes. The manikin did not seem to do much but cling to his mount. That was the only one of the new attackers that didn't glow with magic light, so I figured it had to be an ordinary animal. Whatever it was, it left a trail of severed devil fingers and torn hamstrings in its wake.

The tide began to turn against Burning Cloud Devil's forces.

"Now?" I asked.

He hesitated before saying, "Now."

I jumped down and made a beeline for the dragon. A beefy fellow tried to brain me with a pair of hammers. I shot him a hard one to the belly and threw him aside.

Two of the red guards got in my way. I took away their spears and stabbed them through the guts. Those white-robed monks were all that stood between me and the dragon. That was all right with me. After the fireworks, I had a yen to see what they were made of.

A big blur of a guy came first. His clothes were white, but I saw his hair as a charcoal smudge. He took a shallow stance that reminded me a little of Burning Cloud Devil. They were about the same size and color, come to think of it. I blinked and squinted, hoping for a better look at his face. It was no good. My blurred vision was better than closed eyes, but not much.

I barely saw him move before he peppered me with strikes. The man was strong, and the first couple of blows hurt. I got my arms and legs moving. He cried out as his fist met my knee spike.

"How do you like that?" I asked him.

He revised his stance. Must not speak devil, I figured. I threw him the big smile.

That was stupid. While I was showing off, he kicked. His heel caught me in the throat. I wheeled away, trying to shield myself with my arms. He followed me close. His fists slipped through my clumsy guard, and I felt a rib crack.

A line of fire came down and set his clothes alight. Burning Cloud Devil had joined the fight.

While my foe did the dance of hot, I gave him a few mementos of our time together. The last punch lifted him from the ground, and I kicked him across the platform. I couldn't see whether he'd gone over, but I sort of hoped he hadn't. We'd have some words later. Up close.

It was hard to distinguish the other fighters, but I spotted the thin white-robed monk. He put himself between me and the dragon. By the position of his shoulders, I got the sense he was holding out an open palm as if it would stop me.

I went in for the kill.

Every punch that should have struck barely missed. The style was all different, but he fought like Viper. He barely touched me, but with a finger he made my fists go where he wanted them.

I swept his legs, but he hopped across to land behind me. When I shot him a spur, he barely touched my arm to pull it out of line. I grabbed for his sleeve to pull him close, but my fingers brought back only scraps of cloth. Figuring to hell with him, I pushed past, only to fall flat on my face as he hooked my ankle.

He was making me lose my patience. I growled a final warning.

When I reached for him again, a white blur ran between my legs. Sharp teeth sank into my calf. My scream could have split stone. The pain was fantastic.

The fox clung to my calf. I grabbed it by the neck and pulled, but it held tight. A punch to the head didn't loosen its grip, so I grabbed the big knife. One quick thrust skewered it through the heart. Still it wouldn't let go. It only whimpered and hung on.

I twisted and pulled until it burst into nine bright stars. The light burned into my skull and left a pounding ache.

The monk spoke at last, but all he said was, "No."

"Wait your turn, old man. You're next."

Then I realized he wasn't looking at me.

"Li Renshu, you stole my beauty and my youth. I come for my revenge!"

The ghost maiden flew down. I saw her face as clear as on the night I visited her tombstone, only now all her hair stuck out like black needles, revealing the ruin of her face.

"Shuchun, I have always regret—" That was all the old man could utter before the ghost dragged him off the platform and followed him down, screaming all the way to the red gate of Hell.

Something banged up behind me. I turned to see that freaky hopping eyeball bearing down on me. A sizzling green spark fell upon its head, dimming its glowing eye. It bounced away in an erratic pattern.

"The way is clear," said Burning Cloud Devil. "Strike now."

I slapped my palms a few times and turned toward the dragon. The reason we'd come here. One good shot, and I could go home in my old body.

I turned at looked up at the dragon.

Its entire body had come through the gate now. Its massive form floated a couple of feet above the platform in massive coils. Until now, I hadn't given much thought to the sheer size of the thing. If I'd known, I never would have thought I could kill it with my bare hands.

Except I knew I could. I felt it in my palms and in my guts. The dragon made no move to attack or flee. Its weird blue eyes looked upon me without judgment or remorse. If it was at peace with dying, there was no reason I shouldn't be at peace with killing it.

One of the damned monks slid into place between me and the dragon. He spoke, but whatever he said drowned in the waves of Burning Cloud Devil's laughter. I'd felt that spell many times before, including on the day we first met. It made my opponent wince and cover his ears. It magnified every screaming pain that had been pounded into my skull.

"Kill him," roared Burning Cloud Devil. "Sweep away the last of these monks and fulfill your oath."

"All right, all right!" I shouted. "Just watch where you're throwing that stuff."

Someone shouted, "Radovan!"

The muted sound of my name made me hesitate for just a moment, but the pain urged me on. One last mook, then the dragon. Then it would all be over.

I squeezed the grip of my new big knife and leaned in for the kill.

Another pair of jaws clamped down, this time on my hand. I couldn't see the beast, but it was bigger than the fox. I drew back the knife for a thrust, but the teeth weren't cutting me. Instead the dog's jaws held my hand and tugged it to the side.

I'd felt that grip before.

"Arnie? Is that you?"

His mouth was full, so he couldn't bark. Still, I knew it was him.

Burning Cloud Devil's magic laugh faded, but he kept bellowing at me. "Strike! Kill the monk, and destroy the dragon."

"Radovan, you must not."

The monk spoke in the voice of the boss.

The pieces of a puzzle floated all around my brain, but they wouldn't come together except in ragged fragments.

The boss was dead, but here he was. I'd seen the body, but now I heard his voice.

Arnisant was here. He'd fetched me for the boss. Or he was protecting the boss.

From me.

"It's all right," I said. "I got this."

"Do not be fooled by their sorcery," said Burning Cloud Devil. "Do as you promised."

I turned to face the sound of his voice. Dozens of figures, bright and dark, waged their battle around us.

"I've got a better idea," I said. I dropped the big knife and drew the mirror from my robe. I turned it to face him.

"Say something, kid."

Black Mountain. Her voice wavered, barely audible above the din.

"Put that away," shouted Burning Cloud Devil. "I will not be fooled."

Husband, she said. *Turn away now. It is not too late. You may do penance for the rest of your years. You are such a great hero that the Ministers of Heaven may yet forgive us.*

Burning Cloud Devil struck the mirror from my hand. I heard it shatter on the platform.

"You have failed me, devil."

"That's one way to look at it." If the Twin White Palms could kill a dragon, they could kill a Burning

Cloud Devil. "I like to think of it as defying you, you motherless son of a—"

Those invisible fingers that had held my life for so many months closed then. They didn't just squeeze my heart. They crushed it to a pulp.

The pain put me on my knees. I had just enough strength to turn my back on Burning Cloud Devil. I wanted to say a few things before I died, and they weren't for the sorcerer. I saw the slim white figure before me and gave him my last words. Turns out, all I had left was one.

"Boss."

Chapter Twenty-Nine
The Dragon's Wish

All the cold of the winter past returned to harbor in my bones as I saw the sorcerer's devil fall and utter its last word. Its body steamed and melted down within its silken robes until all that remained was the figure of my bodyguard, Radovan.

The din of battle faded, yet I could hear vividly such trifles as the hem of my robes snapping in the breeze. My awareness pulled away from me, as though I were no longer myself but some disembodied observer of my fate. Above me sighed the souls of heroes drawn through the radiant blue Gate of Heaven. Below me the essence of fallen devils howled down into a crimson maelstrom.

I longed to rescue my friend's body from the field, but the battle was not yet won nor lost.

Fewer than half a dozen royal guards remained to protect the princess and Jade Tiger. Some of my brothers bolstered their defense, while the rest battled the devils and their hell hounds. Yingjie was a whirlwind of blades, a snake halberd in one hand, a monk's spade in the other. Mon Choi heaved himself back to his feet, blood streaming down his battered skull as he made thunder with his twin hammers. Karfai fought back-to-back with a senior brother, as did a few other desperate pairs. Calling out instructions as they fought, Kwan and Deming assumed command in the absence of the injured Master Wu.

Venerable Master Li was gone. There would be no one to heal our injured.

Assuming any survived.

We would have lost already except for the astonishing appearance of the kami. Despite reinforcement from the gates' own guardian foo lions and qilin, as well as those brought by the temple masters, the kami had suffered their own losses.

Radovan—or rather, the devil he had been—smashed the fox into nine tiny fragments of itself, each too feeble to pose a threat to the forces of Hell. The enormous spider lay near the edge of the platform, its broken legs twitching as an insect-headed mite tended its wounds. The dragon turtle moved with agonizing slowness, a rime of frost covering its massive shell. A miniature storm cloud rained sleet down upon the foes of a screaming goblin-thing who slashed with a great ringed sword, flung porcupine needles from its back, and buffeted foes off the platform with gales of its noxious breath.

Arnisant came to my side. His presence would have been a comfort, if comfort had not died with Radovan. Still, the hound was an advantage even in a futile struggle. I showed him the sign for stay.

The one-armed sorcerer who had killed Radovan stared at his clenched fist. Gradually he released it to gaze upon his open palm. When he lifted his gaze to the dragon behind me, I knew there was ice in his heart.

I intended to shatter it.

The Shadowless Sword in hand, I flew toward him. He barely seemed to move, but when my blade should have pierced his heart, he was elsewhere. His open hand struck my chest and hurled me backward through the air.

My head struck the platform, and I slid across the mist-slick marble toward the brink. First my arm, then my shoulder went over.

An unshakeable grip caught my robe and pulled me back from doom. Arnisant butted my face with his massive head. The stench of Hell was on his breath from fighting. I welcomed its awful pong, for it shook the confusion from my brain.

Nearby, Master Wu groaned as he struggled to sit upright. Blood streamed from his ears and nose, and he held a broken arm against his chest. He drew in a rattling breath and bellowed, "Burning Cloud Devil!"

The object of his cry was the one-armed man. The Shadowless Sword was in his hand. Not only had he batted me away as if I were a child, but he had stolen the blade that Princess Lanfen had entrusted to me.

Burning Cloud Devil bent his thick legs and flew toward the Celestial Dragon.

Every surviving monk ran toward him, but not even Kwan could come within striking distance before the peerless blade descended. It sliced through the scales as if they were no stronger than paper. The dragon's chest parted to reveal an iridescent orb within.

Its heart was the size of a man's head, its pebbled surface radiant with the holy energy contained within. It pulsed, and I felt my own heartbeat match its rhythm.

Excepting only the dragon and Burning Cloud Devil, everyone screamed in sympathetic pain. Two voices rose high above the din.

Princess Lanfen floated above the center of the platform, suspended by some invisible power. Exquisite light radiated from her breast as an unseen force slit her chest and pulled open the wound to reveal her beating heart. All the sinews and arteries of her mortal body withdrew from the life-sustaining organ, which pulsed in synchronicity with the dragon's own.

Jade Tiger also rose from the court floor. As the cloth wrapping the eunuch's breast parted, it flew away to reveal the secret I had never suspected.

Jade Tiger was a woman.

The dragon's voice was thunder. *What virgin offers her heart for mine?*

"I do!" cried Jade Tiger. "My wish is to rule as the Queen of Quain."

With her robes in disarray and the heavy cloth that had bound her breasts torn free, the truth was suddenly obvious. Her voice, always soft, was now undeniably feminine, as were the smooth jawline and perfect skin I had mistakenly taken for evidence of youthful castration.

It made sense. No one approaching a royal court— let alone a member of the royal family—could ever hope to shroud herself in illusions. Such magic would be revealed in an instant by the magical wards and guardians common to such places. Yet to disguise one's self through purely physical means would be so simple as to be—

"I offer my heart." The voice of Princess Lanfen rang out clear and strong, despite the dreadful vulnerability of her body. "My wish is for peace among all the warring states of Lung Wa."

Two virgins— The dragon's voice faltered as its heart cracked in half, forming two perfect hemispheres.

374

"Be silent, both of you!" Burning Cloud Devil pointed the Shadowless Sword at each of the women in turn. "I am the one who opened your heart. These girls are but the sacrifice. Grant my wish, or I will kill them both and send you down to Hell."

"He can't," croaked Master Wu.

What is thy wish?

The sorcerer's eyes flashed in triumph. "Reunite me with Spring Snow, my beloved wife!"

The dragon raised its face to the sky, its brilliant blue eyes casting beams through the clouds and beyond. All on the platform stared in wonder as it communed with the Court of Heaven. Around us, the fighting subsided as mortal and kami and devil alike stared in awe at the celestial emissary. It hovered there for minutes that crawled like hours.

Black Mountain . . . Burning Cloud Devil, Heaven grants your wish.

"Do not toy with me, wyrm." The sorcerer stepped toward Princess Lanfen. Kwan and I put ourselves in his path. "If I destroy these mortal hearts, you die, if only until the next ceremony."

The dragon's head slumped, its strength spent. The twin hemispheres of its heart spilled out of its chest and clattered to the court floor.

Released from the dragon's magic, the maidens floated down as well. Kwan and I caught Lanfen. The mouth of her bloodless wound trembled and began to close. "Take me to the dragon quickly. It must not perish."

We carried her to the dragon, but Burning Cloud Devil stood in our way.

Kwan struck first, moving with incredible speed. He leaped past the point of the Shadowless Sword and

375

struck Burning Cloud Devil before his foe could respond. The bearded man's expression belied his surprise, but from his open mouth boomed his terrible laughter. The sound battered Kwan down to the platform and pummeled my hearing. I felt the warmth of blood fill my ears and nose.

I threw a flying scroll and felt an inferno swell within my belly. With a mighty shout, I let the fire rush out of my mouth and into the sorcerer's face. The blast set fire to his clothes and hair. He slapped at them with his arm, but he refused to relinquish the Shadowless Sword.

"I have seen your face in dreams," he growled at me, still hovering above the platform. "Your meddling cost me my disciple and my revenge."

Before I could comprehend his meaning, his face was only inches from mine. He displayed a horrible grimace of pain and triumph. I smelled his sour breath and felt the heat of his sweating body.

I felt the blade of the Shadowless Sword where it transfixed my chest.

"Brother Jeggare!" Kwan and the princess cried out. I heard the shriek of the last devil as one of my brothers cast him back to Hell.

Burning Cloud Devil pulled back the sword, but I gripped his hand tight. He tugged again. I knew my failing strength could not defy his a third time.

"Hurry, Prince Tengfei," said Lanfen. "Give my heart to the dragon."

"But Princess—"

She cut off his protest with a gesture. He reached into her chest and lifted her heart.

Burning Cloud Devil jerked the sword from my own.

Kwan leaped up to the dragon and placed the princess's beating heart in its breast. As he fell back toward the platform, Burning Cloud Devil raised the Shadowless Sword to strike.

"Husband." A calm voice called from the center of the platform.

"Snow!" The sorcerer dropped the sword. I fell back hard upon one half of the dragon's sundered heart. I turned my head toward the new voice.

She was a young woman, yet her eyes spoke of decades of sorrow. Her simple beauty spoke of peasant origins, but there was a charm about her overlapping tooth. She held her head with the perfect equilibrium of a woman devoid of pride and pretense.

She held her hand out toward Burning Cloud Devil. "Come, Black Mountain. The dragon grants your wish."

"It is no illusion." The sorcerer stared in disbelief. He ran to her and knelt at her feet.

She placed a hand upon his head as he embraced her. She stroked his hair, but her gaze swept over the ruins of our battlefield. When she looked upon Radovan's body, an expression of mourning darkened her eyes. At last she looked upon me, and I felt an apology in her face. Still she said nothing.

The mists at her feet parted, revealing an abyss ringed with black clouds and indigo lightning. Her skin crackled and blackened, peeling away to reveal the ravaged flesh of a damned soul.

"No!" howled Burning Cloud Devil. His flesh blistered. Flames sprang up in his hair.

"Hush, darling," she hissed through lipless jaws. The dark vortex sucked them through the platform and down toward Hell. "Together . . . forever . . ."

The last moment of their tragedy might have been touching had I a few more moments of life to imagine its previous acts. But beside me, the princess was dying.

With my waning strength, and against all hope, I tipped half of the dragon's heart into her chest.

Upon touching the princess, the protoplasmic contents of the half-pearl slid out like an oyster, leaving the empty shell behind. The celestial substance wriggled and formed branches reaching out to her veins and arteries, molding itself to the cavern of her chest. I watched as the wound sealed itself once more, and the color of life returned to her skin.

"Not her," croaked Jade Tiger's voice. "Me . . ."

I watched helplessly as Jade Tiger flicked her deadly fan at Lanfen.

Swiftly Kwan put himself in the path of the darts. They barely bruised his skin as the blunt ends struck.

Jade Tiger hissed her anger as she realized what had happened. The first thing I had done with her stolen fan was to invert the darts in its spine.

She gasped an order to the royal guards and snapped the fan open to cover her mouth.

The resulting blast destroyed her face even as it snapped back her head to break her neck.

Kwan stared at the gruesome death of the false eunuch before he turned to me, a mixture of horror and appreciation on his face. Apart from me, he alone knew that I had painted the explosive sigils upon her fan.

I smelled Arnisant's breath and reached out to stroke his fur. "Good dog."

Kwan knelt beside me. He pressed his hand upon my wound, but there was no stanching the flow of blood.

Another hand touched me, this one small and warm. It was a gesture for which I had often longed, but I felt no thrill in it now, only a waning regret.

"Brother Jeggare, you must live," said Princess Lanfen. The pearlescent glow of the dragon's magic suffused her skin. She appeared to me to be an angel come to collect me for Pharasma's judgment.

"Bury me beside . . . the one who defied . . . Burning Cloud Devil. All honors to him."

"To that devil?" Kwan's voice was incredulous.

I tried to shake my head, but Kwan gripped my face and held it fast. The white light grew brighter, and I felt Lanfen's hands intruding upon my wound. Whatever she did there felt warm for an instant, but then all warmth drained away.

"Not a devil," I said. "My brother."

Chapter Thirty
Return to the West

Nowhere had I encountered so many different smells as in Lanming, the city we visited after the terrible day at the Gates of Heaven and Hell.

My master had taken me to towns and cities before, but only one was so big, and it was not nearly so full of people. There were parades with music on every street, and the corners crackled with fireworks. The Goblin would have loved it.

None of the other kami dared to enter the city. We said our farewells outside the gate.

"Come with us," said Judge Fang. "I will appoint you Marshal of the Northern Kami."

"A dog marshal of kami?" the Goblin snorted. "That's stupid. He's not even really one of us."

"Arnisant is a great hero among the beasts," said the Whispering Spider. It had taken a long time, but she had woven casts around her six broken legs.

The Hopper peeped agreement.

"Well, I'm a great hero among the kami." The Goblin puffed out his chest and leaned on his mighty sword. We all agreed he was right, but Gust wet him with her laughter.

"We will send your regards to the Phoenix and the Four-Winds Turtle," Judge Fang promised.

Those most powerful among our army had left us as soon as we emerged from Iron Mountain. The phoenix seemed sadder than ever after the battle. The Turtle was anxious to resume his vigil over his treasure trove.

I saw Stone Guardian Chu and Bronze Sentinel Wing again, too. They were among the defenders of the Dragon Ceremony. Afterward they remained at the Court of Heaven and Hell, taking the places of two of their brothers who had died.

No one saw what became of the Dancing Courtesans. I was afraid they had gone searching for the Phantom Virgin and couldn't find their way back. Not even Judge Fang could explain why the Virgin dragged the old man down through the Gate of Hell. When I asked, the Phoenix shed a tear. The others looked away. I knew better than to ask again.

I nuzzled the faces of the nine little kits. It would have been good to see the Fox again, but it would have been harder to say goodbye to her. When I thought about it, I felt like running away.

I would miss all of them, even the smelly Goblin. But it was time to go.

I had another job.

The trail was easy to follow, even though the streets were crowded and he had not been on fire. Men and women jumped away as I ran into the house and up the stairs. A naked man ran out of one of the rooms shouting that he had been robbed, but I could smell that he was lying.

My quarry sat at a low table with three women who smelled of perfume.

"Arnie, this ain't a good time, pal."

One of the women screamed when she saw me. She spilled a pot of tea all over Radovan's lap. He jumped up, slapping his scalded legs and shouting curses. Then he froze and squeezed his brows together.

"That really hurt." He turned slowly toward the woman with the teapot. "You burned me!"

The women recoiled, but Radovan grabbed their hands and danced around the table. He whooped and hollered.

Radovan had been acting strange ever since he woke after the battle. He kept looking around and touching his chest. He seemed surprised to be alive.

"It burned!"

The women smelled more and more frightened. I took Radovan by the hand and pulled him away. He followed, resisting only long enough to throw a few golden coins to the women, and then to everyone else we passed on the way out.

"I got burned!" He shook a fist at the sky. "The damned thing is gone!"

Outside the brothel, Radovan didn't need pulling anymore. Instead he followed me through the streets of Lanming. He paused a few times to give coins to beggars or to buy firecrackers. He lit some and gave the rest to children.

I had never seen him so happy.

He stopped before a cart full of trinkets and bought a little mirror. He studied his face for a minute, frowning and thinking.

"I don't look any different," he said. "Huh."

His good cheer returned as we continued down the crowded street. He kissed a few girls and knocked down a man who objected before throwing a coin at his feet and continuing on our path. His mood changed when he saw where we were going.

Radovan looked up at the sign and groaned. "Aw, no, boss."

Maybe he could smell the wine from here, too.

I led him upstairs to the second floor of the tea house. My master sat by himself at a table full of wine flasks.

He also had been different since the battle.

After the princess put the other half of the dragon's heart in his chest, he slept for a long time. The surviving defenders wanted to kill Radovan. Judge Fang objected, holding up his spinning prayer rod that glowed with divine light, but the humans could not hear him.

I told them to stay back. They didn't listen until I showed them the big smile. They looked at the fingers on the floor of the Court of Heaven and Hell and backed away.

When my master awoke, the other survivors had bandaged their wounds and were ready to leave. Master told them that the devil Burning Cloud Devil had slain was Radovan, but Radovan was not the devil who killed their friends. It was too difficult for me to understand, but the surviving monks accepted his explanation. They knew as I did that my master is wise.

While he was glad to see Radovan alive, my master kept looking at the princess. She leaned on the arm of another man as they descended the long stairway. Wherever they went, my master watched. The longer he looked at them, the sadder he became.

He became even sadder when we reached the city. The monks begged him to come back to the temple. Their leader said that my master could become their master, but he still refused. One stout monk looked especially sorry to leave him behind. I saw him weep as he looked back one last time.

"Come on, boss. The party's outside."

My master looked up at Radovan, but he did not smile. "I am disinclined to celebrate this particular occasion."

Radovan called for a servant and ordered food. He moved a chair close to my master and sat beside him. He touched three flasks of wine before he found one that wasn't empty. He filled my master's cup and poured one for himself.

Radovan lifted his cup. "To the ones who got away."

My master frowned. He began to correct Radovan, but then he closed his mouth and raised his cup. They drank. When my master reached for the flask, Radovan moved it away. For a moment I thought they might fight. If they did, I wouldn't know what to do. I would have to help my master, but I did not want to bite Radovan. He might bite me back.

"You want to hear some good news?"

My master pretended he did not care, but he is always curious. Radovan told him about being burned by the hot tea, and my master pinched the bridge of his nose and thought.

"It seems plausible that the devil whose form you have taken is no longer connected to you."

"Burning Cloud Devil killed him," said Radovan. "He thought he was killing me, but I was too slippery for him."

"Too lucky, you mean."

"Desna smiles on handsome devils." He drank the rest of the wine from the flask.

"Or semi-devils, as I've heard some of the Tian call you. I prefer that to the pejorative 'hellspawn.' But this list of names you say the Phoenix Warrior divined from your blood—that is fascinating. It sounds as though she somehow divined every infernal branch of your family tree. It is a pity we never learned the name of the one who has been, if you will pardon the expression, pruned."

Radovan snorted wine through his nose. "Was there a master of puns at this temple?"

"I don't suppose you would be amenable to a few simple experiments to determine—"

"Forget it."

"You see how miserable I am. You could at least humor me."

"There's limits to every friendship."

When the food arrived, my master refused to eat. Instead he kept trying to persuade Radovan to let him cast magic on him. Radovan pretended to listen. He ate a few steaming dumplings and threw the rest for me to catch.

Radovan is my best friend.

When the dumplings were gone, Radovan slapped the table. "Let's at least get out of here."

I followed them out of the tea house and into the street. While they spoke, I stayed alert for danger. My time with the kami had been exciting. I would always remember them, but it was good to be back on the job. I like working for my master. His rules are simple.

"It was the wisest possible choice that Lanfen should marry Tengfei," said my master. "There will be peace between Lingshen and Quain for years if not decades."

"Yeah," said Radovan. "Still, you know she would have—"

My master made the gesture for silence. For once, Radovan obeyed.

"At least we've got that husk you wanted."

"If only its halves can be rejoined. But yes, King Wen was most generous. His chief eunuch gave me a letter of introduction to a conjurer who can transport us back to Absalom."

"We're going to need porters to carry all those gifts."

"We'll hire a few when we leave for Goka. And this time, you select the guards."

"You got it, boss."

Ahead of us, the crowd parted for a group of men with red hats and long spears. Radovan and my master moved aside with the rest, but the guards went straight to them and stood at attention.

With the guards were four other men in bright robes, the ones my master called eunuchs. They bowed before my master. Something about them reminded me of the Minister of Hell.

One stepped forward and bowed down to the ground three times before my master.

"Count Varian Jeggare of the Chelish Empire, Venture-Captain of the Pathfinder Society."

My master returned the bow, but not as low.

The eunuch bowed again. At a gesture, another eunuch presented my master with a long box. The first eunuch opened the cover to show a sword inside.

"A gift from Princess Lanfen."

My master opened his mouth to speak, but he closed it without a word. He had done that twice since the battle at the Court of Heaven and Hell, but I had never seen him do it before. Like me, he must have learned a few new tricks.

The eunuch gestured for his fellows to withdraw. He whispered in my master's ear, but I heard what he said.

"Her highness also sends the message: 'My heart is divided. Wherever fate leads you, I beg you to safeguard the other half.'"

My master did not move or speak. For a moment I thought he might weep, but Radovan accepted the box for him.

"Thanks, boys—uh, folks," he said. "I'll take it from here."

They looked at him blankly until Radovan slowly repeated his words in their language.

We moved through the crowds until we reached the city gates. There Radovan talked to some men about fetching my master's things from the inn and carrying them to a place called Goka.

Armed men arrived and reported to Radovan, who picked the ones he liked and gave them instructions. When he pointed to me, he pretended to bite his fingers and warned the men not to play with me.

When Radovan turned away from the men to talk to my master, they both seemed pleased, but I couldn't follow their conversation. No matter how carefully I listened, I understood fewer and fewer of the words. At first it was confusing, but it was much easier to understand them without all of the extra words.

By the time we left the city, I ran beside the smoke-colored horse my master made with his magic. He made one for Radovan, too, a big green steed with a mane like seawater. Radovan was surprised at the appearance of his horse. His used to be red, but maybe it learned some new tricks, too.

They rode out of Lanming together, leading the porters and guards. Before the sun set, I understood their words only when they gave me commands, but I could tell my master was becoming a little less sad.

Soon things would be as they were before we came to this place. My master would have new jobs for me. When I did them well, he would reward me.

And when he wasn't looking, Radovan would reward me, too.

About the Author

Dave Gross was born in Michigan and grew up in Virginia. After grinding out a Master's degree in English, he worked as a technical writer and teacher before editing magazines for TSR, Wizards of the Coast, and Paizo Publishing. He's been writing short stories and novels on the side since 1995. His previous Radovan and Jeggare stories for Pathfinder Tales include the novel *Prince of Wolves*, the Pathfinder's Journals "Hell's Pawns" and "Husks" (published in the Council of Thieves and Jade Regent Adventure Paths, respectively), and the short stories "The Lost Pathfinder" and "A Lesson in Taxonomy." In addition, he's also co-written the Pathfinder Tales novel *Winter Witch* with Elaine Cunningham.

Dave lives in Alberta, Canada with the best things in life: his wife and their small menagerie.

Acknowledgments

For notes on the outline and drafts, I thank Thomas M. Reid, Amber Scott, Gareth-Michael Skarka, Lindy Smith, and "Mean" Russ Taylor.

Many fine fellows have instigated or otherwise enabled my love of Chinese fantasy and action movies. Among them are Dave "Zeb" Cook; Robin D. Laws; James Lowder; John R. Phythyon, Jr.; Chris Pramas; Gareth-Michael Skarka; and Pierce Watters. Special thanks and eternal admiration go to Anthony J. Bryant for his inimitable musical translation of the Japanese subtitles and Chinese audio for *Mr. Vampire*.

Glossary

All Pathfinder Tales novels are set in the rich and vibrant world of the Pathfinder campaign setting. Below are explanations of a number of key terms used in this book. For more information on the world of Golarion and the strange monsters, people, and deities that make it their home, see the *Pathfinder Roleplaying Game Core Rulebook* or any of the books in the Pathfinder Campaign Setting series, or visit **paizo.com**.

Abrogail II: Current ruler of Cheliax.

Absalom: Largest city in the Inner Sea region.

Abyss: Plane of evil and chaos inhabited by demons, where many evil souls go after they die.

Acadamae: Notoriously effective and amoral school of magic in Korvosa.

Andoran: Democratic and freedom-loving nation formerly controlled by the Chelish Empire.

Andoren: Of or pertaining to Andoran.

Arcane: Magic that comes from mystical sources rather than the direct intervention of a god; secular magic.

Asmodeus: Devil-god of tyranny, slavery, pride, and contracts; lord of Hell and patron deity of Cheliax.

Avistan: Continent north of the Inner Sea, on which Cheliax, Varisia, Taldor, and many other nations lie.

Avistani: Of or related to the continent of Avistan.

Cantrip: Minor spell or magical trick cast by an arcane spellcaster (such as a wizard or sorcerer).

Cayden Cailean: God of freedom, ale, wine, and bravery. Was once mortal, but ascended to godhood by passing the Test of the Starstone in Absalom.

Celestial Bureaucracy: Tian term for the gods and other entities that rule the afterlife.

Celestial Dragon: Legendary creature honored by the residents of the southern Successor States, who appears every twelve years at the Gates of Heaven and Hell to exchange its "heart"—actually an enormous, magical pearl—with that of a maiden, granting her a wish in the process.

Celestial Order: Tian term for the natural way of things, the eternal balance between good and evil and other such opposing forces.

Celestial Wheel: Tian term for the cycle of existence and the progression of souls through the world and the afterlife.

Chelaxian: Someone from Cheliax.

Cheliax: Devil-worshiping nation in Avistan.

Chelish: Of or related to Cheliax.

Court of Heaven and Hell: Location in the Wall of Heaven mountains where the Dragon Ceremony takes place every twelve years.

Decemvirate: Masked and anonymous leaders of the Pathfinder Society.

Demons: Evil denizens of the Abyss who seek only to maim, ruin, and feed.

Desna: Good-natured goddess of dreams, stars, travelers, and luck.

Devils: Fiendish occupants of Hell who seek to corrupt mortals in order to claim their souls.

Dragon Ceremony: Ceremony in which a maiden offers her heart to the Celestial Dragon and receives a wish. Traditionally undertaken by a princess of Quain.

Dragon Temple: Monastery in Quain where monks are trained to accompany the royal emissary to the Dragon Ceremony every twelve years.

Egorian: Capital of Cheliax.

Elves: Long-lived, beautiful humanoids capable of interbreeding with humans.

Elven: Of or pertaining to elves.

Empire of Lung Wa: Ancient empire that collapsed and broke apart into the Successor States.

Fiendish: Of or related to creatures from the evil Outer Planes, such as devils and demons.

Flying Mountains: Region in Quain where strange magnetism causes entire mountains to levitate.

Flying Scroll: Little-used Tian magical technique by which a wizard can transcribe part of a memorized spell onto a piece of paper, then cast it by flinging the paper.

Garund: Continent south of the Inner Sea, renowned for its deserts and jungles.

Gates of Heaven and Hell: Portals that open at the Court of Heaven and Hell during the Dragon Ceremony.

Goka: Port city on the western edge of Tian Xia.

Golarion: The planet on which the Pathfinder campaign setting focuses—the greater world of which Tian Xia and the Inner Sea Region are both part.

Golden River: Major river running through Quain.

Greensteeples: Count Varian Jeggare's manor house.

Half-Elves: The children of unions between elves and humans. Taller, longer-lived, and generally more graceful and attractive than the average human, yet not nearly so much so as their full elven kin.

Heaven: Plane of good and lawfulness ruled by angels, where many good souls go after they die.

Hell: Plane of evil and tyrannical order ruled by devils, where many evil souls go after they die.

Hellknights: Militant organization of hardened law enforcers whose tactics are often seen as harsh and intimidating, and who bind devils to their will. Based in Cheliax.

Hellspawn: A human whose family line includes a fiendish taint, often displayed by horns or other devilish features. Rarely popular in civilized society.

Infernal: Of or related to Hell.

Inner Sea Region: The region on which most of the Pathfinder campaign setting focuses, situated on the opposite side of the globe from Tian Xia.

Iron Mountain: Famous landmark in Quain and doorway to the Court of Heaven and Hell.

Irori: God of history, knowledge, self-perfection, and enlightenment. Often favored by monks.

Kami: Guardian spirits from Tian Xia, often tied to particular places and things.

Ki: Mystical force or life essence which warrior monks often learn to master, allowing them to perform exceptional feats of strength and agility.

King Huang: Ruler of Lingshen.

King Wen: Ruler of Quain.

Korvosa: One of the most important cities in Varisia.

Lanming: Capital of Quain.

Lepidstadt: City in Ustalav noted for its university.

Lepidstadt Scar: Dueling scar gained during a ritual popular among students of Lepidstadt's university. Considered a badge of honor.

Lingshen: Successor State to the north of Quain.

Mandate of Heaven: The will (either direct or presumed) of the Celestial Bureaucracy.

Metamagic: Magical study devoted not to discovering new spells, but to improving and empowering those an arcane spellcaster already knows.

Minkai: Island nation on the eastern edge of Tian Xia.

Monk: Someone who devotes himself to enlightenment and self-perfection, often through mastery of the physical body and its use as a weapon.

Nagas: Intelligent monsters with the heads of humans and the bodies of snakes.

Nagajor: Region in southern Tian Xia ruled by nagas.

Nethys: God of magic. Also known as the All-Seeing Eye.

Ogres: Hulking, brutal, and often inbred humanoids with little intelligence and an enormous capacity for cruelty.

Oni: Evil spirits that lack physical bodies unless they make them. The natural enemies of kami.

Orcs: Savage humanoids with green or gray skin, protruding tusks, and warlike tendencies.

Paladin: Holy warrior devoted to a god and ruled by a strict code of conduct.

Pathfinder Chronicles: Books published by the Pathfinder Society detailing the most interesting and educational discoveries of their members.

Pathfinder Society: Organization of traveling scholars and adventurers who seek to document the world's wonders. Based out of Absalom and run by a mysterious and masked group called the Decemvirate.

Pesh: Type of narcotic drug.

Pharasma: Goddess of fate, death, prophecy, and birth. Ruler of the Boneyard, where mortal souls go to be judged after death.

Po Li: Successor state to the east of Quain.

Qadira: Desert nation of the Inner Sea.

Quain: One of the southernmost Successor States.

Riffle Scrolls: Magical scrolls shaped like flipbooks, which are activated by flipping the pages rapidly.

Rovagug: The Rough Beast; god of destruction.

Sarenrae: Goddess of the sun, honesty, and redemption. Often seen as a fiery crusader and redeemer.

Shelyn: Goddess of art, beauty, love, and music.

Shiver: Type of narcotic drug.

Shiziru: Tian goddess of honor and swordplay.

Song of the Spheres: Desna.

Sorcerer: Spellcaster who draws power from within himself, and does not need to study to cast spells.

Spellbook: Tome in which a wizard transcribes the arcane formulae necessary to cast spells. Without a spellbook, a wizard can cast only those few spells held in her mind at any given time.

Starknife: A set of four tapering blades that resemble compass points extending from a metal ring with a handle; the holy weapon of Desna.

Successor States: Collection of sometimes-warring nations formed when the ancient empire of Lung Wa collapsed. Includes Lingshen, Po Li, and Quain, among many others.

Taldan: Of or pertaining to Taldor.

Taldane: The common tongue of the Inner Sea region.

Taldor: Former empire in the Inner Sea region, now mostly fallen into decadence.

Thassilon: Ancient empire that crumbled long ago.

Thassilonian: Of or related to ancient Thassilon, as well as the name of its language.

The Tines: Raised fork on which Chelish criminals are sometimes impaled. Also the name of a rude hand gesture from Cheliax, which suggests that the recipient should be impaled in such a manner.

Tian Xia: Continent on the opposite side of the world from the Inner Sea region.

Tian: Of or pertaining to Tian Xia.

Tien: The common language of Tian Xia.

Ustalav: Fog-shrouded nation of the Inner Sea region, rife with superstition and often said to be haunted.

Varisia: Frontier region at the northwestern edge of the Inner Sea region.

Varisian: Something from Varisia, or else a member of the often maligned Varisian ethnic group, which is known for its music, dance, and traveling caravans.

Venture-Captain: Leader in the Pathfinder Society; in charge of directing and assisting lesser agents.

Wall of Heaven Mountains: Massive mountain range running down the western edge of Tian Xia.

Wizard: Someone who casts magical spells through research of arcane secrets and the constant study of spells, which he or she records in a spellbook.

For half-elven Pathfinder Varian Jeggare and his devil-blooded bodyguard Radovan, things are rarely as they seem. Yet not even the notorious crime-solving duo are prepared for what they find when a search for a missing Pathfinder takes them into the gothic and mist-shrouded mountains of Ustalav.

Beset on all sides by noble intrigue, curse-afflicted villagers, suspicious monks, and the deadly creatures of the night, Varian and Radovan must use sword and spell to track the strange rumors to their source and uncover a secret of unimaginable proportions, aided in their quest by a pack of sinister werewolves and a mysterious, mute priestess. But it'll take more than merely solving the mystery to finish this job. For shadowy figures have taken note of the pair's investigations, and the forces of darkness are set on making sure neither man gets out of Ustalav alive . . .

From fan-favorite author Dave Gross, author of *Black Wolf* and *Lord of Stormweather*, comes a new fantastical mystery set in the award-winning world of the Pathfinder Roleplaying Game.

Prince of Wolves print edition: $9.99
ISBN: 978-1-60125-287-6

Prince of Wolves ebook edition: $6.99
ISBN: 978-1-60125-331-6

PRINCE OF WOLVES

Dave Gross

In a village of the frozen north, a child is born possessed by a strange and alien spirit, only to be cast out by her tribe and taken in by the mysterious winter witches of Irrisen, a land locked in permanent magical winter. Farther south, a young mapmaker with a penchant for forgery discovers that his sham treasure maps have begun striking gold.

This is the story of Ellasif, a barbarian shield maiden who will stop at nothing to recover her missing sister, and Declan, the ne'er-do-well young spellcaster-turned-forger who wants only to prove himself to the woman he loves. Together they'll face monsters, magic, and the fury of Ellasif's own cold-hearted warriors in their quest to rescue the lost child. Yet when they finally reach the ice-walled city of Whitethrone, where trolls hold court and wolves roam the streets in human guise, will it be too late to save the girl from the forces of darkness?

From *New York Times* best-selling author Elaine Cunningham comes a fantastic new adventure of swords and sorcery, set in the award-winning world of the Pathfinder Roleplaying Game.

Winter Witch **print edition: $9.99**
ISBN: 978-1-60125-286-9

Winter Witch **ebook edition: $6.99**
ISBN: 978-1-60125-332-3

Winter Witch

Elaine Cunningham

The race is on to free Lord Stelan from the grip of a wasting curse, and only his old mercenary companion, the Forsaken elf Elyana, has the wisdom—and the swordcraft—to uncover the identity of his tormenter and free her old friend before the illness takes its course.

When the villain turns out to be another of their former companions, Elyana sets out with a team of adventurers including Stelan's own son on a dangerous expedition across the revolution-wracked nation of Galt and the treacherous Five Kings Mountains. There, pursued by a bloodthirsty militia and beset by terrible nightmare beasts, they discover the key to Stelan's salvation in a lost valley warped by weird magical energies. Will they be able to retrieve the artifact the dying lord so desperately needs? Or will the shadowy face of betrayal rise up from within their own ranks?

From Howard Andrew Jones, managing editor of the acclaimed sword and sorcery magazine *Black Gate*, comes a classic quest of loyalty and magic set in the award-winning world of the Pathfinder Roleplaying Game.

Plague of Shadows print edition: $9.99
ISBN: 978-1-60125-291-3

Plague of Shadows ebook edition: $6.99
ISBN: 978-1-60125-333-0

Plague
of
Shadows

Howard Andrew Jones

In the foreboding north, the demonic hordes of the magic-twisted hellscape known as the Worldwound encroach upon the southern kingdoms of Golarion. Their latest escalation embroils a preternaturally handsome and coolly charismatic swindler named Gad, who decides to assemble a team of thieves, cutthroats, and con men to take the fight into the demon lands and strike directly at the fiendish leader responsible for the latest raids—the demon Yath, the Shimmering Putrescence. Can Gad hold his team together long enough to pull off the ultimate con, or will trouble from within his own organization lead to an untimely end for them all?

From gaming legend and popular fantasy author Robin D. Laws comes a fantastic new adventure of swords and sorcery, set in the award-winning world of the Pathfinder Roleplaying Game.

***The Worldwound Gambit* print edition: $9.99**
ISBN: 978-1-60125-327-9

***The Worldwound Gambit* ebook edition: $6.99**
ISBN: 978-1-60125-334-7

the WORLDWOUND Gambit

Robin D. Laws

A warrior haunted by his past, Salim Ghadafar serves as
a problem solver for a church he hates, bound by the
goddess of death to hunt down those who would rob her
of her due. Such is the case in the desert nation of Thuvia,
where a powerful merchant about to achieve eternal youth
via a magical elixir is mysteriously murdered and his soul
kidnapped. The only clue is a ransom note, offering to trade
the merchant's soul for his dose of the fabled potion.

Enter Salim, whose keen mind and contacts throughout
the multiverse would make solving this mystery a cinch, if
it weren't for the merchant's stubborn daughter who insists
on going with him. Together, the two must unravel a web of
intrigue that will lead them far from the blistering sands of
Thuvia on a grand tour of the Outer Planes, where devils and
angels rub shoulders with fey lords and mechanical men,
and nothing is as it seems . . .

From noted game designer and author James L. Sutter
comes an epic mystery of murder and immortality, set in the
award-winning world of the Pathfinder Roleplaying Game.

Death's Heretic print edition: $9.99
ISBN: 978-1-60125-369-9

Death's Heretic ebook edition: $6.99
ISBN: 978-1-60125-370-5

Death's
Heretic

James L. Sutter

NOVELS!

Tired of carting around a bag full of books? Take your ebook reader or smart phone over to **paizo.com** to download all the Pathfinder Tales novels from authors like Dave Gross and *New York Times* best seller Elaine Cunningham in both ePub and PDF formats, thus saving valuable bookshelf space and 30% off the cover price!

PATHFINDER'S JOURNALS!

Love the fiction in the Adventure Paths, but don't want to haul six books with you on the subway? Download compiled versions of each fully illustrated journal and read it on whatever device you chose!

FREE WEB FICTION!

Tired of paying for fiction at all? Drop by **paizo.com** every week for your next installment of free weekly web fiction as Paizo serializes new Pathfinder short stories from your favorite high-profile fantasy authors. Read 'em for free, or download 'em for cheap and read them anytime, anywhere!

ALL AVAILABLE NOW AT PAIZO.COM!

PATHFINDER

CAMPAIGN SETTING

THE INNER SEA WORLD GUIDE

You've delved into the Pathfinder campaign setting with Pathfinder Tales novels—now take your adventures even further! *The Inner Sea World Guide* is a full-color, 320-page hardback guide featuring everything you need to know about the exciting world of Pathfinder: overviews of every major nation, religion, race, and adventure location around the Inner Sea, plus a giant poster map! Read it as a travelogue, or use it to flesh out your roleplaying game—it's your world now!

EXPLORE YOUR WORLD!

SWORD & SORCERY LIVES!

Planet Stories is proud to present these classics of magic and perilous adventure from three unparalleled masters of heroic fantasy: Robert E. Howard, A. Merritt, and C. L. Moore.

· ·

"Howard's writing is so highly charged with energy that it nearly gives off sparks."

Stephen King

"[A. Merritt] has a subtle command of a unique type of strangeness which no one else has been able to parallel."

H. P. Lovecraft

"C. L. Moore's shimmering, highly colored prose is unique in science fiction."

Greg Bear

Can a single Earthman hope to overthrow the terrible devils that enslave the savage world of Almuric?
ISBN 978-1-60125-043-8
$12.99

A mysterious artifact from ancient Babylon hurtles amateur archaeologist John Kenton onto the seas of another dimension.
ISBN 978-1-60125-177-0
$14.99

Jirel of Joiry, the first-ever sword and sorcery heroine, takes up her greatsword against dark gods and monsters.
ISBN 978-1-60125-045-2
$12.99

Available now at quality bookstores and **paizo.com/planetstories**

CHART YOUR OWN ADVENTURE!

The PATHFINDER ROLEPLAYING GAME puts you in the role of a brave adventurer fighting to survive in a fantastic world beset by magic and evil!

Take on the role of a canny fighter hacking through enemies with an enchanted sword, a powerful sorceress with demon blood in her veins, a wise cleric of mysterious gods, a wily rogue ready to defuse even the deadliest of traps, or any of countless other heroes. The only limit is your imagination!

The massive 576-page *Pathfinder RPG Core Rulebook* provides all the tools you need to get your hero into the action! One player assumes the role of the Game Master, challenging players with dastardly dungeons or monstrous selections from the more than 350 beasts included in the *Pathfinder RPG Bestiary*!

The PATHFINDER ROLEPLAYING GAME is a fully supported tabletop roleplaying game, with regularly released adventure modules, sourcebooks on the fantastic world of Golarion, and complete campaigns in the form of Pathfinder Adventure Paths like Kingmaker and Serpent's Skull!

Begin your adventure today in the game section of quality bookstores or hobby game shops, or online at **paizo.com**!

Pathfinder RPG Core Rulebook • $49.99
ISBN 978-1-60125-150-3